MICHAEL MCGRAIL

The Forbidden War

The Companion Chronicles

First edition

Editing by Anna Marie Editing Services
Cover art by Rebekah Bowman at bean-designs
Illustration by Rebekah Bowman at bean-designs

This book was professionally typeset on Reedsy.
Find out more at reedsy.com

For my mum,
who taught me ... well, everything ... but specifically, that you are
never too old to do something new. I miss her.

And my beautiful daughter, Seren,
who not only makes me smile every day but also makes me strive
to be better.

Contents

Acknowledgement

Writing this book has been a long time coming. I have toyed with the idea of writing for years, but never pushed to publish anything as I moved from self-doubt to pure fear when thinking about people reading my story and hating it. Although, I don't think that fear will ever go away.

One person who has been there from the very start (a long time ago), through all my procrastinating and self-doubt, encouraging me all the way, is Gaz. He has consistently provided honest, and sometimes jarring feedback while nudging me to continue and get better for it. For that Gaz, I will be eternally grateful. I would never have written this book without your support.

You can never achieve anything without your family. Thank you, Seren & Claire, … for being patient with my mood swings, the time I have dedicated to writing this book, and ensuring there was always tea and snacks available.

Special thanks also need to go to Anna, my editor, sounding board, and all-round writing guru. She has been quite simply amazing. She has not only been brilliant with her edit of the book, but she has helped and encouraged me every step of the way as she dragged this oblivious newbie through the intricate, and sometimes confusing, journey to publishing the first of many stories … (which I hope she will still want to work with me on after working with me for so long on this one).

Thanks also go to Rebekah, who managed to take the idea I had in my head for my cover and design something better - and in my mind, amazing.

Once you start thinking of the journey you have been through and those you need to thank, the list starts growing. I could be here all day. So, this thank you is to everyone I had conversations with about my ideas for my story, those who oooh'd and aaah'd in all the right places, even if it was only to be polite … it all helped me build my confidence and take the next step.

And last but not least, thank you to my readers. I hope you enjoy the book and look forward to the next instalments of "The Companion Chronicles."

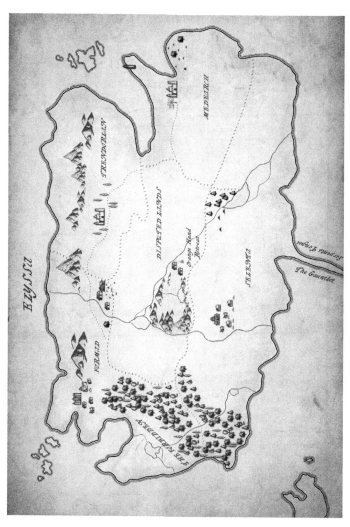

Map of Elyssa

CHAPTER ONE

Nala bundled through the forest, branches snagging his fur, and the undergrowth pulling at his legs, trying to bring him to the ground. If it hadn't been for Swiftwind's instructions in his mind, he wouldn't have made it more than a few metres into The Forbidden, and he would have been caught by his pursuers.

Suddenly, up ahead, a large rock stood in a clearing, and he jumped to the top. An instinct he had never had before, encouraged him to raise his head and sniff the air.

"We must keep going, Nala," Swiftwind pleaded in his mind, interrupting his thoughts.

He smiled at her. "Don't worry, Swift, they won't follow us in here," he replied, soothing her fears.

In Selenta, children learn from an early age that The Forbidden is a place to be feared. Tales of monsters and vicious demons are told to keep naughty children in check, and as they grow older, this is reinforced with every step they take throughout their education. The fact that there are no first-hand accounts of what lurks within The Forbidden serves to strengthen that inbuilt fear.

"I understand, but we must keep moving," Swiftwind continued to plead.

He shook his head, exhaustion overruling Swiftwind's better judgement, and he flopped to the ground and closed his eyes.

The morning's events flooded back to him ...

In his anger, grief, and horror, he had taken a dangerous step. An action the professors at school called the *Forbidden Step*. He had given up his body to become one with his wolf companion.

Alongside their indoctrination into the caste system, Selentans are taught that this act removes all ability to think logically; handing your life over to your animal companion and providing it with a flesh and blood body that it can use as it desires ... while you watch on helplessly.

To his surprise, he had retained control, along with his identity. His memory, grief, and more importantly, his anger remained intact. Yet more of a shock, was that the wolf body he now occupied ... did not resemble Swiftwind in any way.

He shied away from thinking about the trigger for his merge, instead choosing to focus on Swiftwind's worries.

Letting his instincts guide him, as he had seen Swiftwind do countless times, he looked back at the trail they had followed into The Forbidden. It was barely visible. He raised his head and sniffed at the air, straining his hearing. He let out a yelp. His mind had filled with a myriad of new sensations and feelings, as sounds and smells created an intricate pattern of images in his mind that threatened to overwhelm him.

He came back to normality with Swiftwind's chuckle.

"Like a cub that's new to the hunt," she teased.

"Oh, so now you're happy to mock me again?" he drawled sarcastically.

She laughed. "We are safe, Nala Yagin. The soldiers

stopped at the barrier as you predicted, let me help you see …"

Slowly, the array of colours started to form blurry moving images in Nala's mind. "Wow," he gasped. "Is it always like this, Swift?"

He felt Swiftwind shake her head in his mind as he marvelled at the images. The soldiers were milling around at the edge of the tree line. Slowly, angrily, they were turning and heading back the way they had come.

"A cub still suckling at its mother's teat has better hunter vision than this," Swift grinned. Quickly … before he could take offence at her taking on the role of his teacher, she added, "They are usually clearer, but we were not strong enough alone for me to share this with you before our merge. I will show you how to understand this world." She paused, letting this sink in.

"It will save me having to ween you for the rest of our lives." Swift couldn't help teasing him, and they both laughed as the adrenaline of being the hunted fled their system.

As they rested, Nala thought about the events of the last few days …

They had been hunting a group of Scarlett Hand members … rebels and traitors, as their desire to make a place for themselves in this world, omitted Selenta. They had been around for generations and threatened the Selentan way of life.

Selenta taught that the rebels recruit the young, corrupting them to their cause. They funded their little rebellion by attacking military installations and kidnapping those who are important for ransom; taking food, clothing, and money as payment. They were more of an annoyance than any real threat.

This particular cell had made an unfortunate mistake and crossed a path used by the military for training. The trail would have been unseen by an ordinary training patrol. However, the Black Hand's Elite was carrying out their annual tracking refresher for the Training Sergeants. A tracker on the course had pointed out evidence of a trail crossing, advising it was probably two weeks old.

Ordinarily, due to the age of the markings, the tracker would ignore and dismiss them as an animal trail, but one of the Training Sergeant's accused the Black Hand tracker of fabricating the evidence, so those being trained looked inept.

With his authority challenged, the tracker decided to use this as part of the training, and followed the trail to identify the creature that had passed by. It soon became apparent to him that it wasn't animal tracks, but signs of a group of people who were not supposed to be there.

The tracker dismissed the Sergeant who doubted him, and called his team in; the hunt was on.

The Black Hand followed the trail relentlessly for two whole days, barely stopping to eat and rehydrate, with the Training Sergeants struggling to keep up.

Finally, after two days, they located the Scarlett Hand in a gorge within the Disputed Lands, not more than a day's walk from where the Formad border meets with The Forbidden.

He suddenly felt uncomfortable. To let his mind dwell on the next part of the memory was not to his liking, and he rose, shaking himself.

Taking a deep breath, he attempted to open his senses again. As before, the medley of images filled his and Swiftwind's mind. This time, he didn't need Swift to tell him what to do

4

next.

An image of the Black Hand Major; strong, ruthless, relentless, and deadly came clear to his mind. He was studying the spot where they had entered The Forbidden.

Adrenaline flooded Nala's body, and he fled deeper into the forest. Death was coming ...

CHAPTER TWO

Major Drangor stood before the barrier to The Forbidden, his blood was up. The scuffle with the rebels had been decidedly unsatisfying. They barely put up a fight, leaving him to oversee a part of his job that he despised.

The rebels they had caught were all disenchanted young men, many not strong enough to get through schooling, and most would likely have faced assignment to the labour teams or the fields. Unfortunately, their courage far surpassed their strength.

All of them had stubbornly refused to tell him what they were doing and where they were going. They either didn't know, or they truly believed in their cause.

He had no other choice but to torture them. Drangor sighed. Information was rarely obtainable or useful when gathered this way; having to sift out the truth from the lies as the victims screamed what they thought you wanted to hear.

As he suspected, it led to precious little information.

"A waste of a life," he muttered to himself, knowing he would do it again if it meant protecting Selenta. But he wasn't aiming his comment solely at the rebels.

During the torture, one of the Sergeants from the training facility had lost himself in the horror of it, choosing the cowards way out by taking the Forbidden Step.

The Sergeant had merged with his wolf companion, becoming a huge, vicious creature that had immediately ripped the throat out of one of his Hand members, and injured two others. Before the fight could turn, it had bolted, instinctively fleeing towards the forest.

The Training Sergeants had taken chase, allowing the Black Hand to tend the injured. It should have been easy enough, but it was a mistake. That decision, coupled with their incompetence, had let the poor creature reach The Forbidden.

To make matters worse, they had been too scared to follow the animal into the forest to fulfil their sacred duty and exact the Blessing.

Drangor felt his anger at the Sergeants rise. Leaving this creature alive was unthinkable. The Blessing needed exacting to protect Selenta. Merged creatures were always trying to return to the cities and villages, causing panic and many deaths, as they fought back when people were chasing them off.

More importantly, killing the creature enacted the Blessing, freeing the weak soul now stuck within the creature, and allowing him to return to the River. He couldn't let him remain a prisoner of the animal whose form he had taken … destined to watch the atrocities the creature perpetrates … for the rest of eternity. Unable to do anything about it.

Controlling his anger, Drangor reached out to his owl companion, Faith. She immediately responded, eager to hunt. Using her enhanced senses, he searched for the wolf, finding him not too far into The Forbidden; resting, confident of his safety.

Drangor smiled as he spoke to his panther companion, "Ready to hunt, Twister?"

Twister gave a low growl in response.

Drangor's body filled with strength, and courtesy of Faith's senses, he identified the best path to take to be silent on the hunt. Adrenaline pumped through his system as he drew a short blade. He was ready … moving towards The Forbidden … the scent of his quarry filling his nostrils, and his eyes taking on the golden glow of his panther companion.

"Major Drangor!" a voice shouted close behind him.

He turned, a growl deep in his belly mirroring Twister's fury at the interruption. Seeing the fear in his Lieutenant's eyes as he took a slight step backwards, he controlled his voice, "Make it quick, Vas. I'm hungry for the hunt."

To his credit, Vas composed himself quickly. "Sorry, Major, but we have just received a message from Councillor Dortige, you are required back at HQ."

Drangor immediately straightened at the news, and Twister let out a low whine of disappointment; knowing that the hunt was over for now.

"Thank-you, Vas. I will join you shortly. Have the Hand ready to move out immediately," Drangor said. Vas nodded and turned; rushing to carry out his orders.

Drangor looked at the Training Sergeants who were milling around aimlessly, concealing a snarl. "They can make their own way back," he said to Twister before he turned back to the forest.

The message was a code which instructed him to make his way immediately to the Black Hand's retreat with his full contingent of Hands.

"It seems you get to live today, Wolf. One day we will meet again."

Drangor internally felt his panther companion's lingering disappointment. He gently soothed him, "Don't worry, My Friend, if The Black wants us to take full back-up, then we will very likely get to hunt."

His companions smiled their own versions of a toothy grin at Drangor, who laughed as he turned and made his way over to his Hand …. ready for the long trek back to the retreat.

CHAPTER THREE

Rico stumbled through the Hall of Recognition's doors in a daze. The adjudicators had ushered him out quickly when his first attempt had failed.

They weren't interested in helping him discover his third companion. He had failed so often; the monthly testing was likely an obligation to prevent them from breaking the school rules. He suspected the tests had only happened to stop them bearing the wrath of the Lord Professor.

If the Lord Professor himself had not assessed him - identifying that he was capable of a third - they would have evicted him from the school in a heartbeat, and put him on basic work duty.

He shuddered at the thought, sighing as he pulled himself together. When he felt he had composed himself, he started moving and trudged down the corridor. Halfway down, he stopped. Waves of misery at his latest failure threatened to overwhelm him. It was unbearable to fail again, he was bringing Phoenix Squad down.

How could he keep failing? He had to be better; stronger.

Phoenix Squad had the two strongest recruits; Eddie and Jenna. His continued failure meant that the Squad was not at full strength. If only he had his third. They would be at the top of the leader board instead of second, having their choice of assignments once they graduated. Because of him their fate, although better than the majority of Selentans, would be determined by a lottery of which Hand wanted them the most, leaving Jonas to have all the glory.

Just the thought of Jonas angered him, wiping away some of his misery.

It was Jonas's Raptor Squad that was currently holding the top spot. Many thought this was favouritism, the school giving leeway to Raptor Squad to please Jonas's father who was Chairman of the Grey Hand, and a significant benefactor to the school. He didn't share this view. Raptor Squad were good. They were ruthless and didn't let anyone or anything stand in the way of their success. If not for Eddie and Jenna, backed up by his and Tia's unique grasp of tactics, surveillance, and classroom work (which his chameleon and snake companions reinforced), they wouldn't have even been close enough to challenge Jonas's Squad this year.

As he mulled it all over, he felt a little bit amused and chuckled. He knew that he brought real worth to the Squad, he just wanted to be better, so that Phoenix Squad was better.

"OK, don't judge me," he said aloud as he looked up at the portraits of past heroes from the school, shaking his head. "I obviously do enough of that myself. And yes, I know the Squad would kick my ass if they knew I was harping on about bringing them down again."

He continued walking down the corridor, still shaking his head, laughing ruefully at himself.

"Now I'm talking to paintings. You have a lot to answer for third. When we do meet ... I am going to kick *your* ass."

Out of nowhere, a deep voice sounded in his mind ...

"You and who's army, Pipsqueak? You can't even tie your own shoelaces!"

Caught by surprise, he looked down at his feet and tripped over them … going headfirst into the marble floor.

Deep, throaty laughter rang in his ears.

Jumping up quickly, looking around to see if anyone had seen and checking his face, he was making sure he'd hurt nothing but his pride. He found nothing; except for the heroes unchanging faces smiling knowingly back at him. He grinned. Despite the fall, he felt like he could fly, and he moved quickly to the doors ready to face his friends.

They would be waiting outside, worrying more about how he would take failing rather than any stupid league position.

His friends were all that really mattered. They were his family; his team, a true team - who would lay down their lives for each other - without giving it a second thought. It was the thought of losing that driving him to succeed.

"About bloody time! Maybe there is hope for you," the voice huffed sarcastically. "But I won't count on it."

He reached for the door, grinning from ear to ear.

The Squad would not understand at first why he was smiling. The Hall of Recognition's lights had remained dark, indicating the testing had failed; he hadn't found his third. They would be prepared to console him, to brush his apologies aside, and encourage him that next time would be the one, but he didn't care anymore. It was all irrelevant … his third had found him.

It felt different from Misty and Rexter, stronger somehow. It was sarcastic, wilful, and had a mind of its own. He knew things were never going to be the same again.

"A *major* …" he whispered, slightly in awe. "And a feeling

12

tells me you have been here for quite some time, just watching."

He pushed open the doors and stepped into the sunlight just as his third chuckled, "This should be fun."

CHAPTER FOUR

Such a small distance separated these two huge continents, but that divide might as well have been another world, Magnar mused as he stood looking out over the Serpents Tongue.

The Serpents Tongue was a narrow strip of land which connected the two continents; barely four miles long and a few hundred metres wide. It rose to the surface of the sea for four hours, twice a day, making crossings dangerous.

If that wasn't enough of a challenge ... a group of soldiers he had found to be entirely incorruptible was protecting the opposite side of the Serpents Tongue.

Every attempt they had made at converting one of them had failed, ending with someone's head getting left in front of his guard's barracks on this side of the strip.

Even trade was non-existent, with the greediest of merchants feeling the risk was not worth the unknown profits.

His eyes roamed lazily over the sea, absently considering this route, but even in that short time, he saw the backs of at least three creatures break through the surface.

No, the Serpents Tongue was the only way to cross between the continents. Taking the sea route was suicide. Not even the most heavily guarded ship could make it.

The sea creatures defended their territory vigorously. Stories of how hordes of sea creatures had pounded ships into kindling meant no one would even waste time building one, never mind sailing it.

Also, there was no way to amass an army and enter the opposite continent by force. It would take time for the troops to gather and cross the divide … time they didn't have.

The soldiers awaiting them would be aware of the assault long before it arrived, and know that they only had to stall for a short time, letting the sea do the work for them.

He looked down at his satchel and wondered again if this was a trap. There was little information on how the Lost Continent had developed over the last five hundred years. No one from this side had ever crossed the blockade in place and returned to tell the tale.

The absence of information had bred myths about dangerous dragons and monsters roaming freely, devouring all in their path, and of heroes protecting the people. Painting a land of mystery that intrigued even the coldest of hearts.

"Children's stories, nothing more," the voice of his companion purred in his ear.

He smiled, not needing to look to his side to be able to see his companion, manifested in all his glory. He reached over, running his fingers through his lion companion's dark mane.

"I know, Cassius, but aren't you intrigued what that world over there holds? Will they be weak and easily destroyed, or are they true warriors that'll give us a battle worthy of the name?" Magnar asked.

Cassius cocked his head to one side to look at him. "I can't say I am. But then, thinking is a job for you and Tink. I'm just the muscle," Cassius replied.

15

A tinkling chuckle sounded from his shoulder, followed by a sharp stab of pain as Tink pinched his ear. "Do you forget, Magnar, that we intend to take this land by subterfuge?" Tink enquired.

He considered Tink's words ...

"No, My Friend, I do not. But rest assured, if history has shown us anything, there'll be people who will fight." He smiled maliciously. "This alliance with The Black is only going to give us a toehold. There are going to be battles, and blood will be spilt before this continent is under our control."

Cassius snuffed, shaking his mane, but it was Tink who answered. "All true, Magnar, let us hope our Generals are up to this, as you can't stay on that continent. Without you here for the people to revere and fear, we could very well have our own rebellion to deal with, and let's not forget the southern front."

He sighed. "I know. This trip is merely to set the ball rolling. We need to ensure The Black is willing to work with us for more reasons than just having a new ally. It seems he will only finalise negotiations with me."

Cassius growled. "And that had better be all he wants from you."

CHAPTER FIVE

The Black stood, considering his plans as he looked over the map of Elyssa. His eyes were slowly running across the different nations that made up this continent; the Formad to the north-west, Trendorlan to the north-east, Medearch to the east, and his beloved Selenta taking up much of the southern part of the continent.

His eyes briefly rolled over The Forbidden to the west, something in his mind telling him to ignore it and move on. He smiled, recognising the River diverting his attention, and allowing it too as he had no interest in The Forbidden … at least not currently.

The final section was the Disputed Lands, an area in the centre of the continent that linked all the countries, with people from each living in villages that were spotted about. This area had been designated as a buffer zone after the last war that took place over fifty years ago. It was a way to keep each country separate and remove the likelihood of border disputes triggering a costly war. The villages inside the Disputed Lands were essentially autonomous, but in reality, Selenta ran these Lands as its own, with the other countries turning a blind eye so long as their citizens living there were left alone.

He sighed and turned his back on the map, looking out over the city. The spires on the Hall of Recognition were dark, so this afternoon's tests had not encountered any new awakenings.

That was not unusual. There were days, even weeks when no pairings between students and companions happened, especially toward the end of the year. But there were also other times when the lights repeatedly flashed for days on end.

He smiled, remembering his own awakenings; not needing the Hall of Recognition. His companions had joined him at a young age, as was the norm in his family, and they had all been formidable.

He watched them fondly in the reflection of the windows, as they lounged in their manifested states. They could stay in this state for an extended time without exhausting them or himself, enjoying each other's company.

Stirus, his great black bear, lay sprawled on the floor; closed off to all outside eyes, fast asleep. It was only the rhythmic twitching of his nose, and the occasional mental image sent to The Black that confirmed where everyone was within his range, that indicated his alertness.

Starglider was more obviously alert. She was sat perched on Stirus's shoulder, her head and eyes always on the move; constantly flitting to the exits and windows. Unlike Stirus, her images transmitted to The Black only when she felt there was a potential threat.

The Black laughed as one of her talons sunk into Stirus's shoulder, teasing the great bear, and trying to get a rise. The most she received was a huff, yet it was a game of baiting they never grew tired of.

Finally, curled up and obviously asleep with his snores reverberating through the room, was the last of his trio of companions; Trable. The little chameleon was curled up deep inside Stirus's fur, his diminutive size and appearance, disguising his true abilities and strength.

"You're staring at me again," Trable's deep voice accused, without opening his eyes.

The Black let out a deep, throaty chuckle. "You don't miss a thing."

Trable moved quickly, and in the blink of an eye, he was perched on The Black's shoulder to look out across the city. "And don't you forget it!" Trable said.

"Never, My Friend," The Black responded, reaching his hand up, caressing underneath Trable's chin and sighing. "We are about to enter a dangerous time, Trable. One false move and we will lose everything we have worked for. We need to be sure that we are taking the right course."

Trable's eye regarded The Black, thinking carefully before he answered. "The course is set, but even now we can halt its progress. Once we meet them and merge the deal, even then we could turn it back. We will need to be strong, as we will have to give everything we have away before we can take the bigger prize." Trable paused, considering. "Once we are through, we will have everything we desire."

"Yes," The Black simply agreed. The course was set, and the time for doubts was over. He straightened his robes. "Time to go to work."

His companions faded from sight as he turned and headed to the door.

"Oh, the fun we have," Trable laughed in The Black's mind.

CHAPTER SIX

K aden watched them through the eyeglass the Medearches had given him as a gift, it felt like a lifetime ago, but it had only been a few short years. The group he was watching had just crossed the Formad border, and they were late. He had expected them two days earlier. His scouts had finally picked them up near a deep gorge in the Disputed Lands a couple of hours before.

These Lands were supposed to be an independent barrier between the countries to keep the peace. But they were governed by the Selentans who moved through them with impunity; training, policing, and recruiting new soldiers … whether they wanted to be or not.

The scout was not happy. There was something about the appearance of this cell of the Scarlett Hand. Kaden put it down to the natural cautiousness of the breed, but as his group had not met this cell before, they needed to be careful.

He watched as a member of the new group broke off as they hit the Formad border, climbing a tree and scouting around; a signal of who they are to anyone watching.

He nodded his head as he closed his eyeglass and turned to his group of rebels.

"A sorrier bunch of rebels, I never did see," a voice mumbled in his mind.

He smiled and replied in the same way, "Yes, but they have come a long way in the last few months."

"Hmm," was the only response.

He looked them over critically, they were young and scruffy, their clothes dirty and threadbare in places. Still, they moved with a new purpose he had started to instil in them. More importantly, their weapons were in perfect condition.

There were always doubts with a new team, and this was no different. He wasn't sure they were ready for real battles, but this was just a simple meet and greet, and shouldn't be too much of a trial.

He shook his head, trying to rid himself of the feeling that something was in the air. Things were set to change, and it would soon be time for real action.

Instead, he roused his group. "Right, you scruffy lot, on your feet. We meet the cell in Whispering Woods ... a day's march from here. I want to be there to greet them so we will be going at double speed."

A few lighthearted groans came from the fifteen rebels in the group. Still, they were all on their feet and ready to move, their eyes gleaming, and their companions eager for the exercise and action.

He smiled at them and turned into the woods. His jaguar companion manifesting in front of him, and taking the lead as they headed quickly into the forest, going to greet their guests.

CHAPTER SEVEN

As Rico burst out into the sunlight, the picture that greeted him took him by surprise.

Eddie stood in the middle of the courtyard beside the fountain, facing off against Jonas and Raptor Squad. His gargoyle companion's form enveloping his tall, gangly frame; providing strength and speed. His lion crouched, poised and ready to pounce on his command, and his wolverine was prowling behind him, covering Tia.

Tia, the smallest and weakest fighter in the Squad, had just launched her crow and owl into the air, and had her jaguar standing beside her.

Butch was off to the left on the opposite side of the fountain. His huge black bear was roaring its challenge beside him, and their size was almost identical, while his turtle was providing strength to his typically vulnerable skin, causing him to shimmer in a green hue.

The most striking, and terrifying of them all was Jenna. She was stood off to the right of the group with her wolf protecting her. Her blue eyes were dancing with flames, and her blonde hair was shrouded by the opaque form of her golden eagle, providing her with strength and speed, while her phoenix coiled around her forearms, ready to unleash a bolt of fire.

There were gaps in their close quarters battle posture. Phoenix Squad were clearly outnumbered without him, especially as Raptor Squad were similarly battle-ready across from them, with all their companions unleashed.

All of this registered immediately, and his instincts took over. In one quick motion, he leapt down the steps, his snake companion lending him speed, while his chameleon blurred his movement. It didn't stop them from seeing him, but it made it difficult for his enemies to predict his next move.

Within moments, he was amongst his Squad, slightly behind and to the right of Eddie, and instinctively giving Jenna a clear field of fire.

"Good of you to join us," Eddie grinned, not taking his eyes off Raptor Squad.

He chuckled, setting himself.

"Stop this conflict," his new companion suggested strongly in his mind.

"That sounds more like a demand than a suggestion," he growled back.

His blood was up, and a good fight would release the stress the testing had caused.

"Get used to it, *BOY*," his third growled back. "But, if it will get through your thick skull … pretty please stop this fight, with sugar on top."

He laughed out loud and laid a hand on Eddie's shoulder, signalling to Jenna and the others to stand down. He was quite surprised at how quickly they released their companions and surrounded him, leaving Raptor Squad looking stupid as they remained in an aggressive fighting posture.

"Buddy, what happened?" Eddie asked, grabbing his shoulders.

"Easy Ed, you'll shake his head loose," Jenna said as she gently laid her hand on Eddie's arm.

Eddie let out a huge belly laugh. "I doubt it, Jenna. He's made of stronger stuff than that. You're overprotective of him."

Jenna blushed, enhancing her already perfect features. "I'm protective of all of you, Idiot," she retorted.

Butch and Tia laughed, both putting their arms around Jenna's shoulders.

"Of course, you are, Jenna," Tia purred.

"Just not as much as you are with your special one," Butch added, winking at Rico who had no idea what was going on. Tia punched Butch lightly on the arm before moving comfortably into his arms.

"Anyway, enough of that," Eddie growled, "What happened, Rico?"

He started to speak, but Jenna interrupted him. "The lights didn't show, but … you feel different."

"That's because …" he started.

"He is different. Even I can feel the strength, and I'm not sensitive," Eddie cut in.

He folded his arms across his chest and looked them both in the eye. "Are you both quite finished?" he questioned in his sternest voice, feeling his third chuckle in his mind. Whether it was at his feeble attempt at authority, or the excitement he could see in his friends' faces, he didn't know, but he would learn his companion's personality soon enough.

He realised his friends were looking at him; waiting. It would take time to become used to the internal dialogue, and make sure it didn't impact on his interactions.

"We can work on that," his third advised.

He grinned with barely contained excitement. "Not here guys, but it's awesome news. Let's go somewhere private."

They all clustered and turned to leave.

"Where do you bugs think you're going? We have unfinished business," Jonas growled.

In their excitement, they had forgotten about the rival Squad.

Each of them turned back when a voice, mild but commanding, came from an alleyway, "And what business might that be, Jonas Quinn?"

Jonas's face hit the floor as they all dropped to one knee; the correct, respectful response for a student to give when the Lord Professor entered their presence.

The Lord Professor walked across the yard. His comfortable stride eating up the ground as his robes billowed around him. It gave him a majestic look; enhanced by his broad shoulders, and eyes that always seemed to twinkle with mischief. He stopped before Jonas.

"I can only assume you were demonstrating a new starting battle position for your classmates?"

Jonas kept his eyes to the ground, but his tense posture betrayed his rage.

"No answer, Jonas?" the Lord Professor asked. "Well no matter, you know the rules of the Hall of Recognition courtyard."

That grabbed everyone's attention. The rules were no companions in the courtyard, even though students snubbed this regularly because they were always working here, helping each other learn new techniques.

"I told you to stop the fight," his third grinned in his mind.

He swallowed hard, fighting the urge to grin at the smugness he felt from his third. The Lord Professor glanced over at him briefly before turning back to Jonas.

"Oops," his third muttered, not missing the Lord Professor's look.

"What's wrong?" he asked.

"I'm going to take a nap … watch your words."

As simple as that, his companion backed away from his mind. His third wasn't gone, but somehow, he felt less. His mind searched for the right word to describe it, but he couldn't get past the fact that his companion wasn't entirely there.

His thoughts became interrupted as he tuned back into the Lord Professor's voice, "… and due to your decision not to explain yourself, your Squad will be penalised by twenty points."

Every head in the courtyard lifted as they stared openmouthed at the Lord Professor. Twenty points was a huge punishment. It was better than expulsion, but the penalty meant that there were now only three points separating the two Squads, with Raptor Squad dropping to second place.

This changed the dynamics of the final three tests. Raptor Squad would have to excel to be able to defeat Phoenix Squad now.

He was impressed with how well Jonas managed to keep his rage under control.

"As you wish, Lord Professor, but rest assured, my father will hear of this," Jonas said, his voice quivering.

The Lord Professor turned to one of his aides, issuing instructions to change the leader board. He turned back to

Jonas. "I'm sure he will. Now, I think you better go and prepare for the final tests. It appears they will not be as easy as you first thought."

Raptor Squad stood as one and saluted, then turned and stalked off the courtyard, Jonas sparing a venomous glance back at them all.

* * *

As Raptor Squad left the courtyard, the Lord Professor turned back to Eddie and the rest of Phoenix Squad.

"Can I assume, Eddie, that this was to do with the Hall of Recognition's lights not coming on for your friend?"

Eddie, as leader of the Squad, answered, "Yes, Lord Professor."

The Lord Professor sighed, "And can I presume there was a reaction from you?"

Eddie nodded. "Yes, Lord Professor. It was only when Rico came out of the Hall and calmed the situation that we backed down."

The Lord Professor smiled and looked at Rico. "Is that so, Rico? You're usually the hothead."

Rico tried to look hurt by the Lord Professor's comment, but he knew that he was right. His lack of a third had made him very defensive and quick to react to any slight, not helped by how protective of him his Squad were.

"Things change, Lord Professor," was his only reply.

"Indeed, they do, Rico," the Lord Professor said as he walked over and laid his hand on Rico's shoulder. Then, looking back and beaming at his aides added, "I told you, didn't I? Everyone's a sceptic, but you can all pay up when

27

we get back."

The Lord Professor turned back to Rico and the Squad. "Can you feel it?" he asked.

Tia, Butch, Jenna, and Eddie all nodded.

"Feel what?" Rico asked puzzled.

"You, Rico," the Lord Professor said. "Your aura has changed. It's difficult to explain as it's not as clear to me as it should be." Shaking his head, clearly perplexed, he took a step back to give Rico space. "Can we meet your new companion?"

Rico gave a mischievous grin. "But Lord Professor, companions are not allowed in the courtyard."

There was a moment of pause … then the Lord Professor rumbled out a huge belly laugh that continued for some time. Rico grinned at the pleading looks on his friends' faces.

"That was well met, Rico," the Lord Professor laughed, finally controlling himself, and wiping his eyes. "But just this once, I will let you off."

Rico nodded, closed his eyes, and looked inside himself. Immediately his chameleon and snake manifested, one on his shoulder, the other around his leg. His new companion didn't appear.

Instead, he felt a slight shake of the head from him, and a barely discernible whisper, "Not today, Professor."

Rico's eyes flew open and immediately met the Lord Professor's, who didn't look surprised. He simply nodded his understanding. Had he heard his third's response?

"It looks like your third is tired from its awakening. It can sometimes take a few days before they have the strength to manifest," the Lord Professor said, as he patted Rico's shoulder.

He turned his attention back to the Squad, not showing his disappointment. "Right you lot, back to work. You have tests to prepare for."

"Thank-you, Lord Professor," the Squad replied as one.

They turned to leave quickly ... the Lord Professor's voice following them, "However, you have been penalised five points. It is only lower because you stopped the conflict."

"Thank-you, Lord," they all replied again, moving quickly before he changed his mind. Even with a deduction of five points, they still had a much better chance of beating Raptor Squad to top spot. Now, there were only two points in it.

* * *

As the Squad scuttled off the courtyard, the Lord Professor's aide giggled. "They are moving as if the gauntlet is closing in on them."

A distracted chuckle came from the Lord Professor, but the aide wasn't upset. He knew the Lord Professor had already moved on to the next job at hand.

"That is going to cost me, Dutton," the Lord Professor whispered quietly.

"No doubt, Lord, but it's nothing we can't handle."

The Lord Professor smiled and looked at the retreating Squad. "They do look to be in rather a hurry, should I call after them?" he teased.

Dutton shook his head, smiling. "I think they've had enough excitement for one day. That might just push 'em over the edge, My Lord."

"You always spoil my fun," the Lord Professor laughed. Not missing a beat, he continued, "We need to keep an eye on Rico and the Squad. His third is strong; strong enough to hide from me and refuse a summoning. We need to use them."

Dutton nodded.

"But Dutton, be careful. I have a feeling that Phoenix Squad is going to be full of surprises."

"Yes, My Lord. I will put Katrina on it. Let's hope they can come first in the testing so you can put them where they are best suited."

"Hmm … the testing," the Lord Professor mused.

Then he turned and headed towards the Hall of Recognition, to deal with the testers who had doubted his assessment, muttering to himself as he went.

"Tradition can be such a bind to plans unless …" was all he caught as the Lord Professor moved away.

He watched him, grinning. He loved the Lord Professor and his simple manner; how quick he was to laughter and mischief. It never failed to amaze him how effortlessly he was able to put the students at ease, so that he could garner the information he needed.

More impressive, was the loyalty he instilled in everyone he encountered; he was a true leader. The kind that could exact actual change.

He realised the Lord Professor was halfway across the yard and skipped after him, wondering what mess he would get to twist to their benefit next.

CHAPTER EIGHT

They flew through the town in a blur, guarding each other's backs, and watching alleyways for ambushes. The faces they saw, analysed, and then dismissed. It was unlikely that Raptor Squad would try anything so soon, but it was better to be safer rather than sorry.

Pausing outside a bakery, Butch darted inside to buy some food. As soon as he emerged, they continued, moving in silence, and only communicating through hand signals and body language as they headed for their headquarters.

It sounded grander than it was; an old structure they had found while training in the forest, outside of the city. It had required a lot of time to fix up so that it was usable, but the effort was worth it. It was the ideal place for them to escape too, enabling them to practice and plan in secret.

Eddie was at the front of the Squad, with Rico and Butch on the flanks. Tia was in the middle with her crow (the only companion they manifested in the town) flying above them, and providing information on routes. Jenna brought up the rear.

They moved quickly, comfortable, and confident in each other, avoiding citizens where they needed to. It meant a few detours, but it prevented anyone from getting hurt or reporting the indiscretions of the students.

Once they hit the outskirts of the city, the companions who loved to hunt manifested and took their positions, flanking the group.

Eddie's lion and wolverine formed a pincer either side of him. Tia's jaguar was to Rico's right. Jenna's wolf dropped back to create a vanguard and keep a watchful eye on its pack. Butch's big black bear was off to the left with a huge grin splitting its face, and his squirrel clung on to the fur of the bear's head, its eyes wild with excitement.

The Squad relaxed a little, smiling at their companions pleasure to just run and enjoy the day. The sky was also a little fuller.

Jenna's eagle and phoenix joined Tia's crow and owl, all flying a shielding pattern above.

"I bet we look badass from up there!" Butch laughed, breaking the tension.

Jenna's phoenix cried out her distinctive call. "Aldela agrees," Jenna laughed.

They quickly left the city behind them and approached the edge of the forest. As they did, the Squad slowed, leaving Eddie's lion and wolverine to enter and check that it was safe.

After just a few moments, the team were moving quickly again; skipping through the trees - each guided by their knowledge of the forest, and their companions' unique natural abilities.

Before long, Eddie stopped, and the rest of the Squad followed suit. A companion of each member moved to the foot of five large trees and disappeared inside. A minute later, the ground rumbled, and stairs appeared in the earth beneath the trees.

Rico, Jenna, and Butch filed down the stairs quickly with their companions, as Eddie turned to Tia. "Set the perimeter."

Tia nodded; her crow companion landing on her hand. "OK, Phantom, set the perimeter eight separate points. Keep a line of sight and stay hidden. You will join me inside; I don't want you to miss the news."

Phantom winked at her and spread his wings. Smaller, identical versions of Phantom started to appear. They started circling Tia, and once all eight were present, they halted before darting off in different directions. All were travelling the same distance from the central point, and then merging into a tree closest to them.

Tia and Phantom closed their eyes. "Perfect," Tia smiled.

Phantom cawed loudly and jumped up to her shoulder.

Eddie didn't even ask if it was set up. He knew it would be. Surveillance and perimeter setting were Tia's speciality, and if she was happy, he was.

"Right, let's go see what Rico has to say," he instructed as they both filed down the stairs after their companions, who seemed just as eager as they were. Behind them, the ground closed, and there was nothing left to find; it was as if the earth had swallowed them up.

* * *

Eddie smiled as he entered the chamber and saw each member of the Squad settling themselves down.

"Creatures of habit," his gargoyle grumbled in his mind, making Eddie's smile wider.

"Don't pretend you don't find it endearing, Dozer; I know

33

you better than that."

"Humf." A quiet shrug of the shoulders was all he received, as Dozer moved off and took his usual perch on the plinth in the corner, overseeing proceedings. He was followed by Jax and Grey Claw, who curled up around the bottom, settling their heads on their paws, each trying surreptitiously to watch Rico; curiosity had infected them all.

Eddie looked over and tilted his head at Dozer who winked, the slight curling of his lip accepting the irony of his earlier comments. Tia slid past him and took her place, as he shook his head at Dozer in amusement.

Then, looking back to the Squad, he took a minute to survey them. Each one was taking their time settling in; making sure their companions were comfortable before settling themselves. It was a ritual of their arrival here, and as Dozer had said, they were all creatures of habit.

Even so, he could feel the excitement in all of them. A lot had happened in the last thirty minutes, and they needed time to thrash it out, to understand what the implications were, and most importantly, plan their next steps.

He looked over to Rico, who had a bemused look on his boyish face, and almost laughed aloud. Rico was used to being the alpha with only his two minor companions; Misty and Rexter, who exclusively engaged on request and took his lead. It was going to take time for him to become used to having a major companion. A strong one, if the vibes he was getting were anything to go by; major companions tended to say what they wanted, when they wanted, and do what they liked.

He sighed, contemplating how this new companion would fit in with Phoenix Squad. Would it follow orders, and more significantly, how would it change their friend?

A movement to his left attracted his attention, and he moved his eyes over the rest of his Squad.

Jenna was having an animated conversation with Aldela, her beautiful majestic phoenix, while Dizzy, her golden eagle, perched on Dancer's back and watched.

Butch was lounging on the floor, with his legs spread and his head rested on Traveller's shell, eyes closed. Wiggy, his squirrel companion, was chattering in his and Traveller's ears before scampering over Traveller and curling up in Fence's black fur. The black bear let out a huff and pretended he was unhappy at this intrusion, which Wiggy blatantly ignored.

Tia, who was the last to enter, moved to her favourite spot in Butch's lap, looking small in comparison. He opened his eyes and gave her a huge smile as she snuggled into his arms. Phantom and Utah, her owl, hopped onto Traveller's shell, as Kalina, her jaguar, settled beside Traveller's head.

Now that they were all settled, he took his position within this circle of friends, resting up against Dozer's plinth. His hands settling absently in Jax's mane, and fondling Grey Claw's ear.

As he sat, the rest of the Squad's conversations stopped, and they looked to him. He nodded as he closed his eyes and the rest of Phoenix Squad followed suit.

It was part of a process Jenna had instilled in them. Each person was to replay the events of the day back from their perspective. It was her and Aldela's idea that when they had a chance, they should each form their views. A trick that they felt enabled quicker decision making on the battlefield, meaning they were not solely reliant on one member to make the decisions. It also allowed everyone to discuss the events from their perspective, highlighting things the others may have missed.

Although today, Rico's huff of frustration disrupted their thoughts. "Are they all this infuriating?" he groaned, his head in his hands.

Each of the companions presented their version of a grin at Rico, and the Squad laughed.

"Welcome to the real world," Butch laughed. "It will take time for you to get used to this, Rico. A major is a different companion entirely. They have a mind of their own, and if you don't get along …"

"Yes, yes, I know!" Rico interrupted angrily, raising an eye from Traveller.

"Pull yourself together," Rico's third growled in his mind. Startled, Rico realised his actions. The Squad watched him physically pull himself together. "That's better," the third stated calmly.

Rico looked over to Butch. "I'm sorry."

Butch nodded, smirking. "No problem, Brother. When Traveller first appeared, he was so stubborn, I spent two weeks terrorising the family in frustration."

Rico smiled his thanks at Butch's understanding.

Before it could get awkward, Eddie leaned forward … "Right, a lot has happened today, and before we thrash out the implications, the most amazing thing is Rico finding his third."

Rico looked up beaming, catching everyone's eye.

"What can you tell us, Rico? The Lord Professor said your third was tired?" Tia asked.

Before Rico could answer, Jenna interjected, "Although I find that surprising considering how powerful it feels."

Rico blushed. "It's a he, Jenna, and he wasn't tired. He just didn't want to appear for the Lord Professor."

The Squad looked shocked by this news, but as Rico spoke, his third began manifesting in the middle of the group.

Rico shrugged his shoulders. "But it appears he has no issue with appearing for you lot."

Rico momentarily tore his eyes away from the creature that was appearing in front of him. He looked around the room, pleased to see the awe on his friends' faces mirroring his own.

The eyes of each of the Squad, and their companions, were riveted to the creature that was appearing.

Jenna's hand instinctively went to Aldela, resting gently on her wing. "Such power," she muttered, met by a muted caw.

"Especially for such a little midget," Eddie laughed, trying to lighten the tension.

Every set of companion's eyes immediately flashed to him, including Rico's third, who was obviously unimpressed.

"What?" Eddie backtracked. "He is."

All three of his companions shook their heads. They looked back to Rico's third, inclining their heads to him in an apologetic fashion.

Rico found this funny. He had always wondered who was in charge when majors were involved.

"Time for you to find out," his third's voice spoke into his mind.

At that, his third disappeared, and then reappeared in front of Grey Claw, looking tiny, but not weak. In fact, it was quite the opposite. He was exquisite and unusual.

A casual glance may categorise him as some sort of small lizard, but that would not do him justice. He was of the lizard family, but not your standard garden variety. His scales shimmered in the light, appearing to change colour as he moved. His hind legs looked powerful, with muscles that rippled across his torso as he sat back on his haunches. His front legs were smaller, but they looked no less powerful. His snout sat slightly out from his face, his eyes offset, giving him a better peripheral vision. Running down his back were two rows of spines, finished off with a wicked spiked ball on the end of his tail.

While Rico had been revelling in the appearance of his new companion, Grey Claw had mimicked his position. They both closed their eyes and touched noses, the contact lasting a brief five seconds. Once the connection was broken, Rico's third moved on to each of the other companion's, greeting minors in precisely the same way as the majors.

He did not approach Dozer and Aldela; instead, he went to Butch, Tia, and then Jenna. Each of them holding out their hands in front of their face, allowing his third to sit there and follow the same ritual he had with the companions.

When there was only Eddie, Dozer, and Aldela left, Rico's third returned to the centre of the room.

He looked to Dozer and bowed his head, not breaking eye contact. Dozer nodded, then sprung from his plinth, landing in front of him. Rico's third smiled, then followed the same process with Aldela. She nodded her head, spread her beautiful wings, and sprung alongside Dozer.

Finally, Rico's companion looked at Eddie, who clearly didn't understand what the third expected of him. He glanced from face to face, hoping for some indication, when the third growled. "Does he insult me again?"

Rico was about to respond, when a beautiful voice that

sounded like music beat him to it,

"No, Old One, he does not. Selentine Rituals are not followed or taught anymore."

It took a moment for Rico to realise that it was Aldela who had spoken.

Every set of eyes in the room went wide with shock; transfixed by the three companions in the middle of the room.

Then, a voice that was deep and gravelly spoke directly to Eddie. "Eddie, the Old One has pledged his protection and loyalty to each of Phoenix Squad. He expects the same in return. However, he does not presume that we are expecting the same from each other."

Rico's third nodded at Dozer and continued, "The Lord and Lady have accepted me, as is custom. As the leader, Eddie … yours is the final acceptance."

Eddie smiled, quickly regaining his composure and control now that he knew what his role was in this. "But you are pretty small, with a cute tail," he said.

Dozer shook his head at Eddie's further attempt to relieve the tension, but Eddie took a quick step forward, joining the three in the centre of the room.

They all bowed, placing their hand, paw, or wing on top of each other.

As they finished, Rico's third appeared on Eddie's shoulder and spoke directly into his ear. Eddie paled … then let out a big booming laugh.

Rico's third re-emerged back in the centre of the room, looking directly at Rico as he addressed the room. "My name is Landragortandir Oldryford." He smiled at their confused faces. "But you should call me Llýr. I am honoured to join

Phoenix Squad." He gave a slight nod to Aldela. "The startled looks on your faces means that you are either dazzled by my fabulous visage, or that you've never communicated with another's companion before. I think it's the first," Llýr laughed.

All eyes were wide and bright, but no one spoke. Llýr grinned. "Huh, even I'm not that good looking. The fact no one has found their tongue, I take it I'm right? You will all get used to that."

The joke, alongside the self-effacing shrug of his shoulders, broke the spell. Everyone in the room started talking at once. It was a cacophony of sound, rather than individual voices.

There were now sixteen of them in total, all vying to have their viewpoints heard. Only the four in the middle of the room remained quiet. After a few seconds, Dozer slammed his huge fists together, the noise reverberating around the room and stopping all conversation short.

"Thank-you, Lord," Llýr acknowledged. "We have time to discuss and answer all questions, but to begin with … I do not know what strengths and abilities this companionship with Rico will bring, only time will tell. Still, it appears the first is communication."

He looked around the room, pleased he had their complete attention. "As you can probably guess … this ability allows those within a group to communicate with each other when they wish to do so. How far this ability goes, we will have to test. But it will get stronger over time. In the meantime, if you have something private to say … then you should do this via your link with your companions. When we are present, all verbal communication will be heard by all."

The Squad nodded, accepting Llýr's explanation without

question.

Eddie took over. "However, time is against us. We have the final tests to prepare for, and thanks to Rico, Llŷr, and the Lord Professor, we have a better chance of victory."

Dozer, Llŷr, and Aldela nodded.

Eddie turned to Jax. "Jax, if you would ..."

Jax moved to his feet, and disappeared through one of the side walls. After a few moments, the wall slid aside, revealing a large table with a scale model of Selenta on the top of it.

Llŷr suddenly appeared on the roof of the Hall of Recognition, looking huge, and imposing. Rico's instinct said this was how it should be, and Llŷr looked at Rico and winked.

Llŷr turned back and considered the model city, then looked over to Tia, and nodded. "Excellent work, Tia."

Tia blushed as the rest of the Squad murmured their agreement. "Thank-you," she mumbled, struggling to restrain her pride.

Eddie strode over. "Right, Phoenix Squad, let's get down to it, and work out how this new skill can be best used to our advantage."

The Squad filed around, taking up their positions. The planning and learning of a new interaction began.

CHAPTER NINE

They moved down the middle of the street, with people diving to get out of their way. Nobody wanted to be the target for the wrath that was clear in their facial expressions. The streets emptying as they prowled along was for the best.

Jonas, flanked by Ruben and Lisa, could feel his companions' anger, fuelled by his own. They wanted to strike out at something ... wisely, he kept them on a tight leash.

Ellie and Thomas brought up the rear. Unlike the rest, Thomas had a huge grin on his handsome face ... not to be confused with happiness ... this was a grin of expectation. He knew there was going to be a reckoning, and he couldn't wait to begin.

As they turned the corner into the market grounds, the crowds again dispersed as Raptor Squad approached the training barracks courtyard. As one, they looked up at the leader board.

"Have they calculated it wrong?" Ruben asked, confusion adding a comical look to his squashed face.

"No," was his reply.

"Looks like the Lord Professor is not a total idiot," Thomas sniggered, as the rest of the Squad grinned.

"He must have penalised Phoenix Squad. So, we remain in the lead," he replied.

"It still makes for a close contest. We could have lost all three of the last tests and still remained at the top, so long as we finished them in the top three," Ellie advised.

"Don't remind me," he growled. "But at least this means we still have the upper hand. We are in the lead, they have to beat us," he said confidently, but looked away from the Squad quickly so they could not see the doubt in his eyes. He needed them to see his confidence, not his doubt.

The lead they had before today was purely down to the first few tests. Raptor Squad had come into the school as a fully formed unit, already tested. His father had made sure of that.

Each member of Raptor Squad had skills that complimented each other. So, while the other teams, including Phoenix Squad, had been getting to know one another, working out how to work as a team, Raptor Squad was already there.

This meant that over the first half of the first year they had built a sizeable lead, coming first in all the tests. Phoenix Squad had jelled quickly compared to the rest, and were always second or third, so Raptor Squad had not run too far ahead of them.

Since then, the two Squads had been pretty much neck and neck, each Squad winning the top spot every other test, and making the lead that Raptor Squad had built in that first half-year, ever more valuable.

The Lord Professor had shattered that cushion of security today. The top spot was up for grabs. He would not lose.

"Are we going to see your father, Jonas, and appeal this?"

Lisa asked timidly, hiding her skinny, insipid frame behind Ellie.

He had to fight from biting Lisa's head off as she interrupted his thoughts. He needed them to be on the top of their game, and a dressing down was not the right course of action right now.

"You are learning to control that temper, Jonas, that is good. A silent boil will always show you like a stronger leader," his companion spoke into his mind.

He grinned. "Yes, Drake, I agree, and they also don't see the dagger until it is hilt deep."

They both laughed as he turned to the Squad. "No, Lisa, we don't need to. It won't do us any good anyway, my father would expect us to succeed regardless."

The Squad nodded knowingly. Jonas's team had all known his father since they were young, and knew his expectations of them. Nothing but first would be acceptable.

"If we want to join the Black Hand, My Friends, we do it ourselves," he continued with fake positivity.

They all nodded back at him, their anger still present, but a new determination in their eyes.

Ellie looked him in the eye. She was the only one of the Squad not truly scared of him. "Can I suggest that we use this, and revisit our plans for the tests? We need to ensure that we have the best possible approach, and enough contingency plans in place to handle any unexpected challenges."

The group nodded and turned to move off, when Thomas's shrike companion alighted on to his shoulder, reporting through its beautiful song. Thomas turned to him. "Looks like Phoenix Squad is taking the same approach, they have headed out to the forest," Thomas advised.

He scowled. "One day, I will find that place and burn it down. Let's go."

Raptor Squad turned and stalked through the streets, making their way to Jonas's home.

* * *

Raptor Squad arrived at Jonas's house; a massive structure that dominated this part of town, its unforgiving lines and personality, mirroring that of its owner. The gates opened before them, and the Squad didn't even have to break their stride.

Waiting for them was his father's trusted confidant, and the man who made the estate tick; Kennedy. He barely paid him any notice other than to demand he bring food and drink to their training area, as he knew where his loyalties lay. A thought struck him. "Kennedy, is my father here?"

Kennedy shook his head. "No, Young Sire, he is busy this afternoon."

He nodded, that was not unusual.

Kennedy continued, "But do not worry, he is aware of the incident with the Lord Professor."

He smiled, hiding his irritation at Kennedy's presumption that he cared. "I'm not surprised, Kennedy. I assume he was angry?"

Kennedy himself smiled, but it looked more like a sea monsters smile before it struck … "Oh yes, Young Sire, he was furious, and asked me to inform you that he would like an explanation as to how you were so stupid as to be caught fighting in the courtyard."

It felt like Kennedy had just slapped him across the face,

momentarily knocking his concentration. His shock quickly turned to anger, but before he could respond, Kennedy had disappeared into the villa.

Muttering under his breath, he turned and led the Squad into their training facility. They strolled through the gym, where every weapon imaginable adorned the walls, and entered the adjoining room.

There were five cushioned alcoves encircling the room. Each member of the Squad split off to their respective areas, their companions manifesting, and taking their own places.

Lisa walked to the wall beside the door and pressed a series of buttons. In the middle of the room, a perfect model of Selenta appeared; magnificently carved in bone and kindera. An orb of light dropped from the ceiling, mimicking the sun. As it moved, it showed the shadows created, no matter the time of day.

Ellie stood, her muscled frame moving smoothly, gently brushing against Lisa as she took her place at the table, and he took his place at the head.

Ellie looked to him, and he nodded for her to begin.

"The first test will be crowd control. There is a full week of events coming up, culminating in the final festival. Our guess is that they will ask the top two teams to cover the final festival, and we will focus our planning on that eventuality. However, we must prepare for all. We will start with the most basic events, and finish at the festival," Ellie finished, looking to him.

"Let's get to it," he ordered.

The rest of the Squad moved to the table and began talking; going through the plans, and their individual parts to play. Within minutes, they were so engrossed in the planning, that they missed the delivery of food and drink.

CHAPTER TEN

He stood at his post, looking down the length of the Serpents Tongue.

This was his favourite part of his duty; being here at the Serpents Tongue. He watched the waters bubbling and cascading in waves, as the earth below clawed its way to rise slowly up to the surface.

Sea creatures, of all shapes and sizes, were scurrying for the safety of the sea before the rising earth claimed them as its own, and left them stranded on land … gasping for the lifeblood of the sea to sustain them.

Once the land settled, a Squad would go out and collect the creatures, which they would then sell for a tidy sum. Some were worth more than others; depending on their rarity, and the profits were then shared between the soldiers in the barracks.

As he heard the gates open below, he spared a look around. There was no one else at their posts. Panic rose in him. So caught up in his evening ritual, he had forgotten about the order to be in the barracks at the next rising.

Instead of turning and running to the barracks, something caused him to turn back, and look out over the Serpents Tongue.

His eyes nearly bulged out of his sockets. This was not a monster collection Squad ... they were the Elite soldiers of the Emperor.

They moved with purpose and strength, and couldn't be confused with anything other than what they were. He sunk to his knees as he realised who was with them.

"Emperor," he whispered in awe.

He had been privileged enough to hunt with him a few years ago, and recognised his broad frame, majestic features, and the way he moved.

"That is a shame," a commanding voice growled sadly.

The soldier opened his eyes, and in front of him was a golem the size of his head, made totally of dark rock. Each part of its body was perfectly proportioned, and no doubt powerful, despite its size.

"I forgot the order," was all the soldier whispered.

The golem nodded gently, with a knowing, almost kind look in its eye. This was the last thing the soldier saw as the golem moved quickly ... extending its arm into a wicked rock stake, and piercing it through the soldier's eye and into his brain; killing him instantly.

"May the Emperor's love carry you through to the other side," the golem prayed, then sighed. "A true soldier lost."

He turned from the now lifeless body, and walked through the window, disappearing into the night.

* * *

Magnar looked back over his shoulder at the fortress that protected this end of the Serpents Tongue. "The first life lost to this venture," he muttered.

49

"It won't be the last," Cassius purred.

He remained quiet, there was no answer required, he knew this to be true. Turning from the fortress, he realised he had slowed and left a gap in the cordon that covered the decoy.

There were fifteen of his Elite guard with him for this trip … his most trusted Elite. Each one had been with him since birth and was completely loyal.

They moved with purpose, eating up the ground along the Serpents Tongue. The five scouts were already almost halfway across. Their job was to report back if there was no exit on the other side.

His position was on the back-left corner of the cordon. There were two in the middle, one wearing the uniform of the *Emperor*. It was not much different from the Elite guard uniform, which was dark blue, almost black. The pants and top looked basic, but they were made with a durable material they had discovered in their battles with the Tendrin's, that absorbed damage, and could deflect even the sharpest blade. Each wore black shoes, designed by the most skilled cobbler in Carasayer; hard wearing and silent on all surfaces.

The sigil of his house was coloured dark grey and placed on his left bicep. The Elite soldiers had the same sigil. Theirs was placed on the right bicep, with marks below, denoting their rank within the guard.

"Almost there," Tink chimed in his ear.

"Moment of truth," Cassius growled.

There was no call from the forward scouts … had they gotten intercepted along the way and killed? Momentarily, he forgot about his morbid thoughts … as out of the mist … the Lost Continent fortress appeared.

It was of a similar size to its neighbour across the Serpents

Tongue, but that's where the similarities ended. This one was all curves, as opposed to hard lines.

With a practised eye, he quickly assessed the fortress. There was no doubt in its ability to do its job. Still, the builders here clearly spent as much time ensuring it was pleasing to the eye, as they did to make sure it was as challenging to assault as possible.

He was relieved to see that the door to the fortress was open. The path across the maze of defences was clear, with the forward scouts waiting as instructed at points along the way.

"We could never take this place by force, Tink," he spoke in his mind. They would not speak aloud until they cleared the fortress.

An affirmative nod of agreement was all the response he received.

Within moments, they were through the gates and moving along a tunnel. It sloped quickly downwards, then moved into a long and gradual slope upwards. He noted various blocking points along the way.

"A killing zone," Cassius mused.

"It looks that way," he replied.

The silence was absolute - their quiet footsteps lending an eerie quality.

After what felt like a lifetime, but was more like thirty seconds, the group broke out into the night, and straight into another killing zone, this time an open courtyard, surrounded by enormous walls full of slots on two levels, with a small door one hundred yards away.

"If they want to betray us, now is the time," Cassius grumbled.

No assault came out of the night, and the group filed unhurried through the door; moving through three similar chambers.

Finally, they entered an area with stairs leading into different parts of the fortress. In front of them stood massive doors; open, inviting them out into the empty countryside beyond.

They didn't wait for an invite … there was not another soul around but for those streaming out of the fortress.

He grinned, feeling the joy at being the first to walk on the Lost Continent in over a thousand years. Not taking too much time to enjoy the moment, he set about preparing himself for his meeting with The Black.

As they cleared arrow range from the tower, a silent order dropped the Elite into an easy lope that would eat the miles, and not tax them too much. This speed would allow them to arrive at their destination on time, but also strong and still able to fight.

"Hmm, that's disappointing," Cassius mused.

"What is?" he asked.

"I was expecting a monster to be waiting," Cassius mocked, laughing.

The tension momentarily lifted as he laughed too.

* * *

As the group from Carasayer moved into the night … a shadow emerged from the roof of the fortress, dropping to the floor in front of the gate.

A hawk appeared on his shoulder and chittered loudly, before leaping into the air, a message in its claws.

It would pass the message on to another soldier, a few miles down the road, to let them know the group was coming; noting its size, compliment, and the shadow's view on who to watch. This message would continue to be passed-on ... until it reached The Black, allowing him to be ready for when they arrived.

CHAPTER ELEVEN

"You are inordinately proud of that kill, Nala." He bared his teeth in a huge grin. Swift continued, "It's such a paltry little thing, barely bigger than our paws."

He buried his nose and teeth back into the rabbit he had caught, savouring the taste and his victory, laughing happily in his mind.

"Please explain why you are so happy with this little thing; it will not fill our belly. You weren't this happy when we brought down that deer yesterday," Swift grumbled.

He felt her confusion coming through. How could he explain that it was not the kill itself that had pleased him, but the manner of the kill? He had tracked and caught the rabbit himself. For the first time, Swift had not helped him decipher the images, smells, and tastes. He had finally achieved something on his own.

How could he explain that he felt he might be able to contribute, maybe even get the hang of being a wolf?

Swift sighed and smiled. "I understand, Nala."

Surprised, he jumped back from the kill.

"But I didn't say anything! I didn't want to offend you."

Swift cocked her head. "Why would I be offended, Nala?

You are simply developing and learning what you need to survive. I'm proud of you. You will be able to survive if I am not here."

He grinned like a child at the praise. It took a few moments before the last comment hit him in the stomach. He began to ask Swift what she meant when there was a loud noise in the forest.

They dropped into a defensive crouch, utilising all their senses to ascertain the threat.

Then, around twenty feet away, a sleek, light brown shape, darted across the trail into the undergrowth. To the right, something bulldozed its way through the forest, in hot pursuit.

Nala realised there were three shapes in pursuit, not one, as they too crossed the trail no more than three heartbeats behind the first creature.

But, whereas the first was sleek, quick, and silent … these creatures were large, blundering beasts, with huge heads and massive jaws and teeth. Their hind legs were slightly shorter than their front.

"Hyenas," they growled together.

A mutual hatred of the animal meant that they instinctively decided to help the prey, whatever it was.

They took off at an angle that would take them parallel to the hyenas, allowing them to overtake, and eventually link up with the prey.

"Swift, take point on this hunt," he said, happy to allow Swift to lead on something this important. His mind flooded with images that showed the forest floor ahead; the fallen tree they needed to jump, and the tree roots protruding from the ground they would need to avoid as not to break a paw.

Swift's expertise at interpreting the outside environment, allowed him to focus on his movement and speed. They worked in perfect unison; flying through the forest, making no noise as they quickly came alongside the hyenas.

He shot forward in a burst of speed, taking him alongside the prey, but the hyenas changed direction suddenly.

Swift, identified that their quarry had taken a turn and was tiring, she could hear it panting. Rather than take a full turn, Swift decided on a gentle curve in case they changed direction again, confident they could catch them easily.

Suddenly, there was a loud, victorious bark from the hyenas. Swift presented the image of a clearing with a sleek she-wolf backed up against a tree, teeth bared, and growling a challenge to the hyenas. They had formed a semi-circle in front of her, yipping happily; confident they had their kill.

Examining the she-wolf, as he and Swift closed the distance, he wasn't sure they would have it all their own way.

A grin from Swift. "And we haven't arrived yet."

The hyenas had no idea that the chances of them getting their prey were about to disappear.

They flew through the last sections of the forest, planning their attack, and implementing it efficiently. They broke through into the clearing in a flash of fur, hitting the middle hyena like a rock, and driving it into the ground with a satisfying crunch of broken bones. Snapping their jaws out to the left, they ripped the flesh from the shoulder of another.

They bounced back up from the impact and landed between the hyenas and the she-wolf.

Previously excited yips had turned to whimpers and cries of pain from the two injured hyenas. The smallest, uninjured hyena, was quickly backing away.

Nala looked the hyenas over ... growling a challenge for them to attack.

* * *

The hyena didn't know where the attack had come from. There had been no warning, and they had waited for days to catch the she-wolf; the boss wanted her.

Now, this wolf stood before them and their prize. It was massive, its snout covered in his brother's blood.

Even if they were uninjured, they wouldn't have engaged with such small numbers. To defeat a creature of this size required the pack, and there was no chance of that, they had spread out to hunt the she-wolf.

He didn't recognise this new wolf; its size alone would have marked it out as a known adversary, but ... add in the white stripe down its flank ... it would have been infamous.

The best course of action was to retreat, and hope the boss was forgiving, or more realistically, pray that the information about this new arrival to The Forbidden ... earned them a lesser punishment.

They yipped as one, and then disappeared into the forest, as quickly as their injuries would allow.

* * *

"I could have handled them myself, you know," a voice growled angrily, as the hyenas retreated into the forest.

Nala's head flew around to the she-wolf. He was surprised and didn't know what to do or how to reply. In his mind, Swift barked out laughter, amused at his confusion. Seconds passed by as he stared at the she-wolf ...

"What?" the she-wolf growled. "You expect me to rub up against you, thanking you for your protection?"

The she-wolf moved, circling around him, then snarled. "Or do you expect me to lie down so you can mount me? So thankful I am for your protection, oh great and magnificent Wolf."

Her whole body shuddered. "Fat chance." At that, she darted off. "Dumb animals!" her parting shot.

As she disappeared, he stood there watching the spot where she had vacated the clearing and headed back into the forest.

"Swift, what just happened?" He received no answer, but he could feel Swift as she struggled to control her laughter and amusement.

"Oh, you found that funny, did you?" he growled confused, getting slightly irate. This made Swift laugh harder, causing her to snort.

He tried to stay angry, but couldn't keep it up. Swift's laughter was infectious, and soon they were laughing together just for the joy of it, using up the last of their adrenaline from the chase.

Shaking his head, they moved out of the clearing, heading to a spot where they had noticed a fallen tree stump, with a hollow covered area at the bottom, that they would easily fit into.

"She was a merged wolf, Nala," Swift explained finally as they walked through the trees.

"A what?" he asked, confused.

Swift smiled in a motherly fashion. "She is the same as you, Nala, and it looks like merged creatures can talk to each other."

He didn't answer, his mind was whirling over the new information.

Swift continued, "and I think those hyenas were merged creatures too."

He considered this and several things clicked into place.

"Of course!" he exclaimed. "The Forbidden. When someone merges with their companion, they instinctively head for the safety of the forest, it's logical that there would be more like us here."

Swift nodded. "Yes, and it seems they can speak too." She started gigging again as they lay down. "Unlike you, Nala. You dumb animal."

They both sniggered as they settled into the alcove in the tree. He resolved to find this she-wolf to learn more from her. Lifting their snout, they took a deep breath, and sent out their senses; feeling and seeing nothing but the natural life of the forest.

With thoughts of a strong-willed she-wolf filling his mind, he drifted off to sleep. Swiftwind smiled fondly as she too rested, lightly guarding her charge while she could.

CHAPTER TWELVE

I t had been disconcertingly quiet since they had left the
fortress at the Serpents Tongue, they hadn't seen anyone,
or come across any troops.

"Yet we have been watched all the way," Cassius grinned in
Magnar's mind.

He grinned back. "They are good, aren't they?" he replied.

Tink shook his head at them both. "Just because they are
good at staying hidden, doesn't mean that they are fighters."

Suddenly, a big booming laugh filled the space as a third
voice cut in ... "Yes, but you have to admit, it's a good start."

"Oh, that's right, you decide to take their side, Gravel," Tink
muttered, throwing his claws up in exasperation.

"Don't worry, Tink, it's just an observation. I'm with
you that we do this quietly." Gravel winked at Magnar and
Cassius. "With the odd fun skirmish."

They all laughed, even Tink. They were all feeling the thrill
of being behind enemy lines, cut off from their own armies,
with no one but those closest for support. It had been a long
time since they were in this type of danger. The unknown
was not something they dealt with regularly. Every move
they made was planned with precision; the repercussions
measured, and the infrastructure to enforce their will behind

any decision he made.

Here, they were in enemy territory, their route home blocked. They were at the mercy of The Black. They only had his promise of safe passage home, regardless of the outcome of their negotiations.

The Lost Continent was not much different to Carasayer, he mused. There were fields producing food, forests in abundance, and small villages and hamlets spread around. However, although the larger structures dotted about the landscape intrigued them all, and had them wanting to investigate … any deviation from the agreed approach could jeopardise these talks. The time to learn would come later.

The main group slowed to a walk as the scouts returned, reporting to the decoy that the destination was just ahead.

A large entrance, and a cleared pathway through a forest, ran off the road they had been travelling on, matching The Black's directions.

The decoy turned and addressed the group, explaining to them what the scouts had said. It was unnecessary, as they had all heard … they did it to disguise the real reason; to get final instructions from him, and his hand signals obliged.

"Move down towards the building, take it slow, keep alert, and no weapons or companions. Five go in as requested."

Instructions given, they headed down the track. The trees enclosed the Elite, and it felt like they were entering another world. Each of them had subconsciously rested their hands on their weapons, and he could feel more than one companion on the point of release.

Out of the gloom, a large house appeared; hugged by the forest on both sides. The builder's obvious intention was a visible effort to intimidate, yet it put Magnar and his men slightly at ease, because unlike the beautiful fortress on the Serpents Tongue, this was more like the buildings of home. It was all dark, hard edges, with huge imposing double doors hiding more than it revealed.

They entered a small courtyard in front of the house, and his decoy gave instructions to the Squad to spread out. Access to The Black's headquarters was restricted to just five people. All communication had stressed this to such an extent, that five appeared to be a very symbolic number to them. A meaning he hoped to understand.

The imposing doors opened, and an old woman stood before them. She looked them up and down, then huffed, as if to say she had seen it all before. If her gnarled visage was anything to go by … she probably had.

She beckoned them in and turned away, clearly expecting them to follow. They did.

"Some welcoming committee," Gravel grumbled.

"It has to be low key, Gravel. You know that," Tink reprimanded.

"They could have at least given us an armed guard," Gravel replied.

The old woman looked back at them, as she guided them unerringly down corridors that twisted and turned. They had no idea which way was back.

"I think they have," growled Cassius. His eyes through Magnar watching the old hag closely. "She is not what she seems."

Taken aback, he studied her more closely, suddenly understanding what Cassius meant.

"A shifter?" he asked Cassius.

"I think so, and a good one at that. I can't really sense it.

It's more her movements, something is not quite right."

"Through here, Gentlemen," the crone croaked, directing them into a well-lit chamber, and winking at him as he passed her.

With no time to dwell on it, he took his position and studied the surroundings. The room was modest with a few portraits of people on the walls, that looked like they illustrated history of some sort, and a table was off to the side with an assortment of food and drink on it, most of which was unrecognisable.

Five Selentans were waiting in the middle of the room, drawing attention. Three of them were nondescript, un-readable, and faded into the background. Magnar quickly labelled them as dangerous, but if they were dangerous ... the other two in the room exuded power, but in very different ways.

To the left of the centre, stood a large soldier, with a hooked nose and hooded eyes. His attire was eerily similar to Magnar's Elite guard, just minus the house sigil. He wore a black beret ... and whereas the other three hid their nature, he was on show for all to see.

He skipped over him too, because the most intriguing, was the final man present. He wore a similar outfit to the soldier, except for a large black cloak, draped across his back.

He could not get a read on him, but he was slightly smaller than the soldier to his left. He was still well-built, and would be considered a good-looking man, but his demeanour clearly defined him as The Black.

He watched him closely, as his decoy stepped forward to introduce himself. The Black simply smiled at him, stopping him short. The decoy was at a loss for what to do, not only at this breach of protocol, but at the surprise that he had so quickly stopped at this man's non-verbal instruction; emphasising the power of The Black.

"Wait," Tink whispered.

Tink, like him, sensed the change in mood but wanted to see how this played out. The decoy began to open his mouth to address The Black, but again The Black simply raised his hand, stopping him once more in his tracks.

Cassius and Gravel laughed in appreciation, but The Black never took his eyes from the decoy.

"This would go so much easier, Emperor Magnar, if we spoke directly, rather than through your proxy."

He was moving before The Black finished his sentence. His Elite would attack first and ask questions later if they felt he was in danger, and their instinct was kicking in. He felt their shift as soon as they realised the ruse was no longer a defence.

"All plans go in the wind once the first battle cry is sung," Tink intoned, as Magnar placed a hand on his decoy's shoulder.

"It's OK, Captain. Stand down," he said as he took his place, the tension in the room relaxing slightly. "Forgive the show, my personal guards take my safety very seriously. They wanted to make sure this was not a trap."

The Black smiled, and it reminded him of Cassius before he devoured his prey on the hunt.

"There is nothing to forgive, Emperor Magnar. I would expect nothing less from dedicated men," The Black replied with a respectful nod to each of the Elite, before returning his attention to him.

A door opened into a private room housing a burning fire,

two large chairs, and a table with two glasses and a beautiful bottle filled with a light blue liquid. The Black motioned to the chairs. "We have a lot to discuss, and not much time if we are to have you back across the gauntlet before morning."

He took a seat as The Black closed the door, leaving the eight soldiers in an uneasy standoff. Neither side wanted their leader out of their sight, but they were powerless to do anything about it.

He laughed as the door closed. "It's good to see your soldiers are just as protective as mine."

The Black took his seat and poured them both a glass of the blue liquid. "It can be quite tiresome, but unfortunately it is necessary."

He nodded in agreement. "When did you identify that the Captain was the decoy?" he asked.

The Black took a moment to respond. He could imagine the cogs turning, and the conversation he was having internally with his companions; did he want to reveal his cards?

"We suspected from the moment you left the fortress. I had one of my best men oversee your arrival. He felt there was something different about you. You moved the same way as the rest of the soldiers, but he felt it looked forced, and that there was an air of authority around you. Then, when you entered the room, I understood his meaning. Your Captain is good, but to the trained eye, he is not an Emperor," The Black answered.

He smiled. "Thank-you, that is something we can work on perfecting."

The Black handed him a glass. "This was made in the far reaches of Elyssa, in the north, a cold region we call

Trendorlan. Nobody knows how it is made, but it is scarce."
The Black raised the glass, and he followed suit. "To a long
and profitable alliance."

They both took a sip of the drink. He found it to be a little
sour and unpalatable, but didn't let it show. Placing the glass
back down on the table, he looked The Black directly in the
eye. "Let's get down to it."

* * *

Five hours later, their negotiations complete, they both sat
back and assessed their position.

He smiled. "It's been a long time since I have enjoyed
negotiations this much."

The Black laughed. "I was about to make the same
statement."

Mutual respect had grown between them throughout the
negotiation, progressing further than either one of them had
thought possible at this early stage. Both rose as one and
opened the middle door, neither surprised to see that the
guards had barely moved, and that the food on the table was
untouched.

He signalled to his Captain, who immediately broke off
and joined him. He spent a few minutes explaining what he
required of him via hand signals. The Captain nodded and
returned to his position.

The Black simply gave the large soldier with the beret a
look; signalling what must have been confirmation of an
earlier conversation. The soldier saluted, and disappeared
out the door, motioning to Magnar's Captain to follow him.

There were no more words shared. After a simple nod

of acknowledgement between him and The Black, the old woman reappeared out of nowhere, and led them back to the courtyard.

His Elite guard was already waiting, ready to set out albeit with a new complement of five of The Black's men, led by the large soldier.

His Captain saluted, then moved into the headquarters with four of the Elite guard. This exchange sealed the negotiations and allowed both sides to learn a little about their new allies. He smiled. He had only wanted to ensure one remained, leaving five behind was a boon. He signalled to his guard to set off back to the Serpents Tongue.

CHAPTER THIRTEEN

Kaden was pleased with his men. They had moved quickly, and arrived well before the cell, leaving him plenty of time to find a clearing and wait.

The rebels spread out in the woods around the clearing, treating it like a training exercise, not wanting to spook the cell. Seeing one man alone was better than seeing sixteen heavily armed scruffy rebels as a welcome party.

"They wouldn't scare a toddler," a voice in his mind groused.

"Behave, Tadic," he laughed back. "Besides, I remember a certain toddler climbing onto your back not too long ago and shouting giddy-up."

Tadic smirked. "Titch is different. She has the heart of a Conqueror Queen, she fears nothing, and even you do as your told."

They both smiled fondly at the memory. Titch was one of the orphaned children in the camp, and in a reversal of roles … she had taken it upon herself to adopt and look after him.

Six-going-on-sixty, and a force of nature, he mused. He suspected she already had a companion who helped her survive, looking after her, and making sure she enjoyed life. It was something they would probably not confirm until they decided it was time.

A scout pulled him from his reverie as they entered the clearing, reporting that they were almost here, and informing him of their numbers before melting into the forest.

He heard them chattering loudly and excitedly before they arrived. His suspicions were confirmed once they started to file into the clearing.

The new arrivals spread out in a Black Hand manoeuvre, covering the perimeter, and moving into positions that made a darting escape impossible. Their clothes didn't quite fit right, and they looked too well fed to be a cell that had been travelling for weeks.

He sighed, looking at the woman who left the perimeter and walked towards him. "Where are the people you are impersonating?" he asked.

A momentary look of surprise showed in the group leader's eyes before she made a minute hand signal of the Red Hand. The group followed the order and pulled a variety of weapons from within their clothing, and eight snarling companions appeared; including panthers and hunting dogs. They all surrounded Kaden.

He felt his own companions shake their heads.

"I hate it when your right, Kaden," his second companion, Tadic, commented despondently in his mind.

"What are we going to do with them?" Huff asked in the same way.

"I don't know, Huff; it really depends on their answer to my question. They are trainers playing at soldiers. Good at theory, bad at execution," he replied without uttering a word.

Aloud, he said, "You haven't answered my question."

"You are in no position to ask questions, Rebel Scum,"

the woman spat at him, followed by giggles from the group, emboldened by their success in capturing him so effortlessly. She continued with a grin on her face, "You should worry more about what we are going to do to you. But, why not tell you ... I'm feeling in a generous mood." She grinned at her companions. "They are dead. We tortured and killed the scum. They gave you up."

The woman laughed viciously at the hurt in his eyes. He shook his head sadly.

He watched her jump slightly as his face hardened, and looked her in the eye. "I really wish you hadn't done that."

He gave a simple nod of his head, and an arrow hit her in the middle of the chest, cutting short any retort she may have had.

There was a flurry of movement in the forest, accompanied by a chorus of shrieks from companions as their hosts drew their last breath, as his men entered the clearing to finish killing off the trainers.

He looked over the scene. It had taken less than ten seconds from his signal to the end of the skirmish. "Always so quick," he muttered.

A couple of his troops were nursing bites from companions; nothing too serious. He was more concerned about those who looked shaken from the encounter. He would ensure that he spent some time with them, to ease the impact of their first conflict.

He was also pleased to see that none of the Squad was relishing the kills. They had responded instantly to his instructions, without question.

"Good work, everyone," he praised the Squad, as the scouts set about stripping the bodies and putting everyone to work.

"A positive first conflict," Huff observed silently.

"Not really," Tadic retorted. "We could have taken that whole group on our own. There were only two Majors between all of them, and they were teachers, not soldiers,"

Kaden inwardly sighed. "The minute they took lives, they became combatants, Tadic. You know as well as I do that Huff is right, they have to start somewhere."

All three surveyed the scene as a third voice filled his mind, "What now, Kaden?"

"You've been quiet today, Bond," he countered, trying to delay answering.

"You know why, Kaden. I feel the future divergences as well as you. What we do today will impact significantly on the way the future pans out. I have been trying to ride the River to get a better perspective to help in the decisions we make, but it's too hazy."

They all took their time … considering Bond's words.

"So, I ask again, Kaden. What next?"

He looked over the dead bodies of the Training Sergeants and reached a decision. His companions all nodded in agreement. "We send a message."

And just like that, the future went crazy with possibilities.

CHAPTER FOURTEEN

The Black's men easily slotted into the Elite guard formation.

"You and The Black could have come from the same litter," Gravel observed in his mind.

"Maybe," Tink and Magnar replied at the same time.

"He was quite a canny negotiator," Tink continued.

"Yes, he was, Tink, and I have a feeling Regent of Elyssa is not all he wants," he responded.

"I should have just eaten him," Cassius offered.

They all laughed.

"No need, Cassius. Besides, I don't know whether we would have come out on top with a conflict."

"It would have been close," Gravel added. "We will have to observe this Major Drangor carefully, and see what he is capable of. It will give us a good barometer; those others were clearly dangerous, and deferred to him."

A myriad of images halted any further conversation, momentarily causing Tink and him to cry out in pain. He stumbled to the ground, and was immediately surrounded by the Elite guard looking for the attack, their weapons and companions unleashed.

* * *

The Black watched Magnar and his Elite guard leave. His companion, Trable, appeared in the reflection of the window. "Is Drangor up to the task?" Trable asked.

He considered for a moment. "We will find out soon enough. What I am sure of is his dedication to Selenta and I."

It was his companion's turn to consider. "I suppose for now that is enough. Do you think Magnar was suspicious of our real game?" Trable asked.

He smiled. "I'm sure he is suspicious of our motives. Something we can count on is that, like us, he will protect his interests. His Captain will have the same remit as Drangor, although I get the feeling they are out of practice with deceit. Our end game will remain secret until we decide otherwise."

They both smiled.

Suddenly, a searing pain filled their heads. Images flashed incoherently through their minds, leaving him vaguely aware of his guards' flooding into the room; weapons and companions unleashed, ready to eliminate any threat.

CHAPTER FIFTEEN

I t had rained all week during the festivals, so as the morning call woke Phoenix and Raptor Squad, they were pleased to see the sunshine streaking through the skylight windows in the barracks.

Buoyed by the excellent weather, they quickly dressed and made their way to the briefing area.

Filing into the room, they took their allotted positions. They were surprised to see that training Captain Bromfell was going to lead the briefing. Bromfell usually only spoke at the beginning of school years, giving a *how privileged you are* speech, he had never given a briefing.

It quickly became apparent why. Bromfell's delivery was emotionless; quietly droning on, assigning Squads to their selected areas, without any explanation or expectations.

He assigned the critical areas to a mixture of Red, Blue, and Black Squads. They were in their first years out of training, which left Phoenix and Raptor Squad with the outer lying areas.

Both Squads groaned. They had hoped for an area where there would be some action. The other Squads smiled at each other, knowing how they felt, having not long ago been in their position.

However, the reaction went unnoticed by the Captain, and he simply dismissed them. A Sergeant would never have tolerated that reaction, and signed off by yelling at them to do their jobs.

As the Squads piled out of the room, several members of the older Squads wished the two training teams' luck or good hunting.

It was noticeable that the Black Hand never spared a glance, or word, towards Phoenix Squad, and similarly, the Red Hand to Raptor Squad. The reputations, and approach of the top two training Squads, already filtering through.

Finally, Phoenix and Raptor were the last Squads left in the room, each taking a last look over the map of Selenta. One by one, they exited the room. Jonas and Eddie were the last to leave, each nodding to each other. Mutual respect for the other's skills and abilities, the closest these two enemies would come to wishing each other good luck.

CHAPTER SIXTEEN

Phoenix Squad's assignment was to the northern section of the city, monitored by a grizzled old Red Sergeant who worked out of the training school.

Eddie took the Squad on a roundabout route, ensuring they did not hit any of the other Squads assigned areas. Their companions' power would set off any of the other Squads checks, and the last thing he wanted to do was end up arguing with them during a test.

As they reached the outskirts of their assigned area, home to workers who held jobs within the Orange or Yellow Hands, the houses were modest yet tall with flat roofs.

"Deploy," Eddie spoke aloud, and Tia stepped forward, releasing Phantom.

Phantom immediately split, and sent miniature versions of himself to outer areas of the district, flying up and assuming his own place in the middle, keeping an eye on proceedings.

Jenna stepped forward and released Dizzy, who climbed quickly into the sky and took her position protecting Phantom, her wings spread wide, riding the wind to conserve her own and Jenna's energy.

The rest of the Squad made their way to the centre of the district, entering the central courtyard. It was modest as courtyards went, more like a small garden. This was a place for people to relax and enjoy the day, rather than a busy meeting place for everyone, like the Hall of Recognition's courtyard.

Tia found a seat in the middle of the courtyard. She sat down, crossing her legs, and releasing Utah (who perched on the chair behind her), and Kalina (who slipped silently into the surrounding shrubbery, to prowl the vicinity).

Tia was the intelligence hub for the Squad. She had eyes on the outskirts of their allocated area, and all communications would go through her. For that reason, Jenna silently slipped into the alcove of one of the buildings to provide protection today, but not before releasing Dancer, who would support and work beside Rico, keeping Aldela in reserve.

Phoenix Squad had heavily debated both these decisions, but Rico and Llýr had finally come out on top. They argued that this was a test, albeit the easiest of the last three, but still … anything could happen. If they lost Tia, they would basically be blind.

It was a significant trade-off, as it meant that there was only three of them left to clear out to the perimeter, but their most definite advantage was knowledge.

Eddie, Rico, and Butch took off in different directions, releasing their companions and clearing each building. They were checking for people who were not supposed to be there. Instructions were clear, everyone was to be at the festival unless given permission not to be. If granted, they had to keep their doors open so the Squads could confirm.

They didn't come across any open doors in this district, which was not a surprise. The Yellow and Orange were unlikely to get permission not to attend.

Rico had cleared about two-thirds of his area, when Llýr identified someone in one of the buildings. It looked like a pretty little home, with flowers on either side of the door.

Llýr appeared on his shoulder. "There is a lady in there having a baby."

Rico looked at him and froze. "What? That's not right, she should be at the White Building," he finally said, his voice tinged with panic.

"I'll let you tell her that once we get in. I'm sure she will jump up and rush over," Llýr replied. Misty and Rexter sniggered.

"Warn me before you do, Rico. I would like to be in another district," Dancer put in as she reappeared from the building that she had been clearing. "All clear, by the way."

Rico shook his head, thinking quickly. Then, his eyes brightened, and he smiled. "Misty, go to the top of the building and signal Phantom to send a message … we need Butch to get over here straight away, and request Tia find a way to inform the White."

Misty skirted quickly up the walls and disappeared.

While he waited for Butch to arrive, Rico took a tool out of his pocket, and set to work on the lock. It was a simple design, and it opened readily.

"Hello!" he shouted as he opened the door, only to hear an answering scream from further inside.

He darted into the next room, poised and ready to fight the danger that had elicited this scream. He stopped still in shock at the sight of the woman who lay naked on the bed. Her swollen belly was evidence of the child she was having. Her skin was glistening with sweat, and her companions, a fox, and an owl were by her side. Both of whom scowled at

Rico.

"Quit staring and help." Butch clipped Rico around the ear as he stepped past, grinning. Immediately he began speaking calmly to the woman, asking her name, questions about the pregnancy, and if anything had happened to bring on delivery.

Rico vaguely heard the mention of a fall, and early, before Butch urged him to go and get blankets and water.

Butch spoke softly to her, "OK, Izzy. I'm going to assess you now if that's all right?"

Izzy nodded.

"I'll explain what I'm doing."

Another nod.

"I will place my hands on your belly, and Traveller will assess the situation internally. I assume your companions have seen this happen before and will not attack?"

Izzy nodded again, just as another contraction overcame her; screaming out in pain. Butch soothed her until the pain passed, then placed his hand on her belly, closing his eyes, and channelling Traveller's healing skills.

It took longer than it would a White to carry out the assessment, but Butch's medical skills were the best in their year.

He opened his eyes and smiled. "Well, Izzy, I have good news, everything is fine. You've just pulled a muscle. You and baby are healthy, and even better, you're having the baby now."

Izzy stared, not quite comprehending.

"N-n-now?" Rico stammered from in the doorway.

Butch quickly looked back at Rico, his eyes imploring him to remain calm, then he winked and turned back to Izzy.

"Yes, now. I'm going to have to help you. Is that OK?"

Izzy nodded as Butch's calm manner put her at ease.

"Now, my friend, Rico, is going to sit with you. Squeeze his hand when the pain is too much. He's a strong lad, he can take it," Butch smiled, taking the blankets and water from Rico, and ushering him to her head.

Butch then spoke to Wiggy and Traveller in his mind, "I'm going to need your help here guys. I'm terrified, and this woman needs us."

A flood of confidence came through the bond with his companions, and he smiled and turned back to Izzy. "Let's have a baby."

Thirty minutes later an exhausted but elated Butch handed a healthy baby girl to an exhausted Izzy, who beamed tiredly.

Rico looked on in awe, both at the baby girl and at Butch, who had just gone up a hero notch in his eyes.

Llýr appeared on his shoulder and asked, "Butch, please ask Izzy if we companions may celebrate the child?"

Butch relayed this to Izzy, who advised that she felt honoured and smiled shyly. Suddenly the room was a little fuller as Butch and Rico's companions, accompanied by Dancer, filled the room alongside Izzy's own companions.

One by one, they approached the child, bowed, then moved back. As one, they raised their heads to the ceiling and cried out a loud congratulatory call. Izzy jumped at the noise, clutching her baby close.

At Llýr's urging, Butch explained that they were informing the River that a new child was born and worthy of their companionship.

"Ahem."

All eyes in the room turned. A matron stood in the

doorway looking imposing in her gown of the White. She stalked into the room, glaring at the companions who quickly disappeared. Rico and Butch backed away to give her room.

She ignored the boys and approached Izzy, whispering to her, and reaching out to touch her and the child; performing her own checks. Only when she'd finished, did she turn to Butch and Rico. Everything about her demeanour changed as she smiled at them both, now looking like a gentle grandmother who treated you to sweets.

"You did very well, Trainee. You would serve well in the White," she said in a tone that brooked no doubt that this was high praise.

Butch blushed and smiled as wide as he did when Tia entered a room.

"Now, go finish your test," the matron ordered.

Butch and Rico saluted the White, then looked to the baby and saluted before they turned and quickly left.

As they exited the house, a blaring cry from Phantom alerted them to trouble.

Dizzy dived, barely missing their head's, as the tips of her wings caressed each side of the alleyway.

"Emergency, south quadrant, NOW!" she called.

Rico and Butch didn't hesitate, setting off at a dead run.

CHAPTER SEVENTEEN

Raptor Squad's assignment was to a southern quadrant of the city, with Jonas leading them on a direct route. He was aware of the impact this would have on the other Squads, but didn't care. He was perversely pleased to see scowling companions of the Reds and Blues appear to check them out, before returning to their stations.

They did not see any of the Black Hand when they passed through their areas, but suspected they had anticipated this approach, and catered for it.

Their area of the city was home to mainly Greens and Whites, and at Jonas's signal the Squad spread out, quickly positioning themselves at each road that ran through the quadrant.

They all released one of their companions; Ruben's bat, Thomas's shrike, and Lisa's hawk all headed into the sky above to provide surveillance and early warnings of danger. The rest of the companions moved out, disappearing through walls, and checking inside for anyone hanging around or showing signs of suspicious activity. They then relayed images of everything they thought may be of interest.

As they slowly moved through the streets, he grew frustrated. This wasn't a test of his Squad, there was no one here.

The Whites would be on duty, and the Greens would never miss a chance to party.

"Jonas!" Lisa called, with more inquiry than emergency in her voice.

He moved to her, and she explained that Jepp, her jackal, had identified a woman giving birth in one of the blocks in her area.

"Not our problem," he scowled. "Send Jasmine to locate a White so they can deal with this, then move on. We still have half the district to check."

Lisa called to her owl companion and sent her gliding into the air with instructions that needed delivering to a White.

He moved back to his position and continued his sweep, comfortable that he had followed protocol. The pregnant woman was not worth his time, and the Black Hand instructor, who was recording their performance silently, would agree and log it as such.

Raptor Squad quickly finished their sweep of the homes and moved to their assigned areas.

Over the next few hours, he stalked from one section of the quadrant to the other, taking reports of nothing happening from each of the Squad. His mood was growing steadily darker, wishing for something to happen.

He was just leaving Ruben, when he called him back. He watched as Ruben's bat landed lightly on his shoulder, and chirped into his ear. His eyes lit up as a smile creased Ruben's face.

"Something has happened at the festival, and crowds are rampaging out in all directions, causing damage, and looting as they go," Ruben relayed.

He couldn't believe it; were his prayers answered?

"They will hit the district from the north," Ruben finished.

They both clambered up onto the roof of the building, looking in the direction of the festival courtyard, smiling as they saw the smoke rising from numerous areas.

He watched the fires for a moment, and saw their containment to the main walkways. The other Squads must have been corralling the rioters down routes that would cause less damage. His instinct was to fight head-on, to overwhelm them with force, and beat them into submission.

"Fun, yes, but not the way to score highly," Drake offered into his mind.

"Unfortunately, I know. The other Squads have shown us the right approach," he replied.

He signalled to Thomas's shrike, and Lisa's owl, to inform the others that he wanted them to report in. Within minutes, the rest of the Squad had arrived on the rooftop. He outlined his plan, and they all dispersed to prepare … and to wait for the mayhem to hit.

CHAPTER EIGHTEEN

The Lord Professor sat on the balcony of Yellows headquarters, with representatives from all the Hands, including the Grey. Everyone was enjoying warm treats and rare drinks, as they watched the festival display below.

The Central Plaza of the city was huge, yet every spare space was full of citizens of Selenta. There was laughter, dancing, singing, and food and drink ... all supplied by the nimble Purples, who darted through the throngs.

This was their day, or at least that's what they believed, the Lord Professor thought as he watched the Purple entertainers scattered throughout the crowds. They were juggling, performing tricks and other acts, delighting in the enthralled smiles on the children's faces.

Off to the right, was the main stage, being prepared for the final official ceremony of the day. The reason for the festivals was to present the final thank-you gifts to the Hands from the people of Selenta, but it was aimed at reinforcing the caste system, and getting the people to be happy about it.

As each person in Selenta belonged to one of the Hands, it was a gift from one Hand to another. A way of representing the unity of the Hands, and showing how they interacted and worked together.

"Your mind almost convinced me of the harmony in Selenta, between the Hands," Esther spoke in his mind.

"I have a public persona to uphold, Esther," the Lord Professor replied.

"Of course, the Lord Professor could not possibly be seen trying to influence the young to think differently, and implement change," Chirp, his second companion, mocked.

"Now, now, Chirp, no need to be so sarcastic. It's not like he holds a position of power and influence, he's just a simple professor …" Caulder, his final companion, interrupted. "Oh wait, yes he does! he's the Lord Professor and …"

"Come on," the Lord Professor cut in angrily. "Enough! You all know how this works. It's not like you haven't been here with me. These things take time. I'm not my brother!"

All three of his companions just grinned back at him.

"I think we need a bigger cart!" Esther laughed.

"Yep, we caught a big one!" Chirp giggled.

The Lord Professor shook his head, realising what they had been doing, and grinned himself as he shook his head. "Thank-you all, I have become a little caught up in things."

Three silent nods confirmed his statement.

"But I can always count on you to bring me back down to earth."

He looked to his chief aide, Dutton, and smiled at him, nodding a silent thank-you for putting up with him. If his companions thought he required an intervention, he must have been nearly unbearable.

"You have been," Caulder interrupted his thoughts.

"It's understandable. There are so many plans and actions that need to be right," Esther said.

"Not to mention that episode last week," Chirp offered, recounting the images that had knocked them off their feet.

"Yes, things are fluid at the moment," the Lord Professor mused. Then his mind was once again back on the crowded Plaza.

"Something isn't quite right," Esther mumbled, feeling the same sense of foreboding.

The Lord Professor tried to pinpoint his feeling. Still, everything below seemed to be as it was previously. The Purples were dancing, the crowd was laughing, and yet he could not shake the inkling that something disastrous was about to happen.

There was a strong sense of anticipation in the air, that hadn't been there before. The Lord Professor was trying to put his finger on it as he watched the gifts file onto the stage.

A hand landed on his shoulder.

"There, Sir!"

* * *

Dutton was pleased as he watched the Lord Professor's shoulders relax. The tension of the last week was draining off him, and a grin returned to his face again.

His companions must have decided it was time for him to give himself a break … especially since the episode that terrified him, and left him in a heap in his rooms. It had caused him to be frantic over the past week, continually checking the plans they had in place, and ensuring they had contingencies in place for any circumstance. He had wanted hourly reports, and was growling and shouting when things were inevitably late, or not changing fast enough.

When he looked to him and smiled, nodding his thanks, he relaxed further.

As the festival unfolded below, he kept his eye on the Lord Professor, ready to respond to any need. He looked out at the crowd, as attuned to his moods as he was. He knew the Lord Professor was trying to figure something out. He was immediately on alert. If the Lord Professor was concerned, he should be too.

He scanned the crowd; logging and analysing everything that was going on. The Hands were filing onto the stage with the gifts, the mass was watching with varying degrees of interest, and the Purple were still performing and sending food around, with children running about.

Then, his mind jumped back a few steps … the crowd were watching the stage more than expected, it was as if they were anticipating something.

A feeling of dread filled his belly as urgency hit him. He began looking for something that didn't quite fit. It didn't take him long … there it was, at an entrance to the southern side of the Plaza.

A figure stood out; powerful, strong, and well-built, eyes looking to the stage. Dutton's blood went cold as he realised who it was. Stepping forward to the Lord Professor, he put a hand on his shoulder and pointed out the figure.

"There, Sir."

The Lord Professor tensed. "The River, protect us," the Lord Professor whispered.

As if on cue, the figure looked up to the balcony, locking eyes with the Lord Professor. He couldn't even guess at what thoughts were going on in those minds, as the contact broke by a simple grave nod from the figure below before he turned, leaving the Plaza behind him.

Music blared as if heralding the departure, but in fact announcing the countdown to the gift unveiling.

"I have a bad feeling about this, Dutton," the Lord Professor whispered.

He watched as boxes lifted into the air, a heaviness forming in his stomach. Any moment now, and the sides of the boxes would drop, and unveil the gifts. The realisation hit both him and the Lord Professor simultaneously.

"The gifts," they muttered as one.

"We need to stop the ceremony, Sir," he whispered urgently, but they both knew it was much too late.

* * *

They watched, hypnotised, as shrieks of terror filled the Plaza. The boxes had opened to the crowd, and eight severed heads, with faces in various states of terror and a red handprint across their faces, stared sightlessly at the people of Selenta.

"This is going to be bad," Chirp observed.

There was no response required.

After the initial screams … a deathly silence gripped the crowd. They were processing what they were seeing.

The conflict with the Scarlett Hand rebels, which had been a story The Black used to terrify the populace and children into obedience, had just become very real.

Panic started to take hold slowly. Parents were pulling their children closer. People were edging away from the stage, staring accusingly at others, that just minutes before, they had been laughing and sharing drinks with.

"They're here!" someone shrieked, and it was as if the flood gates opened.

More screams tore into the peaceful afternoon, as people began running, trying to escape to the safety of their homes.

"Many will use this to settle scores, and air grievances that are always rumbling," Caulder observed, watching small groups talking and looking around menacingly.

"Let's hope the Squads are up to protecting the city and the innocent," Dutton said, as if hearing Caulder's comment.

"And that the Whites are able to cope with the injured," Esther added quietly, while looking at the carnage and pandemonium on display in front of them.

"At least one question is answered by this whole mess, Tobius," both his and Dutton's heads snapped around at the voice. Dutton's face was red with anger.

"That's Lord Professor to you," Dutton growled.

The Lord Professor laid a hand on Dutton's arm to calm him, the shock and anger of what they had just witnessed, making this usually controlled man, unpredictable. A fight with the tall and imposing Angus Quinn was not what they needed right now.

"Dutton, please go and start making preparations," he instructed. Dutton quickly composed himself and moved away.

"You need to keep a tighter leash on your dogs, Tobius," Angus Quinn taunted, as Dutton walked away.

Dutton had found his calm again, and he smiled as he turned the corner, leaving the Lord Professor to handle Angus Quinn.

"Enough, Angus. Your childish taunts have no place here today. Explain yourself?" He stared his old training rival in the eye. Before Angus could start talking, he smiled and added, "And, Dutton was right ... the correct address, is Lord Professor."

He was pleased to see the same rage he had seen in Jonas this morning, flash across Angus's eyes. Unlike Jonas, where it was plain for all to see, if he hadn't been looking, he would never have identified it. He had to be careful in his handling of Angus; he was the Chairman of the Grey Hand, the political element of Selenta.

The Grey Hand's role was to represent the interests of Selentans. They made decisions that impacted the Hands, and they had arranged this week's annual celebrations to bring those Hands together.

The Grey Hand, historically, were puppets for the other Hands, each pushing their own Hand's agendas and never agreeing on anything. Angus had changed all that, and the establishment was now gaining real power. A power and influence that seemed to suit Angus very well. Once he had taken over the Grey Hand, he had quickly turned the existing members to his side. They were now sycophants, taking his lead on all matters, and they all stood behind him now, watching these powerhouses spar.

This increase in the influence of the Grey, was not for the better in the Lord Professor's opinion, reinforcing his fears and belief's, that the system was in ruin, and easily manipulated.

"Of course, you are correct, Lord Professor."

The Lord Professor smiled. He was impressed that Angus did not spit his words out.

"It's just the shock of what has happened," Angus finished.

"Understandable, Chairman Quinn," he replied, using the

honorific title of Angus's position to soothe any wounds caused by his protection of Dutton.

Those watching, visibly relaxed, as they naively thought that ended the conflict, little did they understand that this had been going on since they were children.

"Now, Chairman, you said this answered one question? All I see are more questions to be answered," he asked.

Angus nodded towards the severed heads. "At least we know where your missing Training Sergeants are."

A malicious smile split Angus's face as he turned and left, followed by the rest of the Grey, leaving him alone … looking at the heads, and pondering the future.

"You were right, this is going to be very bad, Chirp," he whispered.

CHAPTER NINETEEN

J onas looked on in approval. The Squad had worked
well, quickly creating barricades, and pushing the
disgusting mob of sheep in the direction he wanted.
Moving them away from the areas with shops and businesses,
and keeping them on a track to disperse into the residential
district.

Ruben and Thomas were at the main barricades, chivvying
people on when they dawdled. They happily knocked the
head off anyone who raised their voice, caused mischief, or
generally didn't move quickly enough when told. However,
this was rare, as the sight of Ruben's squat form, together
with the scowl on his squashed face, had the sheep scurrying
by.

The crowds quickly passed and slipped away to their
homes, hiding until the next day. As the last few were
filtering by, Ellie took to the rooftops, checking each section,
and confirming they were all still in place and secure.

He made his way to Lisa's barricade, that blocked access
to a critical exit from the city. He had placed her there just
to score points. If this was an outside attack ... it was the
right course of action to stop the perpetrators leaving the
city. When he reached her section, he couldn't see her.

"Charter, assistance please."

His white tiger companion obliged quickly, flooding him with strength and power. He darted to the edge of the building, jumping across to the next, clearing the gap easily. He quickly made his way to Lisa's barricade. Jumping down, he landed gracefully in front of it and looked around.

"LISA!" he shouted.

She was nowhere in sight, and worry started to flood through him. Lisa may not be powerful, but she was diligent in her duties. She would never leave her post unless ordered to do so, or because something terrible had happened.

"LISA!" he shouted louder, with more urgency in his voice.

He heard a groan from behind the barricade, and moved quickly up and over, finding Lisa lying on the floor, barely conscious with a gash on the side of her head. It was evident that someone had attacked her.

Immediately ... Charter, Drake (his centaur), and Treffin (his raptor) manifested, taking up positions to cover him. Treffin raised her head and cawed five loud piercing calls that echoed down the streets, alerting the Squad to danger, and bringing them to him.

Lisa's eyes fluttered open, reacting to the alert.

"So fast, didn't see them," she mumbled, before she slipped back into unconsciousness.

Ellie was the first to arrive, her companions quick to manifest.

"Watch her," he growled, as he took off down the alleyway. Someone was going to pay. His rage was mirrored and fuelled by his companions as they loped around the bend, Charter catching a scent that led the way.

Ahead, they saw a figure slip around a corner. Adrenaline

flooded through him, and he sped forward, flooded with strength courtesy of his companions ... making him feel invincible.

As one, they turned the corner, growling, catching the figure three-quarters of the way up the alleyway.

"Halt!" he shouted.

The figure stopped but didn't turn around. Instead, the figure inclined his head slightly, but cast in shadow, he couldn't see him clearly. The figure spoke. His voice was calm, clear, commanding, and somehow familiar. "Boy, retreat now."

Something about his calm demeanour should have warned him of the danger, but his anger clouded his thinking.

"You don't get to give orders," he said, stepping menacingly forward. "Get him!" he instructed his companions.

He was barely aware of the shake of the figure's head.

"Trap!" Drake cried out. The hit came instantly from all directions, the damage not enough to wipe out his companions, but more than enough to prevent them from retaining their manifested states. He felt a blow to the back of his head, and his legs gave way, the ground quickly coming up to meet him.

"Stop!" the powerful command cut through his haze, a voice he would never forget.

Fighting unconsciousness, he strained to listen, and learn anything he could.

"He's just a child. My message has been sent, and we do not kill children."

His breath caught as he realised how close to the River he was.

"Yes, Sir, but did you see his companions? They are

powerful. He could be a future danger."

There was an eerie silence, filled only with retreating footsteps. He imagined the silent conversation the Commander was having with his own companions.

"The Hand has spoken, Rogers," another voice instructed.

He opened his eyes in panic, he was close to the Scarlett Hand. He had to see him ... but he only saw the hilt of a sword as it came down to impact upon his head, sending him into dark unconsciousness.

* * *

"Yeah, but he didn't say anything about me not leaving him with a headache."

Rogers looked down at the unconscious child, then grinned at his friend, before joining the departure from the city.

CHAPTER TWENTY

Rico and Butch were set to work straight away. As they had raced to the south quadrant, a small version of Phantom had alighted on each of their shoulders; advising them of the situation, and Eddie's plan.

Aldela had scouted ahead and reported back what was happening. There was a situation in the Central Plaza that had caused mass panic, and some unhappy citizens had taken it as an opportunity to create further chaos and damage. Squads closer to the Plaza had dealt with many of those culprits already, which meant the groups approaching them were a bit more docile, and just wanted to go home.

Tia, Jenna, and he had set up a staging area that Jenna was controlling; splitting up the group, funnelling those with children down one route, and couples and singles down the other.

Rico and Butch were taking control of the exits, one on each side. Once a family, couple, or singleton showed their home keys, they could progress through.

Tia was on the roof above them, keeping an eye on the large group that was out in front, but also ensuring that those they let through, did not cause any further problems, or move off their course.

He was in reserve and dealing with any incidents, either at the gates or with those who went through. Thankfully, everything went smoothly, and they were able to handle adverse situations, like a child wandering off or an impatient singleton, quickly and easily before they escalated. This was mainly due to the improved ability in their communication, available via Phantom, who sat on each Squad member's shoulder.

Once the last family passed through the staging area, he instructed Tia to cast out her net to the outskirts, to ensure that nothing unusual was happening. Reports from the citizens about heads covered in blood, and the Scarlett Hand attacking, had put him on edge. He and the rest of the Squad set about dismantling the barricades.

"Well that could have gone much worse," Rico stated.

"Don't count your chickens yet," Llýr muttered absently from his shoulder, as Rico moved a large fence panel with him, and put it back in place.

"Eddie ..." Phantom spoke on everyone's shoulders, relaying Tia's words.

"Go ahead, Tia. I'm listening."

"There is something odd going on in the east quadrant," Tia replied. Her tone showing her confusion. "Phantom and I can't get a fix, and I have had Utah do a fly-by. There is nothing obvious, but something is not quite right," Tia continued to explain.

"Can you elaborate, Tia?" Jenna asked. "Is it like anything you have seen before?"

There were a few moments of silence, as Tia consulted with Phantom. "The best we can describe, is that it's kind of like when we track Rico in full Misty mode. But even then, we can get a useable trace."

He looked around the Squad. "Ideas?"

"It could be nothing," Jenna offered. "It has been a long day, and we are all tired."

"Possible," he nodded.

"It could be a straggler from the Plaza, trying to get home quietly without causing a problem," Butch suggested.

"Again possible, but unlikely someone living in this area can avoid detection from Tia and Phantom," he said.

They all nodded as Rico shrugged. "It could be another part of the test, or even worse, one of the Scarlett Hand trying to escape."

"Tia, is the phenomenon on the move?" he asked quickly, Rico's suggestion hitting home.

"Yes," she replied immediately.

"Can you guess at a destination?" Jenna asked.

"I think so," Tia advised. "It is moving back and forth, but steadily heading towards the edge of the city; opposite Tinten Falls."

He considered everything quickly. "OK, let's cut whatever it is off." He smirked, and his sudden excitement was mirrored in the grins showing on the Squad's faces. "But we are not going to chase it, we will let it come to us. Jenna, you and Butch will close the door behind it when it enters the last alleyway leading to the falls, and Rico and I will block the exit."

The Squad nodded.

"Tia, make your way over the rooftops at a distance, then close off that escape route. Let's put it in a box. Let's roll."

They took off at a sprint to set their trap, not noticing that the grizzled Red Training Sergeant was releasing his robin, and sending it back to the city.

* * *

Hush moved quickly and quietly through the now silent city. He had been set the task of establishing contact with some of the local dissidents. Unfortunately, they had not shown. He wasn't angry … there was no point … merely disappointed. He assumed they had gotten spooked by the Plaza show.

He smiled; he would have loved to have seen the faces of the Hand leaders, who were watching up on the balcony.

The Scarlett Hand was sending a huge message … and the future was about to get a whole lot more interesting.

As he neared the outskirts of the city, he began to relax, turning into the last alleyway. The disappointment he had been feeling was wearing off, as he chalked up the ease of his exit to another success.

"Always congratulating yourself too early, Hush," Shadow (his black panther companion) spoke.

He looked up to see two figures blocking his exit, and he shrugged, annoyed that he had not foreseen this.

"No bother, they can't see us. We will just double back." As he turned around, two more figures stepped into the alleyway.

"Going up is out too," Shadow advised unhelpfully.

Hush sighed and turned back to the two in front, examining them more closely. "They're only trainees. We should be able to dodge them, and get into …"

Before he could finish his sentence, the trainees released their companions; a blatant display of power. Around them appeared a gargoyle, phoenix, black bear, lion, wolf, jaguar, golden eagle, and a figure that melted into the background … but not before he glanced a small lizard type creature he didn't recognise, perched on his shoulder.

"This could be problematic," Hush muttered. "Are you sure they can't see us, Freddy?" he asked his chameleon companion.

Before Freddy could reply, the remaining figure in front stepped forward. "Are you lost?"

Hush shook his head. "Well, I guess that answers that question."

* * *

"Serpents balls," Donte muttered, as he watched the group of trainees cut Hush's retreat off.

He lined up the shotbolt, getting ready in case Hush needed him.

"Shoot," Kip hissed, Donte's second in command.

Donte didn't even glance at Kip, meaning he didn't miss the display of power, as the trainees released their companions.

"Hush has gotten himself out of much worse predicaments. Besides, I'm not even sure I could hit a kill shot from here," he explained, his voice slightly strained after seeing the opposition Hush faced. "And, looking at those companions … if I injure the host, or any of their group, they will likely take it out on my ass … and I quite like my ass in one piece."

He looked at Kip, shaking his head at the petulant scowl, before looking back to where Hush had appeared and set himself in the alleyway.

"Now watch and learn."

* * *

Eddie stepped forward. "Are you lost?" he asked to the empty alleyway. He was compensated with the appearance of a squat, powerful-looking man, dressed in what looked like an old soldier's uniform.

The man looked at him like he would if he was sizing up a fighter before a bout, with his head cocked slightly to one side, as he closed his eyes.

He signalled quickly to the group to be ready, and fighting staffs were extended into the Squad's hands as chaos broke loose. The target burst into life, his companions flying out, aiming towards Jenna, Butch, and Eddie. Their own companions moved just as quickly to defend them, but before they hit, all of the target's companions disappeared, and so did he.

"Tia?" he shouted.

* * *

The feint had worked. With the trainees focused on the illusion in the chaos, Hush managed to slip past the big guy with ease, his panther allowing him to be silent, and his chameleon masking his movements.

He looked back as he exited the alleyway, a smile creasing his face. He turned to dart into the distance, confident they wouldn't catch him now.

* * *

Rico had taken a step back away from the group at the urging of Llŷr, instinctively extending his own staff, as Eddie gave the signal.

"Focus on the target," Misty advised.

With the help of his companions, he watched as the target's companions burst from him, aiming for his friends. Instinctively, he tensed, wanting to act, but even as he thought to move ... he realised they were an illusion; intended purely as a distraction.

The target shimmered, already moving as he melted into his surroundings, an improvement on the blurring image he and Misty achieved when they moved.

"We will achieve this soon," Misty stated confidently.

He smiled affectionately. His minors had grown in confidence and strength since Llŷr's arrival, which was helping to improve their abilities.

The target made no effort to attack the Squad, but moved quickly around them ... avoiding the spot he had initially been in.

Unfortunately for the target, this brought him within striking distance of where he now waited. The target looked back, as the illusions disappeared. He had a smile on his face as he turned around, ready to vanish into the open and secure his freedom.

* * *

Donte and Kip smiled as Hush slipped past the recruits, silently congratulating him on an escape.

Out of nowhere, a figure appeared and struck out with a staff ... intercepting Hush, and knocking him out cold.

Kip groaned, shaking his head.

103

They packed up their gear quickly, and slipped into the forest ... they would need to report this to the Scarlett Hand immediately.

* * *

Every member of the Squad turned at the sound of Rico's staff striking the target across the forehead, and knocking him out cold.

"Nice," congratulated Butch, as they gathered around the prone form.

Tia landed silently beside them; Phantom already sent out to reconnoitre the perimeter.

Jenna instructed Dancer to head into the fields and the forest, to see if anyone was lurking, waiting for the target.

"Belay that order, Trainee!"

They all turned to see the grizzled Red Training Sergeant enter the alleyway, followed by a Squad from the Red Hand. This Squad were no raw recruits, they had the look of veterans; all business, clinical, and efficient. They secured the perimeter, while the Training Sergeant spoke to Phoenix Squad.

"Excellent work, you will get full marks for this test."

They all beamed.

"So, this was part of the test?" Rico asked.

The Training Sergeant looked to the Red Captain, who nodded.

"No, we don't know what this is, but we suspect it is something to do with the events in the Plaza." He held up his hand to stop the questions he knew were about to erupt. "Any further information is on a need-to-know basis I'm afraid, and in the interest of security, you must not discuss this with anyone."

Phoenix Squad nodded their understanding; having had it drilled into them from an early age to follow orders.

"Now, head back to the barracks and rest. Good work today," he congratulated. Phoenix Squad saluted, and basked in the nods of appreciation from the veteran Red Squad as they left.

The Red Captain stood beside him. "They did very well here today," he said.

"And then some, Captain," he added. At the puzzled look on the Captain's face, he continued, "Do you have any idea who that is on the floor?" The Captain shook his head.

"That is Hush."

The Captain's eyes widened, looking again at the man on the floor, recognising him now he knew what to look for.

"Then, how did they?" the Captain questioned, looking towards the disappearing Squad.

"I'd like to know myself," he replied. "But even the best underestimate people, and they are a Squad who are not to be underestimated."

The Captain looked between Hush and the departing Squad, shaking his head in disbelief. "Do you think this will get out?" the Captain asked.

He shrugged. "I doubt it. They have no idea who this is, and for once, the Selentan upbringing works in our favour." He paused momentarily. "Besides, those trainees worship the Red Hand and care about the people. I don't think they will say anything. They probably think that keeping quiet is a part of the test."

The Captain nodded and turned to his Squad, issuing

105

instructions. "Time to make this go away."

They picked up Hush, and disappeared silently into the city.

CHAPTER TWENTY-ONE

"The merge did nothing to improve your patience, Nala," Swiftwind commented as he tore into the hog they had caught.

The last week had been uneventful, as they had followed scents, honed their hunting skills, and explored the forest. He had learned quickly, picking up the nuances of the hunt effortlessly. He also became distracted easily, eager to meet others who had merged and tease open this new puzzle. There had been numerous occasions over the past week when they had felt like someone was watching them. Still, it was always at the edge of their range, disappearing the minute they moved to investigate.

"I am not impatient; I just feel we are being avoided."

He felt Swiftwind's desire to console him and tell him he was wrong, but the truth was ... she agreed with him. The areas they were investigating were often abandoned, and at times, it looked like it had been in haste. The dens they found were empty, with the scents and tracks always distorted.

There were plenty of animals about, but they were of the standard variety, and even with all this life ... there was an empty feel to the forest. It was as if someone, or something, was missing.

"I agree, Nala, but we have to be patient," Swift finally said.

"Hmmph," was all he replied. He buried their nose back inside the hog, something he knew Swiftwind hated, and he grinned as she grimaced.

"You do know that doing that distorts our ability to smell on the ..." their head whipped up, and their ears perked, as they heard a noise up the trail.

A sleek green fox, dappled with patches of light brown, emerged from the trees. It stopped and casually looked up the trail, then turned, looking back down ... its eyes alighting on them. What could pass for a grin creased its face, and he decided in his frustration that it was laughing at them.

"Wait!" Swiftwind cautioned, but she was too late, he had taken control and was quickly bolting down the trail after the fox.

Within seconds, he felt her natural caution become eroded by his excitement, and she gave herself over to the hunt. The fox didn't bolt straight away. It waited until they were halfway down the trail. The fox was obviously a merged creature ... it was too confident and controlled. It winked at them before darting into the undergrowth, confirming their suspicions.

"Swift, I can't smell him. There are gaps," he stated, as he dived into the undergrowth after the fox, using sight and sound alone to track it.

"That's because of the blood, it distorts the scents," she replied, shaking her head.

"Damn it!" he growled. He snorted as much of the blood out of his nostrils as he could while running. "But no mind, I can track this one by sound alone."

At this, he changed direction; shooting forward with a

burst of speed to intercept the fox, who seemed to be treading on every piece of detritus there was on the forest floor.

* * *

They slowed, feeling frustrated. They had been tracking the fox for half an hour, but it was always just out of their grasp. They had come close to catching it a couple of times, once when it had changed direction. They had pre-empted the change, but the fox had slipped through a tiny gap in a clump of thorn trees, and their bulk had prevented them from following. The second time, they had almost stood on the fox as it had laid up to catch its breath, resulting in a bite mark on their rump where it had nipped them before racing away.

"When I catch this ..."

"If ..." Swiftwind interrupted his angry growl.

"*WHEN* I catch this fox, I am going to teach it that it's not smart to torment a wolf," he finished. Swiftwind chuckled, trying to break into his frustration. "OK, Swiftwind, what do you suggest?" he asked.

Swiftwind looked at him in their mind with mock humility. "What ... little old me have an idea?" Her grin was mischievous. "When the big bad wolf is doing such a great job ..."

Finally, he burst out laughing. "I think the she-wolf is right - I am a bit of a dumb animal."

Swiftwind scowled at him. "Never insult yourself, Nala Yagin. There are plenty of others in the world who will do that. Besides, it's not endearing ... it's annoying," she growled.

"I'm sorry, Swiftwind," he responded quickly with sincerity.

"Besides, it's not your fault. You are new to this and let your instinct take over, and you draw me in with you. We need to stop thinking like a wild animal and start acting like a merged one."

He considered this for a moment, the situation finally dawning on him. "We can't catch this fox alone, can we?" he said simply.

"No, Nala, but we can trap him," Swiftwind grinned wickedly.

Once they started thinking differently, they had more success. Rather than chase the fox directly, they began to corral it; loping ahead to scout the terrain, and choosing a spot to set their trap. Added to this … their sense of smell was coming back, but it would be at least another hour before it fully returned.

Once they'd chosen their spot, they circled the area the fox was in; making sure to make lots of noise while doing it. Then they went silent, using every trick they could muster to ensure the fox could not pinpoint where they were heading.

They had picked out a small gorge, about half a mile ahead, that they suspected the fox was heading to as it had numerous spaces where it could hide, or disappear into. But the destination worked just as well for them to set a trap.

They made their way there as quickly as they could, quietly entering from the top, and being careful not to leave any tracks or scent to alert the fox to their presence. They took cover in a hidden spot that gave them a good view of the entrance to the gorge, and waited silently for the fox to appear.

When it finally arrived, it looked agitated, darting back

and forth, and making enough noise to attract any predator within hearing distance.

The fox shook its head and wandered slowly into the gorge, its mouth moving as if muttering to itself. They both grinned as they heard the words *stupid wolf* muttered as it passed underneath them.

They waited patiently until the fox reached the point where they could corner him, then pounced, landing behind him. The fox jumped, backing into the corner as they had planned. Slowly, they stalked towards him ... growling menacingly.

"Clever, Wolf," the fox muttered, its eyes darting everywhere, looking for an escape.

They both grinned in triumph, while stepping across a bed of leaves the fox had just backed over. They felt soft underfoot, but this was peripheral thought as they had their prey.

The fox's body language changed. It stood up calmly, controlled; no longer the cowering prey, and grinned. "Well, maybe not so clever," it said.

Instantly ... the surrounding area, the fox's frustration as it entered the gorge, the soft surface beneath his feet ... all hit him like a sledgehammer. He shrugged apologetically at Swiftwind. "Well, that didn't go as planned," he said, as the ground gave way beneath them, and everything went dark.

* * *

They came around slowly, with Swiftwind taking control before Nala woke. She knew she couldn't once he was fully awake. She was aware his instinct would be to jump up and rage around, but she wanted to be sure they hadn't broken any bones. Only when she was confident that they had only bruising, with a few minor cuts, did she relinquish control.

To her surprise, he didn't go crazy. Instead, he stood and shook their fur before exploring their cell. It was a cube approximately eight by eight feet, barely big enough to hold their bulk. The ground was a soft spongy moss, which explained the lack of broken bones or any other serious injury.

Nala looked up. The opening they had fallen through was closed over, and not letting in any light. It was also too high for him to get any leverage to try and uncover it. He stopped prowling, moved to the middle of his cell, and taking on board what Swift had taught him, he sat and started breathing deeply, sending out their senses.

Unfortunately, the earth around them and the covering muted their senses, preventing their hunter vision from working. However, they could hear what appeared to be many muffled voices. They were able to make out the odd word; *Tame, Huge, Kill, Free*. It wasn't a stretch to guess that their captors were deciding their fate.

"Well, what now, Nala Yagin?" Swiftwind asked.

He considered what to do, and was about to answer that he had no idea, when they heard clear and crisp, "A dumb animal." At hearing the words and voice, the craziness Swift had been expecting earlier appeared …

Nala flung himself at the wall, trying to climb out. The soil gave way, leaving him in a heap on the floor. After a couple of attempts, he accepted that he was stuck.

He began shouting, "SHE-WOLF! LET ME OUT!" over and over.

Swiftwind shook her head. "That's not going to work.

You're not even barking or howling; all you're doing is giving me a headache."

Swiftwind expected an angry retort, but instead, he told her, "Of course, you're a genius, Swift."

Swiftwind had an answer to her confusion quickly, as she felt Nala concentrate on making an actual noise. Realising what he was doing, she tried to encourage him. "Remember what it was like to speak to others."

He tried, but it was difficult. He had never had to consciously think to speak before. As a human, it was second nature. Their survival depended on his ability to think this through briskly, and he decided to approach it as children did when they learned how to talk, sounding out the words bit by bit to make a full word.

Taking a deep breath, he placed his front paws as high up the wall as he could, and focused on his desire to speak. "SHHHHHEEEEEEE-WWWWWWOOOOOLLLLLFFFFF!"

Both he and Swift waited, hoping it had worked. After what felt like an age, and when he was about to try again … a corner of the covering opened, and a tiny monkey face peered in at him. He looked at it in what he hoped passed as a smile, but the monkey's flinch said that he'd not been successful. Quickly, before it closed the cover, he tried again. "LLLLLEEEETTTT MMMEEEE OOOOOUUUTTT!"

The monkey jumped at the words, dropping the corner, and they heard it scurrying away.

"Well, either that worked, or it is running to tell them we are escaping," Swift surmised.

"Either way, we have their attention," he grinned, pleased with himself.

They sat back and strained their hearing, but it was next

to impossible to hear through the earth and cover, although they felt an increase in volume followed by silence.

There was a shift and a movement above as someone opened the cover. A giant silver-back gorilla was staring back at them.

His shoulders sagged, he hoped it would be the she-wolf that came.

"That was a very human gesture, Wolf."

His head snapped up as the gorilla spoke.

"Were you hoping for someone else? Someone a little more to your taste?"

He shook his head, but to those above, it looked like they were shaking their fur in frustration.

"Hmmm," the gorilla mused, his large hand reaching up and cupping his chin. "Maybe I am just looking for the human reaction in you." The gorilla started to turn away.

"Hurry, Nala, say something," Swiftwind encouraged.

"Shhee-woolllff!"

It came more natural to him this time, using the same words he had tried earlier.

The gorilla's head snapped around, and from beside him, the she-wolf's angry face appeared at the edge of the cell. Nala's eyes went immediately to her.

"I told you before I wasn't going ..." the she-wolf started to retort angrily, but then a realisation hit her, and she pulled back out of sight. "Not such a dumb animal," she muttered as she disappeared. Was that guilt he saw in her human eyes before she went?

The gorilla once again replaced her at the edge. "Well, it looks like I was right ... the wolf was hoping for someone else." The gorilla chuckled, accompanied by others who he couldn't see as he glanced back to who he assumed was the she-wolf. Whatever retort she gave, caused the gorilla to belly laugh. Once the rumbling sound subsided, he finally looked back down at them.

"OK, Wolf, we need to go a little primitive in communication. I'm assuming you are new to the merge and have never spoken in this form before?"

He tried to nod a yes to the gorilla, who shook his head slightly.

"The gestures you made as a human, such as shaking your head or smiling, come across differently," the gorilla lectured. "Your wolf form does not understand them, and so interprets it in a different way. It's a bit weird, really. Our companions live with us for so long and notice our gestures through mental communication, but in their natural form … they just don't grasp the concepts."

A growl from behind interrupted the gorilla, and he grinned. "But I digress, we have little time, so I will ask yes or no questions. If your answer is yes, walk round in a circle. If it's no, walk to the corner and back. Do you understand?"

Quickly, he walked round in a circle.

"Good," the gorilla responded. "Have you been merged long?"

He moved to the corner and back, no.

"Were you chasing the fox for food?"

Again, he moved to the corner and back, no.

"Were you trying to find us?"

Another walk to the corner, no.

The gorilla looked confused, and muttering and scuffles came from behind him.

"Ah," the gorilla looked back down at Nala, a twinkle of

mischief in his eyes. "The she-wolf?"

A circle.

The gorilla sat at the edge of the cell considering them for a long time, his arms folded across his ample midriff, with his fingers absently tapping against his teeth ... giving this creature a vicious look. It reminded him that if this strong, powerful, and deadly gorilla decided he was a threat, he could drop in on top of them, and that would be the end of things.

The gorilla interrupted his thoughts. "I'm in a quandary, Wolf. You see, you are a fabulous specimen, and you would be a valuable asset to the River Runners ... but you could also be a deadly enemy," the gorilla said with a menacing look now in his eyes.

He quickly walked to the corner and back.

The gorilla peeled back his lips in a grin. "You catch on quick." Then, his whole visage changed again, as his full animal nature was unleashed.

The gorilla seemed to grow wider and taller as he stood towering over the edge of the pit, roaring down at him, beating his chest, and clearly asserting his authority. Finally, he looked him in the eye, and growled menacingly, "But if you harm any of mine, I will hunt you down, and tear you to pieces."

Swiftwind tried to stop what she knew was coming, but was too late, as his blood boiled.

The threat had stirred his alpha instinct. He dropped to a fighting stance, growling back at the gorilla, and baring his teeth in a challenge.

After a few moments, he walked a slow circle to acknowledge he understood the threat ... not taking his eyes of the gorilla. When he finished his loop, he and the gorilla continued staring at each other a while longer.

"Back down, Nala," Swiftwind pleaded.

It was her tone, more than her words, that convinced him to break the confrontation. He nodded his head, breaking eye contact, accepting the gorilla's authority, and acknowledging the threat. He waited.

Swiftwind was pleased to see the gorilla go through the same process of bringing his own nature under control. Once he had, he spoke calmly and with authority, "My name is Gervais Badan, welcome to the River Runners, Wolf."

Gervais signalled to someone to remove the cover.

A large rock dropped in front of them, and both he and Swiftwind smiled. They took a step back, and quick as lightning, they jumped onto the rock and out of the hole.

CHAPTER TWENTY-TWO

"He's coming round," the voice shouted, sending shooting pains and bright spots of light through his head. "Go fetch his father."

Jonas tried hard to open his eyes, but it was a struggle. He could barely discern the shapes milling around him, and it hurt immensely to try any harder.

"Sleep, Jonas," Treffin gently cooed in his mind, careful to not cause any more pain. "You have done the hard part; the White will wake you when your father arrives."

Jonas didn't need telling twice, he stopped struggling, and let the darkness swallow him.

* * *

Angus was already on his way to visit Jonas, as the White orderly bumped into him, and let him know Jonas was waking up. He smiled a grim thank-you, and stood at the entrance to the door.

He watched as anger flooded Ellie, while Ruben looked just as furious.

"You said he was waking up, what just happened?" Ellie growled menacingly at the Whites in the room. Her voice was low and deadly, vibrating with venom, as she took a step forwards towards the Whites. Ruben started grinning from ear-to-ear, hoping for an argument to ensue, as he knew that Ellie had Saskia on the verge of release. The ordinarily unflappable Whites were backing away.

He was pleased to see their loyalty to Jonas, but now was not the right time. He stepped into the room. "Back down, Ellie," he said in a calm, commanding voice. He was pleased to see Ellie immediately swallow her anger.

"Yes, Sir." Ellie immediately reacted to his voice.

The rest of Raptor Squad jumped to their feet, nodding their heads in reverence to him. Not taking his eyes of Ellie, he acknowledged the thankful expressions on the Whites faces with a gentle smile.

"Now, Ellie, what the Whites will have said, is that Jonas has done the hard part. He has returned to a level where they can help him and remove his pain. The mind is a dangerous thing to heal ... until the subject shows some signs of consciousness; there is nothing they can do."

He suppressed his anger at the blank look on Ruben and Thomas's faces, his companions having to remind him that he had not linked them with Jonas for their brains ... but for their power, abilities, and loyalty. Ellie's loss of control was more of a concern. Jonas and Ellie were the brains of Raptor Squad. However, based on the report, Jonas had not been using his on the day of the festival.

"May I, Chairman?" Ellie asked, having seen the confusion on the Squad's faces, her anger now under control.

He nodded, and Ellie explained to the Squad. "The brain needs to be active for healing to work. White skills essentially use the body's own healing abilities and amplifies them. As the brain controls the body … if that's not working properly, a White's skills would actually cause the opposite effect, and destroy the body from within."

Thomas and Ruben nodded, not really understanding the detail, other than the Whites had done the right thing.

Shaking his head, he turned to the White matron and nodded. She, and the other White in the room, approached Jonas, each placing a hand on his head and taking his wrist in their hands. They closed their eyes, and went into a trance, each issuing a gentle humming noise. After about two minutes, Jonas's eyes snapped open, and he jerked upright.

* * *

"The Scarlett Hand … he's here," he shouted, his eyes slightly wild.

"Easy, Jonas," Treffin spoke in his mind, calming him. "Look around, we are safe now." Slowly he settled, taking in the anxious faces of his Squad, the serene looks of the Whites, and finally settling on the stern visage of his father.

"Damn it!" he grumbled, letting his head drop back onto the pillow. "How long have I been out?" he asked.

"Three days, we were worried about you," Lisa answered quickly.

An image of her lay unconscious on the ground flashed through his mind, and he looked over to her quickly, cataloguing any sign of injury or issue. "Are you OK?" he asked her. Lisa simply nodded.

"Not to break up this heartwarming concern, but …" his father interrupted, "Jonas, report."

He quickly looked back to his father. "Yes, Sir," he hissed.

Still, before his father could dress him down, he continued, "I assume you know up to the point I found Lisa unconscious at the barricade?" His father nodded, but did not respond. All the better he thought, but he never took his eyes off him. "I identified a suspect fleeing the assault on Lisa, and took off in pursuit."

At this point, his father did interrupt. "On your own? Your Squad left you to go alone?" The accusation that they would abandon him evident.

"I ordered them to stay and protect Lisa. It was one suspect; I could handle him."

His father huffed a laugh. "Obviously not."

He saw the pleasure in his father's eyes, as the Squad's rage at his insult was written plainly on their faces and in their body language. Only their fear of his father was stopping them from acting on it.

Instead of reacting, he decided on a calm, and measured response. "No, Sir. As I pursued the suspect, I entered the alleyway where he was waiting for me, and I instructed him to stop. He told me to retreat, but I refused, and was about to attack when I was ambushed."

He watched his father catalogue the information and ask his questions. "How many attackers? Would you recognise them? Anything else?"

He nodded. "The figure stopped the ambushers from killing me. He said they don't kill children. I don't know how many attackers there were, and I only saw the back of the figure, but they referred to him as *The Hand*. That's the last thing I remember before I was knocked unconscious."

"He was here?" his father growled. A slight tick of anger flickered across his face, but it was gone as quickly as it had appeared. "As for you, Jonas, this information is important, but it does not alleviate this failure of large proportions."

Thomas and Ruben instinctively took a step forward, then halted at a signal from him. His father looked at them both until they cowered and returned to their positions.

"As I was saying … a failure. You split from your Squad, and entered into a confrontation against assailants unknown. A tactically unsound move," his father shook his head.

He smiled at his father, hoping the fire he felt inside showed through. "I agree, Sir."

* * *

Angus looked at Jonas, impressed that he was not trying to explain his actions, and admiring the steely resolve he saw in his eyes. Something good may have come from this debacle after all. Jonas had changed, he had become colder.

"Perhaps this has not been such a failure," a voice considered in his mind.

"It won't happen again," Jonas continued, and as simple as that, Jonas had closed the book on it.

He didn't doubt Jonas's words, so quickly moved onto the next matter at hand. "Phoenix Squad came first in the test. They achieved the best score ever recorded, and are now on equal points with you."

He was pleased to see the anger on Jonas's face. The incident may have changed him, but his desire to win was still burning. Jonas started to get up. "The next test is tomorrow," Jonas argued, as he placed a hand on his shoulder, pushing him gently back onto the bed.

"Rest, Jonas. The tests have been put on hold for now.

After the fiasco in the Central Plaza, all Squads are on patrol duty; putting down disturbances, and making sure everyone knows who is in control. It will take a few more days before things move back to any sense of normality."

Jonas looked confused. "Debacle in the Central Plaza?"

He let out a genuine laugh at Jonas's words, and was pleased to see him smile. "I think you are the only one who doesn't know what has happened," he said, as he patted Jonas gently on the shoulder. "I would like to talk you through it, but I left a meeting with the council to check on you. If I don't get back soon, they will have sent troops into The Forbidden."

They all laughed. He could see that Jonas was slightly stunned by the affection he had just shown. "Your Squad will fill you in on the details, but join me this evening for dinner. We can discuss the implications, and you can fill me in on your plans for the final few tests."

With that, he turned and left, leaving five stunned faces behind him.

* * *

"What just happened?" Thomas asked, slightly mystified.

"I have no idea," he whispered, looking on after his father.

Putting this aside, for now, the Squad turned to him and started to fuss. He allowed it this once, quite enjoying the attention, and listening intently as they all clambered to explain what had happened over the last few days.

CHAPTER TWENTY-THREE

As Phoenix Squad filed out of the classroom, Eddie saw Raptor Squad lounging in the communal area. This reaffirmed his thoughts … they hadn't been quick enough.

Jonas looked over and nodded to him, then turned back to his Squad.

"I preferred him when he was sneering," Grey Claw observed aloud … silently referring to Jonas's change of demeanour since the first test.

"I agree. At least then you knew what was going on in that warped head of his," Aldela responded, as everyone else nodded in agreement.

They sat down and closed their eyes, going over the second test as they took their usual place in the corner, waiting for the other Squads to finish. It had been routine; basic battlefield tactics from a Hand's perspective. A battlefield had been set up on a table showing opposing sides, with pieces to represent the different strengths and skills of the units involved. They filtered information continuously, changing the circumstances, and the pieces on the field of battle.

The aim of the test had been to utilise their forces to

defeat the invading army, which outnumbered them two to one. They had been successful, but as the invading troops retreated, they had detoured, and commandeered a local village; taking all the inhabitant's hostage and threatening to kill them if they did not stop harrying the retreat.

They had paused the pursuit, aiming to give the impression that they were complying, and devised a plan to save the hostages. They succeeded in rescuing the villagers, but it had meant that the enemy General, and a contingent of his soldiers, had escaped.

"Everyone ready?" he asked. They all nodded.

"What could we have done differently?" He was not surprised that Rico got straight to the point.

"We could have taken the village without stopping to plan a rescue, we would have lost maybe 50-75% of the villagers, but the Commander would not have escaped."

Tia looked a little pale. "But that would have been unacceptable, right?" she asked.

Traveller responded, and his gentle manner made the delivery kinder. "For us, yes, Tia. But for Selenta? Probably not. We can repopulate the villages easily enough. However, soldiers are more difficult to replace."

As Traveller paused, Llýr took over. "And by letting the General escape, one day he could return to invade again, which would mean more losses." The group all understood this concept and Llýr continued, "Traveller is correct in his view that it is unacceptable to us. Yes, letting the General escape was part of the problem outcome, but defending the villagers was not the major mistake, I will let Eddie explain."

He smiled, ruefully, but acknowledged Llýr referring to him with an appreciative nod.

He spoke quietly. "My mistake was using everybody to rescue the prisoners. I should have sent a few Squads to circle the village and overtake the retreat, tasking them with making sure the General and his high-ranking officers did not survive." He paused. "No matter the cost."

He watched the implications dawn on the Squad. Tia paled further. Jenna's hand instinctively looked for Aldela. Butch and Rico both sighed deeply, clearly thankful the burden of command was not theirs.

"Now rest, take some time to sort through this, and let's learn from it. The final test is in a week; that is our focus now," he instructed.

A grim determination fell over the group, as each of them relaxed as best they could, waiting for the remaining Squads to complete the testing.

* * *

Over the next few hours, the other Squads emerged from their rooms in various states of frustration; some in tears, and others utterly shell-shocked, but all exhausted and slumping into their chairs. Some of the students were not cut out for the pressures of battle and quick decision making.

As the last Squad emerged, the trainers disappeared into the staff area to discuss the results, leaving the students to wait for the final scores, and for someone to dismiss them. But Phoenix Squad saw none of this, as they had all fallen asleep.

Llŷr smiled, "It's good that they can rest."

Dozer and Aldela joined him, smiling. The three were overseeing the Squad's protection as they slept, allowing the other companions to recharge.

"Yes, it is. Today took more out of them than they'd like to admit. They hate to fail," Dozer huffed.

"Was it a failure? I'm not so sure. I'd rather not see them automatically send people to their deaths, even if it is only a war game," Aldela countered.

Llýr looked over the sleeping Squad. "But there are times when it is called for, Aldela, to prevent a greater loss. Eddie understands this. But I agree, it's good that it isn't their first thought. Life is to be preserved where possible."

"I feel darker times are coming," Aldela whispered.

"The Scarlett Hand has seen to that," Dozer growled.

"Not just that, Dozer," Aldela countered. "There is something more at play, I can feel it."

"I agree, Lady Aldela," Llýr whispered. "The River flows are chaotic and uncertain. We are entering a time when even actions from individuals can have a profound effect on how the future pans out, and I fear these children are right in the middle of it all."

Llýr watched, as Dozer and Aldela looked within themselves, teasing their intuitions and knowledge of the River, with each of them coming to the same conclusion.

"Do we tell them what we fear?" Aldela asked.

Both Llýr and Dozer shook their heads slowly. It was Dozer who answered. "No. Telling them may impact the decisions they make, causing them to worry, and potentially even second-guess every choice they need to make. No, it would be undue stress on their young shoulders."

"And besides, they have the three of us to guide them, and do the worrying for them," Llýr put in. They all gave a rueful laugh and bowed their heads slightly.

"The River runs, may it grant us safe passage," they prayed as one.

* * *

As the door to the staff area opened, Phoenix Squad jumped up from their slumber, mirrored by all the other Squads, and saluted the trainers.

One of the new trainers stepped forward and addressed them. "All in all, a disappointing bunch of test results. We expected better from some." He looked directly at Phoenix and Raptor Squad. "But … when mediocre is the average, good succeeds."

Rico was as shocked as everyone else, but spared a glance to see Jonas's reaction. He remained motionless, looking collected, composed, and every bit a leader.

"Calm? The Scarlett Hand may have taught him a valuable lesson," Llŷr queried into his mind.

"I preferred him when he was more readable," he replied, as the trainer started reading the results.

"The top five Squads in descending order are as follows; in fifth place is Snake Squad, fourth is Fox Squad, third is Eagle Squad … second and first was a tie, both the top Squads made a different, yet disastrous decision, which meant a key deliverable was not met."

The trainer looked at both Squads in turn. "Other than the error, you could not be separated. You will be handed a full breakdown of the test by the clerks as you leave. Dismissed," the trainer finished.

All the Squads, other than Phoenix and Raptor, quickly headed for the exits. They both sat down and waited, trying not to look at each other, each Squad obviously eager to understand where the other group fell short. Finally, one of the clerks broke off and handed Eddie and Jonas their score sheets.

* * *

Rico watched Eddie as he placed the result on the table, and the Squad gathered around. Each of them read and digested the report, while trying hard not to skip to the end to see if they had analysed their own failure correctly. Once they had read it, they all sat back in their spots.

"Well, at least we know we were right about where we went wrong," Butch said.

"Yeah, that bit doesn't bother me so much," he groused. "It's them marking us down for moving a Squad off the front line to take out those bolt shooters that bothers me. They would have played merry murder with our flank, or in the village while we rescued the villagers."

They all laughed at him. Taking out the bolters had been a hotly debated topic, and Eddie had authorised it based on just that argument.

"Not everyone sees a threat in the same way, Rico," Fence growled in his deep timbre. Everyone had jumped when Fence first started communicating, not realising that he wasn't angry, that was just his voice.

"Fence is right, these scores are based on a classroom set of outcomes. In the scenario set out, the shooters probably didn't play a part, but in the hands of a smart General, that platoon could be deadly," Dizzy said.

"And not one of the trainers are ingenious Generals," Tia

sniggered. They all laughed again, the tension draining from them now that they knew the result.

"I wonder where Raptor Squad went wrong?" Jenna said, voicing what the others were thinking.

"I honestly don't care. They did, and that means it's equal between us going into the final test next week," Eddie answered. With that, Phoenix Squad rose to leave.

* * *

Jonas sat back and digested the report, before passing it on to Ellie. He understood where they had gone wrong and suspected that Phoenix had done the complete opposite. He surmised that a middle ground was the desired outcome.

He had ploughed through the village and taken out the retreat, wiping them out to a man. The losses in the village had been high, 85% the report said; acceptable losses as far as he was concerned. They were simple labourers who were replaceable.

His father had advised him that within the test, the scoring took in to account each Hand's approach, and that there would be sections dedicated to each of the Hands. The Blue section was to protect a VIP from injury while they visited the battle. The Green section was to understand the battlefield; knowing where best to fight to have firm footing, and where to not get drawn in. The White and Yellow sections were to ensure that they set up the reserves, supplies, and medical support correctly. Finally, the Red and the Black Hand sections were geared to assess their military skills, one specialising in intelligence and threat reduction, and the other looking at the defence and protection of Selentans.

By ploughing through the village, he had failed the Red Hand element. Ellie and Lisa had asked if that was the right course, but he'd been caught-up in the final chase, wanting the General's head. Looking back, he should have taken time to save the villagers, and sent Squads on a roundabout route to cut off the retreat. It was something for him to consider, but not now ... the decisions had been made.

"And you would make the same one if faced with it again, Jonas," Drake advised in his mind.

He laughed. "Yes, Drake, I would. However, I need to ensure I don't act on the emotion of the chase in future." Then, to the Squad, he asked, "Anyone have any questions?"

They all considered what he was asking.

"They wanted us to save the villagers?" Thomas spat out in disgust, his true nature momentarily showing through his handsome visage.

He nodded.

"Why? There's plenty more of them," Ruben added angrily.

He considered his answer before responding. "It was a test, geared to involve each of the Hand's, saving the villagers was the Red element of that test." He stopped himself mocking Thomas as the light dawned in his eyes. He might be a little slow to pick things up, but he was loyal, powerful, and would carry out any order he gave him.

"They wanted us to sacrifice troops for the villagers?" Lisa asked.

It was Ellie who responded. "Yes, Lisa, but as Jonas said, it was a test. I, for one, don't regret our approach, and if we had to make that choice again, I think we would follow the same decision path."

He nodded, smiling. Ellie understood him well. "Right,

let's get ready for the last test, we win this one at any cost."

Raptor Squad all stood and filed out after Jonas.

CHAPTER TWENTY-FOUR

ngus Quinn usually enjoyed presiding over meetings of the Grey, continually manoeuvring, and manipulating the rest of the Hand towards his goals. But today, all he felt was frustration.

There were eight people within the Hands' ruling council, including himself. Then one for each of the other Hand's, with specific staff members assigned to sort the administration, and to implement the council's orders. Historically, they had been long-standing members of their Hand's and were no longer of any use. By assigning these members to the council, it gave them the honour of representing their Hand's in the Grey, allowing them to spend their time organising events and festivals.

"Until they decide to expire," a voice piped up in his mind.

He laughed, carefully schooling his outward expression to feign interest. Membership in the Grey was changing, it was becoming a Hand that people wanted involvement in. He had bribed, threatened, and extorted his way to taking up the position as Chairman of the Grey, then gradually took on extra responsibilities ... responsibilities that the old books detailed as the reason why the Grey Hand was first created.

He had ensured things moved as slowly as was necessary,

bite-sized chunks here and there, but never too much, selling it as the Grey relieving the pressure on the overly busy Hands.

The other Hands were yet to fully see the subtle shift in power. The one Hand he had gained no real control, or oversight over, was the Orange Hand. The old books detailed this separation of powers, deducing that it was because their roles were similar. Add in the current Lord Professor, and it was no surprise that he had not gained the control he wanted.

Where the Grey united the Hands as one ... the Orange were to educate the Selentan children in all areas of Selentan society; including how each of the Hands worked, their responsibilities, and ensuring that the students moved into the right Hand to benefit Selenta. They had to make certain that those with a knack for farming went to the Green, anyone with strong organisational skills went to the Yellow or Grey, natural entertainers went to the Purple, and healers went to the White. It was then the responsibility of the Hands to assign the new members according to their strengths.

Today, this was the source of his frustration. The Lord Professor was presenting to the council, explaining the plans for the final test and the requirements they had of the Grey to help prepare for the event, but the Grey was having no say in the proceedings.

The final test was going to take place over several days, with the students starting at a designated location, and making their way to the finish ... all while having to negotiate various obstacles and dangers.

Representatives of the Hands leaderships were based at the Orange retreat for the full event, attending several meetings, negotiations, and parties, as they decided which of the students they wanted to recruit into their own Hands.

The students believed their placement was a random decision. However, the Orange slotted each student to a given Hand, based on their views of each one's abilities and strengths. Only then were the other Hands able to negotiate for the students, explaining why they felt certain ones were a better fit within their own Hand.

The less attractive Hands tended to get the lower achievers, alongside those who never even went to the school. They would then attempt to give their whole allotment of recruits for one of the stronger recruit's, one who would excel across all the disciplines, but this was rarely agreed. It was the Black and the Red Hands who took the cream of the crop … keeping the top Squad together, rather than splitting them up.

"Do you think we will be able to place the new Squads where we want them?" a voice asked in his head.

"The Lord Professor is good," he replied. "If he wasn't, I would have already had it set. But with a bit of luck, and if Jonas can come first, we should be able to do it."

Aloud, he interrupted the conversation. "Lord Professor, I assume the proposal again this year will see the top Squad go as a full unit to either the Red or the Black Hand?"

The Lord professor smiled; he had clearly expected this question. "Yes, Mr Chairman. There is some thought currently going into what happens with the runners-up."

* * *

The Lord Professor watched for a reaction in Angus, but didn't get one. Instead, it was one of the other members who replied. "What do you mean, Lord Professor? It has always been that the other Squads are split up and placed where they are best suited."

He turned to the speaker, but did not miss the smirk that creased Angus's face.

"That is true, but this year is different from the last twenty years. We have two Squads going into the final test neck and neck, and as is our role, the trainers and I are considering what is best for Selenta."

The speaker scoffed at him. "Don't dance around the issue, Lord Professor. Everyone knows that one of the Squads in the lead are your favourites, and you are just finding a way to protect them."

His anger, that was usually slow to the boil, rose quickly, threatening to erupt.

"School yourself, Tobius," Esther spoke calmly, but with authority, aiming to break through the red mist. He took her advice, and instead of answering … stared at the speaker.

It didn't take long for the speaker's defiance to wither under his stare. He gulped, and his quick glance towards Angus confirmed this had been a set-up.

"As I said, we will consider what is best for Selenta, and that is the route we will recommend. But as usual, it is open to all the Hands to finalise any decisions and negotiate where the students end up," he said, purposely ignoring the favouritism accusation.

"Mistake," Caulder whispered too late, as they all saw the vicious smile that appeared on Angus's face.

"Thank-you for clarifying the position, Lord Professor," Angus smiled sweetly. "I'm sure all the Hands will take your recommendations seriously, and if splitting the second-place Squad is the right thing to do … then it will happen."

This time his companions did not try to calm him. "Never,

in my time as Lord Professor, has a recommendation ever been overruled. And you, Mr Chairman," he hissed. "You do not have the purview to have a vote on this."

* * *

Angus wanted to jump down, and get into it with the Lord Professor, the only man he felt was his equal, but that would weaken his position. He had won this round. The Lord Professor losing his cool was a rare occurrence; one to savour.

Instead, he spoke calmly and evenly, "I totally agree, Lord Professor. I was simply pointing out, that the Hands can split any Squad that does not finish first … if they feel it is the right thing for Selenta, for the skills of the Squad to be spread out."

"Of course, Mr Chairman," the Lord Professor snarled, then turned, and stalked from the meeting hall.

The Grey sat quietly, discussing things between themselves. He remained silent, watching the Lord Professor leave.

"He won't take this lying down," his companion observed.

"I would be disappointed if he did. We have some work to do this next week," he said, motioning to an aide, and issuing some instructions. As the aide scurried off, he addressed the rest of the Grey. "Let's get this meeting back on track, shall we … what's next?"

The speaker, who had sprung the trap on the Lord Professor, stood. "It is the Yellow, Mr Chairman, to discuss the treasury, and any support that we can give."

Buoyed by the last meeting, he smiled. "Excellent, let's not keep him waiting, bring him in."

* * *

Dutton watched as the Lord Professor stormed out of the Grey meeting hall. He scowled at the attendant who handed him his cloak, and bit the head off one of the Grey clerks who needed his signature on a document. As he flashed past, he simply took his place behind him, matching the Lord Professor's aggressive stride.

Once they had left the Grey head office, and entered the streets of Selenta, the Lord Professor took numerous turns down long roads and dark alleyways … seemingly wandering at random to clear his head, before he slipped into a bakery.

The server nodded as they moved behind the counter, and through a door into a room in the back. He waited at the entrance to make sure nobody had followed them, and only when he was confident that they were in the clear, did he join the Lord Professor in the back room.

As he entered, a shadow detached itself from the back corner, making him jump. "You know I hate it when you do that."

Katrina smiled, batting her beautiful green eyes at Dutton, and blowing him a kiss. As always, he blushed. He regularly dealt with the most powerful men in Selenta without blinking, but this beautiful redhead could disarm him with a simple smile.

"Enough flirting, you two," the Lord Professor teased, with no sign of his previously angry mood evident. "Katrina, we don't have much time, report please."

Katrina turned to the Lord Professor, and her manner changed, becoming the dangerous spy she was. "Yes, Sir. Phoenix Squad is a tight unit. They socialise with the other

Squads, yet this is all on a very high level. They help where they can to bring those other Squads on. Still, there is nothing of any substance, other than educating, in their interactions."

He and the Lord Professor both nodded, this was information they already knew from the trainer's reports.

"They keep any of their own training and tactics to themselves, and I believe they have a training facility, outside of the city within the forest. I can't get close without detection when they are there. Their perimeter is excellent."

Both of them smiled; this was high praise indeed.

"Lord Professor, you did say that you didn't want them to become aware of the surveillance, so I did not test the perimeter too much. However, I did search the area once they left, and I couldn't find any evidence of their training, or a structure ... although I did get a feeling that there was something in the area."

He took a note to do some research.

"All in all, the group are quite well drilled. They work well as a unit and seem to be able to communicate with each other easily," Katrina reported.

"Well, using voice and hand signals is common," he interrupted.

Katrina glanced at him, not needing words, as the look in her eyes was all the insult she needed to throw, and he visibly quailed.

Katrina continued explaining. "This is different, it's almost like they can communicate with the whole Squad, including each other's companions."

The Lord Professor leaned forward, intrigued. "Interesting," he mumbled, then looked to him. "I wonder if they have communication?"

Recovering quickly from Katrina's stare, he looked quizzically at the Lord Professor. "No one has had that skill in centuries, Lord Professor." Turning back to Katrina, he asked, "Can you explain what makes you think this a little more?"

Katrina wasn't sure what they were talking about, but continued, "In the crowd control test, they worked individually, clearing the buildings. They had a companion from one of the other's with them, talking to them like they did their own companions, and when the shit hit the fan, Tia's companion, Phantom, separated into multiple versions, and had one of his splits perched on each team member's shoulder. Their coordination while they cleared the crowds was uncanny."

Both he and the Lord Professor sat back, thinking.

"Rico's new companion?" the Lord Professor suggested.

"Possibly, Sir. We don't know much about it, and it doesn't conform to any creature our trainers have ever seen before."

"What do you mean? It's a dragon," Katrina interrupted, surprised they didn't know what the creature was.

"A dragon?" both he and the Lord Professor questioned as one.

"But it's so small. Are you sure?" he asked her.

Katrina's laughter tinkled through the room, making him grin like a schoolboy. "You, men! always preoccupied with size," she teased, shaking her head. "You should know size does not always matter with companions, and Llýr is a dragon. He matches the images in my grandfather's old books that I used to read as a child."

Neither he, nor the Lord Professor, questioned Katrina's opinion. She never gave one unless she was sure, and their minds had already moved onto the implications this had for Selenta, and for their plans.

"How did the meeting go with the Grey?" Katrina asked, interrupting their thoughts.

"As expected," the Lord Professor answered. "Angus wants to strip down Phoenix Squad. He sees them as a threat and will do anything he can to split them up. Unfortunately, he will succeed unless they come first. If they do win, it will work in my favour … I will be able to split Raptor Squad. Although, we have a potential long shot if they don't come first, thanks to Dutton."

The Lord Professor explained the plan and assigned Katrina her next task. As she moved to leave, she stood on her tiptoes and whispered in his ear, before kissing his cheek, and disappearing into the streets.

"Right, Dutton, back to work. We need to get representatives in from all the Hands. Angus needs to think he has outflanked us, and that we are trying to garner support for our plan."

"Yes, Sir," he answered as he absently followed the Lord Professor out into the street. His mind was still whirring over the whispered praise that Katrina had bestowed upon him.

CHAPTER TWENTY-FIVE

Major Drangor looked out over the city. The fog clung to it like a leech, remaining even as the day moved on. It would likely be late afternoon before it lifted. It gave the city a dark blanket that muted sound, lending to its drab, dismal appearance.

Had he been a Purple … he would no doubt pen poetry to describe what his eyes saw. Providing a beautifully crafted story detailing the sense of finality, isolation, and desolation that hung over the city and the rest of the world.

He had seen beyond the Gauntlet. Initially, he had been impressed by the fighting force that Magnar had at his command. They were well-drilled, well-equipped, and efficient. It had been hard to find fault, but the deeper they moved into Carasayer, the more he realised why.

Carasayer was purely a military state. The citizens worked to feed the military machine. They were all dirty and dishevelled, and many looked to be on the verge of starvation. Curious glances or interest were stamped out, met with severe punishments, or orders to keep quiet and work.

Rather than be more relaxed, the Elite soldiers were even more alert as they had moved closer to their home. The little he had been able to learn, told him that the Elite were in constant fear of an assassination attempt.

He gave a little rueful laugh, it seemed that despite his military might, there were still those who found a way to get close to Magnar. This thought sustained him, as he turned from his vista and considered his room ... or was it a cell? It felt like a cell, but as they went, this was not a bad cell to be in. It was well furnished, with a separate bathroom, kept clean by mute servants, and he was well fed. Despite this, his movements within the castle were restricted, and someone passed his room every hour checking that he was still there. He hadn't felt like this since he was newly recruited into the Black Hand.

He was beginning to think that getting into bed with Magnar was a terrible idea. The Black needed warning ... if Magnar's army got unlimited access to Elyssa, he was sure they could not stop him taking control, just by sheer numbers ... despite their well-laid plans. He needed to find a way to get a message back to The Black.

He needed access to, and to understand more, about this land and the tools he had at his disposal. The only chance he'd had to explore options so far was a quick visit to the city. Although he had a chaperone that kept an extraordinarily close eye on him, he had learned a lot.

The everyday citizens scurried out of their path, looking terrified, and just as dishevelled as their countryside kin. Next to them, there was a middle-class, who looked like administrators, and moved quickly out of the way, bowing their heads in deference. This reaction, and the easy acceptance of the Elite, led him to surmise that they owed their limited positions and allegiance to Magnar. The final group were obviously more affluent. They walked around with their own guards, and took their time getting out of the way of his Elite chaperone, firing glances of hatred when they thought they wouldn't get noticed.

He had been intrigued, and wondered whether he could use them, the little trip putting into perspective the alert status of the Elite when they entered Carasayer. Despite all the evident troubles, what had surprised him most was the lack of companions on show. He had not been able to investigate any further, as not long after they had passed the more affluent citizens, his chaperone had become agitated, and ushered him quickly back to the castle.

"What about the others?" Twister asked.

"I don't think we can trust them, Twister," he responded.

"I agree. The glimpses we've seen have shown us that they seem very comfortable here … slipping into the Elite's routines, and enjoying the perks that come with them," a third voice finished. He sighed. He had seen them apparently free to roam on his limited movement through the castle.

"Traitors," Twister growled.

"Tracker may be right, Twister," he observed. "But let's not label them traitors just yet."

"What else would you call them?" Tracker asked, his voice tinged with disgust. "Unlike you, they have full access to the building, and they come and go as they please, having the same access to Magnar as the Elite do."

"And, you are little more than a glorified prisoner," Twister finished for Tracker.

The words hit home with him, he'd had the same thoughts, but to hear them said aloud …

He shook his head in disappointment. The Black had warned him that Magnar would be a skilled manipulator, and that he should be on his guard, advising that he would try to turn them against him and use their knowledge. He had dismissed this as nonsense … he knew his heart and soul belonged to Selenta and the Black Hand. He would never be coerced.

"But are you sure about the others?" Tracker finished his train of thought.

As if on cue, there was a knock on his door. As he went to open it, Tracker advised, "Hold your counsel and anger, Drangor."

* * *

Magnar finished the council meeting, a tradition he chose to adhere to. It gave the more powerful families a chance to air their views and opinions, and made them feel like they had a say in the governing of the Empire. But realistically, it was just another tool he used to control them. It allowed him to see who were in opposition to his plans, only giving them decisions to make that had no impact on his own policies, or where he knew the outcome would be unanimous. He made any real decisions by himself and enforced them through the Elite and his military.

The council today had been uneventful; a few incursions on the lands of several of the councillors. They had agreed to send some soldiers in to root out the aggravators. He had information that this was purely the councillors wanting to frighten their workforce into working harder, as their quotas were perilously low. He didn't mind letting his men knock some heads if it helped to feed and clothe his army.

Thinking back on his visit to Elyssa, numerous things

about that state intrigued him … including the puzzle of the silos, which ate at him. He didn't like unanswered questions. Unfortunately, the four Black soldiers, whose loyalty he had so easily swayed, knew nothing of these silos. They seemed genuinely confused by his questions and thought he had seen things. He had surmised that they were not the cream of the crop, probably more of a distraction away from Drangor, who he saw as the real prize.

"I don't think he will be swayed," Tink put in.

"Me neither, he is the Black Hand's heart and soul," Gravel added.

"What do you think, Cassius?" he asked.

"I think he would be the only one worth having, but you won't have him even if he says so. And just to reiterate … you should have let me eat those other four, they're nothing but snivelling weasels."

They all laughed. Throughout the conversations he'd had with each of The Black's men, Cassius had continuously asked to eat them. In his view, they were too quick to turncoat on Selenta and answer all of his questions. The way the military lived in Carasayer had already turned their heads.

"They will prove useful, Cassius, but once they are no longer of use to me, they're all yours."

A satisfied grunt was all the answer he received.

He turned down a corridor headed towards the common soldiers' area.

"I assume you have decided to make your pitch," Tink surmised.

"In a manner of speaking. I have put off a conversation with him for far too long."

Stopping outside Drangor's door, he dismissed the guard and his own bodyguard. They obeyed, but immediately set off at a sprint. They wouldn't challenge him themselves, but they would go to the one man who would. He grinned, thinking about the look that would appear on Matrix's face as he raised his hand and knocked on the door. It didn't take Drangor long to answer, and to his credit, he wasn't taken aback by his being there.

"Told you he's the only one worth having," Cassius commented, then lapsed back into silence.

"Emperor Magnar," Drangor greeted, nodding in deference to his position, as he would to anyone of importance.

"You can drop the *Emperor*, Drangor. But as a minimum, call me Lord. The Elite get a little tetchy about disrespect." Drangor acknowledged this with a simple, respectful nod.

"Now walk with me, we have much to discuss."

Drangor fell in step to the left of him, slightly behind, showing deference, but staying in his peripheral vision.

"Does this man do anything that is not impressive?" Gravel observed, before they all lapsed into silence.

As he led them into the middle of the castle, all eyes were on Drangor.

* * *

Drangor logged everything as they went, the number and types of rooms, where the guard stations were, and the general layout. He did it carefully, using Tracker, Twister, and Faith rather than his eyes. He had to keep his focus on Magnar. He suspected the next few minutes would determine the success or failure of his mission.

He was intrigued that Magnar had not started talking straight away, no apology for keeping him waiting. Instead, he just moved through the castle … taking what felt like aimless directions.

"We are heading to something, Drangor, and I wish he would hurry up about it," Tracker observed sarcastically.

He suddenly realised what was happening … this was a peace offering. He hadn't been allowed to explore any of the castle since his arrival … and Magnar obviously wasn't going to apologise. Instead, he was giving him a tour.

He smirked. This is exactly the play The Black would make; unpredictable and clever. Which meant this meeting was not going to go the way he and his companions had thought it would.

* * *

Magnar saw Drangor's grin, and knew it was time to start talking. "What do you find so amusing, Major Drangor?" he asked.

Drangor composed himself before he replied. "I was thinking how similar you and The Black are, Lord."

The answer was so honest and straightforward that he smiled. It hadn't been the evasive answer he had been expecting. "Thank-you, Major Drangor."

He saw Drangor's eyes sparkle a little, because he had recognised it as the compliment it clearly was, reaffirming the discussion he and his companions had earlier … that this man idolised The Black, and comparing anyone to him, was the highest accolade Drangor would give.

At that moment, he made a choice, immediately turning,

and carefully observing Drangor to see if he recognised the change in energy. He had a destination now firmly in mind.

* * *

Drangor watched as Magnar's body language changed ever so slightly, he had decided something, and took off around the corner. There was now intent to this meandering through the hallways, they were going somewhere.

"Be prepared for anything, this one is crafty, cunning, and deadly," Tracker cautioned.

"Exactly, Tracker. I didn't compare him to The Black to boost his ego," he replied.

Outwardly, he straightened his uniform, and kept pace with Magnar. This time neither he, nor his companions, took their eyes off the Emperor.

Within minutes they entered a vast room. It had a high ceiling, and the outer area was ringed with empty benches. In the middle of the room, there was various marked areas, with racks of training weapons of all shapes and sizes, ranging from simple batons, to what looked like a boltshot, but a little longer. There were staffs with dark wooden heads that looked like a blade, and various sword-shaped weapons.

He glanced to the racks, fighting the urge to walk over, and test the quality. He despised training weapons, they were usually poorly made, and lighter than the real thing. Training with them was pointless; once you had used an authentic piece, it was like having to relearn again. Instead, he followed Magnar, waiting for him to make the next move, and deciding patience was currently his best weapon.

* * *

Magnar avoided numerous checked areas on the way to the auditorium, he knew that if the General arrived before they started, he would put an end to this. His heart was racing.

"This is dangerous, Magnar," Tink put in, having understood his intent.

"But necessary," growled Cassius and Gravel in anticipation.

"Put aside that those two are bloodthirsty, this is necessary, Tink. I need to show him trust. He will never be ours, heart and soul, but ..." he explained.

"Yes, I know," Tink interrupted, finishing his words. "But this will at least make him a true ally and help our plans. I agree with your reasoning, Magnar. I'm just not looking forward to Matrix's wrath."

They all grinned wickedly. Tink was looking forward to that as much as this, it was just his natural caution that meant he always voiced his position.

"But I will be testing him as well, Tink," he finished.

The situation discussed and agreed, he stopped in the middle of the room, coming to a standstill within a marked area that was approximately ten by ten meters.

He turned to Drangor. "So, Major, what do you think of Carasayer so far?"

Drangor didn't even pause. "It's difficult to build a true picture, when you are a prisoner, Lord."

He nodded, accepting the gentle reproof.

"Only because we will take it out of his flesh," Cassius growled happily.

Drangor continued at his nod. "However, from what I have

seen of it, it is interesting. In summary; the military holds sway. There appears to be four tiers; the military, the manual workers, the rich, and the administrators, who appear to be closely linked to the military." Drangor stopped, his delivery simple and business-like.

"A good summary, Drangor, but that's nothing a simple farmer couldn't observe. It's definitely not the summary from someone I would expect The Black to send as his emissary."

He turned, and walked to a weapons rack, and started sorting through them.

"So, I ask again … what do you think of Carasayer?" he asked, with emphasis on the "you".

There was a momentary pause as Drangor considered, he must have decided to go all in …

"Lord, there is significant unrest between the tiers. It's not obvious, but it's seen through the actions and interactions. The lower hate the rich, the rich hate the poor … they both hate the administrators and the military. There is a constant undercurrent of fear. The rich have guards of their own, the other two tiers scurry around quickly and efficiently, never making eye contact or staying in one place for long. Your military don't like to be out alone in the city, and you even have checkpoints within the castle walls. I suspect that there is an undercurrent of violence. Although, I have seen no evidence in the little time that I have been free to roam. I also suspect that there is a huge underground criminal or rebellious element that eats up a lot of your military time and resources. If my reading of you, and the people under your command is correct … I will surmise that you are aware of all of this, but get limited information in the reports you receive.

You're informed that it's under control, yet suspect that is not the case. Your power is so absolute, probably ruthlessly obtained and controlled, no one wants to be the one to provide you with bad news." Drangor paused momentarily to take a breath. "Then you add to that this being a military state - you need to keep Carasayer growing, and make sure that you keep the troops busy. Bored troops have their own risks. So, it is often thought that expansion or war is required … soldiers do not make for good unemployed, disgruntled farmers."

Drangor looked directly at him. "Was that a better summary than a farmer's, Lord?"

"Oh, I really like this one," Gravel laughed. "Can we keep him?"

He didn't respond. Instead, he selected two training staffs created to imitate a Scaltar: a staff about six-foot-long, with a wicked eighteen-inch curved blade on the end.

He turned to Drangor. "A very direct response, and dangerously honest. I get very little of that when the news is bad. Now, due to your honesty, I will give you some free information … don't trust your compatriots. They took my offer, and they now work for me."

He was impressed that Drangor didn't let his anger show outwardly. He felt, rather than saw, the internal rage. He began to stalk around Drangor, who was in the middle of the square.

"Now, I will not disrespect you, Drangor. I'm not even going to try and convert you, as I believe that you are The Black's. Any acquiescence on your part would be false."

He watched Drangor move to keep him in view as he circled him.

"But I don't even think you would do that. You appear to be a man of honour, and I need your help. I want you to give me that help freely, and to the best of your ability … as you would any General that The Black requested you to work under." He stopped, casting a glance to the entrance. It wouldn't be long before Matrix arrived. "So, in return for your help, Drangor, I will answer any question you ask."

He didn't need to turn to see the surprise in Drangor's eyes.

"But there are limits. I will not discuss mine and The Black's plans, and you must earn the right to ask each question."

He stopped prowling, faced Drangor, and threw one of the staffs towards him. As Drangor reached, and plucked it out of the air, he moved quickly and silently to attack.

CHAPTER TWENTY-SIX

"I wish they would just get this started," Rico moaned.

They had arrived at the barracks outside the test zone a few days earlier.

Butch laughed. "You're always impatient, Rico. Just relax. We're going to have enough to do over the next few days."

"He's right," Jenna added. "Eat or sleep. There's nothing else to do. We are as prepared as we can be."

He grumbled, and continued to pace the room. His agitation was not merely his impatience ... he had a bad feeling he couldn't shake off, and it had been eating at him over the last few days.

The door opened as Eddie and Tia entered the room. Tia, as always, immediately going to Butch.

"Any news?" he asked, hopefully.

Eddie smiled. "No change, there is nothing in this camp that gives a clue about what lies ahead. There are so many barriers up to stop us snooping on the zone, even Tia can't get through."

Butch and Jenna chuckled at the tone Eddie used, having reported the same outcome numerous times the last few days.

"We could use the trick we have been practising?" he

offered. Such was his agitation; he hadn't noticed Eddie's attempt at levity.

"No, I would rather keep that up our sleeve. If we do something now, and anyone sees, they can prepare a counter in the test," Eddie replied.

He grunted, but didn't argue, he knew Eddie was right.

"Besides, we will see soon enough; in a few hours."

His eyes lit up, and both Butch and Jenna sat up more alert.

"The last group just reached the halfway point; we have been given the final call."

They all looked around at each other, excitement, anticipation, and nervousness in their eyes. This was what they had been training for the last five years.

Llýr appeared on the window ledge. "Well, what are you all waiting for? Get yourselves ready," he instructed.

As if a spell had been broken, the Squad sprang into action.

* * *

Jonas paced the squad room; he knew he was letting his impatience show, but he wanted to get going. The rest of the Squad wisely stayed away from him, keeping their own counsel.

Thomas was fast asleep and snoring in the corner. Jonas considered walking over and kicking him, but decided it was beneath him. He was just jealous that Thomas could sleep in the middle of a battle.

Ruben sat on the opposite side of the room, slowly sharpening his knife, a sure sign of his nervousness. The slightly distracted look in his eyes, showing that he was in conversation with his companions.

Lastly, Lisa lay on the bed with her head rested in Ellie's lap, dozing, but her eyes snapping open at every noise. Ellie gently stroked her hair, as she kept her own eyes closed. She was also preparing herself for the coming trials.

Their turn to start the final tests had been delayed a couple of times, meaning the last Squads had not crossed the halfway point or given up yet.

His father had explained that the final test was a time trial. The lower-ranking Squads being the first to attempt to cross the course. No one knew how it was set up until they entered the valley. Even the mighty Angus Quinn didn't know.

He was about to go outside, and get some fresh air, when there was a light knock at the door. Lisa jumped up quickly and answered, taking the message. She came back into the room, her eyes bright with excitement. "Final call," she told Raptor Squad.

He grinned. "Finally." Then, turning to the rest of the Squad, he said, "Let's get ready to kick some ass!"

They all jumped into action, finalising their packs with the contents Jonas had prescribed.

* * *

"Looks like someone was more impatient than you."

Tia smiled as she heard Llýr tease Rico. Phoenix Squad were walking down the approach to the training valley, where Raptor Squad was already waiting.

"Did any of you feel that?" she whispered, as she felt a tingling.

"I don't feel anything," Jenna answered.

Butch and Rico shook their heads, neither of them had felt

it.

"Gravel says that it's probably a scouting barrier. We didn't feel anything, but it's likely you did because of Phantom," Eddie explained.

"OK," she answered, and decided on impulse to step back, so she could feel the barrier. "Phantom, do you think we could work out how to do this?" she asked.

"I don't know, maybe. Let's learn a little more, shall we?" Phantom replied eagerly.

The rest of the Squad waited patiently. They watched as a spectral vision of Phantom appeared around her head, his wings appearing to sprout from her ears, and his head above hers. After a few seconds, Phantom's image disappeared, and she opened her eyes to see a big grin on Butch's face. "What?" she asked shyly.

Butch simply walked up to her and kissed her. "You are beautiful," he whispered in her ear.

She hugged him hard, then broke away, looking at the rest of the Squad. "What are we standing about for? We have a test to win."

They all laughed as they made their way down to the starting area, to await the arrival of the last three Squads.

* * *

The Lord Professor watched as the final three Squads arrived shortly after Phoenix and Raptor Squad, each looking nervous, flustered, and in some cases ... very upset. He sympathised with them; today would be the last time they did anything together as a Squad before they were split-up. This test was almost cruel for them, as it wasn't a task that suited their skill set.

These Squads were the nearest to Raptor and Phoenix Squad in the scoring, but they were still a way off from being close to having their abilities. Their skills in tactics and combat were average at best. None of them were a good fit for the Black or Red Hand. Horse Squad were more suited to the Purple and Green Hands. Bear Squad had three powerful healers who would join the White. The other two members were developing strong Blue attributes, as they spent their time protecting their healers. The last, Armadillo Squad, were suited to the Orange, and possibly Yellow, Hand. They were able to interpret and implement the concepts of all the Hands to an average level, always eager to help other Squads, while displaying good organisation, and a strong ability to train.

He supposed they could become good foot soldiers in the Red and Black Hands. Still, with the debacle in the Plaza, the Orange needed some new trainers.

He waited patiently for them to get into position; it didn't take long. "Good morning, Squads," he said when they were all ready. "Before we start today's test, I would like to say how proud I am. You have all advanced and honed your skills."

He was pleased to see the Squads perk up at his compliment, knowing they would need all their confidence and abilities today.

"Don't tell them how difficult you have made the course then, and how everyone else has failed," Caulder said in his mind, grinning.

"Not just failed, Caulder. They epically failed, none even reaching halfway," Chirp put in.

"You know very well the course was not set up for them,"

he snapped.

Outwardly, he smiled benignly at the Squads before con-tinuing. "Your final task is to get from one end of the course to the other."

He pointed to a board that gave an outline of the shape of the course; highlighting the start and finish. But there was no detail on the map; nothing about the terrain or the obstacles they would face.

"You will notice that there are two coloured dots for each Squad," he continued. "As well as getting from start to finish, you have to recover an injured VIP, and transport them from your allotted point A to point B ... alive."

He watched the cogs turning, this was an extra element added to the test that had never appeared previously.

"You can decide to leave the VIP if you wish ... but eight hours will be added to your finishing time for not succeeding, and an additional fifty points awarded if you succeed."

He let this sink in. The final test was essentially two races; Phoenix and Raptor Squad competing for the top spot, and Bear, Horse, and Armadillo Squads vying for third.

"There are two hundred points on offer for finishing the race, and a bonus of twenty-five points for coming first," he finished, trying his best not to laugh at the scowls he received from Jonas and Lisa.

"You are so not their favourite person," Esther laughed.

Effectively ... by attaching a higher points award to the delivery of the VIP, rather than finishing first ... he had given Raptor and Phoenix Squad no option but to recover the VIP. They had to if they wanted to win this final test.

"You have five minutes to finalise your plans and position yourselves along the wall. Good luck to you all, may the best

Squad win!"

He raised his hands above his head and clapped loudly, indicating the test had begun.

The Squads were on the move immediately, as he retreated to the viewing balcony and joined the Hand leaders. All were present, except the Red and Black Hands ... their identities were closely guarded secrets, and proxies represented them in their stead.

He turned and watched the start of the proceedings. It always interested him to see who went to the board from each Squad. It was typically the Squad leader, as seen with the previous four groups.

"He trusts his Squad's skills," Esther spoke.

"That he does," he replied, as he watched Tia from Phoenix Squad approach the board with her crow, Phantom, perched on her shoulder.

The rest of Phoenix Squad moved to their chosen starting position. However, when Tia returned to the group ... she spoke briefly, and the Squad moved to the southern end of the starting wall.

"I thought you said this Phoenix Squad was good? They moved from a prime spot to the furthest point away," Angus Quinn, who was representing the Grey, mocked.

He schooled his face and spoke lightly, "I'm sure it seems that way. But I assure you, there are potential tactical benefits to that position." He paused, thinking. "I wonder ..." he said to nobody in particular, momentarily forgetting Angus was there.

"You wonder what, Lord Professor?" Angus asked, intrigued.

He considered, and could see no harm in telling him.

Raptor Squad was already in the field and had taken the point position, it was unlikely that Phoenix Squad would have identified the weak area.

"Similar to the shield that covers the training area ... to stop snooping before the test ... a few hundred meters in front of the wall, and about ten meters above the ground, is a defensive screen set up by the Red's. It's a scouting screen that allows them to know that a manifested flying companion has slipped through."

Angus nodded. He had suspected as much. "And I assume a Red will then instruct the defenders own companions to go to that point to prevent the Squads from getting an early view of the field," Angus surmised.

He smiled. "Exactly, pretty ingenious really."

"But what has that got to do with where Phoenix Squad have set up?" Angus asked.

"That's the *I wonder* part. Where the Red has set up the screen ... the closest point it is to the wall, is where Phoenix Squad has set up. It's only about thirty metres away from the wall there."

He recalled how Angus's tactical mind was equal to his own, demonstrating how dangerous an enemy he is, as he quickly assessed the implication of Phoenix Squad's position.

"So, they could make a quick dart out, release their scout, and get a view of the battlefield before the defenders know what has happened. By the time the defenders realise, it will be too late, and their scouts will have reported back." Angus summarised his thoughts.

"Precisely. Let's watch!" he answered, caught up in the moment.

The bell rang to signal the five minutes were up, and the

161

Squads sprang into action.

As suspected, Phoenix Squad darted out of cover … Eddie and Rico flanking Tia, none of their companions manifesting, leaving the other Squads hidden behind the wall. He watched closely. As they reached the thirty-meter mark, Tia turned to Eddie and nodded. They advanced another ten meters and stopped. Tia's crow manifested on her shoulder as she beckoned to Rico, who approached her and reached up as if stroking the crow. When he stepped back, Rico's chameleon companion was perched on the crow's back.

"What are they doing?" Angus asked, leaning in to get a better look, excitement in his voice. He'd also become caught up in the start.

"I have no idea," he replied, as they both moved forward like old friends figuring out a puzzle.

They were both captivated as Eddie came forward, and the crow jumped onto his arm. Eddie ran forward and launched the crow into the air. It took a few seconds for it to become accustomed to the extra weight, but once it did, it climbed quickly into the air and then suddenly vanished from sight.

He and Angus Quinn looked at each other in amazement, neither able to explain what they had just seen. Their minds were mulling over the implications as Phoenix Squad returned to the cover of the wall.

"She said they were full of surprises," Esther chuckled in his mind, reminding him of Katrina's assessment.

"What did we just see?" Angus Quinn questioned.

"A new tactic that we are going to have to learn how to defend against," he answered.

Any further conversation was then halted by a huge thunderclap off to the left.

* * *

As the Lord Professor clapped his hands to start the test … Eddie motioned to Tia to check the board; she was their navigator within the test, so best placed to mark the locations of their VIP. The scoring meant that they had to rescue the VIP if they wanted any chance to take first place.

He led the Squad to the starting spot they had agreed on, while waiting for the other Squads to arrive, and waited for Tia to join them. As Tia walked back, she paused slightly, a look of concentration on her face.

"What's wrong?" Rico asked Tia, the moment she was back in the safety of the group.

Eddie was pleased that Rico noticed they had to look out for each other.

"Nothing bad," Tia answered absently. "Just give me a second."

They waited patiently. Suddenly, her eyes refocused, and she smirked at them. "Change of plan, move to the southernmost starting point."

No one questioned her, they just moved quickly, taking up their new position.

"Spill," Jenna said, once they were in place.

Tia shrugged, smirking. "I'm playing a hunch." At their questioning looks, she explained. "When we entered the training zone, I took some time and felt the crossover with Phantom."

"We remember, Beautiful," Butch winked.

Tia smiled lovingly at him before continuing, "Well, as we walked over, Phantom and I extended our senses without manifesting, like we have been practising. By doing so, we felt a similar signature to the one earlier out front." She indicated to the test zone … "It was faint, and not as strong as the one on the outside, so we explored it as best we could, and identified that it is closest to the wall at this point," Tia finished.

"Do you know what it is, or what it does?" Eddie asked.

"We're not sure exactly what it does, but we think it could be some sort of alert system. It's focused on one thing, and feels almost alive," Tia answered.

"Do you think it might alert the defenders when we pass through it?" Jenna asked.

Tia considered what Jenna was asking and consulted Phantom. "If we had to guess … it's when companions pass through it, not hosts, but that's just a hunch. Phantom feels it much more than I do."

Eddie looked around the group, watching them assimilate the information. "OK, based on Tia's explanation, I would guess at a scouting screen. The basic plan still stands, but with one slight tweak."

They all looked at him, grinning.

"All plans go to pot at the first breath of battle," Rico smirked.

Eddie laughed; they were prepared for this. "Rico and I will head out, protecting Tia. Once we clear this barrier, whatever it is, we will release Phantom and Misty. No manifesting until we clear the barrier."

They all nodded.

The bell rang, signalling the end of the five minutes, and they sprang into action. Eddie and Rico flanking Tia as they sprinted into the open. Jenna and Butch kept an eye out for any surprises. There were none, as the three made their way quickly across the ground. Eddie suspected that the defenders would not expect this move.

He looked to Tia as they approached the thirty-meter mark, and she nodded. "We just passed through."

"A little further, just to be sure," Eddie instructed.

After another ten metres, they stopped. Phantom manifested on Tia's shoulder.

"Your turn, Rico," she smiled.

Rico walked forward and placed his hand on Phantom's back, asking Misty to manifest, which she did immediately. "Look after her?" he asked Phantom, who cawed in acknowledgement.

Misty looked terrified, but she was a pivotal component of the plan.

Eddie then stepped forward, and Phantom hopped onto his arm. This was the tricky part, as Phantom needed to take off with Misty on his back. Tia and Rico were too short to provide enough momentum to launch them into the air. Eddie took a few quick steps forward, and Phantom vaulted from his arm. Collectively, they held their breath, as Phantom fought for control. It was only moments, but it felt like hours, until he caught his flow, and swung gracefully into the air, to a full outward release of breath from the Squad.

As he started to climb, they suddenly merged into the sky, and for all intents and purposes … disappearing out of sight.

"AWESOME!" Butch shouted, as the three turned and rushed back to cover, keeping an eye out for any sign that they'd been spotted, but none came.

Tia dropped to the floor inside the protective cordon of Phoenix Squad, as she connected with Phantom, and quickly sketched the battlefield. They only had a few minutes, as they didn't want to overly tax Phantom and Misty. Hopefully, that would be enough.

Suddenly, a huge thunderclap from the north caught everyone's attention.

* * *

As the Lord Professor clapped his hands to start the test, Jonas headed to the board to check on the VIP position, having brought his anger under control.

The Lord Professor had done his best to stack the odds in Phoenix Squad's favour. By limiting the first-place finish to just twenty-five points, he was forcing Raptor Squad to slow down. Their original game plan was to focus on their speed and strength, avoid trouble where possible, or simply bulldoze their way through. The addition of the VIP element nullified this approach.

He joined the rest of the Squad, who had taken position at the forward point he had chosen. This spot gave the most options for when they started moving. He checked Lisa, Thomas, Ellie, and Ruben were ready and looked around.

Horse and Armadillo had moved into positions slightly to the north, Bear was to the south in-between them and Phoenix Squad, who had gone to the southernmost tip of the starting wall. He wondered what they were doing, but didn't get time to ponder on it as the bell rang to signal the start of the test.

He watched as five of the Squad's companions manifested; Jasmine and Achos, Lisa's owl and hawk, perched on each of her shoulders. Merl, Ellie's raven, and Harur, Thomas's shrike, were likewise perched. Jonas looked to Ruben ... who was having an animated conversation with his thunderbird, Indran. He was a medium-sized bird, but his size hid his real power. Jonas gave him a few moments, Indran was key to the plan. Let the other Squads beat the bushes and flush out the defenders, he thought. He was sure they wouldn't send their full defence, but it would give an idea of potential numbers.

He watched, as birds from the other three Squads, took off into the air to try and give them a view of the battlefield. He wasn't surprised to see an immediate response from defending birds, appearing from various locations to intercept.

He scowled. "Amateurs," he hissed, as he watched the Squads allow their birds to be struck by the attackers, meaning that they would get injured and take something out of the host too.

Turning away from the other Squads attempts in disgust; he addressed his own Squad. "Go north fifty metres, then climb quickly. There is a slight gap that should give a little more time before they converge," he instructed. "Remember, do not get embroiled in a fight. Get as much of a view as you can, but do not take any kind of injury. Or you deal with me," he growled.

They all nodded.

He turned back to the test area. The moment the last defender's bird disappeared out of sight, he instructed them to go.

Their companions took flight in close formation. Indran was in the lead, Jasmine and Merl either side of him, Achos and Harur immediately behind, and giving the illusion that there were only three birds. The Squad was watching, tense with anticipation. The outcome of this could mean the difference between first and second.

The birds hit the fifty-metre mark, then as instructed, rose quickly. As they started their ascent, the defenders reappeared ... this time in more significant numbers. He grunted in satisfaction; he had expected this. The birds continued to climb as the defenders converged on them.

"Ten seconds," Ruben muttered.

As he spoke, Indran pulled up in the air, and hovered, facing the oncoming defenders who were racing to meet them. The other four continued several meters, before Jasmine and Merl pulled up and hung in the air, letting Achos and Harur pass. As they did, both Jasmine and Merl flapped hard, giving them a wing-blast, and adding additional speed to them as they continued to climb. Once their job was complete, they disappeared, returning to Lisa and Ellie.

Below, Indran cried loudly, flapping his wings. His cries were accompanied by a huge thunderclap, the shockwave pouring out from him and into the oncoming defenders, knocking them out of their flight. Over half of them disappeared, either from taking too much damage, or by their host calling them back if they recognised what was about to happen.

Indran called loudly, mocking the defenders, and their inability to stand up to him.

He mirrored Ruben's grin; this was not Indran's usual style. He was normally quiet, reserved, and deadly. However, the plan required the attention be on him for as long as possible ... allowing Achos and Harur precious seconds to climb unencumbered.

The defenders recovered quickly, with their numbers increased substantially. This time with deadly major companions amongst them. The defenders changing tact was a testament to Indran's threat, but it also highlighted that there were some stalwart defenders out in the testing zone, showing again that the Lord Professor had not made this test easy.

Indran bowed to the new arrivals and disappeared.

A shrill "Aak, aak," that was followed by a sharp, "Beek," dragged his eyes back to Achos and Harur.

Two defenders had broken off, and followed the climbing pair on a course which prevented them from getting the view they required.

Harur had decided Achos was better set to complete the mission. He had broken off from Achos, and was diving full speed at the two sparrow hawks. There was no way Harur could beat either of the hawks directly, but that was not his plan. He chittered loudly, baiting the sparrow hawks to fight him, they split slightly to let Harur pass between them unencumbered, before they themselves dived to finish him off cleanly.

Harur let out a victorious, "Beek," before he disappeared, letting Achos flash through, taking advantage of the space the sparrow hawks had left. They had no chance to catch her, she was by in an instant, and able to take her time looking out over the battlefield … providing images back to Lisa so she could document the terrain. Lisa smiled as she sketched.

"Tell Achos to return, Lisa. She's done her job, and they are converging," he instructed.

Achos gave one last cry and disappeared, leaving the defenders frustrated. She reappeared on Lisa's shoulder, looking down at her sketch, and chittering if she felt Lisa had missed a detail.

When Lisa had finished, she passed him the sketch.

"Excellent work, all of you," he praised. "Now the hard part."

They all gathered around the map. "This is what I propose …"

* * *

"Nicely done," Eddie applauded, as he watched Achos disappear. Then he turned back to Tia. "How's it going?" he asked.

Tia looked up. "Worked like a charm," she answered, showing the map she had sketched. It contained details, not only of the terrain, but the number and placement of defences, and a feel for the estimated power of defenders, based on the companions released to head off Raptor Squad.

"Phantom is tiring quicker than we expected, they have had to make some urgent turns to avoid patrols," she added.

He turned to Rico. "How's Misty doing?"

Rico smiled fondly. "Other than being terrified, she's doing OK. She's just a passenger. Phantoms doing all the hard work."

He thought quickly. Both of these companions were crucial to their plans. "OK, call them both back. We have more than enough information to start with, let's not overtax them too early."

Both Tia and Rico closed their eyes and sent messages to their companions, once they opened their eyes, they nodded to let him know it was done.

"You're a bad influence on her, Llýr," Rico laughed, responding to a conversation going on in his head. Realising he had spoken aloud, he chortled. "Misty says, let's not do

170

that again," he explained to chuckles from the Squad.

Since Llýr's arrival, Rico's two minor companions had become much more confident and vocal, mirrored by improved abilities and strengths, and becoming more like majors than minors. It was evidenced by Misty having the ability to camouflage the others, and not just Rico … providing the Squad with a new bag of tricks.

"OK. Well, at least not until tomorrow," he joked, and the rest of the Squad laughed, as Misty appeared briefly on Rico's shoulder, and stuck out her tongue before disappearing again.

He shook his head, focusing on Tia's map. "Right, down to business. Ideas on our route …"

Tia placed the map on the stone table in front of them where they were all gathered.

"We could head directly for the VIP, hitting the lowest scout point? Their numbers are small, and their strength is middling," Butch offered.

"I'm with Butch," Rico said.

"I agree. We have enough up our sleeves to take that approach, but …" Jenna said, "I think we hug the south wall, then come up through the zone between the defence emplacements." Jenna smiled, tracing the route with her finger. "We use the forest cover to get close to our VIP pickup, avoiding the risk of conflict until that point. I'm fairly certain there will be a surprise waiting for us there."

He nodded. "Tia?"

Tia considered all of this as she talked with Phantom. "We think avoidance at first is the best plan. We're going to have to fight our way through at some point, and must assume they have a communication route. If we use our advantages frivolously, or too early, they won't help us when we really need them."

"Good point, Tia," Rico conceded.

Butch winked at her affectionately, agreeing with her point. They all then looked to him ...

"We will take the southern route and come up in between. I'm worried about entering the forest without full information, so we will send Dancer and Grey Claw ahead to scout once we are close. This should be fun," he smiled.

Decision made; they took off quickly into the valley.

* * *

As Jonas finished outlining their plan, Ruben and Thomas grinned wickedly. This suited their skill set ... hit hard, and fast ... not giving the defenders time to regroup.

He planned to hit the middle defensive position, then skirt the wall as if heading north, before they hooked back south ... following the edge of the forest as they made their way to their VIP pickup. He was anticipating significant resistance when they collected their VIP, and the plan was to break that pursuit early, rather than have a protracted chase.

He stood, looking at the other Squads, watching as Phoenix Squad rose and quickly headed south. It was tempting to tweak his plans and follow them, but he had made his decision, and was confident of his own success. He was about to instruct the Squad to move, when Horse, Armadillo, and Bear suddenly sprang into action.

Armadillo headed north, Bear heading slightly to the south ... both directions would bring them close to the defensive positions so were not his concern. Horse Squad, however, was a different story. They had picked a route almost identical to the one he had chosen, probably by pure luck.

Ellie came up beside him. "We use them as a distraction, and save our strength?" she asked.

He grinned. "Just what I was thinking. Ruben, send out Sly to keep an eye on them, report back as soon as they encounter the defenders."

Ruben's fox companion appeared, and slipped into the field, his colours shimmering into the background as he moved, keeping a steady distance from Horse Squad.

"Once they're intercepted, we head north and skirt them. Let them take the brunt of the heat."

He laughed at the disappointment on the faces of Ruben and Thomas. "Don't worry, there will be plenty of chances at combat over the next few days, I'm sure," he reassured them.

"They're out of sight," Lisa advised.

"OK, let's move," he instructed, and they took off in the wake of Horse Squad.

CHAPTER TWENTY-SEVEN

Jonas was pleased with the Squad's progress. They had slipped past the defenders easily enough, as they were pre-occupied with Horse Squad, making it much more straightforward than anticipated.

Horse Squad had put up a pretty good fight, surprising him, and because of this, he had let Ruben and Thomas hit the defensive position which only had two Blues guarding it. The pair had slipped in and eliminated them from the rest of the test. Each combatant, including the Squads, had breakable seals at various points on their bodies ... some much easier to break than others. If broken, the combatant was deemed injured or dead, with White healing able to fix some of the seals if broken. Ruben and Thomas had broken the ones on the Blues necks, quietly and efficiently.

They then headed north; ensuring their direction was obvious, before splitting wide, and heading south quickly towards their VIP, this time disguising their tracks.

He wasn't worried that they would be defeated by the defenders, his concern was that they'd slow them down, and Phoenix Squad would be quicker.

As they moved south, he had his suspicions confirmed, as he caught a glimpse of a bird in the distance; Jepp, Lisa's jackal, reporting back not long after. He had seen Phoenix Squad enter the forest slightly to the east.

He felt tempted to send some of the companions to alert the defenders to Phoenix Squad's position, but decided against it, as it would leave them undefended and open to attack. Instead, he put his mind to the job at hand.

According to Lisa's map, there were two guard posts slightly to the south-east of where they were now, they would be expecting an attack. Raptor Squad's VIP was close by, and to ensure victory ... Raptor Squad had to collect it.

He trotted up to Ellie. "They know we're coming," he said.

"Saskia and I were just having the same conversation."

He smiled; this was why he had mentioned it. Saskia was Ellie's chimera companion, and was as vicious as they came. "Does Saskia have any ideas?"

Ellie grinned. "She does, but Ruben is not going to like it one little bit."

An hour later, they lay waiting for the signal ... Ruben was the bait. After Ellie, he was the fastest in the Squad, but unlike Ellie, he had the stamina to maintain his pace. His job was to casually walk in-between the defensive posts and draw them out. He wasn't there to fight them, just kick the kennel.

This was the tricky part of the plan. They didn't want them to give full, immediate chase. This would leave Ruben isolated and easy to defeat ... they just wanted the defensive position to look that way. Ideally, anticipating that Ruben's appearance was a ruse, and delaying any pursuit while consolidating their forces to pursue, to overwhelm the trap. It all depended on how good the Commander of these defensive positions were. They needed a good Commander.

One that recognised Ruben as bait, and therefore likely to go out in force … just not too good to guess that he needed to also look the other way.

The first defence posts had ten people in them, and left two behind to defend the post. If that was the setup throughout the training area, then it meant a potential sixteen soldiers prepping to head off after Ruben.

Lisa's eyes glazed over as she spoke with Jepp, who'd made his way as close to the posts as he could. He had decided to keep surveillance away from the birds for the time being. They had tested scouting earlier, and every time they took off into the air, defenders' companions were immediately onto them.

"They're not taking the bait, Jonas. They set off, but a Captain from the northernmost post stopped them. He looks to have them set up on a scouting net to cover an attack. There's a group heading off towards our VIP area," Lisa explained.

He growled. "Probably just checking we've not slipped by."

"We can take them all out?" Thomas offered.

"Tempting as that may be … Phoenix have to drop their VIP off in this area. If we wipe out both posts, we make it easier for them," he said, and saw the disappointed look on Thomas's face. "OK, change of plan. Ruben will have to catch us up. Thomas, go with Ellie and clean out anyone left at this lowest defence post. We don't want to eliminate them all, but I want the nest stirred."

They both nodded.

"Then wait for Ruben to join you. We are going to get the VIP."

Ellie nodded.

"Silent or loud?" Thomas asked.

"Silent, to start. Treffin will stay with you, and when she starts kicking up a fuss, head to me quickly and noisily."

Merl suddenly appeared on Lisa's shoulder, getting a look from Jonas. Ellie explained, "When Merl nips Lisa's ear, Ruben has arrived."

"Good call," Jonas answered, and disappeared into the dusk with Lisa on his heels.

* * *

"The calm before the storm?" Jenna murmured to no one in particular.

Llýr appeared on her shoulder. "Don't jinx it, Princess," he grinned, and vanished again, appearing on Rico's shoulder, and winking at her.

She laughed.

"Ignore him, Jenna," Rico advised. "He's just sulking because he didn't get to fly on Phantom."

Llýr huffed and turned his face away in an exaggerated sulk. The Squad grinned at their attempt to relieve the tension. They had made it this far without any trouble thanks to Phantom and Misty, but it had been long enough now that defence posts and patrols could have changed.

Phantom had reported, that although the ceiling of the scouting net was higher out here, it was still there. It was preventing him from getting more than a view of the immediate vicinity, and was risky because the ceiling seemed to be rising and falling randomly. Eddie had called Phantom back, he didn't want to risk giving away their position, especially when they were about to enter the forest.

Dancer, Grey Claw, and Wiggy had gone on ahead into the forest to check it was clear, or at least give them a feel for what they were about to face. Wiggy was waiting for them as they approached the edge of the forest. He was chittering loudly, letting them know that all was safe to enter, and to follow him to a small glade they could hold up in while they planned their next steps.

The forest was denser than it looked; lots of low-lying bushes and shrubs to tangle feet, and not well travelled. It would take a lot of care to move through the forest quietly. Within a few minutes, they entered the glade where Dancer and Grey Claw waited, and Tia set the perimeter, all on their guard.

"We're clear for the moment," Tia whispered. "There is a track not far from here that has been used recently, possibly a patrol route."

Eddie turned to Jenna and Dancer. "Can you follow the track to see where it leads and stay out of sight?"

Dancer nodded, and glided silently into the forest.

Eddie looked around Phoenix Squad, each of their eyes shined, the tension was evident, but they were clearly enjoying this. He had to admit … so was he. He grinned at them through the gloom of the dense canopy.

"The plan is to move quickly through the forest, hugging the edge as best we can, which will give us as much light as possible. Wiggy will act as our eyes on the forest edge, keeping pace with us. Anyone disagree?" He looked around as they all shook their heads. "If we move quickly enough, we should be in scouting distance of the VIP at dusk. We can check the lay of the land and look to hit as darkness falls."

Dancer reappeared next to Jenna and reported. "The track

178

is well used and fresh today, it leads back to a number of other well-worn tracks, shooting off in various paths. I heard voices from two different directions to the north, so I think at least two patrols, but it feels a little lax. I didn't go much further as I didn't want to risk being seen, and they're likely to have their own companions out scouting."

The Squad considered Dancer's report.

"They're probably not expecting anyone to enter the forest from the south this early. Raptor have to collect their VIP before they move up, and there are three Squad VIP starting points to the north," Jenna offered.

"That makes sense, they won't be expecting us," Butch agreed.

"Well, what are we waiting for then?" Rico added. "Let's use it to our advantage and be up and past them before they think to check."

Eddie inclined his head. "Well, you're taking point, Rico. After you."

Rico winked and moved out in front, blending smoothly into the forest with the help of Misty.

Tia called back Phantom, and the Squad rose quickly, with Wiggy skipping from tree to tree, and heading to the forest edge. Kalina, Grey Claw, and Dancer took up flanking positions.

* * *

"So, what do you think?" Eddie asked.

"Much too quiet," Llýr answered after a few seconds for Rico, who was busy and hadn't heard.

Eddie glanced over and smirked at the *what can you do* look on Llýr's face, but neither interfered. They knew Rico was studying the area.

He and Rico had crept as close to the VIP point as they could, with Misty providing them cover. After a few minutes, Rico huffed, slightly annoyed. "It's a trap, there's no doubt about it. They've had plenty of time to prepare, and I can't pinpoint all of them." Rico sketched a small map to share with the others before they made their way back to the trees.

As they arrived back, Butch handed them some bread and meat, simple fare, but they took it gratefully.

"So how does it look?" Tia asked.

Rico handed her the map, which she studied and passed onto Jenna and Butch.

"Six defenders you can see, which leaves at least six more hidden," Tia observed, as Butch and Jenna looked it over.

"That's if they keep to size, based on our reconnaissance," Rico added.

Butch finished examining the map and placed it in front of Rico. "So, how would you do it?" he asked Rico, whose head shot up to look at Butch in surprise.

Llýr appeared on Butch's shoulder. "Well?" he mocked.

He interrupted before Rico could start arguing … "He's right, Rico. You're our best tactician. If we were to estimate that there were six more defenders, where would you put them?"

Rico scowled at Llýr playfully, before setting his mind to the task.

"Well for me, the six we can see were too easy to spot. They are a diversion … made obvious, so we take a different route to get to our target," he said.

"What makes them obvious?" Jenna asked.

"There's just too much wrong with their positioning. The ground just doesn't quite match the contours of the area cleanly. It's nothing major, but even a novice Commander would see it and dig them in deeper ... make it look more natural. They're trying too hard to be seen while pretending to hide."

Jenna nodded her understanding before Rico continued. "That being the case ... I would make sure my other troops were out of sight, with nothing to give them away until I was ready for them to be seen." He pointed to where the sandbank met the trees. "I'd put them along this route, probably above the sandbank. They will expect us to come out of the trees, or to skirt the sandbank to the north. Once we start the attack, they will be on the move, half of them to cut off our retreat, and the other half to corral us into a killing zone."

They all played Rico's scenario out themselves.

"There's more than twelve of them aren't there?" Jenna stated what everyone else was thinking.

"That's my reckoning - at least another six. The Lord Professor won't make this easy for us," Rico answered.

"So how do we get the VIP out?" Butch asked.

He grinned. "Right from under their noses," he said, as Rico reached out and touched him. "Misty, if you please," he asked, and on cue ... they disappeared from sight.

"Get in!" Butch laughed appreciatively.

"All very impressive, but one big problem," Jenna put in. "This VIP will likely be injured or hurt, you'll need to take Butch with you, just in case. Can you cover three?"

They reappeared. "Probably not," Rico admitted. "But we'll be able to blur the movement. It should be enough in the dark, there's cloud cover, so moonlight won't give us away."

His mind began whirring through options, then he decided. "OK, Rico and Butch will go in once darkness falls, take out the two guards quietly, and bring out the VIP."

Butch and Rico fist-bumped.

"Tia, Jenna, and I will make our way up to where the forest meets the sand, it's likely the defenders will head that way when their plan A doesn't work. We can take them out before they know what hit them."

Tia and Jenna nodded, automatically checking their weapons.

"Wiggy can come with us so we can communicate."

There was a look of hurt on Tia's face, she expected Phantom to do this task.

"It's probably best not to have any manifested companions as they approach the VIP. The defender may have more scouting nets set up." he said gently to her.

Tia gave an apologetic *of course* look.

"Regardless of whether things go well or not, head back to the glade we started from." He rose with Jenna and Tia to head to their positions. "One hour, and good luck," he instructed.

"You too," Rico and Butch both answered.

CHAPTER TWENTY-EIGHT

D rangor was not surprised by the revelation about the other members of the Black Hand. He had expected as much, but the weapon that came flying towards him did take him unaware.

His mind had been sorting through the questions he wanted to ask, but luckily Tracker and Twister had anticipated the attack. He caught the thrown staff easily, but in an awkward position. Twister flooded him with speed and strength, while Tracker pushed his instinct to move, and fast. He hopped back and slightly to the right, giving him just enough distance to avoid the strike from Magnar, that would have carved him in two, had it hit. His right hand reached out and struck Magnar's upper arm, aimed at the nerve to deaden it, and make him drop the weapon. All he got for his attempt was a grunt from Magnar, who finished his attack by flowing into a fighting crouch.

He moved slightly away, swinging the staff experimentally to get a feel for its weight and balance. He was impressed; the weight was excellent. It felt like a proper weapon and cut through the air nicely. He set himself across from Magnar, the spear in a position to allow swift movement.

Magnar observed him, then spoke, "You have one question,

Drangor. You scored a hit. But as it was a minor hit, you only get a minor question."

He smiled, watching Magnar for any signs that his arm was numbing, and admiring the feel of the weapon in his hand. He knew his first question.

"The training weapons, Lord, how do you make them like the real thing?"

As he finished his question, Magnar struck, his staff coming in at speed. He moved into Prowling Panther, a defensive pattern he had learned as a child, sweeping body movements which hung his body position, and constantly conserving his energy as his wrists flipped from the side, trying to get a feel for Magnar's favoured style.

Not breaking stride or slowing his attack, Magnar answered the question. "The same weapon-smith that creates our combat weapons created these. One of the regions we took over had trees of different weights when cut, allowing the smiths to create weapons that did not kill trainees. It meant no time was wasted acclimatising them to the new weapons, making them battle-ready quicker."

"Watch left!" Tracker warned.

He grunted, disgusted with himself. He had been lulled by Magnar's words and had watched the staff that Magnar had used as a distraction, using it as a pivot to lash out with his right foot and striking his upper thigh. Aiming as he had earlier, for a nerve to deaden the leg. Tracker's warning had meant that he moved enough so that Magnar missed the nerve, but the strike was viper quick.

He quickly made a defensive manoeuvre, sweeping the staff fast and hard. It expanded energy, using enhanced strength and speed from a companion. Yet it gave him time and space, so that rather than take the hit, opponents would take a step back as it was easy to avoid.

Unfortunately, Magnar was not just any opponent. He planted his staff and placed his foot beside it to give it a solid barrier, then stepped forward to engage him with his hands. He bared his teeth, letting go of the staff as it struck Magnar's to deflect the punch that came at his chest. He dropped into Frightened Bear, another defensive pattern that allowed him to stay big, and focus on defence and finding room. He fumed internally while deflecting additional blows. It was taking him too long to understand Magnar's fighting style. Although, in fairness, his style changed constantly.

Magnar's first attack had borne a passing resemblance to Probing Hyena, but the kick mixed it with Striking Viper, quick and deadly. His defence was like Solid Rhino. Magnar's latest assault was firing a flurry of attacks right out of three differing styles.

Suddenly, Magnar stopped and backed off. His eyes flashed goldenly, and he growled deeply at him, "Why do you serve The Black?"

He was speechless. It was a question he had never answered before. He bought himself some time by walking to the closest weapons rack and picking up a version of a short sword and a mace.

He turned back to Magnar. "That's a difficult question to answer; it is simply because I do. I always have, and I want to."

He was surprised that Magnar simply nodded, accepting the answer without question. He then moved to the weapons rack himself and selected a small circular shield with wicked spikes at four points, and a short training version of a Kira double-bladed staff.

"You should know, my next question will be ... what's your history with The Black?"

"He has a thing about loyalty, doesn't he?" Twister mocked.

He grinned at Twister. "To be honest, I want to see the real Magnar. Everything we have seen so far is a mask, a persona he wears."

"I agree," Twister said. "Let's up the ante and attack, but with no attempted killing blows. I think his anger is just below the surface, and if he thinks you are going easy, he might reveal his true nature."

He nodded. "But I'm not so sure I would get to take a killing blow," he said, as he slid across the surface and moved into Crow's Assault, ready to rain quick sharp blows at Magnar.

"I know, isn't it fun!" Twister laughed, as he brought the mace down quickly towards Magnar.

* * *

Magnar grinned wickedly, as Drangor slid across the floor, the steps akin to Rapid Fire. He was quickly concerned at his choice of weapon. They were short, quick, and deadly, but the Kira was not a defensive weapon. It looked like Drangor was going to try to attack him with speed, testing his defence.

The mace came down hard at his head, and he dropped into the Mongoose. His shield moving quick and directing the mace at an angle, making sure not to take a full blow which would break or impale the shield, rendering it useless. At the same time, he slid backwards, and then pivoted to attempt a sharp attack, but found he couldn't go on the offence. Drangor was moving quickly, already on the assault, and his short blade was moving towards his throat. The light staff was no good for deflecting swords, so his shield arm whipped up in defence.

"Mace," Gravel warned calmly.

Drangor had somehow manipulated the mace from the downward attack and brought it up rapidly, aimed at his lower body. He laughed happily as he had to drop his weapons and summersault back to avoid the blow.

"A worthy opponent!" Cassius growled.

He landed on the edge of the square, weaponless, his legs spread, and his left hand on the ground. He kept watching Drangor, trying to anticipate his next move, and working out a way to get to a weapon himself. He didn't wait long. Drangor moved steadily in for the kill, the mace casually held at his side as he stalked towards him.

"He's good, Magnar," Tink murmured.

"Why isn't he attacking quickly?" Cassius growled.

"He's expecting you, Cassius. A cornered enemy uses all weapons, and from what the other Black Hand soldiers told us, they fight side by side with their companions," Gravel explained.

He grinned. "And I was about to lose my temper, thinking he was going easy on me."

"Magnar, you are cornered. If he went any easier you would be unconscious," Tink commented drily.

"Sarcasm noted, Tink, but Gravel and I have a plan."

They both grinned as Drangor changed the mace to his left, and short sword to his right hand.

"Watch and learn, Tink," Gravel said as Drangor moved fast, the mace sweeping in an arc from his right thigh, aiming towards his right side.

"The mace hit its feint. It's a brawler weapon, not good for clinically finishing a kill," Gravel explained, as they slipped inside the blow. "It was designed to move us to Drangor's right, where the short sword will do the damage," he continued, as he moved to slip back under the mace and Drangor's left hand. Drangor moved just as quickly.

"Looks like he knew you would read that," Tink muttered.

Instead of coming at them with the short sword from the right … Drangor had moved the sword to his centre, and his attack was a stabbing motion which catered for both a dodge and his more aggressive move. He growled and twisted his body, still taking a heavy glancing blow to his shoulder, but getting under and past Drangor. He landed a punch with his uninjured arm to Drangor's kidney area, before moving to a weapon rack.

This time Drangor did not stalk. He moved like lightning, weapons raised, not wanting to let him get a weapon.

"HALT! OR I'LL DROP YOU WHERE YOU STAND!" a voice from the entrance bellowed. General Matrix had arrived.

He watched, as in the blink of an eye, Drangor stopped, his weapons dropping to the ground, and raising his hands in submission.

"NO!" he roared, fury and rage pouring out of him at the intrusion.

He stopped, pointing at the door, and releasing Cassius, who bounded across the floor towards Matrix and the soldiers who had entered with him. An incarnation of the rage seething through Magnar … Cassius caught the closest solider in his jaws and flung him into the others.

"GET OUT! ALL OF YOU, OR I WILL GUT EVERY ONE

OF YOU WHERE YOU STAND!" he screamed, accompanied by a deafening roar from Cassius.

* * *

"Well, finally!" Tracker murmured, as they watched on in awe.

Magnar's companion, a massive black lion, leapt out of him. Directed by Magnar's rage to the oncoming Carasayer soldiers, its roar was a mirror to Magnar's anger.

The fact that the Elite had held back near the door … wasn't lost on Drangor. They had stopped and retreated the minute he dropped the training weapons. The lion clamped its massive jaws around a soldier who screamed in agony, as the lion threw him into the onrushing soldiers.

"GET OUT! ALL OF YOU, OR I WILL GUT EVERY ONE OF YOU WHERE YOU STAND!" Magnar screamed in a fury.

"Is it wrong to like him even more? But damn, that lion's huge," Twister observed.

He laughed, watching the uncertainty on the faces of the soldiers. They cast fearful looks towards Magnar, then pleading looks to the man who stood, dominating the doorway.

Magnar took a menacing step forward, and two small figures appeared either side of the huge lion. These creatures could not be more different. One was small, and the size of his hand, made of what looked like a rock, with each part of its body perfectly proportioned, looking powerful.

"A golem," Tracker whispered, fear in his voice.

The other was a hybrid. It had the head, body, and antlers

of a dear, and the hind legs and tail of a tiger. Both oozed pure power … despite their small stature.

"And a manticore. River, I hope The Black understands what he's dealing with," Tracker observed.

He didn't respond. He was enthralled with the events unfolding in front of him. Whether it was Magnar taking a step forward, or the appearance of the two companions, he wasn't sure. Still, the soldiers vanished as if the demons of the River's bank were on their heels. Only the man in the doorway remained, his arms folded over his chest.

The lion growled but remained unmoved. This was a battle of wills. He knew there had to be someone who would stand up to Magnar, especially where his safety was involved, but there had to be a limit … even then. This limit came when the golem took a step forward and signalled for him to leave. Only then, did he see a flicker of fear in the man's eyes.

He looked to Magnar, nodded a salute, and as quick as his pride allowed him, he retreated into the corridor. He had no doubt he was just out of sight.

"Well, that was suitably terrifying," Tracker observed.

They watched as Magnar slowly composed himself. Magnar's three companions turned back, and the lion lay down to watch him, licking his lips with an all too self-satisfied expression on his face. The other two companions moved, and perched on his paws, either side of his head.

"I don't think it's over yet," he observed. "We need to calm Magnar down. Go and join Magnar's companions … let them see you."

Tracker, Twister, and Faith all manifested, and as casually as they could, joined Magnar's companions.

"River, get this over with quick. These three are strong

enough to send us back to the River on a thought," Twister complained.

"My apologies for General Matrix's interruption," Magnar spoke, his voice slightly coarse.

He marvelled that he had composed himself so quickly, although, fire and barely controlled fury, still danced in his eyes.

"By my reckoning … one question each. But I suspect you would have gained another by the time I armed myself, and if you include the interruption, that gives you three."

He nodded to Magnar, who continued, "But the questions can wait until this evening. We have time for one more round before the General and Elite tear down the building to get me out of here."

He didn't hesitate, knowing any avoidance on his part would bring the rage back. He turned to the rack and selected his weapons. He chose two short staffs of a similar size to the fighting staffs they used in Selenta, the difference being a slim, one-inch double-sided blade at the end.

Running through a few simple warm-up routines, and testing the balance and weight of the staffs, he felt like he had his own staffs in his hand.

"That's good. I have a feeling this last bout is going to be the real thing," Tracker stated, his concern evident.

He agreed. Magnar had steam to blow off. How he fought here would determine how Magnar dealt with him. He had to go all in. He suspected that the lion would have him as a light snack if he held back. Still, he couldn't win outright, as that would destroy him with the soldiers in Magnar's guard, and no doubt earn him a trip to the River.

"A tightrope?" Twister whispered.

"Exactly," he replied as he turned to Magnar, who himself was going through a warm-up routine.

Magnar had chosen two training Katana swords; long, curved, and deadly in the right hands. As he watched him warm up, Drangor was impressed. The blades seemed to flow as part of him, simple extensions of his arms. He moved effortlessly through some complex routines.

"Steadying himself, you can forget using his anger against him," Tracker murmured.

He knew he was right the minute Magnar turned to face him. His eyes had calmed. His breathing was under control.

Magnar stepped forward into the square and stopped, bowing his head, and lowering his knee to the ground … the blades extended out and behind him, resting on the ground like vipers ready to strike.

He recognised this as a ceremonial start to a bout, and that Magnar was honouring him. He similarly dropped into his Black Hand's River salute, his legs set in a fighting stance, his fighting staffs crossed over his chest, and head bowed into the V they created.

Then Magnar whispered, "Fight me. Fight me with everything you have, or I'll let Cassius decide your fate."

He kept his eyes on Magnar, but heard the huge lion, whom he guessed was Cassius, lick his lips. It was followed closely by his own companion's gulp.

"I preferred him when his rage was obvious," Tracker groaned.

He couldn't reply as Magnar growled, "Begin," and the two fighters burst to life.

CHAPTER TWENTY-NINE

Kaden's group had swelled as they made their way back from Selenta across the Disputed Lands. They had skirted wide of the training zone, moving quickly, as a large number of Black and Red Squads were on their heels, with more milling around the area because they were preparing for the final testing.

While they travelled past the testing ground, an idea had begun forming in his mind to upset the testing. It was an idea that was quickly shutdown by Bond, who cryptically stated it would cause problems for the River, and he had not elaborated further. He was right. They had already stirred up a hornet's nest, there was no point in waking the volcano.

Donte and Kip had joined them quite early in the withdrawal, both upset by the events and the capture of Hush. He was surprised by Hush's capture, but not overly worried. He suspected, as usual, that Hush would find a way out, but made a mental note to find out more about this Squad that had captured him.

His faith in Hush was proven justifiable when they'd reached Lake Silverfish. He found Hush sat beside a fire, cooking the beautiful fish from which the lake had gained its name. A substantial black eye testament to the story Donte and Kip had told.

Hush didn't remember anything after his capture, except waking up outside the city. He had quickly made his way to the rendezvous. There had been at least twenty other rebels waiting there, all back from their own missions, having picked up the pace when they had learned what had taken place in the Capital, and not risking capture in the Disputed Lands alone.

He didn't want to hang around too long either and pushed on quickly from the lake. A scout group of Formad military greeted them on the Formad border, not long after, and ushered them through, leaving the scouts to ensure they had been efficient in covering their tracks. Hush had overseen this, making sure that they were not traceable. He had no doubt the Formad would be impressed and send another group of scouts for a training session. Their payment for sanctuary in Formad.

He sighed, relaxing slightly, and thinking of having a nice long sleep when he found his bed. He was exhausted and needed to recharge, but as they crested the rise, he knew this was a pipe dream. To hide his frustration, he examined the camp, and was pleased to see it had changed substantially while he'd been away. It was turning into an actual village.

It was clear the Formad had lived up to their side of the bargain ... the engineers and builders, who had arrived just before they left, had been busy. Buildings had sprung up to replace the sprawl of tents, with some of them larger than others. More impressively, it looked like the work was nearly complete. There were only a few tents, and a small number of buildings still left under construction. He surmised that another week's work would have them finished, based on achievements so far.

His shoulders sagged, as he acknowledged the fact that he was going to be stuck without rest for the next few hours. Standing at the edge of the village was a welcoming committee, with everyone eager for information about the incursion into the Disputed Lands.

"Just wait until they hear about our trip to the Capital," Bond chuckled.

He groaned. "It was necessary, Bond. We need to change the dynamics of this fight."

"It's not us you need to convince," Huff answered.

He felt his face scrunch up in a scowl.

"That's not the face to show for our exalted council and Formad envoy," Hush chuckled next to him.

He barely resisted the urge to throw a dig at Hush, schooling his face as they reached the first building and approached the waiting assembly. Oliver, the Chairman of the rebel council, stepped forward and bowed, formal as always.

"Scarlett Hand, welcome ba …"

His welcome was interrupted by a loud screech, "KKKKAAAADDDDDDDEEEENNNNN!"

A small figure flew from the top of the two-story building directly at him. Bond flooded him with strength and speed. They both moved instinctively towards the figure, catching it in mid-air, and swinging the smiling, giggling Titch around, landing her safely on the ground.

Titch crawled up his arms and wrapped her hands tightly around his throat. His adrenaline still flooded his system as he hugged her back.

"What are you doing, Child! What if I had avoided rather than caught you? Or one of the others had thought it was an attack? You could've been hurt or worse," he scolded.

Titch pulled back slightly, and looked at him with those beautiful brown eyes, as if he had grown a second head.

"Don't be silly," she said, tapping his nose playfully. "Bond would never have let you avoid me. He helped you move to me." She smiled, those eyes knowing more than they should. Then, she nodded her head behind him, "And Huff, Tadic, and Hush would never let anyone hurt me."

She giggled at the confusion on his face. He hadn't even realised his companions had manifested as he was so intent on catching Titch.

"Well, just be careful," he said, mustering up as much scold as he could, while hugging her hard with a big grin threatening to split his face. Then her face hardened. She wriggled out of his arms and went over to Hush, who had been trying to avoid detection.

"Who hurt you?" she growled, in a voice not wholly her own, while indicating Hush to kneel closer to her.

He would have laughed at this hardened warrior scout, timidly obeying a six-year-old, if he knew he wouldn't have done the same.

"I underestimated an enemy, Little One," Hush whispered, answering her honestly.

Titch folded her arms across her chest, considering. "Well, don't let it happen again." She reached out and gently ran her fingers over the bruise. He couldn't be certain if the bruise lost a bit of its colour, but he was sure of the surprise in Hush's eyes and the wink Titch gave him.

"Now, Mister, you better have brought me a treat," she threatened, once again the little six-year-old on the verge of a tantrum.

Hush laughed. "Of course, Little One."

He reached into his pack and pulled out a sealed box, opening it for her. Inside were four salted silverfish fillets. This time he did laugh, as Titch licked her lips and threw an excited thank-you hug around Hush's neck. She turned to the rest of the returning rebels and welcomed them all back, many by name, before returning to Kaden with Huff and Tadic in tow. She grabbed his hand, motioning for Hush to follow.

"We have made dinner for you," was all she said, as she led him through the centre of the welcoming committee. No one made a move to stop this little typhoon from getting her own way.

He gave them his best *what can you do* look, thinking about ways he could spoil Titch for her timely intervention, and relieved that he would get some time to rest before the onslaught. He grinned as he imagined the council's faces when his men refused to give them any information until he had given his permission. He figured he would only have a few hours before even the protection of Titch wore off.

* * *

Titch smiled as Kaden and Hush sat back from the table, both had that satisfied, full look on their faces. Kaden looked at her and smiled. "That was delicious, Titch!" he complimented.

"The River to that, Titch. I haven't eaten that well in ages," Hush added.

She beamed with pleasure. "It's just something we whipped up in preparation of you coming home."

"Be careful, Little One," a mild voice spoke in her mind.

"You slip up often with these two. They will start asking questions."

"I'm sorry, Mother, but can't we let them in? They could help us."

"I know you trust them, Little One. With your safety and wellbeing, I do too. They love you as I do. But with knowledge of me, I'm not so sure," the voice paused momentarily, feeling her unhappiness. "Yet. Let's give it some time and see if the River helps us with the answer," she said, placating Titch. "Now, Kaden is asking what you've been up to these last weeks while he was away."

She looked at Kaden and shrugged. "This and that. Oh, and I built our home," she smiled, her arms outstretched, taking in the building she had brought them back to. "Isn't it beautiful? It's bigger than the others," she grinned mischievously.

"It is also away from the chaos of the rest. It's absolutely perfect, Titch," Kaden complimented.

She giggled at the praise and leaned in, beckoning them closer and whispered, "I bribed the Formad builders with my special treats."

Hush's eyes lit up. "No wonder it's so amazing," Hush answered distractedly, his eyes now roving around the room. "Do you have any left?" he asked.

"Let's go see."

She grabbed Hush's hand then looked back at Kaden and instructed, "You sit and relax, your evening is going to be busy."

* * *

Kaden grinned happily, listening to Titch admonish Hush

like he was a child and she the adult. She was making him promise that he would do his best to keep out of trouble before she would let him have a treat. Titch was happy and obviously thriving, he didn't doubt for a moment that she had cajoled the builder into building this home for them. She was a force of the River.

As he watched her growing, he was increasingly convinced she had a companion who was looking out for her. She had slipped up a few times today.

"What are you going to do about it?" Huff asked.

"Absolutely nothing, Huff," he replied.

"I agree," Bond added. "The companion, whoever it is, looks after that child. She is allowing her to live as a child would, while giving her enough advice to keep her safe."

He nodded in agreement at Bond's explanation, as Huff and Tadic digested it. He had been thinking the same for a while. Those in Selenta would want to pull Titch into training to help her develop that relationship, yet in his mind, this companion knew better than anyone how to develop that connection. He suspected that it would be stronger for it.

Bond interrupted his train of thought. "Besides, every time I try to get a feel for Titch's future, I see mist. It's hidden, but I can't shake the feeling it's an important one, for everyone."

He jumped in surprise. This was new information.

He had to school his face quickly, and log this for a later discussion, as Titch and Hush returned with a plate covered in pop treats. His mouth watered as he anticipated the flavour he'd get; would it be sour, sweet, tangy, or would he find the Edgarberry?

"Thank-you, Titch." He reached out and grabbed one,

popping it into his mouth and grinning as the flavour of sweet fruit burst into his mouth; a refreshing taste that you couldn't help but smile at.

Suddenly, a grunt of disgust came from Hush. His face screwed up. He and Titch both rolled about laughing as the smell of Edgarberry floated through the room. After they'd stopped laughing, and polished off the plate of treats, they sat and talked, listening to Titch telling the tale of the house build, and how she had laid the first and last stone. It was obvious that the Formad engineers were as fond of her as the rest of the Scarlett Hand camp.

Then it was their turn to detail the events of the last weeks, but they omitted the gory details. Titch was particularly interested, as was he, in the Squad that had captured Hush … wanting to know details about the companions they had, and what they looked like. Hush's enthusiastic description of the beautiful phoenix made her eyes sparkle in childish delight. They hardened in concentration as he described the creature on the shoulder of the one who struck the blow to Hush.

Finally, he watched Titch's eyes start to get heavy. She curled up with Tadic and Huff, who had manifested and snuggled in close to her.

"Right, bedtime, Little One," he instructed and received no argument. Titch simply got up and went to get washed and ready for bed.

"We will stay with Titch," Huff stated, and he and Tadic padded off after her.

Once settled in her bed, flanked by his companions, he and Hush kissed her goodnight.

"There's a package next to the door for Cassie. Give her

a kiss for me," Titch murmured through a yawn, that ended with her eyes closing as she settled into slumber.

He returned to the sitting area and heard Hush's own snores. He had obviously decided he would stay and watch the house and Titch. He smirked, Hush could fall asleep in the Riverbed, but he knew he would wake and be alert at the tiniest sound or threat. It wasn't just his own companions who were protective of Titch.

He moved to the door. It was time he spoke to the council. Remembering, he grabbed the package for Cassie; hopefully, he would get a chance to see her this evening too.

CHAPTER THIRTY

Nala sniffed the air, something felt off.

"Don't worry, Nala," Slaven said, smiling at him. "She will be back when she's ready."

The River Runners found it amusing that he fixated on Leandra. To them, she was a fearsome warrior, a scout, and very much a loner. She isolated herself from the rest of the Runners, obsessed with hunting members of the Death Dealers.

Gervais had taken great pains to explain to him, that years ago, when Leandra had taken on the *True Merge* (the name the River Runners gave to the Forbidden Step, where someone relinquishes their body to permanently take on the form of one of their companions), she had done so on purpose with her husband. They had become disillusioned with life in Selenta, and aimed to forge a new life in The Forbidden. Unfortunately, not long after they had entered the forest, they had encountered the Death Dealers … leading to a fight that killed her husband, and left Leandra suffering severe injuries and abuse.

Gervais and a group of River Runners had come across the Death Dealers and chased them off, saving Leandra's life … but too late to prevent the scars the encounter had written on her soul.

His thoughts were disturbed again by a sharp, tangy smell that hit his nostrils.

"What's that smell, Slaven?"

Slaven cocked his head to one side, sniffing the air. "I can't smell anything other than the forest?"

He shook his head; he must be imagining it.

Slaven had merged with his dog companion, a strong working dog, with dark shaggy hair. He had been patient with him; helping him to learn how to communicate and find his way in the River Runners. He had been amazed at how these creatures had developed into a community, each helping one another. The smaller creatures with hands would tend crops, and butcher kills from the hunting animals to store and share. Nothing went to waste. The larger and stronger creatures in the Runners provided the protection for them all.

His enthusiasm, and desire to be helpful and useful, had endeared him to many. His position as a trainer in Selenta, meant that he had knowledge of disciplines from all the Hands, and was able to support all areas. He worked closely with the smaller creatures, helping them with new ways to store the food, or showing them tricks to speed up growing crops. With the fighters and hunters, he showed them ways to improve their patrols and security. Within a very short time span, he had become Gervais's second in command. Rather than be jealous ... the other River Runners had accepted him quickly. Deferring simple queries and issues that they would normally have taken to Gervais, directly to him.

Gervais was happy too, he now had someone who would

challenge him, and mix up the status quo ... going as far as telling him that he had brought some much-needed life into the River Runners.

In return, they had taught him everything they knew. They explained how some chose the True Merge while others had it thrust upon them. That depending on the person, the level of the merge was different. The young and weak-willed, taken over by their new animal instincts, becoming the animal they turned to; the person and their companion's consciousness returning to the River.

This explained why The Forbidden was always full of animals of all varieties.

With his thoughts interrupted, he jumped to his feet. There was that scent again. He couldn't believe that Slaven couldn't smell it ... it was so strong.

"Swiftwind, some help here ... what's that scent?" he asked.

"I'm sorry, Nala. I don't know what it is, but I think I can take you to where it is."

He turned to Slaven who looked unconcerned.

"I'm going to investigate this scent. It doesn't feel right."

Slaven merely nodded, obviously thinking that he was acting ridiculously. He turned and followed Swiftwind's lead, moving steadily across the forest floor, and sliding between crops and working River Runners, before stepping outside the cordon of the hunters.

Swift led him to a small hollow, a short distance from the Runners' camp. He stopped at the top, looking out across the small ravine. He saw Mavis, a small monkey with a broad face surrounded by a mane of white, she had been a grandmother before her merge. She was now walking below the trees collecting mushrooms and herbs in a small basket, which she used to make poultices to help injuries.

"There!" Swift growled, dragging his attention away from Mavis.

In a tree, not too far ahead of Mavis, a leopard waited. It was deathly still, waiting for its prey to pass beneath it.

He and Swift acted as one. Silently and quickly, they darted through the forest so not to alert the leopard, and arriving behind the tree just as Mavis came into sight and the leopard pounced.

He was faster. He knocked into Mavis, easily pushing her out of harm's way of the initial attack, but taking a knock to his head that momentarily stunned him.

This left Mavis open to a killing blow from the leopard, who had landed a few feet away. The strike didn't land, however, as a light brown shape hit the leopard hard in the side … its teeth tearing at the leopard's throat.

He was up quickly to help his ally … watching helplessly as the leopard kicked out its claws at its assailant, trying to get it to let go to avoid having its stomach ripped open.

He realised it was Leandra. He turned quickly, making sure Mavis was OK. Thankfully, she had wisely slipped behind him.

Not wanting to anger Leandra again, he waited before interrupting the fight.

* * *

Leandra grinned as she saw him wait while she faced the leopard. He learned fast, but this was a fight she couldn't win alone. The leopard was bigger, stronger, faster, and a much better solo fighter; she needed pack help.

"Anytime you're ready …" she said, barely finishing before he moved like lightning, his massive jaws opening.

"Eager to die are we, River Wolf?" the leopard grinned, thinking Leandra was aiming her words in its direction.

This was a merged creature, and probably one of the Death Dealers. They could do with it alive. Instinctively knowing it was too late to stop Nala's attack, she grinned evilly.

"Not today, Leopard," she responded, happily watching as Nala's huge jaws clamped down hard on the leopard's head and crushing it in one swift bite.

The leopard's body stayed upright for a few seconds until it realised it was no longer getting any signals.

"Show off," she joked.

Nala turned to her, grinning. It looked quite endearing, in a gruesome way, as bits of the leopard's skull covered his muzzle.

"You've got something in your teeth," she teased, and immediately regretted it … seeing the elation in his eyes turn to embarrassment.

Before she could say something to soften the blow, everything started to go blurry. She felt her body begin to waiver. Embarrassment turned to concern in Nala's eyes.

As if she was in a bad dream, she heard him call to Mavis, who rushed over. She tried to tell them not to worry, but the words wouldn't come. Somehow, she found the strength to look at her flank and saw blood dripping from long gashes. The leopard had gotten a hit in after all, she mused.

She felt herself drop to the floor, barely registering the commotion above. She needed to tell them that the leopard was a Death Dealer, compromising the camp, but she couldn't focus or form the words.

As she fell into unconsciousness, her last thought was that she had failed them all.

* * *

"Nala! Concentrate! Call the Runners!" Mavis shouted.

Seeing Leandra dropping to the ground had sent him into a state of shock. She realised she was not getting through to him, and changed tactic. "Swiftwind, I need you to take control here. Get the Runners and my helpers to bring a stretcher here ... NOW. I need to stop this bleeding." Her tiny hands were darting over Leandra's wounds, doing their best to staunch the bleeding.

Swiftwind understood, and raised their head and howled the emergency call, two to alert to danger, and then two more to signal they needed help to carry an injured Runner.

"Now, I need you to get your head under her rump, but from the front. It means you will get blood over your ..."

Swiftwind moved quickly and raised Leandra's back end.

"Face," she finished. "Thank-you."

Then, as she worked, she talked, as was her habit.

"You have raised her wound above her heart. It will help slow the bleeding a little, but more importantly, you are pushing the lacerations together. This also slows the bleeding and allows me to close some of the wound."

She continued her litany, as her tiny hands, which had produced a needle and thread, moved quickly and efficiently over the injury.

Swiftwind watched her closely while no doubt keeping an eye on Nala, and hoping her calm demeanour would get through to give him some comfort.

It felt like it took forever for the Runners to arrive, but it could only have been minutes. Six of the big cats arrived and immediately created a defensive perimeter. On their tails, five chimpanzees swung down the valley, one carrying a pole stretcher.

They gently moved Leandra onto the stretcher and started back to the camp.

She turned before she left and looked at Swiftwind and Nala. "Thank-you both for saving my life, now I will go and save hers," she said, with a grim determination in her eyes. With that, she turned and sped after the chimps ... leaving Nala looking lost in the wood.

* * *

Nala watched Mavis disappear out of sight over the top of the hollow. "Swift, will she die?" he asked, like a child looking for comfort.

Swiftwind thought about her answer. Her instinct was to comfort him and tell him everything would be OK, but he had fallen in love with the idea of this she-wolf ... if she did die, and she'd said she would be fine, he would never forgive her; irrational as she knew that was.

She decided on middle ground. "I don't know, Nala. It was a serious wound, but she received help straight away, so I think she has a chance. We were lucky Mavis was on hand."

"She had better save her," he growled. "It was her fault she was injured. If we hadn't been trying to save her ..."

Swiftwind felt shocked by the venom in his voice, feeling her own anger rise to rival his.

"Now you listen to me, Nala Yagin!" she snapped. "That

leopard was a Death Dealer. By stopping her, we stopped more of the River Runners from getting hurt. If we had not caught it here … imagine the damage it could have done to the rest of the Runners."

She calmed as she felt an immediate shift in Nala's mood. "What did you just say?" he asked her.

"I said, although her injuries were bad, it's better than …"

"No, no. The Death Dealer bit," he interrupted.

"Oh, yes. The leopard taunted Leandra just before you hit," she said.

"The River!" he hissed, raising his snout to the air, but all he could smell was Leandra's blood. "Damn, I can't smell," he shouted, shaking his head in frustration.

"What's wrong?" Swift asked.

"Death Dealers, Swift. If they are this close to the camp, there will be more than one of them."

He turned to the panthers, there were three left, as two had gone back with Mavis to protect the chimps. He instructed two of them to do a sweep to the north. He and the other one would go to the south and sweep around the camp.

"Belay that!"

His head snapped up angrily at the interruption. Gervais stood at the top of the hollow, the light shining behind his huge form and giving him a majestic look, which was lost on him.

"There are Death Dealers here," he growled angrily.

Gervais cocked his head. "I know," was all he replied.

His calm response cut through to him, his brain finally started firing. Gervais obviously had something planned. As if in answer to the unasked question … "I have initiated plan Hawk, the camps in movement." He motioned to the

209

panthers, "I need you all back there to protect the rest of the Runners."

The panthers didn't hesitate, they moved quickly, darting past Gervais, and moving to their assigned areas in the camp.

Moving up to Gervais's side, he asked, "Plan Hawk?"

"We go to ground. We have several hidden areas around the camp, all the non-combatant creatures will make their way to these with anything of value. Each group has two protectors and a scout, who will find them a safe route to our alpha site. The plan is for everyone to get there safely."

He considered Gervais's answer. "So, we run?" he rumbled.

Gervais again cocked a head to him. "What would you expect us to do?" he asked, as if educating an errant student.

He responded by prowling around. He had to be doing something, someone had to pay. "Fight," he snarled.

Gervais looked at him, his eyes wide with faint shock. "Really?" he questioned. "You would expect Mavis to beat them to death with her tiny hands? Or Slaven to take on a boar? Do you care so little for them that you would want to see their broken, lifeless bodies strewn around the forest floor?"

"No!" he responded vehemently. He had grown fond of all the Runners, and the thought of what Gervais described made him sick to the stomach, but his anger didn't want to let go just yet. "But we can't run in fear of them forever, we have to take a stand."

Gervais grinned viciously, his teeth sparkling in the light. "There is always a time and a place, Nala. I have seen what happens to merged creatures not aligned with the Runners who the Death Dealers have caught … it's not pretty. That will not happen to the Runners on my watch."

He sagged slightly, the adrenaline leaving him. He knew Gervais was right.

* * *

As he watched Nala's body sag, Gervais knew he had gotten through to him. His reaction and desire to hit out was understandable. It was a result of his shock and rage at Leandra getting hurt, but he didn't want him to lose all the fire for revenge, they had work to do.

On impulse, he decided to sow the seed he had been mulling over since he first met Nala. "But I have an option you might like, which will scratch that itch."

Nala's head jerked up instantly, and his body language changed from defeatist to controlled energy, his eyes that little bit brighter.

"We don't have time to discuss it now. We need to get the River Runners to safety. You and I have a vital job to do first," he stated, as he made his way back to the camp.

He was pleased to see Nala fall in behind him. As they arrived back at the camp area, Nala let out a whimper. It was so quiet for an area that was full of life a short time earlier.

He, on the other hand, was pleased to see how quickly the plan had been enacted, and because of this, he was confident they would all make it to the alpha site safely.

"We stay until the end; we have to protect Mavis and the chimps as they work on Leandra," he paused, as Nala's head had shot up at the mention of Leandra. It took all of Gervais's self-control not to laugh at the puppy-wolf look in his eyes. Instead, his own eyes hardened. "You must follow my lead, no matter what happens."

He waited for Nala to nod his agreement before continuing. "Mavis said it wasn't safe to move her until she has stopped the bleeding and cleaned and dressed the wound. Our job is to make sure they're safe and make it to the alpha site. But I repeat, you must follow my lead."

Nala nodded absently, his eyes darting to the cave. They had arrived at the small cave area where Mavis worked with the ill and injured. Four chimps were waiting to carry the stretcher Leandra was on, once they had permission.

"Now, go clean your face. Let's see if we can get that nose of yours working," he ordered.

Nala reluctantly complied, casting longing glances to the cave, but moving to the small waterfall that supplied water to the camp.

He shook his head, watching him before poking his head around the corner of the rock. "How's it going, Mavis?" he asked quietly.

"Better than expected. The River watches this one," she replied. "I've stopped the bleeding, and I'm just stitching her up; ideally, I would give it at least an hour before we move, then I will be confident that she will fully recover."

She held her hand up to stop him telling her they didn't have an hour. "I know we don't have that time. If you can give me thirty minutes, and we move slowly, Leandra will have a fighting chance. She's lost a lot of blood."

He sighed. "You have half an hour, Mavis, then we have to go." He looked at Leandra. "She has survived worse, Mavis," he said, remembering when he first found her.

Mavis looked at him with sadness in her eyes. "Yes, she has. But now, her survival is important to our survival. If he is going to do what we need … he needs to be with us, and not on a rampage, getting himself killed."

He nodded to her. "Then keep Leandra alive," he instructed with finality.

When he returned to the outside of the cave, Nala had followed his instructions and was snorting his nostrils to clear them as best he could. As Nala saw him appear, he approached, a clear question in his eyes.

"Mavis says she's doing well. If we can give her thirty minutes to rest, and then move slowly, she has a fighting chance."

He was pleased to see Nala's eyes shining again at the news, and he immediately went to work to give her the half hour she needed.

Nala prowled around, his head raised, sniffing the air. When he had completed half a circle of the area, he stopped and growled. "That scent … it's back."

Then, looking back at him, with fear replacing the light in his eyes, he said, "I don't think we have thirty minutes."

As the words left his lips, he heard a cackle from the woods. In front of him was a leopard, slowly stalking out. "You're right there, Wolf!" it purred menacingly.

"It's nice for him to be right once before he dies, Sister."

He looked around and saw another leopard on the ground above the cave.

"I wonder if one of these miserable excuses for a creature was the one to kill our sister?"

Another leopard appeared from the side of the spring, lightly jumping over the water still slightly tinged by Leandra's blood.

"Neither. The injured one in the cave would be my guess," a fourth voice said from the opposite side, moving towards the cave entrance.

He watched Nala spring from his position, and place himself between the last leopard and the cave entrance, recklessly exposing his back to the leopard behind.

"And who might you be?" he calmly asked the first of the leopards to appear, not missing the confused glance from Nala.

"My name is not for you to know, Primate," she spat, her barely controlled rage becoming more evident.

"He's stalling for time, Sister," the leopard on the cave stated.

"Are you, Primate?" the first asked.

"I don't think so, all your fighters are gone. You're all alone and at my mercy. Now tell me, who killed my sister? If you refuse to tell me we will kill the rest of you slowly."

He saw Nala ready to speak and cut in quickly. "Ah, so you were listening in, were you? How clever."

The leopard growled menacingly, lowering her head as she moved towards him. "Listen to me, Runner. The only reason you're not dead already, is because I want my sister's killer to suffer."

* * *

"Be patient, Nala," Swiftwind calmed.

"But you heard them. They know it's just me and Gervais left. We have to attack quickly to have a chance," he replied, growling.

"NO, NALA!" Swift shouted. "Gervais asked us to follow his lead. Now follow it."

Swiftwind's sudden outburst shocked him into realising

that his emotions were still very much in control. Giving himself a mental slap, he started reassessing the situation clinically. Firstly, looking to Gervais as he spoke to the leopard ... he was calm, controlled, and laid back, while the leopards were all sat on their haunches and ready to attack at a moment's notice. Gervais explicitly telling him twice to follow his lead ... it dawned on him, Gervais was not expecting to fight.

"Thank the River one of us listens, Swift," he whispered.

But what was going on? Was he playing for time? His mind was whirring over the options when Gervais started speaking, and this time his voice dripped with scorn, obviously aiming to anger the leopard. "And here was me thinking you were a good little soldier, waiting for your boss to arrive."

The leopard's face turned vicious. Its lips peeled back, baring long deadly canines, as it spat, "He's hours away. I don't have the time, nor the patience, to wait for him."

"And, there's the game," Swift chuckled, as they watched a grin peel back on Gervais's face. He wasn't stalling, he was gathering information.

"Let's kill them all slowly, Sister," the leopard on the cave crooned.

"Yes," the other two hissed, taking another step forward.

He watched them all tense, as Gervais stood and shook himself off. They were afraid of him ... that was good to know.

"I think your right, Sister ..." the first leopard started to say, but stopped short, taking an involuntary step back, as Gervais raised his arm, shaking his finger.

"Tut, tut, tut. Impatience is not a virtue. I think you would all enjoy a little nap rather than killing us." He winked at the lead leopard, who realised too late that it was a trap.

He heard four blow darts fire from the trees around them, each hitting a leopard cleanly. He had watched the crazy marmoset monkeys preparing these darts. They coated them with a virulent poison the snakes in the Runners provided, mixed with some herbs they collected in the forest. They used these darts to bring down big prey quickly and cleanly, and he had been amazed at how fast it had taken effect. He wasn't disappointed now as he watched it work just as fast on the leopards. Each barely having time to register what was happening before their legs gave way, and they hit the ground. The Marmosets dropped from their hiding places.

"Why didn't we know they were there?" he asked Swift.

"The blood in our nostrils. They're small, and give off little scent, especially if they are still and prepared to ambush. We can only smell powerful scents when we are this clogged up."

They both snorted again, trying to clean out the rest of the blood.

Gervais walked forward and bent down to the lead leopard; whose eyes were full of hatred. He whispered so quietly; he could barely make out his words. "Know this, you are only the first. The Riverbank will swim with your brethren by the time we have finished." Then he stood up and stretched. "Finish them off," Gervais ordered, as he turned away. His mind was already on the future, as the marmosets pulled out tiny bone blades, and with practised ease, they slid them into the throats of the leopards.

He watched on impassively as he allowed his adrenaline to return to normal, marvelling at how cleanly Gervais had dealt with the threat.

"Learning are we, Nala?" Swift mocked, eliciting a smile

from him.

Dex, the green and brown dappled fox who had so easily captured him, appeared out of the woods, and approached Gervais, who issued him instructions. He then disappeared back into the woods. He waited until he had finished before he approached Gervais.

"I'm sorry, Nala. I couldn't tell you the whole plan."

He merely nodded, the result showing it was the right play.

"You expected this?" he asked instead.

Gervais nodded in reply. "This, or at least something similar. We've had reports of a group of leopards who work for the Death Dealers," he explained. "Part of me had hoped Zagane would have been here; unfortunately, I'm not that lucky. At least we know we have time to let Leandra rest."

He looked at Gervais in awe. He had just made sure that Leandra had the best chance of survival, and for that, he would always be in his debt.

"I assume Zagane is not going to be happy," he chuckled, breaking the silence, and motioning to the dead leopards.

Gervais laughed hard, beating his chest. "Most definitely not. These were one of his best Squads. He will be furious, and that will mean he will want to hurt the Runners more than ever before."

"So, what happens next?" he asked.

He decided to learn from Gervais, who thought many moves ahead. He kept letting himself think in the moment with his emotions, and that needed to change.

"We can't fight him directly yet; we have more numbers, but they're not all fighters. Those around him are the most vicious misfits that ever took the True Merge, creatures that thrive on pain and suffering."

He watched Gervais considering things before he turned to look him in the eye. "So, how would you handle this enemy, Nala?" he asked.

He and Swiftwind spoke as one … "Thin the herd."

Gervais's toothy grin was infectious. "Exactly! Zagane will be furious, and he'll double his efforts to find us. That's where you come in …" Gervais flopped to the ground and beckoned him closer. "Let me explain."

They were still refining the plan as they left an hour later, making their way to the alpha site.

* * *

An hour after Nala and Gervais had left the cave, two enormous wolfhounds trotted into the clearing, followed closely by a pack of hyenas who circled the area. The wolfhounds walked slowly around the bodies of the leopards, then took up positions on either side.

Once the hyenas had finished checking the area, and had taken their place, they gave a low bark. Moments later, a large boar, jet-black with a ring of white around his torso, appeared from the forest edge. But what caught the eye … were his huge tusks; protruding high up over his nose, and two, half the size, pointing down; all four were razor sharp. The boar was flanked by a small bear with a golden chest and snout, its teeth and claws also razor-sharp.

The bear stopped, as the boar walked towards the leopards … the wolfhounds their silent sentinels … and their positions ensuring that the boar had plenty of room. The bear fidgeted slightly, examining his claws, as the boar stood motionless, casting his eyes over the dead leopards. His silence and calm was putting them all on edge … when he was quiet, it was a sign he was at his most deadly.

"Where is Lanine?" he asked calmly.

No one answered.

"I asked a question," he growled from deep in his belly.

The bear stepped forward, cautiously. "We don't know, Zagane. We have scouts out looking for her, but we suspect she is dead too."

He snorted.

"For once, Vepar is correct. I have just found Lanine a little way into the forest area. She had her head crushed. There were signs of a fight."

All heads, other than Zaganc's, turned to the sound of the voice that appeared from the wood. It came from Gremor, a sleek wolverine, his fur a mixture of brown and green, giving the impression he was one with the forest.

Gremor shrugged when Zagane finally looked up. "It appears she lost."

As Gremor walked past Vepar, he bared his teeth, hissing. Vepar growled in response. "Enough, Gremor. You too, Vepar," Zagane ordered.

Usually, he enjoyed the conflict between his two Lieutenants, but not today. His anger was simmering below the surface, and he had to concentrate on acting, now was not the time for internal conflict. "The filthy River Runners have declared war on us here today. I intend to wipe out every last one of them."

"Yes, Sir," both Gremor and Vepar responded briskly, grinning evilly.

"Double the patrols and find them. Then we destroy them once and for all."

Gremor and Vepar disappeared into the woods to set things in motion.

Zagane took one last look at the leopards, and then slipped back into the forest, flanked by the wolfhounds.

CHAPTER THIRTY-ONE

General Matrix had not gone far when he retreated from the training arena, ensuring he was able to hear what was going on. Magnar's protection was his key concern. He usually wouldn't have backed down; it was the one area where Magnar had agreed he could challenge him publicly.

However, Gravel supporting Magnar's instruction was enough to convince him that Magnar was in no real danger. Besides, Tink terrified him. Once he heard Magnar issue the direction to fight, he slowly made his way back to the entrance. He watched as Magnar and the Black Major circled, probing each other's defences.

During a brief lull in the fighting, Tink looked back and nodded to Matrix. That one movement let him know it was OK to watch, but if he even considered interrupting, he was in trouble.

Suddenly the fighters burst into life, flowing from formation to formation. Magnar was powerful and deadly, slipping from Raptor Strike to Leopard's Prowl. The Black Major drifting quickly, but no less deadly, through steps unknown to Matrix, but with similarities to Viper's Strike and Cheetah's Flight; moves that eased from defence into attack. The echoes from the weapons clashing together rang throughout the room.

He recognised an opportunity and turned, signalling to the Elite that they could enter silently, and watch only. They needed to see the movements of the Black Major, and understand the different ways of fighting, to learn how to fight them, or encompass some of these moves into their own training. They had been working with the other Black Hand soldiers to learn what they could, but their fighting skills were poor compared to the Major's ... which were exceptional, and right now they had to be.

Magnar was one of the best fighters in Carasayer, but he was out of practice as no one would fight him and put in their all, so he had given up trying.

Watching, he found himself mesmerised by the fight. The weapons flashing through the motions, trading blows and hits, none major, but when the defence was not quick enough, or a footstep faltered even by a minute amount, the opponent was ready to score a hit, albeit meaningless as they were nothing their companions could not absorb.

He shook himself, he had to concentrate, not admire. He was surprised to see the training area had filled quickly. All the soldiers were watching with rapt admiration on their faces. As it should be ... they were watching a conflict between two extraordinary fighters. Many of them had never seen their Emperor fighting with all his skill. Stories of this bout would circulate all over Carasayer by late evening.

Twenty minutes passed, and there was no sign that the fighters were anywhere near finished. He was considering intervening when he noticed a falter in the Major's step. He had changed his mind on a formation, getting confused by a step-away made by Magnar. He grinned; it was all the opening Magnar needed. He had played the Chameleon Gambit, a formation that attacked hard and looked like a step-away, but it actually set-up for an attack.

The Major, not having seen the manoeuvre before, had tried to switch quickly from defence to press an attack; a mistake. If the Gambit worked ... and it had ... then it would expose the Major. If he had continued defending, Magnar himself would have been vulnerable. The Major brought his staff down hard and quick, but was greeted by two blades coming up, knocking the staff clean out of his hands. Magnar slid past, letting the Major's momentum put his back to Magnar.

Magnar twisted swiftly, taking down the Major's right leg at the knee, and swinging his sword to his throat.

"Yield?" Magnar demanded.

Drangor moved as brisk as a viper, bringing his staff down at Magnar's foot, who grunted as he slammed his second blade into the middle of Drangor's back, driving him to the floor.

"Death then," Magnar breathed heavily.

* * *

"Death then," Magnar breathed heavily, as he watched Drangor drop to one knee and release his staff. As it fell to the floor, the noise was obscenely loud.

"Choose your next step wisely," Tink muttered in his mind. "I know what you want to do, but I also know what you want him to do. You have a large audience."

He wanted to help Drangor to his feet, congratulate him

223

on a fantastic duel, and discuss techniques. Some of his movements were amazing, lightning-fast, and he had not fought an opponent like this in years.

"It feels dishonourable," Cassius grumbled, as he made his decision.

Schooling his face to scorn rather than admiration, he turned his back on Drangor and walked away. He was mildly surprised to see the size of the crowd; he had not even realised they weren't alone … the fight absorbing all his attention.

"What are they looking at?" he growled, his anger at the necessity of the situation boiling in him.

"They are a little in awe of you both. That duel was mesmerising. I will replay it for you later," Gravel explained.

"Really?" he asked, suddenly an intrigued child.

Before they could answer, he reached Matrix.

"Put your face straight, General. You're no raw recruit," he snarled angrily … winking to let him know it was for show.

Matrix jumped to attention and saluted, dropping into step beside him as the Elite slipped into a protective cordon as they left the arena.

The soldiers cast awed glances at him, then back to the arena, confused by his attitude towards Drangor.

"Damn. If they're impressed, Gravel, I need to see it."

He glanced back to see that the awe was not just for him, but also for Drangor. Many of the soldiers had moved to help him and bombarded him with questions.

"It was worth it then," Cassius purred, happier now.

"Thankfully, Cassius." Then aloud, once they were out of earshot of the general soldiers, he said, "General, make sure Drangor has access to all areas of Carasayer … without the need of a guard."

Matrix nodded, "Yes, Sir. Does that include the inner areas?"

"Everywhere but my personal quarters, Matrix. And Matrix, I want you to personally speak to Drangor, in private, and apologise for how I left at the end of the duel. Let him know it was necessary, and that I will explain over dinner as soon as my schedule allows. He can then ask the questions he earned."

He saw several twitched smiles from his Elite, showing Drangor had earned their respect also. It must have been some spectacle to impress them to the point that they were concerned at how he had treated Drangor.

"Let's get back to my quarters," he ordered, and upped the pace.

"You need to bathe those bruises?" Tink joked.

"Exactly, Tink. I've not had a fight like that in years."

"And I suppose it's nothing to do with the fact that Elena is back?" Cassius grinned.

"Damn. I forgot," he shouted aloud and upped his pace, leaving Matrix to pass on his message.

* * *

Drangor dropped to the bed, staring at the ceiling. He ached in places he never knew he had. It didn't help that he'd felt dejected, ever since Magnar drove him to his knees, and left him immobile in the middle of the arena ... not even honouring him with a finishing salute.

Getting mobbed by the soldiers, including a few of the Elite ... who all looked at him with new respect in their eyes, had not helped his mood. He had failed The Black. Chosen to get close to Magnar … he needed to make himself indispensable, but a simple misstep in the bout had turned the Emperor against him.

Once he had been able to extradite himself from the arena, he had taken his time getting back to his room. He had taken numerous wrong turns along the way, not coming across anyone to give him directions. Come to think of it, his guard had not been following him … that would have made it easier.

He closed his eyes to rest, and plan his next move, only to be disturbed by a knock at the door. Tempted to ignore it, he instead decided not to leave his bed and shouted. "Come in."

He heard the door open and feet patter in.

"Just get it over with. I'm too sore and too tired to fight," he moaned, hating the petulance he could hear in his own voice.

"I'm rather glad of that," a deep voice answered. "After watching you in the arena … I'm not first on the list for a training bout."

He opened his eyes and recognised the soldier who had tried to interrupt his duel with Magnar.

"Thank-you," he answered, dragging himself up off the bed to greet his guest with honour, feeling the satisfaction come across his companion bond. "I don't think your Emperor agreed."

The soldier turned and checked the corridor, then closed the door and turned back to him.

"I am General Matrix, Lord Magnar's second in command. He has asked me to speak to you on his behalf."

He cocked his head, intrigued. He became momentarily distracted by a commotion and the noise of running water in the next room. He looked questioningly at the General ...

"A peace offering," Matrix answered. "But first, Lord Magnar sends his deepest apologies for the way he treated you at the end of the bout."

"You mean the total disrespect?" he asked angrily.

Matrix had the good grace to look abashed before he answered. "Lord Magnar treated you with dishonour for a reason. He has plans, and he needs your help. I suspect he needs people to think you and he are at odds, but he will explain everything to you over dinner once his schedule allows."

His head was spinning. The same way it did when he spent time planning with The Black. Add the exhaustion from the bout ... his mind was not picking up what was going on, so he had not formulated any questions.

Matrix took this as acceptance and continued, "He also says he will answer all your questions, which you more than earned. In the meantime, he has instructed that you no longer require a guard, and you have unlimited access to anywhere in Carasayer. However, I would suggest if you go anywhere outside the castle, that you take two soldiers with you as protection. There are a number of them, who have asked for the honour after watching your duel, but you can pick for yourself."

Matrix extended his arm, and he stepped forward immediately and took it, grasping forearms as a sign of respect.

"A fabulous duel, Major. You have earned the respect of our Emperor and I. When you're fully rested, I would be honoured to spar with you."

He nodded his gratitude.

Two young, pretty castle maids attracted his attention

towards the door to the bathrooms, where they were waiting and smiling shyly in the doorway.

"These two are here to look after your injuries - and *any other needs* - they have drawn you a bath filled with some herbs that will help you heal faster. Now relax, Drangor, and get to know your surroundings. I suspect once the Emperor sets out his plans, you will be very busy."

With that parting statement, Matrix opened the door and left.

Exhaustion flooded him, both physically and mentally. Feeling as weak as a kitten, he let the two maids' undress and guide him meekly to the bath.

"You look like an old man! No one would guess you nearly bested the Emperor less than an hour ago," Tracker laughed.

He just grinned. He had not failed.

CHAPTER THIRTY-TWO

As darkness had fallen, Ellie and Thomas had incapacitated six defenders in the outpost, before meeting up with Ruben. They were now following Ruben and his bat companion, Chitter, as they made their way to the VIP point from the defence post, where they would wait for Jonas's signal.

After they had taken out the defence post ... which had been all too easy ... she had discussed their next steps with Saskia. She reported their musings to Jonas through Treffin, who had nodded Jonas's agreement. As they neared the VIP area, they encountered a number of scouts, and took them out cleanly and silently. It helped that they had been looking the other way, not expecting an attack from the direction of the post, and instead focusing on an attack from the south, or from the forest.

Treffin nuzzled into her side and disappeared. Shortly after, Merl appeared on her shoulder.

She tapped Ruben and Thomas, signalling for them to be ready. The seconds passed by slowly, when out of the darkness she heard a loud roar, as Charter announced his presence. A whistle through the air, followed by a heavy thud, told them that Drake had begun his deadly work loosing arrows into the defenders. They wouldn't kill as he would deaden the tip. Still, they would eliminate the defenders from combat.

"Wait for it," she whispered, holding back Thomas and Ruben, who were all too eager to join in the fight. As if on cue, the area in front of them became bathed in a dome of light. Out of the darkness, a shape emerged, looking terrifyingly magnificent; Jonas, his fighting staffs extended at his sides, and flanked by Treffin and Drake, with Charter prowling out front. Lisa took up position to his left, slightly back, with Jepp by her side, and Achos and Jasmine perched on either shoulder.

Everything was silent for a moment, as all eyes watched the spectacle … then all hell broke loose as defenders appeared out of nowhere, surrounded by their own companions, and intent on defending the VIP.

"Hold," she muttered, as much to herself as to Ruben and Thomas.

Jonas instructed Treffin and Charter to handle the companions; it was akin to letting them loose from a leash. They dove straight into the fray, and the defenders' companions disappeared before their claws and teeth.

"Ruben, skirt the darkness and eliminate anyone on the peripheral." She had barely finished her instructions before Ruben had disappeared.

She looked back to the battle developing in front of her. After the initial contact, Jonas and Lisa's companions were now pegged-back, by sheer numbers rather than strength. Jonas and Lisa had also been engaged by several defenders. Two already lay at Jonas's feet, and he was holding his own against a further three, leaving two to bare down on Lisa.

"Wait for it," Saskia hissed in her head, sensing her desire to protect Lisa.

The battle halted momentarily, as a loud, shrill scream pierced the night to the north, in the direction where Ruben had disappeared.

Then, things moved quickly … a figure appeared to hover on the southern edge of the light. It evaporated before getting replaced by a large contingent of defenders, who burst into the light … headed across the battlefield towards the scream.

She noted the Commander's position. This was what they had been waiting for. The Commander will have held back some defenders until he knew the whole Squad was engaged, the scream to the north had convinced him that the last three members of Raptor Squad were there. A big mistake.

"Now!" she hissed to Thomas.

They exploded from their hiding place, with Saskia appearing, and rampaging into the exposed flank of defenders who were heading towards Ruben. She was flanked by Thomas's gorilla and buffalo companions; Hammer and Smash. Saskia's lion head was snapping left and right, breaking seals, as Thomas's companions lived up to their names.

Thomas waded in behind, his whip snapping out to inflict damage or to divert an attack, and using his knife to finish off injured defenders.

She skirted the conflict, and utilising her cheetah Zahara's speed, she aimed for the spot where she had noted the Commander. His attention was on the carnage being inflicted to his reinforcements. She felt a moment of pity at the look of sheer confusion and terror on his face. Then she slipped easily beneath his guard to take out his left leg, before rising quickly to deliver a thump to his head, aiming to incapacitate rather than kill.

The defence didn't last much longer.

The sound of Saskia's goat heads cackling laughter, was encouraging the remaining defenders to retreat rapidly to the west, leaving Raptor Squad alone in the dying light.

There were seven defenders lay on the floor, seals broken, so incapacitated, with just two in Thomas's wake classed as being dead and eliminated.

Ruben entered the light, grinning from ear to ear as moans of pain came from the darkness.

"You're supposed to use none lethal methods, Ruben," Jonas grinned back.

Ruben smirked. "He's still alive, just in a little bit of pain. The same can't be said of Thomas's victims."

Ruben motioned, winking at Thomas to show it was a compliment. They all laughed, the adrenaline coursing through their veins. Lisa approached the VIP and hissed.

"What's wrong?" she asked.

"They've put a White puzzle on the VIP."

Jonas stalked over. "Lord Professor!" he growled.

The VIP was a big doll, that right now, resembled a flat blob. The White puzzle meant they had to heal the VIP to make it easier to transport. Unfortunately, the White disciplines were not a strong area for Raptor Squad.

"Do what you can quickly, so Thomas and Hammer can carry it," Jonas instructed.

Lisa nodded, closed her eyes, and called on Jepp and Jasmine to help.

Jonas turned to her and the rest of the Squad. "Five minutes and we move. They will regroup and attack again. I want to be gone by the time they pluck up the courage."

They all nodded. All elation at the victory dissipating, as they set about getting ready to move.

"Ruben, head for the trees and find us somewhere we can rest up. It'll give Lisa some time to work out this White puzzle. Charter will go with you," Jonas instructed.

Ruben and Charter melted into the darkness.

"I'll go and keep an eye on the defenders … and cover our rear," she said, moving in the opposite direction with Saskia and Zahara.

"I'm going too," Drake said to Jonas, and followed her.

As she moved into the darkness, she watched as Jonas turned back to Lisa. From where she was, she could see that Lisa had passed the first few levels, as the VIP had coalesced into a solid form.

"How's it going?" Jonas asked Lisa.

Lisa looked up. "It's a difficult puzzle. I think I can clear another couple of levels, but it will take time. This is the best I can do for now."

"OK, over to you, Thomas." Jonas instructed

Thomas spoke to Hammer, who stepped forward. He slid his hands under the VIP, bent his knees and started to lift, letting out a grunt of frustration, as he realised it was heavier than he thought. He repositioned himself and tried again …

* * *

Rico and Butch watched the two guards planning their next move. One guard sat at the fire as the other walked a slow circle around the VIP. With one on the move constantly, they couldn't sneak in and take them out at the same time. The plan was to stage their bodies, so that they could remove the VIP, while the observers on the outside thought nothing was wrong.

"It's going to have to be silent, in and out," Llýr whispered.

To the outside world, it would sound like a night animal stalking its prey. Both he and Butch nodded, rising slowly, and keeping low, watching their steps, so they were as silent as possible.

Halfway to the VIP, they came across a low run of thorn bushes that were disguised by the contours of the land. It was less than a full stride in width, so they could easily cross. They gathered themselves, ready to jump together so not to break contact.

"STOP!" hissed Rexter, appearing around their arms.

He immediately froze, poised to jump, but it took Butch a fraction longer to react. He pivoted on one leg, the other dangling over the edge of the bushes, as he fought to hold his balance. A misstep now would blow the whole operation. Butch hovered there for what felt like a lifetime, his arm circling like a windmill, as he tried to steady himself. Finally, he gained his balance, and looked questioningly at Rico, who exhaled a breath he had not realised he held.

"Well?" he asked Rexter in his mind.

Rexter slithered around both his and Butch's forearm. "Snakes in the grass," he hissed, flicking out his tongue.

An image of two defenders, lay up against the thorn bushes on the other side, jumped into his mind. If they had stepped across, they would have quite literally landed on them.

"We need to take them out, quietly," he said in his mind.

"Leave that to Rexter and I," Llýr answered.

Rexter slithered down his leg and joined Llýr, who had

appeared at their feet. They both slipped silently into the thorn bushes. A few seconds later, two dull thuds and a whispered, "Damn it," broke the silence.

Llýr and Rexter appeared back on his shoulders.

"It's OK to go now," hissed Rexter, a vicious, satisfied glint in his eye.

"Just jump a little further," laughed Llýr.

Progress was painstakingly slow, every step had to be exact and measured, so as not to raise the alarm. They had to plan their route before moving, so that they could slip through the patrol route of the guard who was circling the VIP.

Finally, they arrived beside the VIP. Butch crouched down next to it, immediately laying a hand on the VIP, and casting out his senses with Traveller's help.

"White puzzle," he signalled to him.

He nodded and signalled back. "How long?"

Butch shrugged, then signalled that there were fifteen levels, and he could complete five in roughly five minutes.

He knew that the puzzle would get harder the deeper Butch went. Butch's hand, signalling that he didn't think he could complete the next five here, that he would need time, and ideally light, confirmed it.

He signalled back to do what he could, turning his attention now to the guards. To his surprise, he saw them both sitting next to the fire and chatting in low tones. He couldn't make out what they were saying, but this was a gilt-edged opportunity.

He tapped Butch on the shoulder and pointed to the guards. Butch grinned wickedly. They moved silently up to the unsuspecting guards, who were discussing the food that the Purples were preparing for the after-event feast. They were unaware that two wraiths were raising up behind them, until they felt hands clamped over their mouths, and knives running over their throat pads … the touch of the blades cracking the seals and eliminating them.

They carefully leaned the guards against each other, and tied them to their seats.

"Now you are staged, don't move a muscle." He whispered his instructions into their ears, then re-established contact with Butch before they disappeared into the night. Just as silently as the attack, they moved back to the VIP, Butch setting to work as he stood guard.

Ten minutes quickly passed by, before Butch looked up. "That's the best I can do here," Butch whispered.

He looked over at the VIP, which had previously resembled a flat blob when Butch had started. It was substantially reduced in size, and beginning to resemble a human. He reached out to lift it, but found it was easily the weight of all of Phoenix Squad combined.

"We can't lift that and avoid a confrontation," he said.

"No, but Fence can. I think the next two levels will reduce the weight; it'll probably take me an hour to complete," Butch explained.

He nodded in the darkness, as Fence appeared and approached the VIP, keeping low.

"Somethings not right," Llŷr observed in his mind.

"I agree, it's too easy," he replied, as Fence slipped his hands under the VIP, setting his legs ready to lift. His eyes scanned the vicinity, trying to identify the cause of his unease. His internal alarm bells were screaming, but he could see no obvious threats. Out of the corner of his eye, he saw the guards they had staged, they were watching Fence get ready to lift, with satisfied glints in their eyes.

Suddenly it all dropped into place, the VIP was booby-trapped. That's why so few guards were here, and why they were sitting so far away from the VIP. He cursed himself, he should have expected this. It's what he would have done to give the defenders time to spring their trap. This all flew through his mind as he watched Fence flex his leg muscles, ready to lift.

"STOP!" he hissed urgently, as Llýr appeared on the VIP, face-to-face with Fence.

Whether it was his warning, or Llýr's sudden appearance, he didn't care, because Fence released the VIP, and dropped back onto his rump with a startled grunt.

"What gives?" he growled angrily.

"Sorry, Buddy, but I think it's a booby-trap," he whispered apologetically.

"Oh, OK," Fence replied with a shrug, his ire forgotten.

He reached up and scratched his neck, thinking. "Llýr, can you identify what we are dealing with?" he asked.

Llýr moved around the top of the VIP. "Now that we know what we are looking for, I think so." Closing his eyes, Llýr seemed to melt into the VIP, reappearing a few seconds later, on Fence's shoulder. "Definitely a trap, there is a stun and flare mine underneath it. The moment Fence raised it … us companions would have been rendered useless, and you guys incapacitated, for a least a few minutes, while the area is bathed in light," Llýr explained.

"Thank-you," he responded, his mind ticking over their options.

He and Butch could go out to the limit of the stun and spring the trap, but then the stun would render Fence useless, and no one else could carry the VIP at its current weight.

An idea formed in his mind, causing him to smile as he looked to Llŷr, whose grin mirrored his.

"I hate it when you get that look on your face," Butch said.

"Why?" he replied innocently.

* * *

"Because it usually means we are going to do something crazy," Butch chuckled. "So? Spill."

He marvelled at the immediate change in Rico ... with his decision made, his body language was no longer that of a teenage boy, this was a soldier worthy of the Red.

"You have your hour," Rico told him instead of answering. "Get to reducing the weight. Once you're done, we are going to need to move quickly. Remember to keep low next to the VIP, so you can't be seen in silhouette, once I move away," Rico advised.

"What are you going to do?" he asked, intrigued.

Rico tapped his pack and glanced at the VIP. "Two can play that game," Rico said cryptically, as he disappeared into the night.

"He's getting good at that," he said, admiring his skill at camouflage.

"He is, but I feel sorry for those defenders," Fence grunted.

He laughed, patting Fence's shoulder. "Me too, Partner," he said absently, as his attention had already returned to the VIP. "But that's not our worry. We have work to do. Stay low and watch my back," he instructed.

"Always," Fence huffed, as Butch and Traveller set to work.

An hour later, Rico appeared next to him, making him

jump.

"Damn, Rico! Don't do that," he hissed.

Rico looked confused. "What? I figured you could see me."

He shook his head. "No, not any more. In the light, sometimes I can catch a glimpse as you move from one background colour to another, but at night ... you're as good as invisible."

"Really? That's good to know," Rico smirked. "How did you get on with the VIP?"

He glanced back at the puzzle. "Surprisingly well. I got through the next two stages in half the time I expected to, and was able to clear more levels while you were gone," he explained, his tone, even to himself, was evidence that he was impressed with his achievement.

"That's Awesome!" Rico congratulated him, showing the correct response to his friend's excellent accomplishment.

"I know, both Traveller and I were surprised. Those stages of the puzzle would have been well beyond us a few weeks ago. We were sure we had reached our White discipline limits," he said, shaking his head.

"Seems to be going around," Rico answered with a smile, alluding to his improved camouflaging abilities.

"A puzzle for another day," they both said simultaneously, laughing.

He looked at the VIP. "It's about two-thirds complete, I think. I'd say light enough now that you or I could carry it if need be. Although, it would be slow going, it's like moving jelly."

"So, Fence still needs to carry it," Rico stated, handing him two poles. "Stake these in the ground near the guards, and stand them up against them lightly. We need them to drop to their knees when the stun hits."

He moved immediately with Fence to complete the task, careful not to be in silhouette by the fire. While he did that, Rico went to the VIP and tied a rope around its middle.

* * *

"Llýr, are you sure fifteen metres is far enough away to be unaffected by the stunner?" Rico asked.

"I can't be a hundred percent certain. The closer you are to the stun, the more impacted you will be. If Butch goes to that depression in the ground twenty metres away, I'm pretty sure he will be fine."

He nodded, pretty sure was as close as he was going to get to confirmation. He'd had this discussion with Llýr a few times in the last hour. Finished with his task, he looked up and saw that Butch and Fence had the guards in position. Moving over, he tied a rope lightly around each guard's forehead, holding it himself to stop them lulling forward. He needed them to be standing until after the stun, to create the right picture for the watching defenders.

"Butch, go back twenty metres the way we came in. You will find a depression in the ground … get down into it," he instructed, then turned to Fence. "Can you un-manifest please? We don't think the stun will go that far, but once it has gone off … I need you in as quick as possible. Don't wait for anything, just pick up the VIP, and head for the trees as if a horde of Forbidden were on your tail."

Fence nodded and disappeared.

"And what are you going to do?" Butch asked. By his tone and body language, he already knew the answer, and was not happy.

He lifted the rope he had tied to the VIP.

"Spring the trap," Llýr answered for him.

"But won't that leave you defenceless?" Butch said, clearly uncomfortable.

"For a few minutes, yes, but we think it will wear off quickly," he answered. "Besides, we have a few surprises of our own for the defenders," he grinned wickedly.

Butch laughed ruefully, knowing he couldn't change Rico's mind once it was made up. "I'll let the guys know they're going to have company," he said instead, as he moved away.

He waited until Butch had settled into the depression, giving him a few minutes to communicate with Eddie. After all, he and Llýr were only sort of sure they would be fine.

Butch raised a hand above the depression, signalling he was good to go. He readied himself, and gave a considerable yank on the rope. The VIP moved immediately on the first try, it was so light. Butch had done an excellent job. That was the only thought that flashed through his mind, as the booby-trap went off less than a heartbeat later. A bright light filled the night, followed quickly by the stun element which drove him to his knees, causing him to drop the ropes. He glanced around, pleased to see the guards drop correspondingly to himself. Hopefully, the defenders would see three attackers falling, and spring their trap.

"That hurt a little," Llýr groaned sarcastically in his mind.

He nodded agreement, it felt too much to try and speak, as he attempted to get to his feet. He couldn't move. Within seconds, Fence flashed by, grabbing up the VIP, and heading to the forest.

"Rico?" Butch asked, a questioning look in his eyes as he

241

dropped beside him, placing a hand on his shoulder.

He felt Butch and Traveller reach into him, looking for the damage caused by the stun.

"You need to head out with Fence, I'll follow shortly," he muttered, struggling to talk.

"The River I will, defenders are coming, and you're out of action," Butch growled.

"W-w-wait for it," he stammered.

As if on cue, three dull thuds went off … followed by several screams of pain.

Butch looked up with widened eyes, then returned his attention to him, shaking his head and smiling. Butch then focused Traveller on reversing the effects of the stun.

"What did you do?" Butch asked while he worked.

He grinned wickedly. "I set some mines of my own. Not as sophisticated as this one," he said, gesturing to where the VIP had been. "Nothing deadly, of course, but they had a good range and packed a punch, so they won't tickle and will slow them down."

As he finished explaining, Butch removed his hand from his shoulder. "Your good to go. It might be a while before the guys can manifest though," Butch advised.

"Let's get out of here then," he stated, stumbling slightly as he stood. Butch reached around to help him, and they both headed for the trees.

* * *

They had to stay still. Tia had scouted the area earlier, determining this to be the quickest route she would take, if she needed to cut off a Squad running from the VIP spot. The trick of their trap was to let the companions pass, dropping in on the defenders, and clearing most of them in the first attack.

Grey Claw was a little further into the wood, positioned to try and draw the defender's companions on, assuming Grey Claw to be a scout for the Squad to the south.

Tia had set up listening posts further up the trail, ensuring Phantom was out of sight of any of the defenders, hopefully giving them plenty of warning. They were going to need it. From the sounds of Butch's explanation, Rico was about to stir up a hornet's nest.

Eddie twisted in his position, feeling slightly cramped, his long legs not suited for the confined spot. He, like the others, had positioned himself up high in the trees, Phantom making sure the foliage hid them from sight below. But he was not comfortable. He looked across at Jenna who was grinning mischievously ... utilising the sign language they had developed as a Squad ... she told him to sit still, and stop squirming like a baby. He smiled. She looked as graceful as always, Aldela's regal demeanour very much a part of her. He looked in the opposite direction to Tia ... she appeared to be floating within the tree. Her legs were crossed, and her eyes closed. The only inkling that she was awake, was the movement behind her eyelids as she continuously scanned the images sent back by Phantom.

As if feeling his gaze, her face screwed up in concentration and her eyes snapped open. She signalled to him that eight defenders were heading this way, their direction fetching them right under their current position.

The defenders had four companions out in front, working in pairs, and the group were running in two lines side by side.

He huffed

"Too confident," he signed back.

Tia just shrugged.

He signed for her to tell him if anything changed and turned, passing the message on to Jenna. She smiled wickedly and opened her palm, a ball of fire appearing with the face of Aldela swirling within it, a questioning look in her eye.

He considered. She was probably right. A well-placed fireball would injure at least half of them and cut the odds substantially. Jax and Dancer could finish the injured off quickly while Jenna, Dozer, and he dealt with the remaining defenders.

He nodded, not even considering telling her to be careful not to injure them for real. Recently, Jenna had become much more controlled with Aldela's power, able to focus it, and hit her target easier.

When he looked back at Tia, she signalled that they were less than a minute out, and that the companions would be here momentarily. As the companions barrelled beneath them, they all held their breath, not wanting to make a single sound.

Two of the companions darted past in the blink of an eye, sleek foxes, one dark brown, and the other a light grey. The second two appeared and stopped directly beneath them, looking around suspiciously. One was a medium-sized white wolf that stood guard, while the other, a dappled leopard, prowled around the bottom of the trees.

Something had caught the leopard's attention as it rummaged around the base of the tree, its paws bashing gently at the ground. Suddenly, a tiny mouse darted out from the bush, disturbed by the leopard's exploration. A paw snapped out like lightning and captured the mouse, killing it instantly. A tiny exhalation of air from Tia had the big cat turn its head, looking in her direction.

He glanced to Jenna, who had a fireball in her hands. His head whirled with options. Should they take out these two, and move through the canopy to silently remove the defenders one by one ... which would take longer than an all-out assault on the eight defenders. It would be more difficult, as they would need to spread out, tripling the risks.

A yip to the south disrupted his thoughts ... followed by a chuckle in his mind, as the foxes engaged Grey Claw. The wolf and the leopard's attention were immediately drawn that way. The yelps of pain from their compatriots had them set off instantly to support them.

He let out a breath and looked to Tia, who was smiling as she looked down at the spot where the leopard had been ... when he looked, he saw that the mouse was still alive. It seemed a little dazed after its ordeal, but after a second, it turned and dashed back into its bush.

He shook his head in exasperation, a damn mouse had nearly blown the whole plan. He quickly diverted his thoughts back to the job at hand, as he heard the defenders ploughing through the forest, much closer now. There was no finesse in their movement, it was all about speed. They had to spring the trap, and they were confident their quarry was where they expected them to be.

"The first rule, always expect the unexpected," Dozer mumbled in his mind.

"The River to that," he replied.

The defenders came into sight moments later, and started to pass under the trees. Everything slowed down, this was not unexpected, as whenever he entered combat, he always felt a little speedier than his opponent ... but this was different, more pronounced. He could see the beads of sweat dripping down the front defender's cheek, and a small branch snap back and make the following defender wince slightly as it hit his head.

He glanced to Jenna, and watched as she released the fireball from her hands with a gentle flick of her fingers, an action that he would ordinarily have missed. He watched it, mesmerised. It glided through the air, with Aldela's face swirling within the flame, winking at him. He grinned as he pounced from the tree, Dozer and Jax manifesting from him halfway through the air. The fireball hit with precision in front of the four defenders, scattering them. Bruising and breaking the seals on their legs and lower bodies, but causing no lasting harm.

He had time to check on Jenna, who had also jumped from her perch. She gracefully glided through the air, Dizzy's wings spread behind her, and controlling her descent. They both landed together in the middle of the last four defenders, extending fighting sticks and immediately attacking the two in front of them. His opponent moved much too slow. He had attacked, struck his knee, and driven him to the ground ... taking him out of the fight, before he had even raised his own weapon.

"Amateur," he hissed, as he looked around for his next target.

He saw Dozer standing over a defender, who slowly dropped to the floor with a confused look on his face. He turned to Jenna who was in mid-strike, moving just as slowly as the defenders. She ducked underneath the first strike, a knee coming up into his midriff, an elbow dropping towards the back of the defender's head to finish him off. However, the last defender was moving in to attack. He had somehow managed to work his way to her undefended side. As she finished off the first, she realised her predicament and brought her staff up to protect herself. She was too slow. He hadn't even realised that he was on the move until he tackled the defender from the side, driving him into the ground, the impact breaking the seals on the defender's arms and legs.

He quickly stood up, taking stock. The eight defenders were down and incapacitated, but not eliminated. Jenna was in front of him unharmed, her mouth moving. It was at this point that everything sped up and sound came crashing back in…

"… you moved so fast," he heard Jenna finish.

He staggered slightly, disorientated by the sudden shift in his perceptions. Dozer caught him. "Easy there, Big Fella," Dozer said, sitting him down.

"I'm OK," he answered. "What happened, Dozer? I've never felt anything like that before."

Dozer shook his head. "I don't know. It was like they were in slow motion."

He thought it through. "It felt like more than that. I could almost read what their next decision would be, before they even made it. Is that even possible?" he asked Dozer.

"Sorry to interrupt, but what just happened?" Jenna asked testily, arms folded across her chest.

"Something new," Dozer answered her, grinning.

Tia dropped down next to them. "Eddie and Dozer were moving much faster than everyone else down here. It was confusing to watch. One moment they're squared off, then the next, the defenders were on the floor. The same when he tackled that last one, I was sure you were going to take a hit, then the next thing I knew, Eddie had tackled him."

He shook his head, trying to take it all in.

"Well?" Jenna asked him.

He laughed. "I don't know, Jenna. Maybe it's the advancement of my abilities, like those you guys have been experiencing." He shrugged. "You all know that in a fight, I always seem to be able to counter attacks, and beat opponents with far more skill than I have. I always thought it was because of my ability to read their body language and next moves. Maybe it was a skill from Dozer that slowed them down or sped me up?" he tried to explain.

"Well, whatever it is, we need to investigate it further. But not right now," Dozer interrupted.

"Dozer's right. We need to make our way back to the meeting place, rest up, and get ready to win this thing," he said, as he stood up, collecting himself. "OK, let's go."

Leaving the defenders on the ground, they moved out without giving them a second thought, they were someone else's problem now.

CHAPTER THIRTY-THREE

Cassie watched Kaden emerge from the house. She had guessed right; he wouldn't leave until Titch was asleep. As she watched him move through the street, she felt something about him had changed while he had been away, he seemed a little harder, and was moving with more purpose. She smiled. What she had learned from the other rebels in his Squad was going to upset a few people … and he wouldn't be looking forward to the conversation with the council.

Nevertheless, she was proud of him. He'd done what needed doing … revenge. By sending an important message to Selenta, they would now know they were dealing with someone who was serious.

She followed him, slipping through the shadows, unseen and unheard. She slid past couples sneaking a kiss, all the time watching him move as he took a roundabout route, familiarising himself with the town and his surroundings.

"Always the General," Kira, her lioness companion purred in her mind.

She grinned, imagining what was going through his head; what scenarios was he playing out? Suddenly, Kaden moved quickly, heading out into the countryside, and becoming

249

much harder to follow. Something had caught his attention.

Instead of trying to keep up with him, she slipped silently up onto the roof of the closest building, closed her eyes, and asked her bat companion, Whispers, for help.

As Whispers went to work, an image appeared in her mind … outlining what was happening in the dark.

"He's testing the sentries," she murmured.

"He's going to be very disappointed then," Flidalis, her final companion observed.

They watched as he approached the sentry post, slipping between them, taking their weapons, and then walking away back into the village without challenge.

His body language had changed. He was now furious, striding purposefully to the centre of the village. She quickly thanked Whispers and jumped to her feet, darting across the rooftops on a course to intercept him. Closing the gap swiftly, she dropped from the building, landing directly in his path.

She was pleased to see surprise and desire flash across his eyes, but it was all too fleeting as rage took back control. She suspected there was more to this flare-up than just poor sentries.

"Is a scowl any way to greet your lady, Kaden?" she purred.

"I'll greet you properly later. Right now, I have business to attend to," he growled, moving to pass her.

"What business could be more important than me?" she pouted, pulling her face.

"Have you seen those sentries?" he shouted. "Anyone could walk in and attack us in our sleep."

"They're not trained soldiers, Kaden," she said mildly.

"Redmund is. I'll tear him apart for this," Kaden raged.

She had to play this easy, his rage was in control. "Redmund was a soldier, yes, but what rank was he?" she asked.

"That's irrelevant. Just because he was a grunt ... a child could do better," he snapped, and she smiled smoothly. Here was her means to calm him.

She prowled around Kaden, running her finger across his shoulder and back.

"Oh yes, just a grunt. No training in advanced tactics, never drilled in how to set and maintain a stable sentry cordon ... just told what to do, when to pee, point him where you want, and he can die for the mighty Hands. Have you done more than let him watch you set a perimeter with a brief explanation?"

Kaden sighed, and she could see that he was struggling to maintain his anger.

"That's not what I meant. The soldiers are lax. I have their weapons!" he stammered, gesturing to his back.

"Then what did you mean, My Darling? Those scouts are raw recruits, learning the war trade. They have been working day and night to impress you with the village when you return," she purred. "How disappointed they'll be when their mighty, decapitating leader returns, and he can only rant and rave."

Satisfied that he was calmer now and chewing over the snippets she had given him ... his beautiful brain thinking along several lines ... she slipped into his arms, kissing him gently.

He growled slightly and pulled her closer, kissing her back, harder, and with a hunger that she knew all too well. He pulled back all too quickly.

"They've done all this to impress me?" he asked.

She shrugged her shoulders, a *what do you think* gesture, and smiled as he shook his head in wonder. She loved that he didn't realise the loyalty and awe he inspired in others.

"And you know about the heads? Who else knows?"

She chose not to answer the question. Instead, she indicated to his belt. "Are those for me?"

Kaden looked momentarily confused, then noticed that she was looking at the package from Titch, which had a pink bow attached. He handed the package to her. "Yes, it's from Titch."

She clapped her hands in delight, realising what was in the package. A brief note attached read *thank-you* in Titch's tiny scrawl.

"Mmmm, pop treats just for me," she smiled, popping one into her mouth and purring in pleasure.

"There would've been more if you had joined us for food," Kaden pouted.

She took her time before answering, enjoying the pop treats. "Don't pout. Titch has been preparing for this evening for weeks. There was no way I was interrupting and taking any of your attention away from her."

Kaden looked lost, and she laughed. "She has bribed, cajoled, and pestered to make sure that home was ready for when you got back. I hope you made it clear how amazing it was to her?"

She was pleased to see an affirmative nod. She wanted to laugh, looking at him now walking beside her, seemingly lost, racking his head thinking about what he had or hadn't said. A stark contrast to the man, who minutes ago, was ready to gut the entire council and his soldiers. Dealing with her and Titch always seemed to leave him with the same bemused look. She decided to put him out of his misery.

"Titch and I have become good friends. I would not jeopardise that for anything. She loves and cherishes you and is happy to share you with me. The gift of these pop treats shows she appreciates my giving her the time."

She moved in close, taking his hand and enjoying the walk, smiling into his arm as he shook his head ... muttering about confusing women.

* * *

"I just don't get women, Bond," Kaden complained.

Bond laughed in his mind. "No point asking me, Kaden. I'm as clueless as you."

His heart rate jumped as Cassie took his arm and cuddled in close as they walked through the town. He realised that she'd played him. Cassie had calmed him, and he loved her for that. He was right to feel angered by the laxness of the sentries. However, his worry about the council's reaction to what he had done in Selenta was fuelling his rage. He knew he had the trust of the soldiers, but there was more to it than that with the rebels ... they needed convincing to escalate their offensive at every step.

"Thank-you," he said, as he kissed the top of her head. He felt, more than saw her smile, and hugged her closer, no more needed saying. "How much do you know?"

A slight shrug was all she responded with; she was waiting for him to explain it before drawing any conclusions.

"We are lucky to have her," Bond said.

He nodded his agreement.

"I had to do it, Cassie," he confessed. "They killed the whole cell and tortured them. There were children in that group. I had to send a message they might listen to."

She stopped and moved in front of him. "Do you think you made a mistake?" she asked, a stern look on her face.

"Absolutely not. They need to understand. Something needs doing to free people in Selenta from the corrupt caste system that oppresses the weak and rewards the ruthless. People need to live freely, and choose their own paths and leaders. I'm just ..." he tailed off.

"Your just what, My Love?" Cassie asked.

"I'm afraid they're not ready, and that I'm pushing them too fast into my agenda."

Cassie stood on her tiptoes and kissed him. "My beautiful lion, you are a General, and the Scarlett Hand leader. Are people going to die? Yes, its war."

He squirmed uncomfortably. "But they're just kids," he said quietly.

"No! They're rebels," she admonished. "They are here to fight for their freedom. If you think they're not ready, train them faster or send them home." She jabbed at his chest, fire dancing in her eyes. "If you think things are going too fast, slow it down. You control the speed we move at." She jabbed him again. "And if they don't agree with you, convince them. Take a vote if it will make you feel better, but make them understand what's needed. You're the only one who can," she finished, breathing slightly heavier.

He smiled at her. She was his rock, always supportive, and pushing him when he may have slowed. She nodded to the building they were in front of. "Now, in you go, and drag them into the future."

Before he could answer, she had turned and walked away

from him, her athletic body sliding from side to side as she moved provocatively, teasing him.

"They can wait," he growled hungrily, watching her.

She looked over her shoulder and winked at him. "Later," she whispered, blowing him a kiss before she disappeared into the shadows.

He watched the spot where she had disappeared for a moment, before he shook himself and turned to the building, preparing himself for the onslaught.

"Here we go, Bond," he said.

"This should be fun," Bond replied grimly.

* * *

Kaden returned home several hours later. Standing outside the door, he replayed the meeting with the council. It had been as confrontational as he had expected.

Redmund had stormed out in fury to deal with the sentries, after Kaden had placed the weapons in front of him with a raised eyebrow. He had mingled with the rest of the council while they waited for Redmund to return, gauging what they already knew about his actions. It turned out; his men had been tight-lipped. He would have to find out how Cassie had learned about it and close that door. However, she was a trained spy ... it may be something he couldn't close, but they were improving.

"They will have to get even better," Bond added grimly.

The meeting was called to order when Redmund returned. He summarised the excursion into Selenta and the Disputed Lands, giving high-level details about conversations with cells, and information gleaned about events and supply routes. He'd left the details about the deaths of the new cell members until last, not out of fear, but expedience. They would never have discussed other essential elements once he explained those events.

Finally, he described how he had killed those who had murdered the rebels and sent their heads into Selenta, switching the final festival gifts with the severed heads of the killers. The resulting explosion had been as expected. Redmund was furious, not concerned by his actions, but because he had risked himself in that way. Oliver was livid, clearly shaken, and supported in his anger by Davies and Gluttun.

Oliver was genuinely worried about the rebels and the harm that could come to them. But he was an administrator, not a soldier, and in his fear ... he was accusing him of damning them all. He was worrying that the Black Hand would hunt them down mercilessly, and even kill them.

Davies was not so vocal in supporting Oliver's views, probably only siding with him because he was in love with him.

Gluttun, on the other hand, was more concerned about his position. He was a short, fat, weasel-like man who enjoyed the power he had gained in the rebel group. Power, a man of his level, would never have had in his previous life.

Gluttun was already on the de facto council when he had joined the rebels. He had always suspected that he had ulterior motives and kept a close eye on him.

Redmund, as expected, supported his play, with Manusa and Harris also on his side, believing they needed to move forward. With the council split down the middle, it led to hours of vigorous arguments about what this meant to them and what to do next, from stopping all operations to an all-out assault.

He stayed out of the discussions, leaving the council to do what it did best … talk. Eventually, they ran out of steam, and he suggested they retire for the evening. It would give them time to think about what they had discussed, and decide on their next steps the following day, when their heads were clearer.

He had another bombshell to drop on them, thanks to something Cassie had said, but he felt they'd had enough for one night, and he wanted to play it around a little first. What worried him more, was that the Formad envoy, Kendin, had kept quiet all the way through the meeting. He had only caught him at the end as they were leaving, asking him to give him a week before heading out again, and requesting a private audience on his return.

He had assured him that he wouldn't be moving in the next week and that he was always welcome to talk to him privately. He made it clear the Formad had earned that, and more, for the support they had given the rebels. Kendin had smiled from ear-to-ear and bowed to him before he left, heading straight to his transport, and leaving the village. He was intrigued about what he would want on his return but decided that could wait.

He took a deep cleansing breath and walked into the house. Hush had found himself a bed from somewhere and was seemingly fast asleep. Shaking his head, he said, "Get some proper rest, Hush. We have a lot of work to do. I need you to be on form."

Hush cracked an eye. "I'm always ready, Boss," he said, then closed his eyes again and started to snore.

He grinned as he walked into Titch's room, finding her curled up with her head on Tadic's belly, and an arm around Huff's neck, whose wing was acting as a blanket to keep her warm. Not one of them stirred as he sat down, watching them sleep. He rubbed his eyes, he was tired. The trip had taken more out of him than he thought.

"You need to rest more," a gentle female voice spoke.

"I can sleep when we have freed Selenta," he replied just as quietly.

"A noble sentiment, Kaden, yet you constantly question yourself and your motives," the voice said.

"She's an old one," Bond whispered in awe.

He felt no awe, but if Bond was impressed, Titch's companion was an ally he needed.

Replying to her directly he said, "I do, Old One. I must question myself every day, to ensure I don't pick *my* fight, instead of the *right* fight."

"Your companion does you credit, Kaden, yet hides rather than talk directly." He could hear the smile and mischief in her voice.

"Old One?" Bond asked, he could hear the confusion in his voice. "You can hear me?"

"Yes, Bond. We can discuss that later … when I want to. But back to the conversation at hand … what is the right fight, Kaden? And is it the only fight?" she asked.

* * *

Kaden left Titch's room a little while later, even more tired than he had been previously. There were more thoughts now running through his head, yet he also felt happier. Who, or whatever, Titch's companion was … she was intelligent, caring, possessed a high degree of morals, and was decidedly well-informed; having hinted at events that he was yet unaware of? Overall, an excellent companion to help Titch grow.

"And powerful, never forget that, Kaden," Bond added.

He huffed, that would be something he would never forget.

Exhausted, he opened the door to his room and found Cassie lying on his bed, waiting for him to join her.

"Have you been here long?" he asked.

"Long enough, My Love. Now, come to bed," she purred.

His exhaustion forgotten, Kaden closed the door and happily did as she proposed.

CHAPTER THIRTY-FOUR

J enna relaxed, as Dancer let them know that Rico and Butch were unhurt, and back at the rendezvous point. It had taken them a while to get back, having to make a significant detour to avoid the defenders at the forest edge. She smirked; they didn't sound too happy. Sharing knowing looks with Tia, she continued to grin. People were often unhappy when they came up against Rico. He had a habit of causing mischief wherever he went, usually coming out of it on top.

Although Rico had calmed considerably since Llýr's arrival - his general, personal image improving - he felt more dangerous for it. What she liked the most was his improved confidence in decision making, whether that be combat, training, or in general life … he was becoming the man they all knew he was, with Llýr making sure it didn't become tinged with arrogance.

As they entered the glade, her eyes scanned over Butch and Rico, making sure that Dancer hadn't omitted anything to stop her worrying. Immediately she knew she had; something wasn't quite right. She looked back at Rico. He looked pale and drawn, and before she could even think about it, she was by his side.

"What happened?" she interrogated.

Aldela provided her with healing as she placed her hands on his cheeks, looking into his eyes, and channelling her meagre White skills to check … only relaxing when she identified it was nothing a few hours' sleep wouldn't heal. Then it dawned on her that Llýr wasn't around, his absence more a measure of Rico's condition.

Llýr had become a permanent fixture due to his ability to manifest at will, without draining Rico and himself.

"Where's Llýr?" she asked as she glanced around, quickly trying to find him, panic tinging her voice.

Rico reached out and placed his hand on hers, smiling. It calmed her immediately. "Don't worry. I took a hit by a stun booby-trap, and it wiped the guys and me out. It'll be a little while before they can manifest again," he said.

She rocked back; the tension she didn't realise she had been holding, leaving her body.

"I'm OK by the way," Butch chimed in.

Her head whipped around. In her panic, she had focused on Rico, not checking on Butch. Then she saw the big grin on his face … he was teasing her. Tia was already in his lap, having checked on him. "And besides, don't give him any sympathy … he did it to himself," Butch added.

She turned back to Rico, hitting him on the arm.

"Oww, what was that for?" he complained.

"For being stupid," she answered, moving away in a huff.

"Thanks, Buddy!" Rico scowled at Butch.

"Anytime," Butch replied smirking.

She watched Eddie as he looked on fondly. "I think you better tell us what happened. Don't leave anything out. We have a few interesting things to discuss too," he said.

Twenty minutes later, they all looked at each other in awe.

"We are getting even more badass," Butch grinned.

"That's an understatement," Eddie said. "You didn't see that fireball Jenna fired."

"Well it will all be for nothing if we don't win this trial," she added, blushing.

"Does anyone have any idea what's going on?" Tia asked the question they were all avoiding.

They all pondered, but no one had an answer, until finally, Rico spoke. "Llýr has an idea, but he's not forthcoming right now. I think he's sulking because he can't manifest," Rico grinned, shaking his head, and causing them to all mirror his grin, imagining the tirade Rico was getting from Llýr. "Well apparently, he isn't sulking," Rico explained with mock sincerity. "He would just like to run his idea past Aldela and Dozer first."

"Ah, so not sulking, just the River forbid he might be wrong," Butch chuckled.

Rico's eyes widened in surprise. "I won't tell you what he said, but needless to say, I am no longer public enemy number one," Rico laughed.

Butch groaned, paling visibly. "Me and my big mouth."

Tia grinned, kissing him. "I like your big mouth." Butch laughed, perking up immediately.

She sighed as Eddie stood up, his demeanour changed, now all business.

"Right, back to it. Tia, choose your spot and set yourself up. The rest of you get some shuteye, we have four hours before I want to get moving again. This is the last chance to rest before we finish the test, one way or another."

The Squad nodded, and found a spot to sleep.

* * *

Rico woke with a jolt to find himself suspended above the clearing, looking down on the Squad, himself included … still lay sleeping.

"What the …?" he muttered.

He looked over and saw Tia, her head lolled to one side. Panic rose to his throat, she had fallen asleep, that meant their perimeter was unprotected and they were open to attack. He tried to shout, yelling to Tia to wake up, but she didn't stir and neither did anyone else, they all lay sleeping.

Suddenly, he felt a change. The scene before him seemed to fast-forward, he could tell by the tossing and turning of the Squad, it was just too quick for sleeping people. Then, time slowed down again, and within seconds he heard a commotion to the north. He tried to shout to the Squad again, to no avail, and it wasn't long before Bear Squad broke through the trees at the side of the clearing, stumbling into the sleeping Squad.

At this point, chaos reigned. He watched as Butch, Eddie, Jenna, Tia, and himself sprang into action, immediately engaging Bear Squad. The companions from both Squads flying out to fight each other. Bear Squad didn't stand a chance. Even roused from sleep, Phoenix Squad moved with an unparalleled purpose. Badass was a term Butch had used to describe Phoenix Squad earlier, but that didn't do justice to what he witnessed.

Squad members and companions worked in perfect tandem, but not just with their own companions. At a word from Jax … he watched himself drop to one knee, disappearing from sight, as Jax jumped over him, taking a Bear Squad's companion by the throat which had been moments away from gutting him. Llýr had recovered his ability to manifest … taking his pent-up aggression out on the enemy companions, flitting from one to the other, his tail finding weak spots, and at one point protecting Tia from an attack, by delivering a blow that caused a companion to disappear. Eddie and Butch were side-by-side, ploughing into the middle of Bear Squad, demolishing all cohesion, and splitting them up for him and Jenna to pick off.

This all registered in seconds as his attention was drawn to Jenna; she looked magnificent. She was standing in the middle of four attacking companions and two of Bear Squad, completely unfazed. She was so heavily outnumbered that he tried to shout the other Squad members to help her. He needn't have bothered. She extended her fighting staff, muttering something under her breath with her head down so he couldn't hear. His eyes widened … her fighting staffs ignited, a white-hot flame running down each, extended at her side, and wreathed in flame. Jenna flicked them out at the circling companions, and a flame whipped out to the sides, reaching to engulf the four companions. She then pulled back the blazing rope, tightening it, and the companions disappeared with a yelp. Jenna tossed back her beautiful blonde hair to stare down the two members of Bear Squad, her eyes dancing with wildfire. She grinned, and casually beckoned them on. Sensibly, they looked at each other and turned away, seeking an easier fight, but none was found.

Moments later, a shouted warning from Tia came, before the clearing to the north once again erupted. Twelve of the test defenders and their companions broke through, crashing into the sides of Phoenix Squad, with two large wolves barrelling into his invisible form.

He woke with a start. He was back in the clearing, and all was quiet. He looked over to Tia and saw that she had indeed fallen asleep.

"What was that, Llýr?" he asked.

Llýr appeared on his shoulder. "I don't know, you weren't here. I lost contact with you."

He closed his eyes and played back a few images of what he had seen in his mind to Llýr.

"Panther!" Llýr hissed in his ear, vanishing from his shoulder, and reappearing on everyone else's shoulders, hissing the same word.

Phoenix Squad were on their feet and spread out in moments, the alert codeword having them all prepared for an attack.

Tia had sent Phantom out to a small perimeter in seconds. They all looked to him, and he wasted no time explaining.

"In a few minutes, Bear Squad is going to stumble into the clearing followed quickly by twelve defenders and their companions."

No one asked any questions. Instead, they vanished into the trees, leaving Eddie with him. Eddie moved to the opposite end of the clearing where Bear Squad would enter, beckoning him to follow.

"We can't take on twelve directly without considerable risk," Eddie muttered.

He didn't answer, waiting.

Eddie looked up and grinned. "So, let's not. It worked earlier ... why not now?"

He nodded, confident to take Eddie's lead, and moved into position ... slightly behind Eddie, where he called on Misty, and then disappeared.

On cue, Bear Squad burst out of the trees and came up short as they saw a figure stood waiting at the opposite side of the clearing.

Eddie stepped forward into the moonlight, addressing the Squad leader. "Lia, we don't have much time. You need to listen to me carefully, then follow my instructions exactly. If you do, we will all come out of this in one piece."

Lia didn't even think about it, he could see the exhaustion in her eyes. "What do you want us to do?" she said.

Bear Squad had been gone no longer than thirty seconds before sounds of the pursuit crashed through the forest, and the trees at the side of the clearing burst open. Companions first; different variations of wolves, foxes, and big cats, their eyes wild with the chase, as they flew past the hidden Phoenix Squad without even a second look, confident their quarry was in retreat.

Next, the defenders came through the trees. As they filed quickly past, in pursuit of their prey, he smiled. He had saved the Squad, even if he didn't understand how ... it was still a win.

As suspected, two defenders hung back in the clearing, waiting to provide backup if required.

He slipped out of his hiding spot and approached them. "Good evening, Gentlemen," he said calmly.

Their heads whipped around; their eyes full of confusion at not seeing anything. However, they clearly felt the blow to their foreheads which broke their seals and effectively rendered them unconscious. They both dropped to the floor, looking up as he appeared as if from nowhere, he winked at them, and then joined Phoenix Squad at the edge of the clearing.

* * *

Eddie gathered the Squad and they set off quickly after the defenders, Rico taking the lead, and disappearing into the forest with the help of Misty. Eddie followed at the head of the spear, with Butch to his right, and Jenna to the left. Tia followed behind to provide backup where needed. Dozer, Jax, Grey Claw, Kalina, Dancer, and Fence all formed a shield out in front of the bulk of the Squad ... ensuring any companions that slipped past Rico were dealt with before they hit.

"Three, two, one ..." he muttered, waiting expectantly ... and being rewarded with the shriek of the defenders' and Bear Squad's companions.

Bear Squad had sprung the first part of the trap right on time.

He had instructed them to continue into the forest for two minutes, and then wait for the forward scouts. Once they arrived, they were to strike them, creating as much noise as possible. He wanted a clear message sent that Bear Squad had stopped running, ensuring the defenders were looking that way.

The standard operating procedure meant they would spread out to create multiple targets as they encircled the enemy, at which point, Phoenix would come from behind, and eliminate them before they knew what was happening.

Rico had removed the main obstacle to the plan without complication, by taking out the rear guard before they could sound any type of alarm. He marvelled at how quickly they moved through the forest.

"Ten metres ahead," Tia whispered, relaying information from Rico. A few more strides found Phoenix Squad amongst the defenders, and the fight was on …

No companions were protecting the defenders, and they were split into two small groups.

"So much for the standard operating procedure," Jax muttered in his mind. He smiled; the confrontation was over before it began.

The Squad's companions fell on the defenders mercilessly, eliminating half in the first hit. Rico took out the Captain, who never knew what had happened, as he, Jenna, and Butch finished off the final dazed defenders.

Immediately, their companions spread out, covering the perimeter as best as possible. He looked over and saw Rico looking disappointedly at Jenna.

"What's up, Rico? That was a perfectly executed plan … and you got to fight," he said.

Rico laughed. "It's not that. I'm just disappointed I didn't get to see Jenna's flame whip again."

Jenna's face screwed up in confusion. "My what?"

Any answer forthcoming from Rico was halted as Lia walked gracefully through the trees with the rest of Bear Squad, one carrying what looked like a large child on their back.

Casting her eyes over the prone defenders, and the lack of injury on Phoenix Squad, she shook her head. "Damn, you guys are good," she muttered under her breath, then louder, said, "Thank-you for your help, everyone."

Bear Squad all nodded, showing their appreciation, even though their exhaustion was evident.

"Anytime," Butch winked at Lia, eliciting an eyebrow raise

from Tia.

Formalities over, Lia got straight down to business. "Butch, how far did you get with your VIP puzzle?"

Butch looked to him and he nodded. "About halfway, I think. The weight dropped, but it's still a nightmare to move."

Lia and the others in Bear Squad looked impressed, and it was Chris who spoke, "That's impressive, Butch. If you lose today, the White could do with you."

"We don't intend to lose," snarled Rico, taking a threatening step towards Chris.

Lia raised her hand to stop any bubbling conflict, as Jenna placed herself between them. "Chris didn't mean to imply you would. It's just awe-inspiring that Butch could reach that level alone," Lia said.

"Explain," Tia stated, testily. There were too many lingering eyes on Butch from the women in Bear Squad for her liking.

"The White puzzle is geared for three stages. The first can be done by one, the second you need two working in tandem, and the final section needs three to be working together," Lia explained. "Butch getting halfway through the puzzle alone … I'm not even sure I could do that." She paused, looking at Butch. "As Chris said - impressive."

She smiled the compliment to Butch, her blue eyes twinkling, and Butch blushed more from the praise than from the appreciative looks cast his way by Lia.

Tia huffed and punched Butch in the arm. "Stop encouraging her," she growled at him, finding it hard to maintain her snarl as he smirked at her and blew her a kiss. Attempting to retain some annoyance at Butch, Tia sauntered off into the forest. "I'll go set the perimeter," she called over her shoulder.

"He's going to pay for that," he said to Dozer in his mind.

"Don't be so sure," Dozer replied, smiling as they observed Butch watching her go with obvious adoration in his eyes.

Lia shook her head wistfully, turning to her Squad. "Chris, Anna, go with Butch back to their VIP and complete the puzzle with him." Chris and Anna nodded, following Butch into the forest, going back to the clearing.

Lia sighed. "He would have made a great White, but you guys have to win. The VIP puzzle is the least we can do."

"Thank-you," he replied. "But you would have done the same for us."

Lia shook her head. "Unlikely. We would have probably been asleep when you barged through, and we could never have taken out the defenders that cleanly."

"That's not your skillset, Lia," Jenna stated simply.

Lia smiled her thanks to Jenna, and then the two Squads made their way back to the clearing, leaving the defenders prone on the floor of the forest.

By the time they had returned to the clearing, Butch, Chris, and Anna had finished the VIP puzzle, and a figure was strapped onto Butch's pack, mirroring Chris's.

The Squads bid each other good luck and headed into the night.

* * *

Lisa smiled as she moved silently from tree to tree, scouting for the Squad. She loved the forest, it allowed her to move unseen, giving her the feel of perpetual night. It had been Ellie's idea that she acts as the scout instead of Ruben, who typically took point. But Ellie had argued he was more of a blunt instrument that would plough through the forest like a bull, stirring up trouble. What they needed was a precision tool that could alert them to danger, and allow them to avoid it if possible, especially as they wanted to move quickly and quietly.

She had found it difficult not to giggle at the scowl on Ruben's face when Jonas had agreed.

A sound out in front of her brought her back to the present. Creeping forward, she used the forest to hide her movements, keeping to the shadows. Her dark clothing aiding ... any eyes watching would only see the foliage, as she melted into the background. She found two defenders leaning against the trees, chatting as they ate and drank. She was so close; she could have reached out and stolen their dinner.

"I'm bored," the first guard moaned. "None of the trainees will come this deep into the forest. They'll skirt the edges where it's easier going. We're just token guards; the edge is where the action is at."

The second guard laughed. "Stop moaning," he admonished. "From what I hear, you don't want action with Raptor or Phoenix Squad, they're pretty vicious. They've embarrassed every defender they have come across so far," he explained.

"Those defenders were all idiots. They treated them like trainees, rather than proper combatants."

She watched as the second guard shook his head and rose. "Whatever you say. I'm going to take a leak."

He moved off into the forest, and she thought quickly. Raptor Squad would be here soon, and these guys looked like they hadn't moved in a while. Decision made, she circled silently around, coming up behind the remaining guard, the small tree between them.

She reached around with her left hand and clamped it over his mouth as she slid her blade across his neck seal, eliminating him immediately.

"Courtesy of Raptor Squad," she whispered in his ear, as she lowered him silently to the ground.

She moved soundlessly across the small clearing, hiding behind a tree, as the second guard came back. His head was bowed as he adjusted his pants ... "And, anyway ..." he stopped short as he looked up to see his partner slumped down the tree, his throat seal broken, and a look of shame on his face.

"River," he muttered, as she appeared behind him, her knife sliding clinically across his throat seal before he could issue another breath.

"Nighty-night," she whispered in his ear, as he too dropped to the ground.

She took a moment to look around, confirming that the defenders were off the beaten track, and not likely to be found easily. When she was satisfied that they were sufficiently hidden, she took off back into the forest to continue her task.

* * *

Ruben was furious, his eyes firing daggers at Ellie. He should be the one scouting ahead and being the first into battle, not that insipid little thief.

"She does have an uncanny ability to move quietly and unseen," Indran spoke, trying to focus Ruben back to the task.

"Yes, that's all true, but when it comes to combat … Lisa's not strong enough," he replied aloud, letting this private conversation show, and therefore demonstrating the depth of his frustration.

"I wouldn't be so sure of that," Jonas answered from just up ahead.

Ruben hurried up beside Jonas to find two guards laying incapacitated, their throat seals broken, with no sign that anyone else had been here.

"You were saying?" Ellie asked from across the way, a smug smile on her face.

He growled, wishing he could wipe that smirk off her face, but Jonas would tear him to pieces if he harmed her, so he contented himself with a snarl.

"Feel better?" Indran asked sarcastically.

"Which way has she gone?" Jonas asked Ellie.

"She is keeping to the heart of the forest," Ellie responded.

"Argh. I'm so sick of all these trees," Thomas groaned.

"I agree," he added. This was something he could focus on, and Jonas wouldn't think he was acting sullen.

"This is slow going. We should head to the edges … we'll make better time. What do you think, Ellie?" Jonas asked, contemplating.

He barely stopped himself from screaming, "Who cares what she thinks!" as he watched Ellie consider.

"Up to you, Jonas. I agree that it would be quicker going along the edge, but we don't have all the information. To go against the scout changes our approach."

Jonas nodded. "I agree. We wouldn't even be having this conversation if Ruben was on point. We follow Lisa's lead; she is proving herself very adept."

He contained his complaint, knowing the decision was final. He watched Jonas gesture to the prone guards with an impressed look in his eyes ... eyes, which then locked on to him and Thomas. "Harness that anger. I will let you both loose when we deliver the VIP," Jonas said.

He grinned maniacally; his frustration evaporating, as he anticipated a good fight.

* * *

They'd been walking through the forest for a few hours, and even Ellie was becoming a little frustrated. Jonas looked over at Thomas and Ruben, and wanted to laugh. Ellie may be uncomfortable, but they looked positively miserable ... branches and leaves snagged on them, catching in their hair. Yet, their eyes were still alert despite their obvious discomfort, continually scanning the forest for threats, or more likely hoping for them.

"Heads up. To the north," Charter purred.

Jonas, appearing to be as comfortable as he would in his own home, looked to where Charter had directed, but not worried that it was a threat ... that warning would have been more defined and followed with a surge of strength.

He watched as Ruben and Thomas both flowed quickly into a fighting posture. They had heard something coming as well, Chitter and Harur no doubt warning them.

Ellie had a little grin on her face, and had not changed stride.

Out of the forest in front of them glided Lisa, but she wasn't the Lisa that Jonas knew, she held herself differently, moving with deadly purpose.

"What are you doing here?" hissed Ruben, breaking the spell.

Lisa's shoulders slumped, and her stride faltered as she seemed to draw into herself, becoming something less, now that she was back under the authority of the others. Ruben had stepped forward ... grabbing her arm.

"You're supposed to be scouting ahead, protecting us," he growled.

If he hadn't been studying Lisa so carefully, he would have missed the flash in her eyes as her other hand flicked up, touching Ruben's. His grip visibly loosened, allowing her to easily pull away.

"I had to come back," she whimpered, as she backed away. But he wasn't fooled, and it seemed that his companions weren't either.

"Did you see that?" Charter asked in his mind.

"Which bit?" he responded.

"The different Lisa?" Treffin added.

"Or the one who just removed Ruben's grip with the touch of her fingers?" Drake finished.

"OK, so you did," Charter answered his own question, chuckling.

"Very interesting. I think we may have underestimated our little owl," he added, as they watched Lisa move into the protection of Ellie, who unusually, had not raced to her side to look after hercf.

"She was watching you," Drake said, in answer to his unasked question as to why.

He looked to Ellie, and realised Drake was right. Their eyes locked, and without words, she asked the simple question ... had he seen? She had been telling him for months that there was more to Lisa than meets the eye, but this was the first time he had seen any evidence that she was right. He considered his options quickly, and then decided to acknowledge her question with a simple nod. Her eyes lit up as she turned back to Lisa. Now Ellie was happy he had seen, she brought herself between Lisa and Ruben, who had composed himself and was about to advance again.

"Not everyone needs to know," Drake said.

He agreed, this was an advantage for him to use.

"Ruben, back off," he instructed simply, pleased to see Ruben stop immediately. "Although, Ruben's question is a valid one. Explain why you have come back?" he asked Lisa.

At Ellie's encouragement, Lisa took a step towards him.

"The forest edge is twenty minutes ahead. It's swarming with defenders. I counted fifteen working together in threes. I managed to slip through, and our VIP point is across the sand. I couldn't go further without detection. However, Jepp could. He got a closer look, and it's about a further twenty minutes across rolling dunes, there are a few defenders there too, scattered in twos, he counted eight."

He mulled over what Lisa had just told him. "Anything else?" he asked, his tone patient, he wasn't exactly sure what was going on with Lisa.

"Yet," Treffin said, and he smiled, they would figure it out soon enough.

"I did overhear some of the defenders talking. Apparently, the majority of them are set up at the final posts to make us fight through. In their own words … 'This guard duty is bogus, that's where all the fun will be.'" Lisa finished, then went quiet … not offering anything further.

This was the Lisa he knew and understood, she had views and answers ... they just needed teasing out. "Do you have any ideas, Lisa?" he asked, ignoring the horrified look on Ruben's face, as he tried to find the Lisa he had seen.

Lisa looked equally shocked. "T-t-t-take them out?" she stuttered, too quietly to hear.

"We can't hear you!" Ruben spat, then cowered at the withering looks he received from Ellie and Jonas.

Lisa gained a bit of confidence, and spoke clearer, "Take them all out. They're not very good. I slipped through easily. I could have stolen their weapons," she said, followed by as scoff from Ruben.

"He needs a good-hiding," Drake muttered.

He agreed, but his mind was going over attack plans, "Can we get close enough? fifteen to five are long odds, Lisa."

Lisa smiled. "I can get us right next to them. If we each take three, we can hit them all at once, their numbers won't matter. They're lazy."

He considered it, looking to Ruben who was suddenly interested. A fight was just what he needed. "Show me," he said, and Lisa sketched the plan for him.

An hour later, he stood looking out from the VIP drop off at the lay of the land. Lisa's intel had been flawless. They'd moved in quietly and taken out the defenders swiftly. They hadn't even set a perimeter, or had any of their companions loose as early warning, overall ... pretty sloppy.

Then, luck had been on their side. Six of the defenders on the sand had come into the forest, an apparent rotation. They'd been a little better, having their companions enter ahead of them, but they had followed in too quickly ... eager to get out of the sun before getting the all-clear. Thomas and

Ruben had made short work of them. Once they were out of action ... Raptor Squad had simply wandered out into the sands, the two remaining guards paying them no notice as they expected to see guards returning. They quickly paid for their mistake.

Thomas and Hammer had been happy to drop the VIP off, mumbling about payback and smashing. Ruben was in his ear keeping him calm, letting him know there would be plenty of smashing ahead. He shook his head ... Thomas had simple needs, but he was loyal and instrumental in a fight.

He could see a defensive post slightly to the south which looked abandoned. He instructed Ruben and Thomas to go look, setting off at a fast march to the east with Ellie and Lisa. There was also a post directly in their path, but he intended to drop south before that, splitting the two posts. He wasn't afraid of a fight. He knew that one was coming, he just wanted to avoid the posts where they would have shotbolts, which if used effectively, could eliminate even the best.

Ruben and Thomas joined them quickly, reporting the southern post was abandoned. At this, he instructed a drop south, although the sand and sun were welcome after being in the dark forest for so long, he would rather battle where there was firm footing. Sand slowed down good fighters.

As soon as their feet hit solid ground, an alert went up from the post to the southwest, they had obviously been on the lookout. In the direction they headed, they saw pockets of guards rise-up in Hands, spaced some distance apart.

Raptor Squad would have to take on each Hand in turn, this element of the test was about combat, skill, and endurance.

"Now this is more like it," Thomas giggled.

"Battle time," he ordered.

Raptor Squad glided into formation. He was in the middle, as Ellie and Lisa moved out to his left. Ruben and Thomas were to the right, their training weapons extended. They moved into a trot. He could feel the adrenaline pumping through his veins, as his companions filled him with strength, sharpening his senses. The gap to the first Hand closed quickly, and he grinned.

"Loose!" he shouted.

Raptor Squad unleashed their companions. The first Hand of defenders were ready, and unleashed their own companions.

The fight was on.

* * *

Jenna looked over to Rico, marvelling again at how much he had changed since the arrival of Llýr.

"All for the better," Aldela said in her mind.

Jenna smiled. "I agree."

Pulling her mind back to the job in hand ... Tia had been overly apologetic since the incident with Bear Squad. If it hadn't been for Rico, then her mistake would have meant elimination for Phoenix Squad. Regardless, the Squad had not blamed her. In fact, Eddie was angry with himself, they had taxed her and Phantom too much, expecting her to do more work than she ever had before, and still perform at optimum levels. Tia had previously maintained a perimeter for three days, using a kind of trance, which allowed her to rest while still maintaining a conscious link with Phantom. But that had been under optimal circumstances ... not in the middle of a final test, in a brand-new environment, with threats and new techniques added to the mix.

They had all agreed to work on other solutions, but Tia was adamant she could do it and would work on her stamina. It had been Tia's idea that had brought them to where they were now. Phantom had scouted ahead to find them a spot where they could set up. The plan was simple ... Bear Squad had helped them reduce the VIP in size and weight. This meant that one of the larger companions could carry the VIP to the drop-off, and if they used Misty, then that could be carried out without conflict, giving them an advantage over Raptor Squad.

Dizzy had jumped at the chance, saying that she could do it easily. Jenna had laughed as she knew she just wanted to be invisible. She had been jealous of Phantom getting the first go.

"Don't worry, Dizzy is much bigger than Phantom, it will be much safer," Rico cajoled.

She grinned. Rico had been trying to convince Misty that it was safe, ever since the idea to fly in the VIP had materialised. She'd been happy to go in on Dancer or Jax, but flying again had her grumbling.

Dizzy appeared in front of Jenna, hopping over to Misty. She leaned and whispered in her ear. Llŷr chuckled, and Misty groaned, but jumped onto Dizzy's back. Dizzy jumped around for a few seconds, getting accustomed to the extra weight. Then she moved into position.

"Set the VIP," Dizzy instructed.

Rico moved immediately, placing it at the edge of the forest, at the end of the runway they had created. Dizzy would move down the runway, gaining speed and grabbing the VIP in her claws as she passed, sweeping out into the open, and keeping low to the deck with Misty cloaking them. She would then drop off the VIP and return to her and Rico.

Dizzy stretched her wings, fluffing them as if stretching for the challenge. "If you please, Misty?" Dizzy asked, and immediately they disappeared. "Awesome!" she cawed.

"The River with you," Aldela and Llýr both intoned.

Dizzy started her run. The only evidence that she was moving was the slight indentation in the undergrowth. Suddenly, the VIP lifted from the ground, seeming to float of its own accord. Moments later, there was a snap of wings as Dizzy took to the air, and within seconds the VIP also disappeared.

There was nothing more for her and Rico to do now other than wait. Aldela and Llýr manifested, and moved away to talk in private.

"They seem to be getting on well," she said, motioning to the pair.

"Yeah," Rico replied absently. "The companions always got on well, but now they can properly communicate, it's a whole new level," he finished.

"It's like they have a sole purpose," she added, watching them.

"They do. Us," Rico laughed.

She pondered on this for a second and could find no flaw in Rico's comment, but something inside her felt that there was more going on. She decided to leave it for another time.

"Anyway, when are you going to show me your flame whip?" Rico asked.

She looked at him, confused. "Flame whip?" she asked.

Rico huffed. "Don't pretend. You were too good with it

to not have practised, but if you don't want to talk about it, that's fine. I understand."

By his tone, it was clear that he didn't. "Rico, I don't know what you're talking about," she answered, testily.

Rico was about to respond when Llýr interrupted. "She may not know, Rico," Llýr said.

"What do you mean? I know what I saw," Rico retorted, eliciting a raised eyebrow from Aldela.

"When will you learn to listen, Boy," Llýr growled, taking a few steps towards him.

"Now, now, Boys," Aldela admonished, landing between the two and spreading her wings.

Both stopped and nodded an apology to Aldela.

* * *

"Now, as Llýr was trying to explain, we have seen many advancements in the Squad's skills since Llýr's arrival," Aldela explained.

At the interested looks from Jenna and Rico, she continued, the earlier argument forgotten in the light of the puzzle they had a few minutes to unpick. "Think about how things are progressing ... Tia's ability to read the shields, Butch's healing abilities, Eddie's ability to slow down time in conflict, Jenna's control of my fire abilities, and Rico, your vast improvements in camouflage, and the latest development prophecy." She had their attention now, so posed the question her and Llýr had been discussing. "What links all of these improvements?" She smiled, as she watched Rico and Jenna mulling it over. The answer was simple ... the trick was asking the right question.

282

As she suspected, Rico came to the answer first. His proficiency with tactics allowing him to analyse situations quicker than most. She and Llýr were pleased to see that he waited until Jenna came to her own conclusion.

"Stressful situations?" Jenna suggested.

Rico nodded agreement. "My thoughts too. The only one that doesn't fit is Tia's. Hers developed before the tests."

Llýr stepped forward and answered. "That had us stumped at first as well. It was only after she fell asleep while on sentry duty did it dawn on us. She has a different type of stressor than the rest of the Squad."

Jenna's hand went to her mouth. "We expected so much of her."

Llýr nodded. "Yes, we did, and her work had started before the test. We rely heavily on her scouting and sentry abilities. She had spent hours going over the plans. The incident with the shield, Phantom carrying Misty ... on their own, none of them would be enough to stop Tia, but all together, in quick succession ..." Llýr raised a questioning eyebrow.

"Drained her heavily," Rico finished. "That all makes sense, but by the time we get to our age, skills should already have shown. We spend the rest of our lives refining those skills. These are new skills."

"But they're not new skills, are they?" Jenna interrupted, directing her question to her and Llýr.

"No, they're not, Jenna. They're variations on the theme," she answered. "Other than Rico's communication and prophecy ... which are likely associated with Llýr ... they're all improvements on what was likely a weak skill you already had, but never used consciously."

Jenna grinned at her. "Does that means we can make a

flame whip?"

Her eyes flashed in excitement, and emulated her own thoughts, as she replied in kind, hearing the anticipation evident in her own voice, "Now that we know it's possible, we won't stop until we master it."

Jenna's eyes glazed over briefly. "Dizzy says they're about thirty seconds out. There are sixteen guards, all looking a little worried. All out in the open, no subterfuge here. Dizzy is going to land, and say hello."

They all laughed ... imagining the faces of the defenders, as a beautiful golden eagle appeared out of nowhere, with a terrified chameleon on its back, calling her disdain, before the pair vanished again.

Rico and Jenna smiled as they experienced it through the eyes of their companions.

Once they returned, Rico stood. "Let's go."

* * *

"Eddie, they'll be here shortly," Tia advised.

"That was quick," Butch observed.

"That's something else we are going to have to consider when we get out in the field. If we can do that, what can others do?" Eddie grumbled.

He was in a bad mood, angry at himself for not seeing that they were overtaxing Tia, and putting the Squad in danger. It was a feeling that had only increased when they had scouted the next section of the journey while Jenna and Rico delivered the VIP.

He was confident the speed of the delivery had given them the advantage over Raptor Squad. Still, they were going to have to fight their way across the next section of the test.

There was the water route that would be simpler, but none of them was keen on that option. After just a moments consideration about what could be lurking in the water ... it was enough of a deterrent for even the bravest warrior. That meant they would take the lottery of the combat, across the plains.

They had decided to head out quickly to the water's edge, and skirt the lake, heading for the ford to the north. Keeping well away from the guard posts, as range weapons kept there was a big worry; they could eliminate any of them.

He laughed at the irony that Rico's fear of these weapons had become his first thought.

Rico and Jenna arrived, and Phoenix Squad set off immediately, heading for the first pier. He dropped beside Rico and Jenna, explaining the plan as they went. Rico peeled off to the north, disappearing to check out the first post, with the intention of meeting them at the pier.

A short while later, they arrived safely, having not encountered any defenders.

"I don't like it," Jax growled.

"I wouldn't either," a voice came from the pier. The Squad all jumped, weapons at the ready, as Rico appeared ... sat on the edge of the pier.

They all relaxed quickly. Butch laughing as Tia thumped Rico on the arm.

"Don't do that again," she admonished.

Rico nodded, smirking, then looked to him. "Once we get through this, we need to think about how we can counter people with my ability."

He simply nodded, having already had the same conversation with Butch earlier.

Rico turned to the Squad. "The defence post was deserted. Looks like we're going to have some company on the way to the ford."

"We suspected as much from the scouts Phantom completed," Tia answered.

He motioned the Squad into a circle, all their companions manifested. He looked from face to face, happy to see nothing but determination in their eyes, and found himself talking easily. "Whatever the Lord Professor has in store for us, we can beat it together. Let's show them what Phoenix Squad is made of."

They all grinned, extending their weapons and running a final check on their gear. When they'd all gone through their own combat rituals, Rico moved out ... taking point ... and disappearing into the sunshine.

"Let's roll!" Jax growled, and they fell into formation.

It didn't take long before they came into sight of the next defence post. Eddie was about to suggest sending Phantom to check it out, when the alert went up, the defenders were obviously on the lookout for them.

At the alert, groups of defenders appeared in the distance. They were set up in Hands, but didn't move to work as one. They were individual units that would intercept Phoenix Squad one at a time.

"Looks like they want to test our skills and stamina," Jenna observed.

"Well, let's show them what we've got," he stated simply.

Dozer, Jax, and Grey Claw formed a wedge in front of him. Dancer and Kalina flanked Tia, and Fence appeared beside Butch, whose skin had taken on a slightly green hue as

Traveller provided his protection. Wiggy took up his usual battle position on Fence's back, looking like he was riding him into battle. Utah and Dizzy took to the sky, their job was to ensure no aerial attacks took the Squad by surprise, and to provide real-time battle info. Finally, Aldela appeared behind the Squad, her wings flickering with flames as she swooped down over them, letting out a war cry, and releasing a fireball in front of the waiting Squad.

Everything slowed down again for him, giving him time to evaluate the situation. Each of the awaiting Squad looked relaxed and battle-hardened, he couldn't help admiring their calm. Phoenix Squad in full flight had made lesser Squads scatter, losing without putting up a fight. But this group waited calmly, preparing themselves for this conflict. It was likely that they had trained and prepared for this specific task within the test.

Once the smoke from Aldela's fireball cleared, they released their own companions, who moved out to intercept them. He glanced around at Phoenix Squad, completing one final check, grinning when he saw Wiggy squawking in defiance from Fence's back. It was almost comical if you didn't know that Wiggy was by far the most vicious of the two.

"They're well prepared for us," Dozer observed, as they watched the awaiting group spread out slowly.

"It seems that way. But I think they're in for a little surprise."

As if on cue, Rico appeared within their midst … taking out their Squad leader with a blow to the back of his head, and eliminating him from the fight. His three companions, heading to face Phoenix Squad, disappeared, and all cohesion in the defenders dissipated in panic.

"They weren't prepared for that," Dozer laughed.

He watched as Phoenix Squad's companions tore through the defenders remaining companions. A defender on the far left looked back to the Captain, and upon seeing that he had just been eliminated, he darted away from the fight, running past Rico, who turned to follow him.

Rico's body seemed to blur slightly as he stopped his pursuit, his head sweeping around to his Squad. "DOWN!" he cried.

CHAPTER THIRTY-FIVE

T he Lord Professor stood, looking at the board. He
had been nursing a drink for the last thirty minutes
as he considered the Squads placements. They had
all pretty much gone as he'd expected, the work he had done
in the run-up had paid dividends.

Angus Quinn had also been busy, working tirelessly to
ensure meeting his own ends, regardless of the outcome.
What worried the Lord Professor, was how easy it had been
because his and Angus's aims were so similar, even if their
endgame would be different.

There had been many arguments and negotiations, especially with ensuring that Lia, Chris, and Anna all went to the
White. Angus's allies in the Blue had argued that it would be
better to spread them out as field medics ... with Lia going
to the Blue. It was a sound argument as they weren't useless
in a fight like most medics were. However, the White had
nearly exploded. These three were the best medics in the
year, and they had to join the White. The White's view was
that their numbers had reduced, with many forced to leave
over the last year for one reason or another, so they needed
these recruits.

Angus had intervened and selflessly played intermediary,

highlighting that maybe the White was right, they needed the best. But the Blue and other Hands required some of the middling medics to support their requirements. He grinned at the memory … the White proxy had played his part beautifully. Spluttering and posturing, but then trying to be magnanimous in agreeing that was the case and offering up a few names. Butch and Lisa were two names he had plied him with.

As he had hoped, Angus jumped on the names, pushing Butch to the Blue.

"An inspired choice," was his description, yet suggesting that Lisa could go to the Grey.

"Keeping those he trusts close," Esther said.

"Yes, but there is much more to that girl, and he knows it," he replied.

"The report we had back from the two defenders eliminated in the forest for instance," Caulder added.

"Hmm, another late bloomer," Chirp offered, reminding everyone of the advancements they had seen in Phoenix Squad.

"It would seem that way," he replied. "Speaking of which, the White will be rather upset to have so easily given up Butch, if the reports are anything to go by."

A Purple server glided past with a tray of meat pies, and his stomach growled at the smell. Ever aware of the whims of their charges, the Purple pivoted and turned to him, conjuring a small plate from his person as he approached.

"Would you like a pie, Sir? They are made of the finest buffalo meat from the southern farms."

He smiled his thanks and nodded. "Yes, please."

Two pies appeared on the plate as if by magic, and the

Purple handed them with a bow and glided away. "If you require anything else, My Lord, please let me know. I know the chef has some fine stuffed pommer's baking for the Grey," he winked conspiratorially.

"They sound delicious, next time you pass by that would be nice," he said, his mouth-watering. He hadn't realised how hungry he was. The Purple smiled and turned away. "But don't make a special trip," he called to his retreating form.

"Of course not, Lord," the Purple answered, and then was gone into the crowd.

"You do know that was a pointless instruction?" a voice behind him said. It was a sure sign of his agitation that he had not heard Dutton approach. "He will make sure he selects the best one from the batch the moment they are ready," Dutton finished.

"I do hate it when they go out of their way for me," he moaned.

"Perks of the job," Dutton laughed.

He turned back to the board as he bit into the first pie … he groaned in pleasure, it was delicious; a little bit of pepper, and a thick sweet sauce, coated his tongue. But the best part was the buffalo meat inside, cooked to perfection, and melting in his mouth.

* * *

Dutton came up beside him. "Looks like everything has gone to plan," he said.

The Lord Professor huffed and he grinned; he knew what was annoying the Lord Professor.

"I know you didn't want Jonas in the Black, but did you

really think you could've placed Eddie and Jenna into the Red if you hadn't conceded on Jonas and Ruben?" He saw the scowl cross the Lord Professor's face and decided to change tack. "Butch going to the Blue is a disappointment for the White, but good use of his skills, and Tia to the Black, although a surprise, will give us an ally there."

The Lord Professor swallowed the last piece of the first pie. "Yes, Dutton, but they have Ellie in the Red, and Thomas in the Green. I wanted Tia to join Rico in the Orange," he growled.

He thought for a moment. "Well, hopefully it will be a moot point. The observers have Phoenix Squad moving into the final phase in the lead."

The Lord Professor nodded. "Chirp let me know earlier, he has been keeping an eye on proceedings. Raptor Squad is not too far behind, and I believe Armadillo is heading for the lowest pier. They intend to use a boat by the looks of it," he advised, as he tucked into the second pie.

"It seems that way, Lord," he replied, then added, "If things go smoothly, they could add an interesting twist in the final straight. We should make our way up to the observation lounge and watch the final phase with the delegates."

He watched as the Lord Professor finished his pie, then wiped his fingers and dabbed his lips with his napkin, taking one last look at the board.

"There is nothing more to be done." The Lord Professor straightened his robes and turned to head to the observation lounge. "Did you have one of those pies, Dutton? They are delicious," the Lord Professor asked.

"No, Lord, but I will try one when they next come past."

"You should, Dutton, you don't eat enough. Now tell me

… who is already upstairs?"

He smiled as the Lord Professor moved onto the next phase. "Most of the Hands are already upstairs, but we need to make a stop along the way, ensuring we bump into the Red Captain before he heads to the lounge."

The Lord Professor nodded. "Lead the way."

* * *

"Can that boy do nothing right?" Angus growled.

His companions laughed. "Give him some credit, Angus. He hasn't put a foot wrong. How were we to know Phoenix Squad had a skill they'd kept quiet?" his first companion argued. "And besides, I wouldn't write Jonas off yet, he and the Squad will do anything to win. If they can pick up the pace, there could be a spectacular finish to the test. I wouldn't put it past them to attack Phoenix Squad directly themselves."

He took a sip of his drink and sighed. "I know, you're right. It was just too easy over the last few days, sorting out the placements. The Lord Professor played his vetoes on insignificant placements."

His companion considered. "I know, it was a little confusing. I expected more of a fight from him."

He looked around as a commotion at the stairs heralded the Lord Professor's arrival. He snarled as he watched the various Hands and Captains' approach to shake his hand and congratulate him on an exceptional year, working hard to school his face quickly, as the Lord Professor looked over to him and nodded in acknowledgement.

"He's up to something. He's just too calm, but for the life of me I can't fathom what it is," he growled, turning back to the viewing area, and watching as the reports came in from the field.

The situation hadn't changed. Both Phoenix and Raptor were moving steadily through the defending Squads. The time they were taking to dispatch each Hand was almost identical, meaning Phoenix would have a five to ten minutes advantage once they finished off the last defenders.

The exciting element was Armadillo Squad, they were halfway across the water. At their current pace, they would hit the top dock just after Phoenix and Raptor cleared the ford, and this would give them an advantage, as they would have a shorter run to the finish. They could potentially complete the test in first place without facing any conflict. They had never attempted to rescue their VIP, instead deciding to just try to get to the finish line. It was a calculated risk, as unlike Bear Squad ... eliminated when they attempted to drop off their VIP ... it gave them a strong chance to complete the test.

"It's going to be a close finish," the Lord Professor said from behind him.

He nodded. "It does look that way," he replied with a calmness he didn't feel.

They both stood in silence, watching the board change ... notifying them that Phoenix Squad had just dispatched their second to last defenders and were moving on to their final Hand. Raptor Squad had engaged their second to last group.

He went to take a swallow of his drink, realising that he had finished it. He absently motioned for a Purple server to bring him another. He moved forward and took a seat as he continued watching the board, this was going to be close. It was only when the Lord Professor took a seat across from him, that he realised how nervous he was.

"What does he know that we don't?" he muttered in his mind, not looking for an answer, but voicing his frustration to his companions.

A Purple approached the Lord Professor and handed him a plate with a stuffed pommer on it. As he watched the Lord Professor thank the Purple, he was sure he saw a slight twitch of a smile on the Lord Professor's face as he tucked into the succulent dessert. It was one he had requested the Purple make exclusively for the Grey. He was about to say something, when his attention was drawn to the board. Raptor Squad had finished their opponents off quickly and gained some time, while Phoenix had just started their final confrontation. The map charting the Squads' progress showed that Armadillo Squad had managed to gain a slight lead, and would not be far from the shore when Phoenix and Raptor headed for the ford.

He watched as the Lord Professor closed his eyes, talking with his companion, then smiling as he opened them.

"It looks like Phoenix made quick work of the final group and are on the way to the finish line. It will be close, but they'll just pip Raptor to the post."

He scowled. "I wouldn't count out Jonas just yet, Lord Professor. He will do anything to win."

A sigh from the Lord Professor was all the acknowledgement he needed to let him know that he knew that to be the case. The board changed again as Raptor finished their final fight. The Lord Professor stood to leave. "It was a fabulous year, whoever wins ... the runners-up can be proud of what they have achieved."

Watching the Lord Professor's eyes glaze over, he assumed

he was communicating with his companions again. He surmised that Chirp was out in the field, and feeding back information first hand.

He tried not to grin as the Lord Professor paled ... his eyes snapping open as he turned to Dutton ... "Get the Red alert team out to the lake, NOW!" he ordered, all business.

Dutton turned and darted to the Red Captain, who issued orders quickly.

The Lord Professor turned to him. "It seems you were correct, Angus. Jonas will indeed do anything to win. Now, if you will excuse me, I need to try and save the lives of some of my students. I only fear that we are already too late."

The Lord Professor turned and caught up with the Red Captain. He watched them go, a smile crossing his face, as the markers showed Raptor Squad taking the lead, with Phoenix headed to the water's edge.

"Told you so," his companion said, and they both laughed in satisfaction, not even giving a second thought to the lives that could be lost.

* * *

"NOW THAT'S WHAT I'M TALKING ABOUT!" Rico shouted excitedly. "Did you all see? That flame whip is awesome!"

Eddie laughed at Rico's excitement. After the mine had gone off in the first fight, he had been surly and frustrated ... having taken the full brunt of the hit for the Squad and losing his ability to camouflage. Butch had been able to heal his wounds, but the shockwave had pushed Rico's companions to the background, removing a significant advantage from the Squad.

They'd been able to handle the fights the same way they would have without Rico's new skill, but his frustration had shown … with him taking a few too many risks. However, they had survived, so he would leave it until they debriefed.

He looked to Jenna, who was grinning as wildly as Rico, her fighting staff wreathed in flames, and a rope of fire coiled on the floor beside her. Three singed defenders lay around Tia, they had made a big mistake and gone after her. Jenna's and Aldela's cries of fury had pierced the air. A whip of flame had taken one of the defenders around the throat, breaking his seal immediately, before whipping out and grasping the other's weapon arm. Tia had stepped in, finishing the defender with a blow to the stomach as a bolt of flame had taken out the third defender, hitting him in the chest and knocking him back a good six feet, leaving Butch and Rico to easily finish off the final two.

He glanced around, noting that Raptor Squad had just engaged with their last defenders, and that Armadillo, who was on the Lake, would make it to the pier in the lead … they had to get moving.

"No time to celebrate. Time to move," he ordered, and they all took off quickly, heading to the ford.

They had been moving for no more than a minute, when they heard a huge thunderclap, and saw a flash of lightning crash through the daylight. Stopping in his tracks, he got a cold feeling in the pit of his stomach as he turned to look …

* * *

Jonas growled as they finished off the final defenders.

297

Phoenix Squad had the lead and barring a massive stroke of fortune, they would never catch them.

He looked out across the lake and saw Armadillo Squad floating across the water, heading for the pier. They would reach it before both them and Phoenix Squad.

A brutal smile spread across his face. "Ruben," he shouted.

Ruben was watching Phoenix Squad with a look of pure hatred on his face.

"Yes?" Ruben answered, reluctantly turning back to him.

He motioned towards the lake. "How does Indran feel about sinking a boat?"

No response was required, as equally vicious smiles spread across each of Raptor Squad's faces. Indran manifested and sprung into the air, swiftly flying the distance to the tiny boat still bobbing across the water. Armadillo Squad were so focused on getting to the pier, they never knew what hit them.

A thunderclap roared above them, the concussion wave twisting the wood of the boat, as a lightning bolt blew a hole in the bottom of it between their feet.

Ruben grinned in delight, as he watched the fear flash on their faces through Indran's eyes. "Hit them again," Ruben instructed, and Indran obliged, this second thunderclap shattering the boat and scattering Armadillo into the water.

He looked over and was pleased to see that Phoenix Squad had stopped to watch, seeing Tia release Phantom into the air. He grinned wildly. It had worked.

Checking the terrain was the first action Phoenix Squad took before they moved. After what seemed like an age, but likely no more than a few seconds, they headed off at full tilt to the lake.

"Weakness," he growled.

He instructed Raptor Squad to follow him, as they headed to the finish line to claim their victory.

* * *

As the second thunderclap hit the boat, Eddie looked at Tia. She was already releasing Phantom into the air. They had time to check out the situation, ensure Armadillo was safe, and still beat Raptor Squad.

"This is exactly what Jonas is hoping for," Jenna said, coming up to his right side as they waited for Phantom's report.

Tia looked around moments later. "Phantom says they all have kindling to hold onto so they won't drown anytime soon. There is also a Squad heading out from headquarters to help, they will be here in ten minutes."

Tia's eyes glazed over as Dozer, Llýr, and Aldela manifested in front of the Squad.

"Something has awoken," Dozer muttered.

"Something big," Llýr added.

"And nasty. I can feel its anger and hunger," Aldela finished.

Tia's eyes opened, full of fear. "Phantom says there is a disturbance on the lake, moving towards Armadillo, he thinks it will get to them in a few minutes."

"River!" he hissed, and started sprinting to the lake. He wasn't sure what they could do, but they had to try. "There's a boat directly in front of us. It looks big enough for two and Armadillo Squad."

Rico and Butch overtook him easily, reaching the boat before him. Fence and Dozer appeared and pushed them out into the water. Moving across the water quickly, Rico and Butch still seemed to be going much too slow to reach Armadillo Squad first.

"It's going to be close," Tia muttered.

He instructed Jenna to release Aldela and Dizzy into the air, he wasn't sure exactly what they could do, but he felt that it was necessary.

* * *

In the boat, Rico and Butch were working in perfect unison. They hated the water, but had practised using boats just in case they ever needed them.

"Give me dry land any day," Rico grumbled.

Butch laughed. "Especially when there's a monster headed our way."

He shook his head. "Why do we always get ourselves into these predicaments?" he asked ruefully.

"We're just lucky I guess," Butch replied.

They arrived at the wreckage of Armadillo's boat quickly, but more importantly … before the creature. They started pulling the Squad members aboard.

He stood in the centre of the boat and watched as the creature closed in on them. "This boat isn't going to protect us, is it, Llýr?" he asked silently.

The creature was closing fast.

"Well, let's put it this way, getting wet will be the least of your worries," Llýr replied.

The creature was moving closer, it was almost upon them.

"Anytime now would be good, Butch," he urged.

"I'm doing my best," Butch replied.

"DO IT FASTER," he ordered, panic starting to tinge his voice.

He heard a thud as the final member of Armadillo Squad hit the deck, they all froze, not daring to breathe. The creature suddenly disappeared down beneath the surface of the water, missing the boat. He released the breath he had been holding and smiled. He started to turn to Butch, just in time to see a huge tail break through the waves behind him. It crashed back into the water, creating a huge swell that violently rocked them. As he was the only one standing, he was catapulted through the air before plunging into the murky depths. The last thing he saw was the boat careening away from him, pulled by the swell, before the suction pulled him underwater.

He started to fight for the surface. He was a strong swimmer, but that was indoors in a pool, not when buffeted by currents and waves. Suddenly, he felt ripped from his body and pulled up above, having another out-of-body experience.

"Not again," he groaned.

He watched, and saw himself break through the surface, frantically looking around for the boat. To the north, he saw Butch rallying and browbeating Armadillo Squad to take control of the oars so they could get to him. In a panic, he started looking around for the creature, his heart turning to ice as he saw it circling.

The creature was completing a lazy circle, ignoring the boat, on course for him as he fought to keep above the water. Faster than he'd have liked, the creature closed the gap. Butch wouldn't even get halfway back to him. At that moment, the beast broke the surface ... it was gigantic. Its eyes were milky-white and menacing.

His mind churned over the information, screaming at him that it was important … but he was distracted by the mouth full of razor-sharp teeth, which opened wide and crashed over him, taking him inside in one go.

The last thing he saw was Butch screaming in rage, before he was back in his own body and emerging through the waves. He looked around panicking, he was still alive.

"Another premonition," he gasped, as water filled his mouth.

"What?" Llýr asked.

"The creature is coming back for me. We have maybe thirty seconds," he looked around, trying to find an escape route.

"What does it look like?" Llýr asked.

"Huge teeth, white eyes, and hungry!" he snapped. "We need time."

At that point, he heard Aldela cry a warning call. He signalled and shouted to her and she flew down quickly, circling.

"It will break the surface twenty metres that way before it eats me, hit it as hard as you can with a firebolt, I need time to get in the boat."

Aldela didn't even question him, she cried acknowledgement, beating her wings hard as she raised above them, hovering as best she could and waiting.

"NOW!" he shouted.

Aldela let loose a bar of white-hot fire. He watched. It was perfectly timed thanks to the premonition. The bar of fire seared a line down the creature's head as it broke the surface, its squeal of pain hurting his ears. He called out with relief as the creature dived quickly beneath him, causing him to swallow some water, and making him splutter.

"Get back to the boat," Aldela called. "It will be back."

He needed no further encouragement. He turned in the water and swam as hard as he could towards the boat, he was almost there.

"It's blind!" Llýr shouted in realisation.

Surprised, he stopped … thinking, realising it made sense. The boat was the bigger target, yet it dived when the last of Armadillo were aboard, then turned its attention to him … who was making noise in the water. What to do now? The boat would make more noise against the tide, and be the tastier target, once it came back angrier than before. A large piece of Armadillo Squad's hull hit him in the shoulder, and he leaned on it to rest while he thought. The wood was about six-foot-long. He looked up to the sky for inspiration, and saw Dizzy alongside Aldela. Suddenly, an idea came to him, as he felt Butch's hand grab his top and pull him up into the boat.

He looked back and smiled. "Thank-you."

Then he signalled to Dizzy, who swooped down and landed beside him.

In the distance, they heard Aldela's call, and saw her send a bar of fire towards the immersed creature. She tried a further two times, then cawed in frustration.

"Aldela can't stop it this time, it's coming back but staying submerged," Dizzy advised.

He nodded; he had expected as much. They would never make it to shore without a distraction, and he leaned into Dizzy and outlined his plan. "Can you do it?"

Dizzy cocked her head, her eyes piercing him as if to say *what do you think,* as she sprung into the air.

She took a few turns, then swooped down over the boat,

303

where he was lifting the piece of debris he had rested on, high in the air. Dizzy grasped it in her claws and pulled away. He watched closely as she flew off in the other direction, noticing the wood slip slightly in her claws. His heart felt as though it briefly stopped and then started again as she caught it fully, she had just been adjusting it, and was now digging her claws deep into the wood.

He turned to the other occupants in the boat. "Do not move. Do not speak. Do not start moving to shore. If you do, we are all dead."

Butch stopped what he was doing, used to following instructions and trusting his Squad. Armadillo Squad were not as comfortable.

Timson, their Squad leader, started to ask a question, but was cut-off when his fighting staff extended with a snap.

"On second thoughts, don't even breathe, or you'll all become monster chow," he growled.

Butch grinned, watching the fear cross Timson's eyes, his question disappearing. Instead, he turned to watch the approaching monster.

Butch kept his eyes on Dizzy. She came in from the west, soaring gracefully out of the sky. She was on course to intercept the monster, the debris hanging low below her.

"Moment of truth," Llýr whispered.

He nodded. It took all his strength not to close his eyes. The plan was for Dizzy to dip the debris in the water in front of the monster, dragging it in a different direction, mimicking someone being in there. The hard part for Dizzy was making sure the wood didn't get pulled from her grasp as it hit the surface. He needn't have worried. She glided low, caressing the top of the waves with the tip slightly submerging without a problem, leaving a small wake behind. Dizzy cried her distinctive call, as if to say *I told you so,* while she continued to glide effortlessly above the water, the wood a reluctant passenger.

Butch and Armadillo Squad waited, silently. None of them sure what was happening, but each aware of the tension in him. He watched the tide instead of the beautiful eagle ... not sure what he was waiting for, but knowing that their lives were on the line.

Aldela flew a few circles then dropped low over the water, passing the side of the boat. "It has turned," she called to him as she passed.

He waited another thirty seconds, then turned to the others. "Quickly, pick up the oars and row as if your lives depend on it ... because they do."

Everyone grabbed a paddle, and at Butch's instruction ... they swiftly moved into a steady rhythm, and headed for the shore, where Eddie, Jenna, and Tia were waiting impatiently.

He stood at the back, watching Dizzy continue to lead the monster around. He felt the boat bump and looked around to see Eddie, Fence, and Dozer pulling the boat further into the shallows. He suddenly got a nauseous feeling, deep in his stomach, and immediately turned back to Dizzy.

"JENNA!" he shouted. "Bring Dizzy back. NOW."

He prayed to the River that Jenna followed his instruction without hesitation. His instincts were screaming that something was wrong, and his heart sank as a second monster rose out of the water in front of Dizzy. It was the same size as the first, she wouldn't have time to avoid it.

A second monster ... he knew it was different, because the scar Aldela had given the first one was not evident as it

305

crashed back into the water, leaving an empty sky behind it.

He turned to Jenna ... his heart in his mouth.

"She's back safely, Rico," she smiled at him.

Instantly, his legs gave way, and he sank to his knees on the boat.

* * *

"Butch!" Jenna shrieked as she watched him fall.

He left Armadillo Squad on the shore, where he'd been checking that they were OK, and jumped back into the boat, placing his hands upon Rico's chest.

"You alright, Buddy?" he asked calmly - his medical instincts taking control of his panic.

Rico looked at him a little vacantly. "You're the doctor," he slurred.

He laughed as he sagged back in the boat, his examination done.

"He's OK," he told Jenna, who had made her way through the water to the side of the boat. "Just a little exhausted," he finished. He looked at Rico, "That was some fine work out there. We would have been dead without you."

Armadillo Squad all nodded gratefully, not daring to speak in case they bore Rico's wrath.

"Let's not do that again. I don't like water monsters," Rico said, as his eyes closed and he dropped to the deck.

Jenna looked accusingly at him and he shrugged, but nonetheless, readied himself to move rapidly.

"What? He's exhausted, that's all. Did you see that thing? It was enormous."

"Yes, I saw it up close through Dizzy." Jenna scowled at

him as she asked Dozer to carry Rico to dry land.

Once they were on the beach, she turned back to him. "Butch, please recheck him."

He was about to argue that he didn't need too ... but at a look from Tia, he grinned and shook his head, kneeling next to Rico. He placed one hand on his chest, one on the side of his head, and then asked Traveller for help. Immediately, he could tell that Rico was fine; a few stretched muscles and his heart rate was a little fast.

"To be expected with what we've just been through," Traveller observed.

He let go and looked up at Jenna. "He's fine. As I said before ... he's just exhausted."

Having mollified Jenna, he made his way over to check on Armadillo Squad. They were sprawled on the floor, catching their breath.

* * *

Eddie walked over to Jenna and placed a hand on her shoulder, squeezing gently. She looked up at him and smiled ruefully, her eyes telling him he was far too perceptive at times.

"They're nearly here," Tia said, referring to the Red Squad that had been making their way from headquarters.

"Thank-you, Tia," he answered. "Right, Butch, if you're happy they're OK, let's pick up Rico and make our way to the finish line. We might have lost, but I intend to finish the test."

Butch stood, having finished with the last of Armadillo Squad.

Fence manifested and growled. "I'll take, Rico."

No one argued. Fence, although fearsome looking, was mild-mannered and rarely made demands. He gently picked up Rico and started moving towards the ford. Phoenix Squad joined him, instinctively falling into formation. They crossed the ford soon after and moved through quickly, nobody wanted to linger for long in the water.

They decided to stay out in the sun rather than go through the forest … skirting the tip to the south. They turned, and the Orange headquarters rose before them; flags and banners flying from various poles and windows.

They saw Raptor Squad a long way ahead, finishing a fight with a group of defenders. Once again, three Hands … all Red … waited for them.

Phoenix Squad moved into battle formation on his signal, Tia slotting into Rico's space as Fence dropped in behind.

Raptor Squad finished off their final test and sprinted for the finish line, just as Phoenix Squad closed with the first group.

He was about to give the signal to let their companions loose, when the Squads in front of them suddenly lowered their weapons and stood aside, inclining their heads in respect. All their companions were manifested, and they were being equally respectful.

He stopped the Squad and walked forward. The defence leaders simply nodded and directed Phoenix Squad through.

He smiled his thanks, and turned back to the Squad. "We go in with all our strength on show."

They all released their companions and walked together to the bridge. The Squad they had just passed fell in behind them and followed.

"What's going on?" Rico groaned, looking around in confusion.

"You passed out, you wuss," Butch grinned, receiving a punch in the arm from Tia.

Rico looked up at Fence who was carrying him. He seemed to be in no rush to put him down. "Thank-you, Fence. I think I will be all right to walk now, but please keep an eye on me."

Fence set Rico down gently, staying close, ready to catch him as he swayed on his feet, getting his balance.

"What did I miss?" Rico asked.

Jenna walked to his side. "Not much. We've lost. Raptor Squad is about to cross the bridge."

There was a muted applause from the large crowd at the bridge, with only a few pockets of cheers from supporters of Raptor Squad.

"Scratch that," Jenna continued. "Raptor Squad have crossed the bridge, but it looks like we have an honour guard all the way in."

Rico looked around. "Then let's not disappoint them," he said simply.

He pulled the whole Squad in for a hug, knowing this was the last time they would be together as a team.

Llýr appeared in the middle, twice his earlier size.

"The River works everything for a reason," he said matter-of-factly.

They all pulled away with tears in their eyes ... putting smiles on their faces, and moving out into fighting formation. He took the lead with Dozer, Jax, and Grey Claw forming a wedge in front of him. Rico was to his left, Rexter coiled around his arm, Misty on his left shoulder, and the now larger Llýr perched precariously on his right. To Rico's left was Butch, his skin tinged green and the head of Traveller appearing above him, Fence and Wiggy taking their usual places on the flank. Tia took a position to his right, with Kalina out on the flank. Utah and Phantom were up above, flying in formation with Aldela and Dizzy. Finally, Jenna took up position on the far-right with Dancer at her side.

"Let's go," he said, giving his final order. The Squad took off at a marching pace, which was just faster than a jog and aimed at eating-up the miles, but not the runner's energy. As they passed the final two groups of defenders ... they all stood aside, acknowledging Phoenix Squad, and then dropping in behind them.

As they approached the bridge, their guard slowed and formed a semi-circle. Aldela swooped down ... barely missing the heads of the Squad as she released a wall of fire. Phoenix Squad released their weapons as they ran through the flames, appearing on the bridge to be greeted by a wave of noise from the waiting crowd; gasps, cheers, laughter, and finally ... heartfelt applause.

* * *

The Lord Professor watched as Phoenix Squad approached the bridge, unmolested by the defenders. Everyone knew what they had sacrificed. If they hadn't decided to save Armadillo Squad ... they would have easily finished the test in first place; having their choice of Hands.

Angus was standing to his right with the victors: Raptor Squad, who he had already offered his congratulations to.

Angus barely contained his rage. Raptor Squad had come in first, and the crowd had barely acknowledged their victory.

He smiled inwardly. The people, although controlled in the main, were still a fickle beast, something Angus didn't really understand. They had experienced several emotions in the last hour, having seen from the viewing boards that something had happened to slow Phoenix Squad down. The scouts, who monitored the test, had reported that one of Raptor Squad's companions had sunk Armadillo Squad's boat. The information had caused considerable debate, with some questioning Phoenix Squad's decision to rescue Armadillo; it was only a bit of water, they would survive.

However, the release of the Elite Red Emergency Squads … who only went out when lives were in danger … had set tongues wagging. Speculation only increased once details on the monster in the lake came in a little later. The crowds' confusion and apathy towards Phoenix Squad had turned to anger at Raptor Squad … and admiration for the sacrifice that Phoenix Squad had made.

They now waited to celebrate the arrival of the losing team that had sacrificed their future to save the lives of their fellow students, as if they were the victors.

"Maybe we can use this to our advantage," Esther suggested.

He had no time to answer as he heard Aldela's cry of warning as she swooped down over Phoenix Squad, releasing a wall of flame across the entrance to the bridge. Moments later, Phoenix Squad burst through the flames, weapons ready, looking like one of the invincible fighting units of history.

It was an entry piece they had used in their first year for the final of the trials, but it had improved significantly. It was truly impressive. The Purples would have been proud of the show.

"You may not like Phoenix Squad, Angus, but you have to admit they've got style," he smiled.

Angus huffed. "Nothing but a party piece."

Angus was correct. It was. Phoenix Squad were showcasing themselves together for the last time, but that didn't matter.

"But the people love it, Angus," he replied.

"The people are sheep who do what they are told, when they are told," Angus answered, his anger clearly loosening his tongue.

He shook his head at the reply. Angus had always believed the people were there to follow, and to let their better's lead. He didn't understand that this view was a disease, eating at Selenta from the inside.

He looked over the crowd, it was clear that they had enjoyed Phoenix Squad's entrance. It created an image that would stay in the minds of every person here, children and adults alike. They were showing their appreciation as they gasped, hollered, hooted, cheered, and applauded. The noise was deafening, and the reception had taken Phoenix Squad by surprise. They hid it well, but he saw the momentary pause as the flames died down.

He saved them any embarrassment by stepping forward … their companions disappearing as they made their way towards him. Disappointment and exhaustion were clearly written on their faces, as he raised his hands to the crowd, asking for silence.

It took some time, but slowly the crowd quietened, and he silently asked Chirp to make sure everyone in the crowd could hear his words.

"Congratulations on successfully completing the test. Now, unfortunately, you have finished the test in second place, but your efforts and your sacrifice have not gone unappreciated."

At his words and his gesture, the crowd erupted again with cheers and shouts of support. He waited for the crowd to go quiet before he continued. "Armadillo Squad, their families, and friends, owe you all a great debt today. Without your sacrifice, they would have been killed by the creatures in the lake."

The crowd, once again, interrupting him with their applause.

"Thanks to your efforts, Selenta will benefit from the gifts the members of Armadillo Squad bring for many years to come." Raising his hands once more ... he presented Phoenix Squad again to the crowd. "The People's Champions!"

The crowd erupted. Covered by the noise, he took the opportunity to address Phoenix Squad. "Don't be disheartened. Go rest, and prepare for the celebrations. Enjoy your time together as many trials lie ahead."

Phoenix Squad waved to the crowd and made their way, as instructed, into the building for a well-earned rest as the celebrations began.

CHAPTER THIRTY-SIX

Drangor stood on the balcony overlooking the stark reception chamber, a fitting comparison to the city outside the castle walls. His mind was churning over the conversation that had happened nearly ten days ago with Magnar.

It had been somewhat surprising ... Magnar was keen to discuss the fighting techniques of Selenta, and pick his mind for ideas on tactics and methods of assault. He had shown a particular interest in how to use companions alongside soldiers in battle, cleverly manoeuvring the conversation to be more focused on ways to defend against it.

He had been a little cagey with his answers at first, thinking he was giving an advantage away to Magnar that he might use against Selenta. He decided to broach this concern directly. Magnar had eased his worries by explaining, with a dismissive remark, that his interest was to do with some minor trouble they were having on the southern front.

Since the meeting, he had done some digging himself, and found that it was anything but minor. Magnar's forces had suffered some heavy defeats in that area, which was a big reason for the dissent running through Carasayer.

That, added to the underlying unhappiness in Carasayer,

had been the real reason for the meeting with Magnar. It was why Magnar had treated him with such disdain at the end of their bout.

"I need you to flush out all the dissenters, Drangor. We are at a critical time here in Carasayer, with battles on all fronts. It is crucial to the success of our agreement with The Black, that these rebels are removed," Magnar had explained. He went on to detail that there was a lot of opposition to him negotiating with Selenta, that there were movements within Carasayer who would do anything to stop this happening. So much so, that one of the other Black soldiers had had his throat slit in the main city. Magnar had put this down to these *rebels*.

He had accepted this assignment from Magnar without argument, and gone about his business, selecting one of the castle guards to be his guide throughout the city. The one he had chosen had been the first to come to him in the arena, and was now standing to his right shoulder as they waited on Magnar. The guard's name was Marcus, and he was a handsome young soldier, bright-eyed, and huge, which proved useful in keeping unwanted attention away from him.

They had become good friends over a very short period, and he suspected that Marcus had more than a few rebellious leanings himself, plus a few useful contacts.

The doors to the reception area opened, and people started to file in. As they did, he felt Marcus stiffen beside him. Taking a closer look, his own blood began to run cold. Half of the people below, were people he had met in the last week.

Quickly, he signalled to Marcus to calm himself. There were two members of Magnar's Elite in the room, guarding the entrances, who would notice any movements they made.

"More likely guarding you," Tracker said.

He didn't need to let Tracker know he agreed.

The last week had been interesting, but altogether a little too easy. He was followed on his first visit to the city. Marcus had been calm throughout, so it had not raised any alarm bells with him. However, he had spotted two different followers; one better at concealing themselves than the other. The second visit, he'd only seen the one ... when they'd popped into a bakery to buy some food. During this stop, a well-dressed woman approached them and introduced herself as a friend. It had turned out that she was a member of a group of disenchanted citizens, and had heard about his conflict with Emperor Magnar ... she wanted to talk to him. Marcus had stood quietly at his side, keeping an eye on the door to the bakery. She had set a time and place to meet, and the next day he had made his way there, leaving Marcus at the castle.

He suspected Marcus had ties to the group, but he had come to like him and didn't want him to get into any trouble.

He had taken painstaking measures to ensure no one from the castle was following him as he met with the group. They were all very cautious at first, each wearing a hooded cowl, but he could tell they were amateurs.

To the trained eye, there was information everywhere ... a watch with a distinctive design, a crest on a trouser leg, a birthmark covering the back of a hand ... all features a spy could easily use to identify them after the meeting. Although, even that was unnecessary ... after they had questioned him for half an hour, they had thrown their cowls back and approached him, introducing themselves. They wanted to know more about Selenta, and his duel with the Emperor ... more precisely, what had he done that left Magnar with such disdain. They had given no thought at all to the possibility that this was precisely the thing Magnar had hoped would happen.

After spending a few hours with them, he realised they were harmless scholars. They were unhappy with the way Magnar ran Carasayer as a military state. Their view was that it was stifling advancement, the strong rewarded, and the clever diminished. But it was all talk. Most of them were younger, privileged, adult children of the more well-to-do and noble families of Carasayer, of which he had learned there were many.

They were no threat to Magnar in any way, they weren't organised and only spoke about what they would do differently, there was no talk of overthrowing Magnar. They were driven more by the excitement of meeting illegally like this, to discuss their Emperor and his errors, or be derogatory of those that pandered to his every need. Still, there wasn't talk of action or any intent to overthrow the regime. It wasn't any different to the conversations that likely took place in households all over Selenta ... where the discussions were in the security of their own home, and with their own family. In Selenta, this kind of meeting would be stamped-on quickly if known about, and the offenders placed on a work duty for an extended period, to remind them things could always be worse.

He had marked almost everyone in the room as no threat, but there was one that was different. The word *threat* was not a strong enough description ... a figure that kept to the shadows, his cowl draping his form. Every time he tried to get a good look at him, he seemed to blur and move deeper into the shadows. Although, the more he thought about it, he decided the shadows grew to hide him from view. He had internally labelled him a man, but there was no way to know for sure. After a few attempts, he had stopped trying. He didn't want to appear too interested. No one in the room referred to the shadow, and they had all avoided him as best as they could.

He had left after a few hours, and felt eyes on him all the way back to the castle. Later, Marcus had led him around Carasayer, taking him to areas of the city he was sure Magnar would rather he hadn't seen. The areas were run-down, the people in them beaten down, many with injuries that he could only have put down to battling. The *refuse of the Carasayer war machine* Marcus had called it. This had appalled him ... anyone who sustained injuries during a battle in Selenta was taken care of, given jobs within one of the Hands, or supported by their community.

Marcus had huffed at that. "You can't get many injuries then," he'd told him, and then would say no more. He had mulled over this and realised he was right. With the power of the White, the majority of people could be healed, even the field medics were able to treat most injuries. Only those too far gone with serious injuries or conditions were unable to be saved. Recalling the recent incident in The Forbidden where one soldier was slain, the two who had been injured were up and fully functional again within a few hours.

He had asked Marcus about healing in Carasayer, and was told that they used herbs as medicines, with only a handful of people able to heal their own wounds ... and in rare cases, others. This made sense and fit with what he'd already suspected. The healing bath after his bout with Magnar, and the fact that Magnar never once asked him about healing in Selenta … they knew nothing of the White. It needed to stay that way for now. Once he swapped back over with the Carasayer Captain, Magnar would learn everything.

"We need to silence the other Black soldiers here in Carasayer," Twister advised.

Drangor nodded. "I think there is someone else with the same agenda, Twister."

He was brought back to the present as the doors to the reception area opened. The crowd below ushered into the audience chamber. At the same time, he and Marcus were shown through a door onto another balcony, one that opened onto a much more impressive room. The Elite guard closed the door behind them, leaving them alone.

"They cannot see or hear us from below," Marcus advised.

He moved to the edge and waved at a few people below who were looking up, none responded, even though he could see them clearly.

"What's happening, Major?" Marcus asked, concern and fear dancing in his eyes.

He put his fingers to his lips and motioned around, making it clear to Marcus that although they were alone, there could be listeners all around.

"It appears that Emperor Magnar has something he wishes me to see, so that I can report back to The Black," he said, as he turned back to the room.

There was a large chair that sat alone on the far side of the chamber, it was the only seat in the room, and he surmised it was Magnar's. He was quietly impressed, the chair wasn't huge and imposing, but it caught the eye, and it likely put people more on edge. It was a message … "The man who sits here does not need a throne to show who is in charge, he is enough on his own." He pulled his attention away and looked around the rest of the room. His trained eyes taking in the observation areas above, and the slits in the walls that allowed someone to fire a bolt into the room. The vast tapestries that adorned the walls, depicting battles he did not know or understand, were moving very slightly, covering secret passages he assumed. After assessing the risks in the room … he turned his eyes to the people who had an audience with their Emperor.

There were pockets of groups chatting together in quiet tones, gawking at the tapestries, and casting what they felt were hidden glances to the throne. He observed three groups of the people he had met with, and they all looked nervous and agitated.

"They give themselves away," Tracker observed.

He nodded, scowling as he watched them all exchanging glances with each other. He looked at the others in the room, they all looked less concerned. Many looked bored, like they had been here before, and would be again. A few had taken out books and were reading, and a number had pens out, writing down thoughts. The one similarity with them all … they looked wealthy. Their clothes were perfectly tailored, and their faces suggested they were well fed.

"Who are the people below?" he asked Marcus.

Marcus stepped forward. "Mainly traders and nobles. That one there is Dorbin Murphy, he's a trader who supplies food for the military. The one next to him is Gregor Tanic, he owns most of the farmland to the north, and is Dorbin's main food supplier …" Marcus went on, describing each person in the room. As he expected, they were all influential and wealthy people within Carasayer. Any one of them could pose a significant threat to Magnar if they decided he no longer served their own agenda, which was likely to stay wealthy.

"I have an awful feeling about this," Twister purred.

He agreed, continuing to let his eyes roam the room. He caught upon two figures that he had missed previously, although missed was unlikely, as no one could miss them, they had probably entered silently from one of the passageways. One was a stunningly beautiful woman, with long dark hair and green eyes. She moved gracefully between the groups, saying a word here, giving a gesture there, and she was dressed simply, yet elegantly, moving with the grace of a Purple. Every movement was purposeful and measured, reminding him of a cobra. The other was young and well-built, he walked with an arrogance borne of privilege. He wore the uniform of the Elite, but there were no signs of rank. It was clear he was not an Elite soldier, that was obvious from the scornful looks the Elite guards around the room gave him as he passed.

This intrigued him, as in his short time in Carasayer, if anything annoyed the Elite, they were not slow in making their displeasure known. Added to this … no one else in the room addressed them, nor looked their way. But the moment they initiated a conversation, people were effusive in their attention … indicating extreme power or fear, maybe both.

"Who are those two?" he asked Marcus.

Marcus looked where he had pointed and paused, taking a gulp.

"Fear then," Tracker said.

Marcus took a moment to compose himself. "That is Elena, the Emperor's consort. It's rumoured that the Emperor denies her nothing, men have disappeared for even looking at her," Marcus explained.

"And the man?" he asked.

"That's Elgrin, her brother. He's a drunk and a waster, strutting around as if he owns the place," Marcus described with obvious disdain. "No one will touch him though, as Elena dotes on him, they don't want to risk the displeasure of the Emperor by angering her," Marcus finished.

"Hmm," he grunted in reply as he watched them mingle.

"What are you thinking, Drangor?" Tracker asked in his mind.

"I'm not sure, Tracker. Something doesn't feel quite right about him." Then aloud to Marcus he said, "Where are they from? Their skin colour is different from everyone else's."

Marcus looked at him with admiration in his eyes. "I can't believe you noticed that from up here," he said, shaking his head as he continued, "They are from Tendrin. It's a country at the northernmost lands that Carasayer controls. We were at war with them for over a decade. No matter what we did, we couldn't take over, they're fierce fighters. It was only after Magnar came to power that they came to the negotiating table."

He nodded. "I assume part of the agreement for them joining you was an autonomous Government, only answerable to Magnar ... and a marriage for the Emperor?"

Marcus laughed, shaking his head. "Yes and no. They wanted autonomy to govern, but they also wanted their soldiers to integrate into the Carasayer army. The marriage was not on the table."

He could imagine how that conversation went, and it was not too dissimilar to the agreement The Black was negotiating.

"I sense a story there," he said, seeing that Marcus wanted to tell him something.

Marcus grinned like a child and moved closer, lowering his voice. "It's all hearsay, only the Elite and Magnar know the true story. The tale goes that Magnar was happy to let them have the autonomy, but wouldn't allow them into his army. The Tendrins were furious, and Magnar laughed at them and rose to walk out of the negotiations." Marcus paused dramatically, letting the severity of the scenario filter through.

He indulged him. "That can't have been ideal. It would have just meant a continuance of a costly war."

Marcus grinned. "Exactly, but Magnar didn't care, he had plenty of soldiers, even though we were losing five to their one. If the war continued, the Tendrins would eventually have had to surrender, as their population wasn't big enough to sustain the war for much longer. Magnar coming to power had given them an opportunity that their pride wouldn't have allowed under the previous Emperor."

He nodded at Marcus to continue.

"So, as Magnar stood to leave, no one rose to stop him. As he made his way to the door, Elena blocked his path and challenged him to a duel. If she won, he returned to the table and continued negotiations, agreeing to consider the integration. Now, it's important to note, that women aren't allowed in the Carasayer military, but the Tendrin women, they account for a large portion of their fighting force. Magnar accepted the duel, and told her to choose the weapons. Elena did so quickly, as soon as the words passed his lips she pounced, the blade suddenly appearing in her hand."

He huffed. "I bet the Elite didn't like that."

Marcus laughed. "No, but no one had time to react. No one, that is, except Magnar. He had been waiting for it, having fought Tendrin women before. He knew they were deadly and viper quick, but even he was surprised at how quick she was. He only just managed to evade the attack and disarm her on the way through, pulling her own blade to her throat. She mocked him and told him that he was slower than she had thought, and Magnar had found that amusing due to their position." Marcus paused dramatically.

He chuckled, he had an idea of how this tale ended.

"But all was not as it seemed," Marcus finally continued. "She raised her left hand and her fingers were wet with his blood. On the way through, she had scored a cut across his chest. Motioning with her eyes, Magnar saw her right hand had another blade pushed up against his stomach. Magnar was besotted with her from that moment. He released Elena immediately, agreeing that select Tendrin's could work within his border forces, but not the Elite or castle guards. All under one condition … that Elena returned to the Capital with him." Marcus paused for breath. "It turned out she was the daughter of the Chief's brother, and it was commonplace for the Tendrins to utilise women in their negotiations. After this, they resolved things quickly, and Elena returned to Carasayer with Magnar." Marcus took a moment, his eyes looking down into the chamber and finding Elena. Then almost distractedly, he finished his tale. "The story after that is sparse, but it's said they visited many of the other border dispute areas, and fought side-by-side as their love blossomed. Now, Elena does what she wants, when she wants, and is not to be messed with."

He stepped up beside Marcus, watching her move through the crowd below. "Definitely deadly then," he said to his companions.

There was a commotion below, as Magnar prowled into the room with Cassius walking by his side, looking huge and majestic. His face was a blank mask, showing no emotion other than when his gaze fell upon Elena. He saw first-hand that there was some truth to Marcus's story in Magnar's eyes, as they sparkled and brightened at the sight of her.

As Magnar took his seat, Elena slipped out of the crowd and approached him, her hand moving out and running across the left side of his chest, before she slid behind him and took a place to his left.

He quickly cast his eyes around the room again, and noticed the Elite had slipped in, taking up positions around the hall. The occupants hadn't even noticed … their eyes were on their Emperor. Elgrin was lounging against the wall, looking bored.

"Good afternoon all. Something has come to my attention that I feel needs to be addressed quickly," Magnar started. There was no *thank-you for coming* … he got straight to the point.

He sighed, Magnar was about to make a big mistake.

"This is bad, very bad," Tracker said.

* * *

Magnar schooled his face as Elena ran her hand across his

325

chest. It was always the same when she greeted him. To outside observers, it would appear to be an affectionate caress - which it was - but it was also a reminder that he should never underestimate her, as her fingers touched the spot where her dagger had cut him when they first met.

He wanted to ignore everyone in the room, to discover everything that she had learned while they'd been apart, and discuss their next course of action on the southern border. That situation was becoming extremely costly, and there were murmurs from the traders that they couldn't keep up with the supply demands. Most of them were grumbling about the risk of losses they were facing going to the front. This was the reason they were here today, he had to get them back into line. He needed those supplies to be consistent if he was to tip the scales.

"So, let's get your mind back on the task," Tink instructed.

He nodded internally, acknowledging Tink. "Good afternoon all. Something has come to my attention that I feel needs to be addressed quickly," he said calmly, pleased to see those in attendance jump at the sound of his voice.

He looked around the room. Only a few were brave enough to look him in the eye. He knew each person in this room had a view on his rule, with opinions on what they felt he could do better. There were even a few that thought they could do a better job, but didn't have the power base, or support of any military elements to make a move. Now, if he was to be killed, there would be a power vacuum that would plunge Carasayer into civil war. He suspected that two in this room could rise to his position, that is if none of his Generals took a liking to the idea. But today was not about their challenges, it was about sending a strong message that he was in charge

… and they had better do as he asked.

"So, before I explain what has come to my attention, I am giving you all the opportunity to come forward and explain your actions." He paused, lending to the image of a magnanimous leader, giving those in the room the chance to come forth and confess. He didn't expect anyone to step forward. No one here would give away information until they knew what he knew first, but quite a few looked uncomfortable. Sweat was appearing on foreheads, and surreptitious glances were being cast about. "OK, but no one can say I didn't give you the opportunity," he sighed, idly running his hand through Cassius's mane. "It's come to my attention … that a number of you have been meeting in secret, plotting against me."

This did elicit a reaction from those present. His supporters growled in outrage, looking around for someone to attack. Others subconsciously took a step back away from him. There were also several people looking around lazily, confident in their own innocence in this regard.

Suddenly, someone broke out of the crowd, moving towards him. "Emperor, have mercy they ma …"

Before any of the Elite could move, or Cassius could issue a warning growl … a whip flashed out from behind Magnar. It was quick as lightning, wrapping itself around the throat of the unfortunate creature, pulling taut, and dragging him to his knees. Elena strolled past him, releasing a knife, and caressing it along the cheek of the individual.

"I knew she had it all in hand," Cassius grumbled.

In his mind, he laughed. "Of course, you did, My Friend."

He watched as Elena leaned her mouth down to her prisoner's ear. He stopped clawing at his throat and fear flooded his eyes as she whispered, her knife sliding into his back, piercing his heart, and killing him instantly. At her urging, her whip released his throat, and his lifeless body flopped to the floor. Leaving her dagger, she casually walked back to her position behind Magnar.

"Does anyone else have anything to say?" he asked.

Whether in shock at watching a friend killed in front of them, or the sheer nonchalance of the way Elena dispatched him, he wasn't sure, but every eye in the room was on the dagger in the back of the victim. Even those who had nothing to fear and supported him looked to be in shock.

He signalled to the Elite, who moved quickly into the crowd, each slipping behind a target.

"This is how I deal with traitors," he said, as calmly as he would when ordering his breakfast.

At the dismissive wave of his hand, the Elite slit the throats of their targets. Lifeless bodies dropped to the floor. The Elite soldiers cleaned their blades and returned to their posts. The rest of the audience turned their eyes back to him, trying unsuccessfully to ignore the carnage. Horror filled many, but there were more than one with grim satisfaction in their eyes.

He turned his attention to Dorbin Murphy and Gregor Tanic, the dead already forgotten. "Are we on schedule for delivery to the southern front?"

Both Murphy and Tanic looked briefly at each other, then Murphy took in a gulp of air … grimacing … there was no doubt that the metallic stench of blood was filling his nostrils.

"We are a little behind, My Lord, but it is nothing we cannot make up for with a little effort."

He smiled and nodded. "Excellent news. I will provide you

with an extra contingent of soldiers to protect the shipment, and ensure it arrives on time, unscathed and fully laden."

If possible, both the businessmen paled even further, glancing nervously around, checking that the Elite hadn't moved. The last few shipments they had sent were light. Bandits and enemy scouts took the blame, but he suspected Murphy and Tanic were skimming the load, making more money by selling the extra to other domains within Carasayer. He had no issue with this, it was an unvoiced rule, that so long as it didn't hinder his plans, he would overlook such minor transgressions. This was a message, mainly directed at Murphy and Tanic, to let them know that now it was impacting his plans and had to stop. Still, it was for all the traders in the room, he needed all the supplies to make it to the southern front if he was to find a way to handle that situation.

"A-a-any help will be greatly appreciated," Tanic stammered.

"Excellent," he replied. "Speak to the Captain on the way out, and he will give you details of the men who will go with you." He paused momentarily. "Now, does anyone have any questions or issues with their own deliveries?"

There was a round of head shakes in the room.

"Then I will bid you all good day," he said, as he rose and walked away, calmly. Elena smiled at the crowd before taking her place behind him.

* * *

As Drangor watched Magnar leave the room, his fists and body relaxed slightly, his rage was boiling beneath the surface.

Until Magnar had gone from sight, he had not realised how much he had shown on the surface. He looked back over the dead, they were just naive children, maybe not in age, but in their outlook on life. The Black would have simply split them up, sending them to work in the fields on the far ends of Selenta, or shackled them in irons and sent them to the mines if he felt they were a real threat. These children were not a real threat, even if left to their own devices.

He heard a door open to his right, and one of Magnar's Elite guards stepped into the room and beckoned him to follow. He took one final look at the room below to stoke his rage, and then followed the guard. Marcus made to follow, but was intercepted by the guard and sent back the way they had come. For a moment, he thought Marcus was going to argue.

"He's in shock," Tracker said in his mind.

He quickly caught Marcus's eyes and motioned for him to leave.

"Thank the River," Twister whispered, as Marcus acknowledged the instruction and left the room.

The guard moved as if to follow Marcus, having noticed his reluctance to follow his order.

"Is Emperor Magnar waiting for me?" he hissed.

The guard seemed to come out of a trance and nodded at him, almost thankfully, then led him through the secret door and down the stairs. They quickly arrived at what looked to be a reception room. There was a table set up in the corner with food and drink, and comfortable-looking chairs set out in groups of four around the room. The room was empty when he arrived with the guard, who instructed him to wait here before closing the door.

He looked around, trying to find something to focus his mind on. Eating was out of the question … his stomach was in turmoil.

"What do we do next?" Twister asked.

"That really depends on what Lord Magnar wants from us," he replied acidly.

As if on cue, the door to the reception room flung open, and Magnar swept into the room, deep in conversation with General Matrix, Elena not far behind. If anything, up close, she looked even more deadly. He had no doubt that she was beautiful, and could understand why someone with the power of Magnar would be captivated by her. Still, she made him want to hide, rather than chase her.

Magnar dismissed General Matrix, who quickly left, taking the other Elite guards with him, leaving him alone with Magnar and Elena.

Magnar turned to him, and motioned to a chair. "Sit, Major. We have a lot to talk about, and I'm sure you have questions."

He sat as instructed, while Magnar took a seat in front of him and lounged back. Elena passed a drink to Magnar as she slipped into the seat beside him, crossing her legs provocatively, and trying to gauge his reaction. He never took his eyes of Magnar, not even for a second, only Tracker caught the flash of rage in her eyes.

"Ask your question, Major."

He considered raging and shouting, but he knew that would likely earn him his death. "Why?" was all he simply asked.

It was Elena who answered, staring at him with venom. "Why? You ask!" she spat, her anger showing her true visage. "How dare you challenge the Emperor's decision; they were filthy traitors, they got off lightly."

Magnar smiled slightly as he watched for his reaction. He simply nodded in understanding; he had dealt with many vicious people in his time.

It didn't help when Twister purred, "Someone needs to put this Forbidden in a cage."

He was relieved from having to comment by Magnar interrupting. "Elena, Drangor has asked a legitimate question. What transpired today has made the job I asked him to complete near to impossible."

He didn't react. He knew Magnar would finish, but he felt his temper boiling, and called on Faith to help him find a calm space. He must have given away something.

"That is right, Major. I knew about this small group, and have done so for some time. They're basically harmless and useless to me, but their deaths will benefit Carasayer."

He considered, running the scenarios through his head as Magnar continued. "I am impressed, however, at how quickly you infiltrated that group. It took months for my operatives to meet them all and gain their trust. For you to achieve this in less than a week was truly impressive, don't you agree, Elena?"

Elena huffed and leaned back in her seat with her drink, watching him closely. He imagined this was how the rabbit felt before the fox pounced.

Then, Magnar's visage turned cold and hard. "So, why did you not inform me of these traitors?"

A smirk came from Elena, and everything dropped into place … Magnar was paranoid. There were obviously other motives for the deaths, but he suddenly felt he was pivoting on a knife's edge; one false move, and he was dead. He remembered how quickly Elena had reacted, and how easily the dagger had slid into her victim. He had fought Magnar … without a weapon he was outmatched, and even with one … he was simply staring at a slower death.

He looked Magnar straight in the eye, and hoped the fear that gripped him, did not betray his tongue. "They weren't the real threat. I needed them, and assumed I was under surveillance. Until I uncovered the whole situation, I would not risk exposure. They were my eventual introduction to the Shadow Dancer."

He was pleased to see confusion cross both Elena and Magnar's faces, as their body language changed, moving from coiled menace to open interest.

"Shadow Dancer?" Magnar asked, intrigued.

With the mood changing, he felt his heart rate drop. He wanted to shout, "The real threat, that I will never likely get to meet because of your idiotic attempt at control!" But instead, with a calm he didn't feel, he said, "When I met the dissidents, there was another person in the room who never introduced themselves, or even spoke. Nobody even addressed it, and every time I tried to get a look, it melted into the shadows. I called it Shadow Dancer."

Elena rose and quickly left the room.

Magnar leaned forward. "Tell me about this Shadow Dancer. What was it wearing? What did it look like? How did it move?"

He closed his eyes, rebuilding the room in his mind, as his training in the Black kicked in. "*It,* is as good a description as I can find. I can't even say if it was male or female. The figure appeared hunched, and moved slowly but deliberately, disguising their movements, and not giving me any clue that

I could use to recognise them later. They wore a generic dark woollen robe which was bulky, that covered every part of their body, and again, I think that was deliberate."

Enthralled, Magnar sat and listened avidly, as he described every observation, even asking some astute questions to clarify his understanding. He watched Magnar's mind tick over as he explained how the shadows seemed to move with them, disguising their movements further. He had just exhausted all of his observations, when Elena walked back into the room. She gave an almost imperceptible shake of her head to Magnar's unasked question. Magnar motioned for her to sit back down, and instructed him to describe the Shadow Dancer again from the beginning.

Elena appeared a little disconcerted with the information. When he finished for the second time, both Magnar and Elena sat back considering everything they had just heard. While he waited, he rose and poured himself a drink, both Elena and Magnar absently refused one as they mulled over the new information.

He sat back down, considering his next steps carefully, finally deciding to push his luck. "You didn't know about the Shadow Dancer, did you?"

Elena glanced to Magnar, who nodded. "No, Major, we didn't." Her tone was now more conciliatory, she seemed like a different woman, all business, but still very capable. "We learned about these young dissidents months ago, after one of our supporters was approached to join their group. Although they were traitors, they could cause no harm now that we knew about them, but we kept a close eye, ready to use them when we wanted to send a message."

He suddenly understood. "You used me to protect your

own asset," he stated simply. He was mildly impressed, though angry. It was something The Black would have done.

"Exactly," Elena said.

He was beginning to see that there was a reason people feared her; she was deadly and extremely intelligent. He surmised that she was much more than just Magnar's consort.

"But we did not know about the Shadow Dancer," Magnar added.

Elena nodded. "Our asset, and none of our observers, have seen this figure you describe." She paused, letting it sink in. "But that is not to say we don't believe you," she added quickly. "It just means that this Shadow Dancer is better than those we sent to watch the dissidents."

He nodded. "I assume they aren't your best operatives, with them being such a minor threat?"

A slight inclination of Elena's head was all the confirmation he needed.

He continued, "Unfortunately, it will now go underground. I will have lost any tenuous trust I may have earned."

Both Magnar and Elena nodded agreement, looking disturbed.

It prompted him to ask a further question. "Is there something I need to know about the Shadow Dancer?"

Magnar sat back, and it was Elena who answered. "We have never come across anyone as you describe. Although, it does bear a slight resemblance to a report that we had from the southern front, of an attack that came out of the shadows, where they were positive there was no one before."

Magnar rose quietly, and walked to the food table.

"There are attacks off in the south that are surgical, hitting fast, and always deadly. The only report came from a raw recruit, who had knocked himself unconscious on a branch. We think the attackers thought he was already dead," Elena finished.

"The question we have now is … what do we do next?" Magnar said, as he flopped back down in the chair, popping a piece of fruit into his mouth.

He thought about Magnar's question before suggesting, "How about we use the same ruse we did before?"

Magnar raised an eyebrow, inviting him to continue.

"I storm out of here, ranting about being used. I will rant and rave to anyone who will listen about the barbarity of the killings. Then you have me ordered out of the castle, sending me to the borders of your lands."

Elena nodded. "I like the idea. We can say publicly that you are fact-finding for your Black, but it will be viewed as Magnar banishing you from the castle, not wanting to simply kill you and harm the deal he is negotiating."

He nodded in agreement. Elena was again showing her intelligence. He added, "I only take one guard. It will further show you don't care if I return alive."

Magnar remained quiet as he considered his options. He could imagine him chatting it through with his companions.

"You will have to head north, then circle the borders to the east, working your way south. Otherwise, it will seem too obvious," Magnar finally said.

"I think I will hear from them long before I reach the southern border," he replied as he rose, nodding respectfully to them both. "Now, My Lord and Lady, I will be on my way. I hope your Elite don't take it upon themselves to make this whole plan irrelevant."

He made his way to the door, and took a deep breath. Upon

opening it, he started muttering and ranting as he went. He didn't have to fake his ire, he only needed to imagine those children's lives being expelled for his anger to return. He just hoped an Elite did not take offence to his mutterings about the Emperor and slide a blade between his ribs.

He had work to do.

* * *

"Do you trust him?" she asked as she crawled onto Magnar's lap.

"I don't trust anyone but you, My Love," Magnar replied. "But I do trust his loyalty to The Black. If the Major feels he is following The Black's wishes by supporting me, he will help where he can." Magnar ran his hand along her leg absently. "As long as he is in the dark for my true plans, I will let him live."

She smiled wickedly, leaning in, and kissing Magnar hard.

CHAPTER THIRTY-SEVEN

"I should go out and check, Swift, it's too quiet," Nala said.

Swift shook her head in disappointment. "What would that achieve, Nala?"

He didn't answer. Instead, he pushed his nose out from his hiding place and took in a deep breath, straining his hearing … but nothing came to him. He wasn't surprised, it felt like he had tried a hundred times, the result had been the same every time. In a way, it was comforting, this was why they had chosen this place for an ambush. It was perfect. The trees and the ground had a way of deadening sound and smell, nothing lived here but the plant life, which thrived … creating a kind of dead zone.

The human in him was intrigued and wanted to investigate why, but the wolf and River Runner in him simply saw it as a tool to achieve their goal. Once he and Gervais had safely seen the River Runners to the alpha site, they had asked for volunteers to join him on a hunt. He had been surprised at how many had wanted to get involved and follow him, but he had relied on Gervais to pick the right Runner's while he focussed on planning to succeed. He was pleased to say, Gervais had been spot-on with his selection.

There were seven Runners assigned to the task; Midnight, a jet-black panther; Dex, the fox who had lured him into the trap the Runners had first set for him; Reg, a black bear; Anita, a coyote; and finally, the Codin brothers ... Ben, Joe, and Fred, all capuchin monkeys. He had been confused at first and confronted Gervais privately. The brothers were a high-spirited threesome, always up to some sort of mischief, and causing general chaos. Gervais understood his concern, yet was clear that they would be a tremendous asset. He had learned the truth of this quickly in the field, they were as deadly as they came.

He was pulled from his thoughts by a loud hoot. It was difficult to place where the noise had come from in the dead zone, but it wasn't any of his team and nothing else lived here, so it had to be the Death Dealers.

They had stumbled onto his team in the middle of the night ... and thanks to prior planning ... his team had scattered, retreating as agreed upon should they come under attack from a larger force. This pack of hyenas was a significantly bigger force, and had caught them unprepared.

It wasn't that he was afraid of a fight, but the River Runners numbers were limited. In contrast, the Death Dealers seemed to have an inexhaustible supply of fodder. He and his team had been hunting them for over a week now. They had eliminated seven of Zagane's patrols, who were out searching for the River Runners' camp. He was thankful that he hadn't lost any of his team during those encounters, but felt it was more than likely down to the quality of their enemies that they had barely received a scratch. He assumed Zagane would keep his best fighters closest to him, and viewed the patrols as expendable, purely there to tempt out the Runners.

He had tried to spread out the attacks as best as possible, so Zagane couldn't focus his troops in any one location, but this meant that his team were always on the move. After a week, they were all tired. They had decided to rest … which was when the hyenas had stumbled onto them by accident in the night. They were just as surprised as the Runners, which explained why they had been able to slip away so easily.

However, they had organised themselves quickly, communicating with another patrol, and were soon on their trail. Thankfully, Anita had highlighted the dead zone earlier to the team, and they had agreed on this area as a fallback.

A small form dropped down beside his head, making him jump. "What's wrong, Boss, lost your sense of smell?" Joe giggled at his own joke.

He growled lightly at him.

"Relax, Boss, the Codin's got your back," Joe said, reaching out and patting him.

He resisted the urge to snap his little hand off. "What's happening?" he asked.

Joe grinned, showing his fangs, suddenly all business. "Ten hyenas are here, and they have a group of four leopards with them. They move with purpose, looking very organised. The hoot you heard was an owl that's with them, working as their scout."

He nodded. "Any view on a plan of attack?" he asked, conscious the Runners had been on the move for over a week and were severely outnumbered.

If it hadn't been for the leopards, he would have just attacked the hyenas. Once you took out two or three, they would back off, they tended not to attack unless they had strong odds of victory. Leopards were rumoured to be

Zagane's Elite guards, akin to those Gervais had killed at the River Runners home.

He watched as Joe scratched his chin, thinking; a very human action that looked amusing on the small monkey.

"The problem is the leopards," Joe mused, echoing his thoughts. "We can take out three, but if they're fast, they will dart into the hyenas and the fight. Which, by the way, you will have to initiate for us to get close."

He mulled this over. Joe was right, if they acted true to form, Zagane's guard would let the hyenas serve as fodder, get them to wear down the Runners, and hit them once they were tired and depleted. Joe's plan was a good one, but it still meant Nala and the others would have to take out ten hyenas and a leopard.

"If I get the leopard out of the huddle, can you take a shot?" Nala asked.

Joe simply looked at him. "Yes, but it will take me time to reload and get into a better position."

He made his mind up quickly. "Let the others know to converge on me. I want us to dictate the timing, let them think they have flushed us out. You and your brothers set yourselves up a few minutes to the west, just before the clearing. I'll howl when we are in position."

Joe didn't answer, he just scampered up through the bushes and into the trees.

* * *

The owl landed on a tree and looked around; she was getting frustrated. Usually, she had a good sense of the environment around her, able to hear the heartbeat of tiny animals in the

341

undergrowth and see their body heat. Here, she was stuck to regular sight, it was so limited. She looked around, seeing nothing out of the ordinary, and let out a long hoot to let the pack know it was safe to progress.

She was about to spring from the branch when something moved. It was only a slight movement of a leaf on a bush, but there was no wind, and there were no natural animals in here. She waited, concentrating on the spot, willing her sight to find something, and straining her hearing. The pack were closing in, making it hard to get a beat on the slight noise she could hear. It sounded like a hushed, urgent conversation, but she couldn't make out any words.

Suddenly, a coyote burst out of the bush she had been staring at.

"Nooo!" a terrified shout came, as a huge wolf with a white scar on its flank rose out of the undergrowth.

"Everyone move. Now!" the wolf howled, and three other creatures rose from their hiding places; a black bear, a panther, and a fox. They all took off after the coyote.

The owl recognised the fox as one of the River Runners scouts. If he had been the one who had broken from cover, she would have been more cautious in her next action, as he was always the decoy. Instead, she raised her head and screeched, letting the pack know they were on the run.

A muted roar came from the leopards, acknowledging her message, followed by the crazed laughing of the hyenas as they took up the chase.

She waited until they arrived below and then shouted. "They are headed west, one of them panicked and broke cover."

The leopards nodded and sent the hyenas ahead of them,

as they spread out and dropped in a few steps behind.

"Scout ahead, make sure there is no ambush and screech if there is."

The owl bounded from her branch and took flight. She followed the retreating River Runners at a safe distance, ensuring they didn't stop or look to set an ambush. They did neither, leaving her confident that they were running scared.

The coyote was still out in the lead, breaking out into the sunlight with the others closing behind. She spotted a branch near the edge of the clearing and landed lightly, feeling her full abilities come back as the coyote stumbled, its leg falling into a fox hole it hadn't seen. The rest stopped to help the coyote up, but it was injured, holding its leg limply.

The owl cast her eyes over the area, looking for signs of heat that might indicate this was an ambush, but there was nothing around except the five in front. The large wolf was moving back and forth, nervously looking from the clearing back to the coyote.

"Reg, pick her up, we need to move," the wolf instructed, his words clear to the owl.

The bear moved to pick up the coyote as the hyena pack burst out of the tree line into the clearing. They stopped halfway to the Runners, yapping and laughing their call, waiting for the leopards' instructions. The leopards stopped below the owl.

"Anything to report?" the same leopard who had spoken to her earlier asked.

"Nothing out there except fox holes," the owl hooted in delight.

The leopard didn't respond, just wandered out into the sunlight, the other three behind him. He slipped through a hole in the ranks of the hyenas to address the wolf, leaving the three other leopards behind the hyenas.

The owl knew that he would offer them a quick death if they gave up the base camp of the Runners, or a painful death if not. She settled down to enjoy the carnage. Hearing a slight noise above, she lazily looked up. The last thing she saw was a grinning capuchin monkey falling on her, slipping a needle-sharp blade through her eye and into her brain ... killing her instantly, while pinning her to the tree.

"Shame you're going to miss the party," the monkey grinned, while reaching into a pack on his back, removing a blowpipe, and loading it with a dart.

* * *

Nala grinned. Now that they were outside the dead zone, his senses had flooded back. He had seen Ben clinically dispatch the Death Dealers owl scout, while watching the Codin brothers take their positions in the trees.

"That's a tempting offer," he replied, he hadn't really been listening to the leopard, who had said something about pain and quick. He had been more focused on assessing the enemy.

Anita had played her part beautifully. Dex was too well known as a distraction, so they had to come up with a plan that meant the scout was deceived ... a panicked coyote worked perfectly. It was pure luck that the owl had landed directly beneath Ben.

The hyenas looked confident, but they were a weak link that was easy to break. They were immensely strong, but slow and weak-willed. However, the leopards were quite the opposite, looking sleek, deadly, and mean.

The leopard looked at him, waiting for a further response. He just returned his stare, gazing at him blankly, he wasn't to know that the Codin brothers were about to fire their darts.

"I'm going to enjoy killing you slowly," the leopard growled, turning away to walk back to the hyenas. As he turned, he heard the Codin brothers release their darts. The leopard saw them as he turned too, and started to shout a warning, but it was too late.

The darts hit all three of the leopards perfectly. The poison that coated them worked its deadly magic quickly, and his senses allowed him to see the legs of those struck, buckling.

"We need to find a way to combat these attacks," Swift observed.

"But not today," he replied. Then aloud to the Runners, he shouted, "Attack!"

Reg released Anita, and the five Runners advanced swiftly on the Death Dealers. He wanted to be on them before they could organise themselves.

He headed towards the lead leopard, who had darted behind the two hyenas that were now confronting him. He was not surprised or taken unaware ... they had been preparing to attack.

He darted in, aiming a bite at the first hyena's throat. He just missed. The hyena was lucky to avoid the snap of his jaws.

Jumping back quickly, he glanced around. Everything had moved at a rapid pace ... the Codin brothers were racing across the field, trying to find a safe route through to join the fight. Dex and Anita were working together against three of the hyenas. Reg was also up against three, but Nala grinned, that was not a fair match for them. He watched as Reg backhanded one of the hyenas that got too close, knocking it through the air; it landed with a thud and didn't move. Midnight was off to the left, stalking around with a wicked grin on her face, as two hyenas tried to circle her.

He smiled as he turned back to his opponents. They weren't attacking, but holding their ground. He felt a touch of panic from Swift and took a deep breath, his mind suddenly filling with the bigger picture. The leopard had moved out of sight. His senses watched it circle quickly and quietly around behind Midnight, she had not seen him move, her focus was on the hyenas. The Codin brothers were too close to the hyena that had been felled by Reg, and as it stirred, it reached out a huge paw and hit Ben hard, sending him flying. He landed and didn't move, and screeches of distress from Joe and Fred followed.

He turned back to Midnight and watched helplessly as the leopard swept in and dragged his claws down her side. Midnight cried out in pain, and as her right back leg gave way beneath her, the two hyenas dived in without mercy, their jaws snapping at her exposed throat.

He howled in rage, then ploughed into the two hyenas facing him. He was oblivious of the bites he received as he ducked low and came up under the first, his teeth ripping through its throat. Turning to the second, he bowled into it, knocking it down. His bigger size was more than a match for the hyena as his claws tore across its belly. Leaving their cries of pain behind, he closed in on the hyenas attacking Midnight. They weren't the real threat, and he watched helplessly as the leopard sunk its jaws into the back of Midnight's neck. She let out a howl of pure agony as the bite severed her spine.

Reg appeared from the side, scooping up the two hyenas and driving them both screaming into the floor, his claws digging deep into them. The leopard looked up from his bite to see him drive into him. They both went rolling along the floor, trying to avoid claws and jaws which snapped and swept, aiming for soft body parts before they both bounded away from each other.

The leopard was backing away from him with a wicked grin on his face. "Her blood tasted good, Wolf," he baited.

He looked around. Reg slowly approached from the leopard's left, with Dex and Anita coming in from the right. Behind the leopard, Joe and Fred were busy … driving their sharp little knives repeatedly into the now-dead hyena that had hit Ben. A bark from him brought their attention back to what was happening. He could see the blood-crazed look in their eyes and was sure they wouldn't control themselves, but they did. After one last slash with his dagger, Joe jumped down, pulling out his blowpipe, and loading it slowly. The leopard looked around … noticing that he was cornered.

"What, are you a coward, Wolf? Can't fight me on your own?" the leopard growled.

He grinned viciously at him. "Not afraid, Leopard, but unlike you, I will live to see all the Death Dealers … dead."

The leopard growled and moved to attack him as a dart hit him in the rump, and Reg's huge paw drove him to the ground.

"Not today, Filth," Reg growled.

The leopard tried to fight back, but his muscles would not obey him. He tried to scream as the poison rushed through his system, causing him excruciating pain. Within seconds, the realisation that he had lost flickered in his eyes, replaced quickly by the darkness of death.

He watched the light leave the leopard's eyes before rushing over to Midnight, she was still alive, but she couldn't move. He didn't know what to do. Midnight would never be able to move again. There was no White in the River Runners, and there was only a handful in history who had the power and the knowledge to heal this type of injury.

"Nala," Midnight whispered.

He leaned his head down to her.

"Is everyone else alive?"

He looked up to where Joe and Fred were hugging Ben. He looked dazed, but he was conscious and alive.

"Yes, everyone's OK, and we are going to get you home. Mavis will be able to help you."

Midnight smiled kindly. "You and I both know that's not going to happen. I got sloppy, and focused on the immediate danger," she paused, gathering her strength, and trying to put the pain to one side. "You're a good leader, Nala. Learn from this, always see the bigger picture, don't focus on what they want you to see. Make sure you save the Runners."

He nodded. He couldn't find his voice, but he could feel the tears in his eyes as the rest of the team gathered around.

"It has been a pleasure knowing you all," Midnight whispered, her strength nearly gone. "Now go, and the River with you all. I'll be watching." She closed her eyes and lay her head down. Slowly, her breathing faltered and then stopped.

The Runners stood looking down at their friend, no one really knowing what to do.

He shook himself, he needed to be strong, even though his heart was breaking. "Reg, please pick her up."

Reg moved in and gently lifted Midnight's body.

"I'm not leaving her here. We will find somewhere to bury her away from this scum," he told the group.

Dex looked back at the dead zone. "Two of the hyenas bolted when you took on the leopard, should we go after them?"

He thought for a second. "No, let Zagane get the message. He now knows he's in a fight." He turned to the dead zone and yelled, his voice full of fury and pain. "Tell Zagane, that I am going to personally rip out his cowardly throat and watch the life drain from his worthless carcass."

A yelp from the tree line showed that his message had been heard.

He turned back to his team, sending Anita and Dex into the forest to scout the way ahead … and find a resting place for Midnight.

* * *

Nala smiled for the first time in a while, as they walked back into base camp. Gervais was waiting for them.

Everyone had been quiet since the loss of Midnight, but if anything, the group had become closer. He had considered what came next, and decided that they needed some rest before they proceeded. The encounter with the leopards had shown him that they were now getting to the difficult part of the plan. The team had been through a lot together in a very short period of time, and they had been successful at thinning the Death Dealers out, essentially dispensing with Zagane's fodder.

He would need to start committing his better fighters to scouting and chasing shadows in The Forbidden. Every

349

encounter from now on was going to be more difficult. They had to get smarter, and develop some new strategies … going in head-on was now playing right into the Death Dealers strengths.

Gervais moved towards him as the team spread out around him. He shook his head.

"No. You all need to go and get some proper rest. We will meet after our evening meal and work through some new plans then," he said. He could see that the group wanted to argue, even though their fatigue was vying for control.

Eventually, they all broke away and moved into the River Runners' camp.

"They look tired," Gervais said from his side.

He just nodded, tired was an understatement. "We lost Midnight," he said. "A patrol stumbled onto us through pure luck. They tracked us, and it came to a final confrontation … we took out eight hyenas, four leopards, and an owl scout."

Gervais grunted. "That's a successful recovery."

He turned, growling. "Successful? I don't call that successful. I lost Midnight. I would never call that a success."

Gervais didn't move or falter. He growled back at him, fighting his rage with a rage of his own. "We are going to lose many more before this war ends," he rumbled back. "You know that as well as I do. Stop feeling sorry for yourself."

He turned on Gervais, a flurry of emotions filling his eyes, his teeth bared as he tried to control his instinct to attack. Gervais didn't back away, standing his ground, not posing a threat, and not acting like prey.

"Think about the success you have had, Nala?" he said, trying to get through to him.

He took a step toward Gervais.

"Nala, you have to look at the bigger picture."

Gervais's voice rumbled through him and his head shot up at the words. "What did you say?" he growled.

Gervais took a deep breath. "The bigger picture, Nala. What's our end game here?"

His head slumped, and he whispered, "That's what she said to me at the end."

Gervais flopped to the floor in relief, and he dropped down beside him.

"I couldn't save her," he said quietly, misery dripping from his words. "I saw it happening, but I couldn't get there in time."

Gervais laid a massive hand on his shoulder. "I know that feeling, Nala. The helplessness. I'd like to say it gets easier, but it doesn't."

He laid his head down on the floor at Gervais's words, exhaustion pushing him down.

"But we must fight, Nala. Midnight was a fighter. She died protecting the Runners. Every one of those who signed up to fight with you, knew that it was unlikely they would come back."

He opened an eye and looked at Gervais in confusion.

Gervais laughed ruefully. "Nala, you were the only one who believed that this was not a suicide mission. We haven't outright won a proper skirmish against the Death Dealers in the last ten years. They come, we run. They come closer, we hide," Gervais explained.

"And what Gervais is not saying ... is that we die. We die without a fight," Leandra stated, as she walked calmly out of the tree line.

His head shot up quickly, his fatigue was forgotten and

his eyes were sparkling. He barely registered Gervais swallowing back a laugh, as he jumped up and stalked around Leandra, checking she was OK. When he was finally sure, he took her in. She had a scar on her left flank; the hair was growing back in, but it was a lighter colour, almost a sister to match his own.

As he finished his lap of Leandra, she interrupted him.

"If you're quite finished, we were having a conversation," she said, a slight tweak of a smirk on her muzzle.

This time Gervais did laugh, the look of confusion and hurt on his face was too much.

"River, help him," Gervais whispered to himself. "We had just finished, Leandra," Gervais said, saving Nala as best he could. "Nala needs to rest." Turning, he told him, "We will meet in the morning and plan our next move." Gervais pulled his bulk from the ground, said his goodbyes, and left the two wolves together.

"Are you too tired to run?" Leandra asked.

He shook his head once again, struck mute by this self-assured she-wolf.

"Well, see if you can keep up!" she called as she darted off.

He didn't need asking twice, he flew after her. She was quick and agile in the turns, but he was able to close the gap on the straights.

Leandra took him through the camp, sliding in-between dwellings and crops, and jumping over cooking pits and streams. He registered all of this subconsciously, and was impressed at how quickly the Runners had managed to get things set up. However, his focus was on Leandra.

As she glanced back their eyes locked just before she pulled away, putting on a burst of speed and disappearing into the forest. He entered a few seconds later to find she had disappeared, but he knew her scent, she hadn't gone far. Raising his muzzle, he sniffed the air, and saw her flitting between trees up ahead. He bounded up the slope after her, struggling to keep up in the more restrictive confines of the forest. Here, she was in her element, and he a dumb cumbersome wolf. They continued to run for maybe fifteen minutes when a tangy, salty scent started to filter into his senses.

Up ahead, the ground foliage grew thicker, obscuring Leandra from view as she slipped through. He dug deep and found an extra burst of energy, speeding up, and jumping through the bushes not far behind her.

* * *

Leandra dashed out into the sun and onto a sandy beach, pulling up quickly before she ran into the water. She moved aside, waiting for Nala to catch up. She had enjoyed the run and keeping ahead of him, and she suspected that if he hadn't been so tired … he would have been harder to evade.

Her thoughts seemed to summon him as he burst out of the trees at full sprint, quickly realising his predicament. She was impressed at how speedily he put on the breaks, but he was not quick enough. He slid across the sand and buckled as he hit the water's edge, flipping around, and landing with a very human-like yelp in the water.

She burst into howls of laughter, falling to the floor in hysterics as Nala stood himself up in the waves, and made his way back to dry land with a grumpy, hurt look on his face, water dripping off his muzzle.

He stopped in front of her and shook himself. Her yelp mirrored his earlier cry, eliciting a smug smile from him as he jumped at her playful nipping. She evaded him easily, realising too late that he was herding her to the water's edge. She tried to slip by him, but he was always there with a gentle nip and a playful glint in his eyes.

Before long, she felt the seawater lapping against her paws. She was not going to get wet. Lowering her head, she bared her teeth and growled at Nala as menacingly as she could muster, but it was too obvious that her heart wasn't in it. Nala dived in, lowering his head, and exposing the back of his neck … slipping under her belly and flipping her into the water.

She heard him laugh as she landed in the sea, slipping below the waves. She came up spluttering and snorting through her muzzle, putting on her best-unimpressed look, determined she wouldn't let him win. She feigned a dip into the water, acting like her hind leg had given way, and regretted it momentarily when she saw the panicked look on his face. He immediately dived in to help her, and as he did … she sprung up, driving him over onto his back, his head and muzzle becoming submerged as she pinned him down.

It didn't last long, his back paws landed on her belly with his claws retracted, and pushed her high into the air. She landed with a splash on all fours as he rose out of the water. The game went on for a while, until she started to feel the ache in her flank … showing that she had pushed herself too far again. Mavis would be furious, but she needed to be ready.

"Enough," she said, and as simple as that, he stopped.

"Are you OK?" he asked.

A spike of anger flared. She didn't need his concern, she wasn't weak. With great difficulty, she bit down on the anger. In her heart, she knew he didn't think that she was weak, he was concerned for her, more because of the apparent infatuation he seemed to have developed.

"It's fine, Mavis's orders. No more than a certain amount of exercise until she gives me the all-clear," she said instead … hoping her voice did not betray any of the anger she felt at her own feelings of weakness.

Almost reluctantly, they both left the sea and shook themselves as dry as they could. She started walking down the beach, heading back towards the camp. Nala dropped in beside her, his eyes flitting from her to the sea and back. Suddenly something triggered in her mind.

"You've never seen the sea before, have you?" she asked.

Nala shook his head, and at that moment she decided something, and the world seemed to sway slightly.

"Have you enough energy for a quick run?" she asked, after a shake of her head.

Nala nodded, and she set off at a casual pace. He kept aside her, clearly enjoying the gentle run, and she suddenly realised that she was too.

The salty breeze that came off the sea, running through her fur and over her tongue, was keeping her cool. The feel of the sand underneath her pads, the gentle lapping of the surf on the beach, and the sound of Nala beside her … making her feel comfortable in his company.

"Full of revelations, aren't you?" she internally scolded herself. She couldn't let people in, she had to rely on herself. Her injury gave a twinge, and she thought that perhaps her subconscious was telling her that she was already too close. It was evident by how she put herself at risk saving Mavis, and then waited impatiently for Nala to return unharmed. She had spent time convincing herself that she only intervened because it was a Death Dealer, but she knew that wasn't true. It was only just before Nala killed the leopard, that she knew that.

Now, Nala was beside her, and it felt right. Automatically, she tried to dismiss it, but there it was, this dumb animal had burrowed his way under her skin. She wanted to snap at him, but couldn't muster the energy or will to follow through on that thought.

A few moments later, they arrived at their destination, and she slowed. Nala ran on a few steps, yapping away. He turned back and looked at her, his eyes sparkling with excitement, she couldn't help but grin back at him.

"It's amazing," he whispered in awe.

She followed his gaze to watch the waves breaking against the tall rocks, black stones that glistened in the sun, and stood in poles out of the sea. Each one was a few feet wide so you could easily jump from one to another ... extending outwards from the beach ... almost like a staircase leading to an altar; to worship the majesty of the sea.

She was about to ask Nala if he wanted to go up the stones when he took off by himself.

"Come on!" he shouted back excitedly. His excitement was infectious, and she needed no further encouragement. She followed behind him, jumping from pole to pole and overtaking Nala, who playfully nipped at her as she jumped by. She stopped at the top, letting Nala catch up. As he reached her, she jumped down onto a platform that was a little lower than the poles and broader, the poles flanking them on both sides.

The sea in all her beauty was spread before them. The moon was just starting to appear in the distance, as the night fought for control of the day. She watched as Nala raised his head and howled his appreciation, it felt like a prayer of thanks to the River and the sea. She found herself joining him.

When they had finished, Nala lay down, and she dropped in beside him, laying her muzzle on her paws.

"Talk to me, Nala," she said simply.

She imagined the confused look on his face. "About what, Leandra?" His response confirming his confusion.

"Everything that happened from when I fell," she answered him.

Beside her, he looked out over the water that was now glistening in the moonlight and sighed gently, before telling her the story.

She listened intently, only interrupting to confirm a detail, or ask why he made a specific call. Not to challenge ... but to understand. She was quiet as he explained how he and Gervais had hatched the plan, finishing with the death of Midnight, and his decision to come back to camp.

The silence as he finished was comfortable, there wasn't much to say. What he had achieved was nothing short of amazing. He didn't need an analysis of what had happened, he just needed someone to listen and not judge him.

It was evident that the deaths, of not only Midnight, but all the merged creatures were laying heavily on him. Part of her wanted to scream that they were evil, that they deserved everything they got. But she didn't. Nala had not gone through what she had, and even then, it was only a handful of the Death Dealers who had hurt her. Who was she to say, that given the opportunity, more of them would not come over to the River Runners?

She wanted to shake herself, she was getting soft. An idea began forming in her mind, but as she grasped at it, trying to make it unfold, it slipped away.

She decided to let it come of its own accord. "I want to come with you when you go back out," she said instead.

Nala didn't respond, did he not think she was capable? Her head whipped around to tell Nala what she thought of that, just as she heard him gently snoring. He had fallen asleep and not heard her question.

She smiled fondly at him; she had forgotten how tired he was.

A breeze picked up … ruffling her fur. She stood and walked to the other side of Nala, laying down close beside him.

"I'm just laying out of the wind," she said, trying to convince herself. She snuggled in close beside him and fell asleep, lulled by the steady beat of his heart.

CHAPTER THIRTY-EIGHT

Kaden stepped down from the podium in the centre of the village. He had just given his final session with the people of the Scarlett Hand, answering questions, and providing an outline of what he proposed for the future. It had been a chaotic week.

The day after he had returned from Selenta, he had raised the idea of a vote with the council, they surprised him by not dismissing it. He quickly realised that they had misunderstood him ... thinking that he meant only members of the council, and a few of the higher-ranking members of the rebels.

When he realised their mistake, he had made it clear he meant that every rebel in the camp was to have a vote ... the reaction had been amusing.

Oliver and Davies had turned white. Gluttun had spluttered in rage and called him a fool, before realising who he was speaking to and subsiding into dark silence, glaring at him. Redmund had laughed approvingly, but appeared more amused. Manusa and Harris had both sat back considering.

It was Manusa who raised the first objection. "Kaden, the simple people don't understand the immensity of the implications this decision will have." It was a measure of her concentration that she'd used his first name, but at her comment, the River opened, and the council went a little crazy.

He let them exhaust themselves, not answering or arguing any points, merely waiting until they finished before turning to Manusa. "You make an excellent point about their lack of understanding, but I disagree that they are simple. We just need to educate them," he replied.

Manusa quickly apologised for her use of the word *simple*, explaining that she meant they led more simple lives.

Everyone but Gluttun had sat back, weighing up the possibilities.

"Educate them? Pfft, they only eat because we tell them to, they are pathetic followers," Gluttun spat.

He had seen Redmund about to get involved, but signalled for him to wait, thankfully he had glanced his way.

Instead, it was Oliver who intervened. "That's harsh, Gluttun. Each of us in this camp made a dangerous decision to leave Selenta and get away from that very sentiment, these people are anything but pathetic."

Gluttun subsided, quickly realising that he was out alone on a very weak branch.

"We could spend time educating them on the potential issues, and what the outcomes could be … through conversations or speeches," Davies added.

Harris leaned forward, intrigued. "Each of us providing our own perspective?" he asked.

Davies nodded, happily in his element. "Yes. We could even have time set aside for them to ask their own questions, and raise their own concerns; they may have a perspective that we haven't considered."

He smiled smugly at Gluttun, deciding not to add that this could also be a method in the future, for the people to choose their own members of the council. That would probably have been too much for them all at once.

They had expected the week to start slowly ... with a small number of people involved. Beginning with a few meetings in the council offices to explain the plan for the vote, and what it was about, then moving out into the town square later in the week, once people's interest was piqued. However, Titch had become involved ... and with the help of Cassie and the soldiers ... she had run all over town, telling everyone that they had to go and listen, and to help make the decision for their future. She had been insistent that they said nothing more than that, apparently yelling, *"let everyone hear the same message,"* at one of the soldiers who had attempted to explain more about what was going on. The soldier had reddened, apologised to Titch, and then finished his conversation by explaining to *just be there.* No one else had dared to say anything more and risk her wrath.

As it was, that first meeting needed moving briskly outside. Davies had been fantastic, arranging for the square to be prepared on a moment's notice. Everyone had sat and listened intently, as he and Oliver explained that the council were going to hold a secret ballot at the end of the week, allowing everyone a vote as to the future direction the Scarlett Hand would take. They made it very clear that the course chosen, would be that decided by the majority.

The people were a bit stunned at first. None of them really comprehending the implications, as almost all those present had never considered that they would have a chance to influence the direction they would take. Slowly, they started asking questions. The first was about how the vote would work. Davies had stepped forward and explained that they would set up a room with two doors, with each person receiving an item that was yet to be determined. Then they would go into the room and drop that item into a box dependent on their views, exiting out the other side of the room. After this the questions had come thick and fast, and went on for some time; clarifying that it was a secret ballot, asking what the options were that they would be voting for etc.

Davies had answered all these questions calmly and clearly, while outlining the timetable he had created for the week ahead. He explained when the council would be providing their own views, and when the people could ask questions… even allowing them to get up and voice their opinions in a five-minute time slot. For this, they needed to request a slot from Davies before the end of the following day.

He applauded Davies's work, and was quick to acknowledge, that without his fantastic ability to organise events, they'd never be able to do this in a week, having never seen this type of event happen before. Considering the enormity of what they were doing, it was remarkable.

Davies had thought of everything, right down to a way to ensure no one manipulated the result. He had smiled at this; he was sure Davies was looking at Gluttun when he outlined that plan. There would be three people in the room to make sure that only one vote was cast per person, but with screens for secrecy.

It hadn't been all plain sailing though. After the first few meetings, where each council member had given their own views on the current position of the Scarlett Hand … there had been several scuffles between his supporters and those of Gluttun. He had no doubt that Gluttun had been stirring the pot, and trying to influence some of the more unsavoury rebels with whom he had close ties. The scuffle had been quick, with no one really hurt before it was broken-up by Redmund.

This prompted an impassioned speech by Oliver about them not fighting each other, the real fight was with Selenta and its oppressive caste system. Thankfully it had the desired effect, and no further fisticuffs broke out. Although, he mused, it was likely that the additional threat of cancelling the vote if this happened again, is what tipped the scale. However, it didn't stop the heckling, people quickly took sides, and groups formed with people banding together based on their beliefs. Fortunately, there were only a few outright extremes, and a quiet word from Hush or Cassie brought them back to an air of civility.

He took a deep breath, anxious about the enormity of what he had started. It all depended on the understanding of the rebels. The people were going to start voting in an hour, and they had three options. Firstly, remain as they were; recruiting where they could and delaying any radical change to see what the future held in two years. Secondly, merge fully into Formad; disbanding the Scarlett Hand. Thirdly, step up the level of the fight with Selenta; actively assaulting the infrastructure that the Selentan elite so cherished, and openly recruiting in towns and villages to bring more recruits over to their cause ... a perilous course of action.

He joined Hush, Cassie, and Titch who were waiting for him at the side of the stage. Titch jumped up into his arms and gave him a kiss.

"You were great!" Titch gushed, making him smile.

"Thank-you, Little One. There's nothing more to do, it is in the hands of the people now."

Hush grunted as Cassie laughed, moving in beside him, as he hitched Titch to his right. "Let's go and get something to eat before the voting starts," she suggested.

He grimaced, his stomach tightening at the thought of food … it was so full of knots, he wasn't sure that he could eat.

He had no idea how the vote would go, and fear gripped him … what if they decided not to do anything, or worse, to disband?

"There's nothing you can do about that now," Bond said matter-of-factly into his mind.

"I know," he replied, slightly agitated. "But that doesn't mean I have to like it."

"Don't pull that face, Kaden. If you succeed … you will have to become accustomed to not having the final say on almost everything," Hush said.

He laughed at Hush reading his mind and making him feel better. Hush was just as nervous as he was. They had discussed the future many times around the fire, envisaging the world they wanted Selentans to live in, one where they decided the course of their own destiny, or at the very least … had a say in their future.

As they turned a corner, he saw Kendin, who bowed slightly, that minor motion asking whether it was convenient to talk. He was always amazed at how much that man could communicate without words. He turned to the group, "I'll meet you all back at the house."

They all nodded, and smiled at Kendin, moving away. All except Titch. She walked with him over to Kendin and bowed slightly, the way she had seen Kendin do on occasion. The formality was cute, but also a little disconcerting on one so small.

"Hello Ambassador, I am happy to see you back safe, but please do not keep Kaden too long ... we must vote soon," she said, beaming.

Kendin returned Titch's smile, going down on one knee in front of her, and bringing himself to her level. "Of course, it is a momentous day for you all." He paused. "And, Young Lady, I am honoured by your manners, but you have no need to be so formal with me. Please, in future, call me Kendin. I would like us to be friends, and my friends have the right to use my name."

He didn't think Titch's smile could grow any wider, but it did. She seemed to grow in stature. Then, she took Kendin entirely by surprise as she jumped forward, hugging him.

"And you can call me Titch. Young Lady makes me sound old." She let Kendin go and said her goodbyes, before heading off to Hush and Cassie who had been waiting for her, while both he and Kendin watched her go.

She turned her head and shouted, "Amba ... Kendin, make sure you join us for the party after the vote has finished." She managed to make it sound more like an order than a request.

Kendin simply nodded that he would, as Titch turned and ran into Hush's legs, knocking him off balance, and running off squealing as he gave chase.

"I am glad she sees me as a friend, not a foe," Kendin said under his breath.

"She is very perceptive for one so young," he added.

"Young?" Kendin mused, not really responding to him, and lost in his own thoughts before he suddenly realised his musing and caught himself. "Oh, young, yes. Yes, she is."

He noticed the pause, it was unlike Kendin to be so distant in any conversation. He decided to file it away for a later discussion. "It's good to see you back safe, Ambassador. It's not quite the same without you here," he said instead.

Kendin smiled, still slightly distracted. "Kendin, please, we are way past the formalities, Kaden."

He watched as Kendin pulled himself back entirely from wherever his mind had wandered to.

"I am sorry to say it won't be a long stay. I have to head back to the Capital for the appointment progression."

"Appointment progression?" he asked, puzzled.

Kendin waved as if it was of no consequence. "I will explain more later at the party, but our leader's term finishes in three months … anyone named as a potential leader must return to the Capital to take part in the appointment process."

He nodded, still confused, but Kendin had promised to explain later so he would wait. "What would you like to discuss with me now?" he inquired.

"I need to introduce you to my replacement. He is young and a little idealistic, not my first choice, but there are other factions in Formad we have to keep happy," Kendin smiled mildly.

"That's not everything, is it, My Friend?" he asked.

"No," Kendin replied. "That is really a formality. He will have no real power and will still report to me. I have arranged a few code words to ensure we know any information that comes through him are genuine," he finished, handing him a rolled scroll. "Just as a precaution," he added quickly.

He recalled, yet again, that Formad was its own country. It had its own intrigues and power struggles just as any other did. He reminded himself to be aware of that; becoming absorbed in your own personal issues was all too easy.

"Now then, to my real reason for leaving. Follow me," Kendin instructed, smiling as he walked on, and continuing to talk, expecting him to follow. "My instinct tells me that the vote will go your way today, that you will step up your fight against Selenta." Kendin held his hand up as he was about to interrupt. "I know you don't want to guess the results, but I have experience in these matters. I've been around the camp a while, so I have a feel for their hearts."

As he finished, he rounded the corner, and outside the Formad Ambassador's home were twenty people, all milling around. At first glance, they appeared to be a rag-tag bunch, their clothing was tattered and discoloured with none of it matching. They were a multitude of sizes and genders, sat playing games or cooking food. He stopped and looked closer. The first thing he noticed was their footwear, although they were different colours, they were all the same; well maintained, appearing comfortable and practical. His instincts screamed that these were not commoners. The way they moved was wrong. They displayed grace and purpose in every movement. As the thought hit him, he identified four who appeared to be lounging on the outside of the group, but to the trained eye ... were in fact sentries. Each had a clear view of the entry points to this area.

"The weapons are hidden well," Tadic murmured in his mind.

He smiled, walking ahead into the middle of the group, and holding his hand out to a dark-haired female. She had a stern face, and a scar that ran from her chin and down her neck, going under her shirt.

367

"Commander," he said.

She looked at his hand and raised her eyebrows, taking it as she stood, and scowling at Kendin as she looked over his shoulder. "Kendin?" she growled.

"I did not tell him anything. I told you he was good," Kendin responded evenly, not fazed by the growl.

The Commander looked back at him. "What gave us away?"

"My experience," he replied. "It's difficult to hide the essentials a soldier needs, such as your boots. The weapons are all well concealed, but there if you know where to look." He shrugged, then continued, "The four lolling at the edges have clear views of all entrances, so sentries."

The Commander nodded, then raised a questioning eyebrow. "And me as Commander?" she asked.

He smiled, enjoying himself, it was easy to forget what it was like being around real soldiers. "You were the only one in a position with a direct line of sight to all the sentries, but I'm making that bit up a little, it was more that you were in a spot I would have chosen."

"Hmph," was all the reaction he received, as she turned and sat back down with her soldiers.

"Walk with me, Scarlett Hand," Kendin said officially.

He turned to follow him, reluctantly, he wanted to interrogate these soldiers, test their mettle, and understand where they had been, and what they were doing here.

Once they were out of earshot, he raised an eyebrow to Kendin. "Scarlett Hand? I thought we were past formalities?"

Kendin smiled ruefully and started talking. "Protocol has to be followed at times, Kaden," he replied apologetically. "As I said earlier, I believe the vote will go your way. You will up the ante in your rebellion. It's no secret that I wish our two nations to be much closer, specifically to progress our trading relationship." Kendin waited for a nod of agreement from him. "What you don't know, is that relationship is just as important for the future of the Formad as it is for Selenta."

He kept quiet, leaving Kendin to explain at his own pace.

"Unfortunately, I cannot go into detail today, but maybe in the future, dependent on how things develop, I can share more. Suffice to say, our friendship is important. The soldiers back there are a gesture of my support and have been assigned to you."

He considered Kendin's words and a few things slipped quickly into place. "Your idea?" he asked.

Kendin nodded.

"Well, that explains the lack of uniform or any identifying insignia," he finished.

Kendin grinned. "They have all been handpicked, and come from close to the border with the Disputed Lands … able to easily pass as from that area if captured."

He laughed. "It seems you have thought of everything."

Kendin suddenly turned serious. "Use them how you see fit. Keep them as border guards, use them for training your men, or utilise their skills within your fighting units … they answer to you. My replacement has no knowledge of their existence."

He thought this over carefully. "I assume they're all fighting soldiers?"

Kendin nodded.

"I will make use of them. Hush can work out a story with the Commander. It's probably best to keep their true origins a secret for their own safety as well as Formad's. If we don't succeed, I don't want you stuck in a war," he sighed.

"A war is coming, My Friend. We will all have to pick sides and build our allies," Kendin said cryptically.

From his body language, he knew that was the end of their conversation. Still, it didn't stop his mind from whirling as he digested this new information. He looked up, realising they had just arrived back at his home.

Titch came running out of the door and barrelled into his legs. "Voting time!" she squealed.

Kendin bowed slightly to all of them. "I will take my leave. Good luck with your vote. I will see you at the party later, where I will introduce my replacement."

He returned the bow as they all bid Kendin farewell, then headed off to change the future.

CHAPTER THIRTY-NINE

"Get in here," Zagane growled.

Vepar looked across the cave entrance to Gremor, taking a little comfort from the fact that he looked just as anxious as he felt. Two huge wolfhounds stood guard at either side of the cave entrance, but that's not what had them concerned … two hyenas had arrived back at the camp earlier and were brought straight to Zagane.

He and Gremor had received a summons to get back here and hear the report. As they had arrived, they had heard an enormous roar and squeals of terror from inside the cave, stopping them both dead in their tracks. At Zagane's instruction, they both took a deep breath and entered the cave.

As they stepped through the curtain covering the entrance, the sharp metallic smell of newly spilt blood stung his nostrils.

"I take it you didn't like what they had to say?" Gremor observed, as he stepped through a puddle of what looked to him like black tar. It seems bleeding was not all the hyenas had done in here.

He was impressed at how level Gremor's voice came across, and was pleased to hear an evil chuckle from the darkness. If there had been a growl, then their survival odds would have plummeted.

As it was, he watched on as Zagane walked into the firelight. His eyes were dancing with the flames of the fire … appearing at odds with the insanity of the rest of his appearance. His fur was coated in blood, and his tusks had pieces of the hyenas stuck to them.

He felt a shudder coming on and fought to subdue it. It didn't pay to show any sign of fear or weakness in front of Zagane. Instead, he asked a dangerous question, "What happened?"

He watched Zagane consider before replying, absently scraping his tusks against the stone of the wall to remove a piece of bone. "The wolf has made a mockery of us again. He has killed Carnage and his pack. He has humiliated us for the last time," Zagane answered calmly.

This time he did gulp, and he was not alone. When Zagane's voice was that calm … it was usually a precursor to extreme violence. He mentally began preparing himself to fight, even though he knew he wouldn't survive. He wouldn't cower as Zagane tore him apart, he would make sure that he always remembered him.

Zagane snorted as his eyes glazed slightly and began pacing around the cave. Both he and Gremor relaxed a little. "The time has come," Zagane muttered, in a voice not entirely his own. "The reckoning is here … a final battle will decide The Forbidden's allegiance in the coming darkness. The traitors' true colours will show as the battle is swayed by a sacrifice."

He watched as Zagane's eyes came quickly back into focus, and a vicious grin split his face. "Pull all our forces in. We move to the north-west. I suspect they are close to the water, and our numbers will flush them out … then we kill every single one of them."

"Yes, Sir!" he and Gremor answered as one.

They turned rapidly to leave, using his orders as a way to leave his presence. Before they could reach the exit, Zagane issued one last request. "No one touches the wolf or his she-bitch. I am going to rut her as he watches, then tear him apart slowly; piece by piece."

He and Gremor both just nodded, not wanting to say or do anything that would drag forth the violence that was simmering beneath the surface.

"Now go, send them in on your way past," Zagane barked.

He exited first with Gremor right behind him. They both breathed in the fresh air deeply, realising only now how thickly coated the air in the cave had been with filth and death.

The wolfhounds still sat outside like statues, their positions never changing, but they were always alert. A group of ferrets stood waiting with various furs and tools in their hands, obviously summoned to clean up the cave.

"He's ready for you," Gremor instructed.

He looked across at Gremor, and their eyes met, they both knew how close to death they had come today. At that moment, they shared a split-second of camaraderie.

All too quickly, a snarl returned to Gremor's face … filling it with hatred as he growled and bared his teeth, before he turned into the forest.

He sighed; it was easier to hate. He began moving automatically towards his own camp, needing to get messages out to the outlying groups. It would take time to get them back, and he had the suspicion that Zagane was not in a patient mood.

CHAPTER FORTY

E ddie stood at the edge of the graduation chamber, waiting with Phoenix Squad for their call to go up on stage, looking out on the huge amphitheatre. The seats were full. He smirked, observing more than a few pale faces of those suffering from the excesses of the night before.

After the Lord Professor had dismissed them, they had headed to a barracks. Despite the disappointing result, and the exhilarating reception they'd received from the crowd ... all of them had promptly fallen into a dreamless slumber.

He had awoken to the sound of voices, and found Dozer, Aldela, and Llýr deep in conversation. He'd marvelled at how close those three had become. It was uncommon for companions, outside a person's own, to become so close-knit, probably because, as companions, they couldn't usually communicate easily.

He'd looked at the ceremonial uniforms that were hanging up along the wall, and the lack of colour on the epaulettes ... his heart had sunk. Whereas previously there had been an epaulette that had a mix of colours depicting all the Hands ... it was now an empty space, awaiting the decision of the ceremony. The weight of the previous days' events had crashed down on him, threatening to drown him as he'd realised that Phoenix Squad would be separated ... likely to never see each other again.

Dozer had suddenly appeared beside him, laying his huge hand on his shoulder. "Things are never as dark as they appear," was all he had said.

In his grief, he had wanted to shout and curse. How could it not be as bad as it seemed? He had wanted to rage about how stupid Armadillo Squad had been to go out on the water ... but he'd seen the calmness in the eyes of the three companions, and something had settled in his soul.

He had taken a deep breath and roused the rest of the Squad, having to throw cold water over Rico, which had caused an amusing squeal and a fun tussle as he sought revenge.

When they had finally dressed and made their way up to the Central Plaza, the party was already in full swing. Groups of Hands had sat together and talked loudly as they drank. They even saw Purples, Yellows, and Greens mingling in with the Blues and Whites. It was only when he'd heard snippets of their conversations that he'd realised that some of these groups had been Squads during their training. It had dawned on him that it wasn't just his Squad that was to be disbanded ... yet them being together at this time, showed that they would always have each other, no matter what the future held. He'd smiled at the realisation and looked at the others. They had all seemed to be as in awe as he was as they'd entered the Plaza.

That was when all hell had broken loose.

The crowd had immediately started clapping and cheering again. Drinks had been pushed into their hands, and he had caught a glimpse of the scowls of rage on Raptor Squad's faces just before they'd all been dragged off into different groups.

Everyone had wanted to hear first-hand about the monster in the lake, how they'd handled the other tests, or to extoll the virtues of their own Hand. Some had even consoled them that they would not lose touch with their Squad-mates.

He had barely seen any of Phoenix Squad as he had been cajoled from group to group.

At some point, Dutton ... the Lord Professor's aid ... had interrupted what felt like his hundredth telling of the monster story. He had dragged him away to a quiet area inside the Orange headquarters, where the rest of Phoenix Squad had been waiting.

Jenna and Tia had rushed over and hugged him, while Rico and Butch had hung back, giving him a reassuring nod. They'd all looked haggard and harassed.

"Do I look as bad as you lot?" he'd asked.

They'd all laughed, and the noise had ramped up as they'd each started talking at once. So much so, that they hadn't noticed the Lord Professor enter.

"I thought better of you than allowing someone to sneak up on you unaware," the Lord Professor had mocked. His calm voice had cut smoothly through the noise.

They'd all jumped, then quickly dropped to one knee in salute.

"Enough of that. After what you all sacrificed for your fellow students, it is I who should be down on one knee to you."

The Squad had all gone a little white at the idea, and the Lord Professor had chuckled. The sound put them at ease, while his next words etched themselves in his and the Squad's minds forever.

"As Lord Professor, I have to keep a certain detachment from the students under my care. However, I must confess that I have followed your progression more than anyone would consider as impartial. Today, I can say with absolute conviction, that I have never been so proud of anyone as I am of all of you. The decision you made was unselfish. It showed that you have hearts, as well as that your bodies are strong. Be that all Selentans had the same approach to each other."

The rest of the Squad had looked awestruck. Rico and Butch's eyes had glazed as they struggled to hold back tears of pride, while Jenna and Tia had openly allowed the tears to flow.

The moment had ended as Dutton had come to the Lord Professor's side and whispered something in his ear.

"Unfortunately, Dutton knows me too well. While I would love nothing more than to remain here and talk to you all, I am sure you're bored of telling the story of your deeds, and I must return to the party and spend some time with the victors."

He would have complained or argued they weren't worthy if he'd not seen the distaste evident on the Lord Professor's face.

"I must also ask you not to return to the party. Your presence is overshadowing Raptor Squad, and they need their victory as much as you."

The Squad hadn't looked disappointed at all; they knew they would enjoy their time together.

The Lord Professor had laughed. "But I have arranged something I think you will find much more to your taste. Dutton will take you there." As he'd left, he had turned and looked at them, earnestly. "Things are never as dark as they may appear." Then he'd gone.

They had followed Dutton to the gift the Lord Professor had arranged. It was precisely what the Squad would have wanted, but it was also bittersweet, as it showed them what they were going to miss. He had arranged for them to attend the Red Hand's private party. There were veterans and newer recruits all together; drinking, and talking, and laughing.

As they'd arrived, they had found themselves ushered into the middle of the room and seated on comfortable chairs, with everyone in the room gathering around. The grizzled Sergeant from the city test had then stepped forward. He'd asked them to tell their story once again, together, with the promise that they would tell their own stories to the Squad in payment.

Nervously at first, they had started to talk about the lake, but they were quickly stopped by the Sergeant. "Oh no, no, from the beginning ... we want to know about the whole test, not just the fun bit," he'd winked. There had been mutters of agreement from around the room, and once they had drinks in their hands, they had set about describing the events of the test.

The listening Reds had kept quiet throughout, being patient with the Squad as they corrected each other, or argued details or perceptions. They had crouched closer with interest when Tia talked about the barriers, Jenna about her fire whips, Butch about his healing, Rico about his camouflage and visions, and him about his speed. Only occasionally had the Reds asked insightful questions to clarify points, and they had laughed at Rico's self-effacing descriptions of his misfortune with mines. When they had finished explaining why they had ended the test the way they had, everyone had smiled and nodded their understanding.

True to their word ... the Reds had then regaled them with their own stories. Some of them were heart-warming, some were toe-curling, and others mocked each other. It was everything Phoenix Squad had ... just on a larger scale.

All too quickly, the night had flown by. Eventually, after Tia had fallen asleep in Butch's lap, and Jenna against Rico's shoulder ... and the other's eyes had become heavy ... the Sergeant had ushered them off to bed, advising them that things would be brighter after a good night's sleep.

He smiled ruefully, looking out now at the crowded amphitheatre before turning back to his Squad; the friends he was about to lose. How could it get brighter? This was a dark picture; to lose them.

* * *

"He's blaming himself," Jenna whispered in his ear, as Eddie turned to look at them with a sad smile on his face.

Rico only just managed not to jump; Jenna had interrupted a similar thought he had been having. He felt an urge to move nearer to Jenna, to be close to her and whisper back, but he didn't understand the feeling, so instead, he turned to look at her and found their faces just inches apart. His heart skipped a beat, and he heard Llŷr's chuckle echo in his mind.

He didn't know whether to be angry or happy. Llŷr had been in a mood because companions weren't allowed to manifest again until after the ceremony.

When he refocused, he felt a pang that Jenna had moved away, her cheeks slightly flushed. The silence was comforting, but at the same time, it felt awkward.

"Then talk, You Fool," Llýr mocked.

He shook his head, a grin splitting his lips.

"Llýr?" Jenna asked.

He nodded. "He's taking it out on me because he can't manifest," he joked.

"I know, Aldela is going a bit stir crazy too, they're so used to being able to do as they please and plot together … I think it's making the isolation worse."

Realisation and horror hit him with a thud. "I never even considered that this would split them up too. I was too busy wallowing that I was going to lose you," he said. "And the rest of the Squad," he added hastily, sending a silent apology to Llýr at the same time as Jenna nodded, her cheeks flushing a little more.

"We won't lose each other, we're too close. We'll find a way." Jenna placed her hand on his, and he felt a flush run through him. Trying not to focus on the touch, he turned the conversation back to Eddie.

"Coward!" Llýr muttered.

"I don't think he's blaming himself … you know."

Jenna looked a little taken aback by the change of subject, followed by a look in her eyes that he didn't recognise.

"What do you mean?" She asked, her question covering the moment.

"I think he knows that there was no other decision to make … and he would make it again. He's feeling the same as us. It was last night … it was a fabulous evening, but it was also painful as it was a taste of what we have lost as a Squad."

Jenna nodded as she processed things from his point of view. He smiled as he watched her.

"What?" she asked, consciously checking her hair.

"Nothing. I just like watching you think," he said. He was saved from any further conversation as Training Captain Bromfell took to the stage, and proceeded to introduce all the Squads that had graduated.

The ceremony started with those in the final position. It took a while, as each Squad member was named individually and allocated to their Hands. They all made their way out onto the stage in turn, walking past Phoenix, who acknowledged each Squad before they moved to their positions.

Eventually, Bear Squad was summoned, with Lia, Chris, and Anna all being put in the White.

Armadillo Squad nodded solemnly and hurried past, ashamed that it was their fault that Phoenix Squad had lost. As they passed, Eddie pulled Phoenix Squad into a huddle, no words were necessary.

"Enjoying your last moments together, Losers?" Ruben's voice laughed.

He tensed, ready to respond, but Jenna's slight squeeze on his shoulder stopped him. As they broke apart, he was pleased to see Ruben scowling angrily.

"Your shoulders look a little blank," Thomas giggled.

"Yeah, I reckon Purple would look good on there for you, Rico; make sure you bring me a drink," Ruben sniggered, finding his own joke amusing.

"Hold your calm, Boy," Llýr ordered.

"It's *Boy* again, is it?" he snapped at Llýr.

"Focused you on me, didn't it?" Llýr teased before he lost it and guffawed.

His laughter was infectious, and he chuckled, turning away from Raptor Squad in time to watch Captain Bromfell introduce the Lord Professor.

He smiled. This was a break from protocol, as the Lord Professor usually only introduced the first-placed Squad. He considered turning and teasing Raptor Squad as he knew this would infuriate them. Unfortunately, his victory would be fleeting, and they would have the last laugh.

As the applause died down, the Lord Professor looked out over the crowd, his mere presence commanding the attention of everyone. "Good Morning," he said, his voice crisp and clear, reaching every ear in the building, with more than a few jumping at his words. "On behalf of the students and the Orange Hand … I would like to formally thank you for your attendance and support for each of these Squads."

A round of applause and a few cheers filled the amphitheatre.

"It has been a great pleasure to watch each Squad develop. Building bonds of friendship … that will spread out across each Hand as these students take their next steps to benefit our whole society."

The crowd responded with another, but slightly muted, applause.

"As with every year, we have some exceptional students who will go on to do great things." The Lord Professor paused, milking the tension. "But this year has been a little different to most. This year we have two extraordinary Squads, who gave us a thrilling end to the testing process as they fought neck-and-neck to the end. Their drive and passion clearly showed the traits we value in Selenta."

There was another round of applause, a little shorter in duration this time, the crowd knew something was coming, and they didn't want to slow the Lord Professor down.

He realised he had gone tense, every bone in his body on edge.

"One Squad even surpassed what I would have expected from any student. Not only did they put their own lives at risk to rescue fellow students, but they did this knowing that it meant they would lose the chance to finish first and choose their own futures. Now, it is not within *my* power to change the appointments of this exceptional Squad." The Lord Professor paused due to angry grumblings from the crowd. He raised his hand to calm them, and it stopped immediately.

He frowned, had there been an extra emphasis on '*my*' from the Lord Professor? When Eddie looked back at him and mouthed, "My?" he knew he had not been wrong.

"But it is in my power to reward these special students. Which is why today, I award them the *Order of the River*," the Lord Professor finished.

The amphitheatre erupted, while he and the rest of Phoenix Squad watched speechless as Dutton walked onto the stage, carrying a case with five glittering medals inside.

This time the Lord Professor didn't try to quiet the crowd. Instead, he raised his voice. "So, let's welcome them onto the stage. Selentans, I give you … Phoenix Squad!"

The Lord Professor took a step back and beckoned them out. It felt like an age as they stood there paralysed, but it must only have been a few seconds. Jenna and Tia took his hands, and they walked out onto the stage together. He spared a glance back at Raptor Squad. They were furious, but he had no time to dwell on it as he was instantly met with a huge wave of noise and excitement.

* * *

As the Lord Professor stepped back and beckoned Phoenix Squad onto the stage, he nearly laughed. They stood terrified. This Squad, that had calmly rescued their stricken comrades from a sea creature, were struck useless by a simple medal.

"You're harsh," Esther admonished in his mind.

"I know. I wanted to see the shock on their faces as I told them ... and it was worth it," he replied happily.

"No, you didn't want it getting out so you could take the glory ... or let anybody interrupt your plans," Caulder added.

He glanced automatically towards Angus Quinn.

A surge in noise brought him back to attention, and he was pleased to see Phoenix Squad had finally started moving. The Squad ambled to the middle of the stage, looking out at the crowd - awe and surprise showing on their faces at the reception they received.

He wasn't surprised. He was badgered constantly last night by guests at the party, with everyone wanting to talk about how amazing Phoenix Squad were. He repeatedly found himself answering the same question; was there really nothing he could do to keep them together? He'd said the same thing to each of them, feeling like it would become an inscription on his tombstone; "The rules of the Orange are clear, I'm afraid. As Lord Professor, I can only keep one Squad together, the others must be put where their skills suit best for the benefit of Selenta." Many of them had huffed and said it just seemed so unfair after what they had done, but there were still others who had grunted, happily observing the right Squad won in the end. He had taken note of them.

He realised his mind had wandered again. It was happening

to a greater extent just lately. Luckily, the reception for Phoenix Squad had not abated. He considered letting it go on a little longer, but noticed that the Squad were starting to look a bit uncomfortable. Instead, he took a few steps in front of the Squad and raised his hands for silence, the crowd reluctantly quietened.

"I apologise for stopping you from showing your appreciation for Phoenix Squad." He smiled broadly at a few cheeky boos. "But I have the great honour of presenting them with a medal!"

He winked at the crowd as he beckoned Dutton over to him, ever the showman, as they erupted in cheers again. He opened the glass case and took the first medal out. It was heavy in his hands, made of a rare, silver metal, mined somewhere in Trendorlan. He gave an involuntary shiver as the metal touched his skin. It always gave him the feeling of being able to learn something important, but it was just out of his reach.

He walked over to Tia and smiled at her as he placed the ribbon over her head, the medal laying perfectly over her heart. He stood aside and presented Tia to the crowd. They cheered loudly. Following the same process, he went next to Butch, Rico, Jenna, and finally Eddie. As he placed the final medal, he leaned down and whispered in Eddie's ear. "The sacrifice you made will not go unanswered."

He moved quickly to the side to allow Phoenix Squad to take a final bow, then smiled and moved back to the pedestal on the stage. Finally, the cheers abated.

"Thank-you, Phoenix Squad, for your amazing sacrifice to save the lives of your fellow Selentans. Now, I have the honour of placing you within your new Hands, where I am sure you will serve with distinction."

He watched from the corner of his eyes as the group took hold of each other's hands.

"Tia Dengen, you will join the Black Hand."

A slight twitch was all the reaction she gave, but the worry in her eyes was palpable.

"Butch Ferris, you will go to the Blue."

No reaction.

"Rico Ongrad, you will join the Orange."

Slight surprise.

"Jenna Hort and Eddie Murgin, you will both represent the Red."

There was no reaction from the two, but the Lord Professor thought he could see their eyes glisten a little bit.

Phoenix Squad turned to him, dropping to one knee in salute of the Lord Professor and then joined their new Squad-mates.

There was angry muttering from the crowd, they were obviously still mad about the result. They had expected him to make an exception that was outside his power.

Ignoring the muttering he raised his voice. "And finally, it gives me great pleasure to introduce to you the Squad finishing in first place this year. Selentans, please put your hands together for Raptor Squad ... who have chosen to serve the Black Hand."

Raptor Squad prowled out onto the stage, their smiles turning to dangerous scowls as they were received with a muted applause from the crowd. There was nothing obvious, as everyone was clapping, and there were pockets of enthusiastic support. Still, compared to the raucous noise that had met Phoenix Squad, it was almost an unbearable silence.

"He's going to say something!" Esther warned.

The Lord Professor glanced to Angus Quinn, who was quietly applauding and watching Jonas closely, a warning note in his eyes.

"Not him ... Jonas," Esther corrected.

As he looked around, he noticed that Jonas was about to explode, and moved abruptly, stepping out in front of him. He distracted Jonas's attention away from the crowd and was pleased to see calm reassert itself. He hoped this would be enough, a tirade could cause more harm than good.

He ushered Raptor Squad to take their place, in the centre of the stage on a platform, slightly higher than everyone else.

He took a moment to cast his eyes around the stage, looking at each student and memorising their faces, lingering on each member of Phoenix Squad. He had done all he could. This year had been an extremely strong year, and there were lots of amazing students who would serve their Hands well.

Moving back to the podium, it was so quiet he could hear his own heartbeat. The crowd were expecting something to happen, but he had nothing left, he had played all his cards, and it looked like he had lost this round.

The smug look in Angus Quinn's eyes made the feeling worse.

He took a deep breath. "The River runs," he intoned.

"And flows as it wills," everyone replied instinctively.

"I have had the great honour to have worked with these students this year, and I will miss each and every one of them ... and I now bring the ceremony to a clo ..."

"One moment please, Lord Professor," a grizzled Red Training Sergeant spoke calmly and loudly from the middle of the crowd, interrupting him.

"And they say the Purples have a flare for the dramatic!" Caulder muttered.

"The last bloody minute. I had given up hope my messages had got through," he replied, then addressed the Sergeant aloud, "Yes, Sergeant?"

The Sergeant took his time, standing slowly, ensuring the entire audience's eyes were on him. "I have a message from the Red Hand."

This sent tremors through the amphitheatre, as conversations flared up all over; what could this be about? The identity of the Red Hand's leader was a closely guarded secret. As with the Black Hand … they could be sitting in the audience, and no one would know other than a few select members of the Hands themselves, usually only veterans of ten or more years.

This grizzled Sergeant fit the bill of someone who might know the Red Hand's leader personally. It was unheard of for many to be privy to even a second-hand conversation from him … outside its members.

"Why don't you come and share the Red's message with us?" he asked, gesturing to the podium.

The Red Sergeant bowed slightly and took his time walking down from the crowd, nodding to the Heads of the other Hands on the front row.

"You took your sweet time," he hissed quietly, so only the Sergeant could hear.

"Well, you need to send clearer instructions on your requirements next time, Sir," the Sergeant replied just as quietly.

He wanted to laugh at the cheek in the Sergeant's voice,

but schooled his expression, taking a step back as he took the podium.

The Sergeant took a piece of paper from his jacket, then coughed to clear his throat. "People of Selenta, I bring greetings from the Red Hand."

He stifled a grin as he realised the paper in the Sergeant's hand was blank.

"The Red Hand congratulates each and every student who has graduated today." The Sergeant turned and applauded the students, the crowd joined in, but quietened quickly, sensing something momentous was about to happen. "But today I come bearing a decision due to sad news. Recently, the Scarlett Hand declared war on Selenta."

The Sergeant stopped for effect, as Angus Quinn sat up straight and darted an angry glance towards him at the mention of the word *war*.

"Angus knows," Chirp stated.

"No, but he rightly suspects something, My Friend," he responded.

The Sergeant continued, "As set out by Selentan Law ... when Selenta is under attack, the Red Hand has a number of rights to recruit whomever it requires for duty." Again, the Sergeant hesitated for effect, and Raptor Squad started moving around uncomfortably as the crowd started murmuring.

"He missed his calling on the stage for the Purple," Caulder murmured, exasperated.

He struggled to contain his laugh once again.

"One of the laws allows the Red Hand to recruit the top Squad of the latest year to the Red Hand, regardless of the students' own choices."

Angus Quinn rose quickly and raised a hand in warning.

Momentarily, he thought he was interrupting the Sergeant, but upon glancing behind, he saw that Raptor Squad had taken a number of steps forward ... rage evident on their faces. They halted at Angus's instruction. Angus nodded to the Sergeant to continue.

"Thank-you, Lord Councillor. However, the Red Hand has no intention of denying the Black Hand of a dedicated Squad. The law also allows the Red Hand to recruit anyone awarded the *Order of the River* to the Red Hand ..."

The Sergeant stopped talking, and let the implications of this revelation sink into the onlookers.

He watched the faces in the crowd change into smiles of triumph. Angus Quinn looked at him, and nodded ruefully ... acknowledging a well-played game and accepting the loss. He smiled back, pleased he would not challenge the Red Hand's move. The fact that there was overwhelming support from the people helped.

"As such, the Red Hand calls upon the members of Phoenix Squad to step forward, and do their duty for Selenta by joining the Red Hand as a fully-fledged Squad."

The resultant noise in the auditorium hit its highest volume yet.

CHAPTER FORTY-ONE

Drangor sighed, he was wet again. The countryside, that had initially been unusual and interesting, had become dank, dull, and monotonous. Even the town and estates they visited were grey and uniform; all blocks with a lifeless population that had the same beaten look in their eyes. They had no spark, and no fire. The only exciting part was when he entered the outlying countries.

The Tendrin to the north were people who reminded him of the Trendorlan; hardy, powerful, and basically free of the same harsh rule the rest of the continent seemed to be under … a testament to Elena's influence.

Marcus had been invaluable on the trip. His knowledge of the areas they were visiting, excellent. The information was apparently drilled into the recruits during their training to ensure that when stationed, they are prepared. He had scoffed at this doctrine, and Marcus had admitted it was only for those with the potential to become officers … ordinary grunts did not get the same education.

But even Marcus's commentary had run dry the further south they travelled. Their stays at each town or village was short, only long enough for him to make it clear he was out of favour with Magnar. Once their hosts understood his disfavour, the whole dynamic changed. Any interest or hospitality shown towards him, disappeared. The officers and leaders in the outlying areas shunned his company, none wishing to tarnish their reputation through association. He was OK with this, as it played well for his plans, but he was getting frustrated.

They were almost to the southern front, and there had been no sign of the Shadow Dancers. There were times when Tracker felt as though someone was watching and following them, but nothing ever came of it, and the feeling quickly disappeared.

Marcus had become quieter, and more agitated, the further south they had come.

"He's not comfortable down here," Tracker said in his mind.

He looked over to Tracker, who was padding along on his left-hand side, Twister was on his right, and Faith was flying above them, keeping an eye out for threats.

"It seems he's not the only one," he observed, referring to the fact Tracker had not spoken aloud.

"Magnar's reach does not extend as strongly all the way down here. That has become more evident the further we travel," Twister said.

"And you think that is why Marcus has gone quiet? Because he is no longer under the protection of Magnar?" he asked.

"It's our nature to suspect, Drangor ... to protect you," Twister explained.

He smiled inwardly at Tracker making him a priority, and making no mention of Selenta or The Black.

"I don't agree with you on this. Marcus has been nothing but helpful to us, and supportive of everything we have done. He didn't volunteer to join us; I had the choice of companion," he argued.

"I agree, Drangor, but we have to be careful, and not let friendship cloud our judgement," Twister advised.

Twister watched as Drangor's brow furrowed ever so slightly, a sure sign that his mind was reviewing and analysing a situation tactically.

Twister looked over to Tracker, and at his slight nod, they both dropped the conversation. They had planted the seed … and he would make the final decision.

* * *

Marcus watched Drangor and his companions trot just ahead of him. He was accustomed to seeing them in their manifested forms now. It had taken some time before he had stopped wanting to instinctively call Drangor a heretic. Typically, only Magnar and the Elite were allowed to flaunt their companions. The majority of those in Carasayer didn't even have access to a companion. If they did, they were either a part of Magnar's army, or kept the fact a secret, never revealing their companions in public.

"But he is not from Carasayer, and from what he has said, everyone in Selenta has access to companions." He stifled a grunt as Severo, his fox companion, interrupted his thoughts.

"Imagine the power they would add to an army? Where everyone in the ranks had three companions," he replied.

"Exactly, but my immediate concern is what Magnar could achieve with those soldiers at his command," Severo said.

Internally, he laughed ruefully. "He could destroy anyone in his path … or have his own power destroyed."

"A sobering thought," Severo muttered.

"Very much so, My Friend," he said.

A sudden cry from above dragged his attention to the skies.

* * *

"What is it?" Marcus asked.

The question momentarily took Drangor by surprise. Whether it was because Marcus broke Black Hand rules by questioning a senior officer about his companion, or because he'd had his train of thought interrupted … he was unsure, but he could feel anger rising nonetheless.

"He's not Selentan," Twister said simply, dousing his anger.

Instead of an outburst, he forced a smile. "It's a convoy, heading this way. It's heavily guarded by Elite and looks quite burdened."

Marcus shook his head in disbelief. "No wonder the Emperor keeps those with companions close and under his control."

He didn't miss the glint of awe in his eyes, but where was it aimed? At him and his companions, or the Emperor's foresight to keep them close?

"I can't believe how you do it, it's so incredible to me," Marcus gushed. "How does it feel with her? Can you see, or does she tell you?" he asked.

He smiled, but internally he growled at Twister and Tracker. "You two have me seeing intrigue where there is none."

He felt both of them shrug … they wouldn't apologise for keeping him safe and alert. He turned his attention back to Marcus, who had come up alongside him. "It depends on what we're doing. Faith can talk to me like you do. So today, when she doesn't see it as a threat, she will talk. But when we hunt, I can see through her eyes, feel the environment like she does, sounds, movement, and even seeing prey that's out of sight in the distance."

Marcus's jaw dropped, and he realised he had never spoken to him about his companions.

"How do you handle that information?" Marcus asked, enraptured.

He laughed. "That's an excellent question, with no easy answer, but I will try and explain."

"Be careful," Tracker warned, as he slipped off into the forest on their left, his dark pelt merging quickly into the shadows.

He heeded the warning, and decided to talk about just the basics. Pulling their horses up at the side of the track to wait and allow the convoy to pass, he looked at Marcus.

"Many in Selenta receive their companions at a very early age. When the companion first appears, their attributes tend not to exist in any real strength, these develop over time. Their type of ability and their strength, are dependent on the host and the companion's characteristics and how they mix ... so they vary with each person. So, you can have two people with the same type of owl companion, with totally different abilities," he told Marcus, watching as he mulled over the information.

"Does everyone cope with the companions? Our history talks about people going mad and the companions taking control."

He smiled ruefully, remembering the wolf that he had chased into The Forbidden. "No, not everyone can cope with their companions' strength. If you have a weak host, and a strong companion, then their characteristics take control."

He saw the horror of that thought in Marcus's eyes so continued quickly. "However, this is now extremely rare in Selenta. We have a system set up that tests the young early, so they can be trained to control themselves ... and their companions."

Tracker laughed in his mind at that, making him grin.

"What's so funny about that?" Marcus asked, still slightly shaken.

He quickly schooled his face back to being serious again. "There is nothing funny about it, Marcus. I was smiling at Tracker. He scoffed at the thought of host's being able to control their companions."

Marcus's brow furrowed in confusion. "Is he saying you don't control them?"

He was saved from having to reply immediately as the convoy trundled passed them. The Elite soldiers had recognised Marcus from some distance away, and simply nodded as they passed.

He waited for the convoy to be out of earshot before he started talking again. "The relationship with our companions is not really one of control. It's more a symbiotic relationship, they become part of us, and we become part of them. One cannot survive or exist without the other."

Marcus nodded, taking it all in. He was about to ask another question when Faith cried from up above.

An image of the convoy jumped into his mind, but that was not Faith's focus. The area around them seemed to be moving and flowing, like waves on the sea. It was unnatural, and immediately he knew that this was an attack.

"Do not move," Tracker hissed into his mind in a warning.

He held up a hand to Marcus and calmly spoke. "Something is about to happen, Marcus. You're going to want to move and help, to support your compatriots, but you cannot and must not ... or we will both be dead before we can move more than a few feet."

Tracker emerged out of the shadows of the trees, and silently took his place next to him.

"Move higher, Faith," he muttered.

At his instruction, she spread her wings and climbed higher into the sky. He nodded and explained to Marcus, who had looked at him, confused.

"This gives me several advantages. It keeps Faith out of reach of weapons like the shotbolt, and gives plenty of time to avoid a manifesting enemy. It also gives me a wider view of the battlefield."

"Battle?" Marcus hissed, and tugged on his horse's reins, his earlier warning forgotten. Any further movement halted as Twister stood in his way, growling from his belly, and the horse froze in fright.

"We cannot help Carasayer if we are dead," he said simply, watching the turmoil in Marcus's eyes.

He was unable to easily explain what he could see through Faith's eyes, so he had no idea of the futility of trying to help. The convoy was already dead, they just didn't know it.

Suddenly, the waves halted momentarily, and he surmised that they were finally in place, whoever *they* were? The attack would happen shortly.

"Now, watch carefully ... any minute detail may provide us with valuable information," he instructed.

"Watch what?" Marcus asked angrily.

There was nothing to see by the naked eye, as the convoy

trundled lazily through the centre of a large open area. Drangor didn't need to answer as the world around the convoy came alive. Wraiths and shadows appeared as if out of nowhere, the Elite soldiers were dead before they even knew they were under attack.

"Chameleons?" Tracker asked.

"I think there are a few, but it's the shadows that interest me. Keep an eye on them," he answered in his mind.

He watched as the Elite soldiers were taken down; knives, swords, axes ... all flashing through the air.

"All hand-to-hand weapons," Twister observed.

"Interesting," was all Drangor replied.

The fight was over quickly. The Elite soldiers were dead before they drew their weapons, and the drivers of the wagons lay slumped in their chairs, also dead. Figures dressed in battle armour, the likes he had never seen, started appearing out of thin air as their camouflage dropped. The odd cowled figure, interspersed within them.

"Shadow Dancers," Drangor whispered to Marcus, as the figures started moving towards the convoy.

One of the figures dressed in armour reached the first wagon and pulled the canvas back. It was the last thing it did as a blade hit it straight in the face, dropping it instantly to the floor. The attackers seemed stunned for a moment, as they watched their comrade drop to the floor. Ten more Elite soldiers streamed from the back of the wagon, weapons drawn and ready to fight. The pause from the attackers was fleeting, but it allowed the Elite to get set. A keening cry went up from the attackers, and they advanced on the heavily outnumbered Elite soldiers.

It had been a good idea, he mused, hiding in the wagon then

coming to the aid of their brethren, attempting to ambush the ambushers. However, they had not counted on how silent and efficient the ambushers would be. It seemed the Elite Captain had opted to do as much damage as possible, before they were slain or captured. His soldiers made good initial progress, cutting down a few of the soldiers in armour. They attacked the Elite, more out of anger than as a trained unit. The Captain's axe took an armoured figure's head from his shoulders. At that point, a shrill whistle sounded, and the attackers seemed to melt away, dispersing from sight.

From Faith's lofty position, he watched the waves on the ground moving into place on either side of the Elite soldiers. The Captain was flailing his axe around, screaming for the enemy to face him.

He looked and was surprised to see that there were only two attacker's bodies on the ground, the rest had disappeared at the sound of the whistle. Through Faith, he heard a strange clicking sound, and moments later, an Elite soldier at the edge of the defensive circle they had formed, disappeared with no sound, reappearing dead on the ground in front of the Captain. This happened again, and again. Elite numbers dwindled ... they couldn't fight what they couldn't see or understand.

All too soon, the Captain stood alone and helpless, looking at the bodies of his men, the rage evident in his body language. Another whistle sounded, and the attackers appeared again, forming a half-circle around the Elite Captain. One of the cowled figures stood facing him, no more than five meters away.

"You have killed two of the Honoured," a deep, spiritual, and very evidently female voice calmly stated.

He was taken aback at hearing a voice after the silence of the battle.

"Not honoured any more, just dead," the Captain spat. "As will the rest of you be once the Emperor decides to finish this."

"We will see, but you will not live to see it," the figure stated calmly.

"Well then tell your men to get it over with. I'm going to take some of them with me," the Captain growled back.

"You misunderstand," the figure said. "I intend to kill you myself ... as a sacrifice to aid the Honoured on their journey to the source."

He watched her carefully, seeing a curved bone dagger appear in her hand, and missing the initial movement of the Captain, who clearly didn't intend to wait. He charged at her, his axe flashing through the spot where the woman's neck was. Having moved no more than a few inches, she was no longer in its path, and the blade flashed harmlessly by. As the Captain followed his weapon, she simply stepped into the area he had vacated.

He watched closely to understand her fighting style, but was disappointed ... the fight was over. The Captain turned to press his attack, but found his axe was no longer in his hands, having dropped it to the ground. His hands moved up to his throat and came away covered in blood. He fell to his knees, looking up at the figure whose blade, Drangor now realised, was dripping with blood. The life quickly drained from the Captain as he fell forward onto the floor. As he took his last breath, the figure raised the dagger into the air, and everyone dropped to one knee, their heads bowed.

"I didn't see that attack," Twister whispered.

"Drangor, you don't spar with these to earn their respect," Tracker simply stated.

He agreed.

After a few seconds, she lowered her blade, accepting a rag offered by one of the other cowled figures, and cleaned it. The ambush had taken no more than a minute from start to finish. There were twenty dead Elite soldiers, in contrast to just two of the attackers, whose total only numbered twenty-five.

"It's no wonder that Magnar is worried," Tracker commented, reading his thoughts.

"Yes, but with that kind of strength, why have they not driven Magnar away from their front with ease?" he wondered.

As they watched, the attackers took their time in recovering their fallen brethren, handling the bodies with reverence. Six of the armoured soldiers wrapped each of the bodies in strips of cloth, carrying them with three at each side. They stopped beside the five cowled figures, who bowed their heads over each.

After a few moments, the soldiers moved off, vanishing from sight. The remaining soldiers followed suit, but he knew they had not gone far. Faith could see the disturbances in the ground as they took flanking positions around the cowled figures, whose attention had now turned to him and Marcus.

The figures slowly made their way silently across the ground in a V formation, the one with the dagger taking the first flanking position on the right. As they came closer, he climbed down off his horse, motioning for Marcus to do the same. Faith swooped down from the sky and landed on his shoulder, Twister and Tracker coming up beside him. Marcus stayed slightly behind.

Stopping before him, the first of the group stepped forward … pulling back its cowl, and revealing beautiful, long blonde hair, that was tied back and decorated in various coloured cloth. She smiled. He heard Marcus's throat catch, and understood why. The woman before him was stunning, her smile portraying innocence and life. She had crystal blue moon-shaped eyes that sparkled, a fantastic accompaniment to her perfect lips, and soft cheekbones.

"A perfect weapon to disarm men," Tracker observed.

"It worked with Marcus," Twister laughed.

He tried not to laugh, schooling his face as he returned a bow and a gentle smile of his own. He saw a flash of something different, something controlled and calculating in the woman's eyes.

"Only a fool would think her a simple bauble," Faith hooted.

A different kind of smile adorned her face now, as she looked directly at him. "Welcome, Major Drangor, to the Lands of the Honoured."

He bowed his head slightly, the same salute he provided to any senior figure. The woman returned his bow to the same depth.

"A schooled diplomat," Tracker observed.

"Greetings from the Black of Selenta," he replied to the woman.

A shrewd smile crept onto her face, a glimpse of the real woman in front of him. "The Black of Selenta? Major Drangor, are you not here fact-finding for the Emperor of Carasayer?"

He smiled himself, she was direct and intelligent, and

evidently well-informed. "You have me at a disadvantage?" he said, deciding to change tack. At the question in her eyes, he continued. "You know my name, but I do not know yours …"

One of the cowled figures behind seemed to shift, and he saw a slight movement in the woman in front of him, and everything stopped.

"You may call me Artic. My true name you have to earn," Artic smiled.

He wasn't sure what had happened, but he recognised it as useful information, cataloguing it away, and deciding not to inquire of the others' names. "And how would I earn that honour?" he asked instead.

He watched her eyes as she considered his question, noting that slight movement again, followed by a knowing smile which split her face. "Earn our trust, Major Drangor." She paused momentarily. "You can start by explaining why you are travelling with Emperor Magnar's son?"

* * *

Artic watched Drangor closely. She'd been impressed by his reaction and control when she revealed herself … most men simply saw a beautiful blonde woman, and were immediately tongue-tied or dismissive of her abilities as a negotiator. She never failed to leave them confused, and having bargained for less than they desired.

This Major Drangor had surprised her, he had been calm, observant, and a minute flicker in his eyes had shown he had not missed the reaction by her sisters. His asking her name, without it offered, was an insult. However, that had been her own fault because she hadn't introduced herself from the outset. She'd been intent on observing him. By not asking about the others, Drangor had again shown that he was a capable diplomat.

"And how would I earn that honour?" he asked her.

She decided to test him, and signalled to her sisters that she was about to do something. She needed them to not interfere … but to leave it to her to deal. The next few seconds would shape their negotiations.

"Earn our trust, Major Drangor, and you can start by explaining why you are travelling with Emperor Magnar's son?" she asked Drangor.

The reaction was almost instant. Artic barely registered Magnar's son, Marcus, as he took a step forward with blades appearing in his hands. His mouth was open, and he was about to shout something. She was too preoccupied with watching Drangor; rage flickering across his face.

There was a flash of light as a blade appeared in Drangor's hand, stopping Marcus in his tracks, as he rested it against his throat. Drangor's companions had also moved to intercede themselves in between the two, growls rumbling in their bellies.

"Choose your next words very carefully, Marcus. They may be your last," Drangor snarled.

Artic watched as Marcus's eyes looked at her briefly. They were no longer full of lust, and she was mildly surprised to see not only anger, but hurt. Perhaps her sister was correct.

"I may be his son by blood, but I am his enemy by beliefs," Marcus answered, again surprising her.

Artic had expected denials or pleading, but this simple statement was much more convincing. Drangor also thought so, the rage disappearing from his eyes, although he didn't lower his dagger.

Her sister came up beside her, pulling her cowl back … revealing her long auburn hair, and plain features that could easily merge into any crowd; a face that was easily forgettable most of the time.

"May I introduce my sister, you may call her Auricle," Artic said.

Drangor again bowed his head slightly, and Auricle returned the gesture.

"What your companion says is true, Major Drangor. He has been working for years to get himself close to Magnar while working against him. We believe Magnar has no idea of his existence," Auricle explained.

Artic smiled at Marcus's reaction. Her sister, who looked plain at first glance, changed once she started speaking. Her eyes came alive, and her features sharpened, filling with life and enthusiasm, the perfect tool for her role. Her words had the desired effect, and Drangor's blade disappeared.

"We will discuss this later," Drangor stated.

She watched Marcus nod, not taking his eyes from Drangor. She realised why he looked hurt earlier … there was a kind of hero-worship there, one that didn't want to disappoint Drangor. Filing this away for later, she smiled.

"We now need to move quickly and unseen. Major Drangor, please recall your companions for the journey, they are welcome to join us once we get to our destination."

Major Drangor responded immediately with a nod, and his companions disappeared.

"Please forgive our precautions, secrecy is imperative."

Artic was once again impressed by Drangor's control. He

didn't flinch when the Honoured appeared out of nowhere and placed a hood over his head, leading him back to mount his horse. Marcus also made no fuss, but she felt that was due more to the fact he felt deflated, rather than that he was aware of what was happening.

Artic waited as the Honoured led them away into the trees, and still, she remained. Her sister, who had killed the Elite Captain, came up beside her. She knew it was her because the smell of blood was still on her robes.

"Do you think he will be up to the task required?" she asked.

"We will soon see, Delasayer."

She felt more than saw her nod.

"Drangor is quite impressive, isn't he?" Delasayer purred, changing the subject.

Artic laughed a tinkling sound. "I'm sure you will find out soon."

The five sisters all chuckled together, as they began to follow them into the trees.

* * *

"What do you mean, gone?" Magnar growled.

Elena sat casually across from Magnar, outwardly calm, she would not show an ounce of fear to Magnar, less his respect for her diminish. She didn't fear that he would attack her; her concern was for her home. Magnar's trust and love allowed her and her home to remain free of the full heel of Carasayer, allowing her people to regroup and strengthen following their war, and letting her do a job she loved. She sighed inwardly. Being Magnar's intelligence chief meant she had many rewards. She controlled everything that went on in Carasayer, having eyes and ears everywhere, with each of them as dedicated to her as they were to Magnar. However, it meant that conversations of this nature needed delivering by her too.

In the last few months, Magnar's moods had become a little erratic. He saw defeats, but little to no progress on the southern front. A few Generals had felt the sting of that continued failure.

"My agents can find no sign of them. They left the last post before the southern front four weeks ago, but never arrived at the front."

"And this is all you know?" he snarled.

She decided to try a different approach. "I know you're not going to listen in this insufferable mood. I'll save my breath for when you are."

She stood, making her way to the door, and swinging her hips as she moved. She had walked no more than a few paces when she felt him come up behind, growling as his arms slipped around her, and his mouth found her neck, biting menacingly. She smiled; she was as hungry as he was.

"If that's what you wanted … you only needed to ask," she whispered, laughing provocatively as he pulled her off her feet, and carried her into the bedroom.

* * *

Sometime later, she rose from the bed, stretching, and strolled to the window, looking out over Carasayer.

"So, tell me what you know," Magnar instructed, all the animosity of earlier gone from his voice, which was now husky and relaxed.

She looked back over her shoulder, and smiled at him, returning to the bed. She leaned in and kissed him.

"As you asked so nicely ..." she purred, diving away quickly, as he playfully tried to pull her back into his arms.

"Like a playful kitten, once he's satisfied," Lacie, her cobra, hissed in her mind.

"A man of his position should scratch the itch with the maids to keep his mood in check," Shift, her cat, giggled playfully.

"He's no tomcat, and we have been gone a while," Carabella, her third companion observed.

Elena smiled at her companions, and at Magnar. "He wouldn't have me if he was," she stated simply.

Then she took a deep breath. Regardless of how relaxed Magnar was, he was going to be furious. The best way to handle this was to give him the final position. "The soldiers we sent to protect the ambushed convoy are lost to a man, and Major Drangor has disappeared."

Magnar surprised her with a gentle sigh, rather than the explosion she had expected.

"Kitten," Shift giggled.

"Give me the detail," Magnar instructed.

"There isn't really much by way of concrete information. Our agents were following Drangor, but had to keep a significant distance so as not to be discovered."

Magnar looked up, confusion on his face. "How would they be discovered? These were our best trackers?" he questioned.

She nodded. "Yes, they are, but Major Drangor is in the habit of allowing his companions to roam free as he travels. His owl constantly covers the air, and his two ground companions prowl the land in all directions. Reports were that when they came within a certain distance, the companions converged, and they had to use all their skill to avoid being discovered."

She watched as Magnar assimilated this information.

"That fits with what I thought when we sparred, his companions are an extension of him, more like an extra arm."

She nodded; it was a good comparison.

"But what I need to understand is ... how they stay manifested for so long without draining him?" Magnar continued. "I have been trialling this with the Elite, seeing how long they can keep their companions manifested, but they are all exhausted after a very short period." Magnar shook his head. "But I digress. Please, continue ..."

She sat down on the bed, her hand absently finding Magnar. "Due to this, the trackers stayed well back, and all was well when they left the final outpost before the front. They surmise from their findings at the place of the conflict that Drangor crossed paths with the convoy, which was subsequently attacked and wiped out by a force of twenty to thirty attackers."

Magnar jumped at this. "That must be wrong. There were twenty Elite soldiers on that convoy, with Dengreer in charge, he is fearsome."

She sighed. "Was fearsome, My Love. He was found beside a pile of his men with his throat cut ... his axe on the floor by his side." She waited a moment before continuing. "The analysis of the scene determined that it looked like the results of a well-placed ambush, but it was out in the open, in the middle of a meadow."

Magnar looked shocked at the worrying news. "And Drangor's body was found there?"

She shook her head. "No. Some tracks matched their horses some distance away. It looks like they observed the attack, but were not involved. Although at one point, their tracks are ringed by the attackers, we think they were led off towards the trees."

Magnar sat up in the bed, she had his full attention now. "We can follow their tracks. We need them back to explain what happened, and what's going on, they will have the information we need. I'll send my personal guard."

She laid a hand on his chest. "I'm afraid it will do no good. As I said, the tracks led off to the trees … but they disappeared before they reached the treeline. Coplin described it as eerie, it was like no one, or nothing, had stepped there. They cast out for miles into the trees, in all directions, and found nothing. They would have gone further, but they started meeting our own patrols from the front, so any tracks would have been lost."

Magnar dropped back onto the bed, and she laid her head against his chest, listening to his heartbeat. They lay like this for a while. She knew he would be talking this over with Tink and Gravel, with Cassius probably grumbling that he wanted to go and eat someone. She smiled at the thought, she loved Cassius's simplicity.

"We have to hope they somehow escape, and return to us with the information we need to fight this enemy," Magnar said simply, his hand running down her side and making her shiver.

"I have already instructed Coplin and his team to cast a net along the southern front, to watch out for them, and assist in any way they can," she advised, her voice slightly husky.

Magnar pulled her to him, kissing her. "Or to bring them back kicking and screaming, I hope," he growled.

"Of course, My Love," she purred.

CHAPTER FORTY-TWO

Leandra jumped the fallen tree trunk, feeling her back paw catch on the edge of it. She looked around and saw the rest of the Squad looking just as tired. They had lost Daan, Calik, and Dremu in defence of the alpha site while the River Runners escaped, and Ganna and Hurf had been captured, as they fell behind on the retreat.

Nala had split up from them at this point, deciding to divert the quickest of the pursuers, who had wanted him the most, away from the others, or else he would have lost the rest of the Squad too.

She was not overly worried about Nala, the chase seemed to have energised him rather than tired him. She'd thought splitting up was a bad idea, but she had to admit that her concern had been personal, and nothing to do with the tactical benefit.

However, his plan had worked and the Runners had a slight reprieve. The wolves and cats had split after Nala, leaving a troop of hyenas on their tail. They weren't fast, but their stamina was relentless, and Zagane followed close behind them with the rest of the Death Dealers.

Nala's successes, and the deaths of some of Zagane's most loyal troops, had sent him into a frenzy. He had recalled every

Death Dealer to him, and they had scoured The Forbidden looking for them. They were a tide that no one could have avoided, and not surprisingly, he had succeeded and moved in on the alpha site.

Many of the Runners had wanted to stay and fight, fed up with moving every time they were under attack. Gervais had put an end to that idea. The alpha site was defendable, but they couldn't survive a siege. The River Runners hadn't been there long enough for the stores and plants to grow. Gervais pointed out that Zagane wasn't stupid, and that he wouldn't throw an all-out attack on a protected area. In the end, the Runners had fled.

They had lost a few Runner's as they fought to give the non-combatants time to get away. Zagane had tried to flank them, but his initial probes had been thwarted by some well-placed traps and ambushes. This had proven too much for Zagane. He'd recognised that the numbers defending the alpha site were small, so sent in his heavies ... two huge gorillas, flanked by a pack of rabid wolves, and preceded by a Squad of large rats.

Daan, Calik, and Remu had vaulted the defence and the incoming rats, intercepting the gorillas. The monkeys' blades had flashed as they took down the first of the gorillas, slicing the flesh behind its unprotected knees. As it fell to the ground, its huge hands had taken hold of Daan's head and driven it forcefully into the earth. The resounding crack could be heard clear across the forest.

Calik and Remu didn't survive long enough to celebrate their victory. The rats and wolves swarmed them, and their cries pierced the air. Yet in their sacrifice, they provided the time that the final defenders needed to get a head start on their retreat.

Nala had been the last to leave, ensuring everyone had gone. He had a dark look in his eyes as they roamed over the place where their bodies had fallen.

Pulling her mind back, she barely avoided striking a low branch. She felt her energy reserves waning ... cursing her body as she considered one last stand before her energy ran out; leaving her as easy meat for the hyenas. At least this way she could take a few with her. However, this thought was fleeting ... it was the old her, and she had changed because of Nala. She no longer had a death wish.

"Dumb animal," she growled. The thought of Nala gave her a surge of hope and energy. "He had better still be alive, or I'll kill him myself," she snarled.

Her threats were disrupted by a yip from up ahead, a signal from Dex that they were nearly at the rendezvous point. Only Dex and Nala had known the destination, it had been a closely held secret.

"Not that it matters," she cursed.

The Death Dealers had followed them with everything they had, she could hear them following behind the hyenas. They had the scent of blood in their nostrils, and they wouldn't stop until they were forced too, or had eliminated the Runners.

Taking a deep breath, she prepared herself for a final burst of speed to give her time to join the others before the Death Dealers arrived, just as her nostrils became assaulted by the tang of sea air.

"What are they up to?" she muttered, confused, and for the first time, truly terrified.

She saw the edge of the forest up ahead, and darted out

into the open air of the beach. The first thing she noticed was that the tide was out, leaving a vast swath of sand in front of her. Her eyes quickly saw the River Runners up ahead with the sea surrounding them on three sides. There was about a hundred of them.

"There's so few left," she whimpered.

Then, from both the left and right, she saw groups of Death Dealers closing in, they had the Runners cornered. Once Zagane arrived, they would be severely outnumbered.

Anita, Reg, and Dex looked to her for instruction. With Nala gone, she was their Squad leader, and she saw the horror of the situation she felt, mirrored in their eyes.

"We join our family, then leave as many of these filthy animals dead before we go," she growled menacingly.

A steely resolve entered the rest of the Squad's eyes, and they ran across the beach, slipping between the two groups before they could cut them off from the Runners. As they closed in, she saw Gervais was with the group, and her spirits lifted slightly, but as she watched, she saw him preparing them as best he could for assault. Even the Runners who weren't fighters were fitted out with weapons; branches, rakes, and skinning knives. It was little protection against the animals that were about to attack.

Gervais turned as she arrived. "Leandra," he said, acknowledging her arrival, then walked forward a few steps. "We lost so many on the retreat, these are all I could save," he said sullenly as his head sagged.

"Nala will be here, I know it," she whispered, fighting the despair she was feeling.

Gervais shook his head. "No, he won't. Joe came in before the Death Dealers cut us off, he watched Nala go down protecting the cubs."

She felt sick and would have fallen if Reg hadn't come up beside her, propping her up as Joe climbed up on her back. She looked into Reg's eyes and saw tears there too. She felt an empty hole where her heart was.

"Get Zagane close enough for me to get to him. I'll be meeting Nala in the River."

Gervais smiled a deadly smile. "We both will, Leandra," he said, giving a slight pause. "When it's time."

Silence followed his cryptic comment as they watched the two groups of Death Dealers finally come together, cutting off any retreat … or last-minute support.

The tree line behind came alive, as the Death Dealers' leading group arrived. All types of creatures appeared; leopards, panthers, mountain cats, a gorilla, monkeys, ferrets, stags, wolfhounds, dogs, rats, possums, the odd wolf, countless hyenas, a few wild boars, and many other animals of the forest … all scarred and menacing.

There must have been close to three hundred of them, yet regardless of the variety of animals on show, all eyes went to one … a huge wild boar. He was easily the size of Gervais if they were side-by-side, and his huge tusks glinted in the afternoon sun: Zagane.

The attention of every Runner was on Zagane. None had ever seen him before, so when one of the Runner's broke ranks and darted towards the Death Dealers, they were halfway there before it registered.

"Slaven, what are you doing?" she shouted, desperately fearing that Slaven was about to throw his life away needlessly. Her thought was instantly gone as he stopped, and turned back to them with a rabid look in his eyes.

"I'm finally going home," Slaven hissed. "I will enjoy watching you all die." He barked a laugh, and then turned back to the Death Dealers who opened ranks to allow him through, Slaven barking greetings to a few.

She looked to Gervais, the realisation that Slaven had always been working against them, hurting. "We're not going to get Zagane now, are we?" she asked, surprised to see an eager glint in Gervais's eyes as he watched Slaven approach Zagane.

"Just don't go getting yourself killed. Nala will tear me a new one if your dead before he gets here," he replied, instead of answering her question.

Suddenly, it all dropped into place. Nala wasn't dead. Slipping away had always been his plan, and that it was because of a valid reason … it only enhanced the ruse. It explained the low number of fighters left here … even given that all the Death Dealers had chased them … there should have been more than double, and none of the younger ones was in this group at all.

"You knew there was a spy," she accused, surprisingly calm.

"Suspected. Hopefully, Nala will now complete the most important part of the plan," Gervais replied.

"Which is?" she asked.

Gervais just grinned.

She huffed and turned away. "I'm going to let the Squad know he's not dead," she growled, as she flounced off.

"Don't take too long, this is about to get interesting," Gervais said, as he watched Zagane begin barking orders … the Death Dealers were moving into place.

* * *

418

"It's been a long time," Zagane greeted Slaven.

"Too long, Brother," Slaven replied, lowering his head as their foreheads met. "You have no idea how revoltingly nice I've had to be while living with those do-gooders," Slaven snarled. "I haven't even been able to flay a damn rat. You took your sweet time finally deciding to finish them off."

Zagane laughed, and most of his Lieutenants jumped, not recognising the noise coming from him, having expected an outburst of anger.

"Don't worry, Brother, you will get your chance to flay a few today," Zagane answered, gesturing to the remaining Runners. "Is that all there is left?" he asked.

"There are a few left who never made it back, getting cut-off. All the reports say your sheer numbers got the jump on them and eliminated the majority, even Nala," Slaven replied.

Zagane looked at him. "Who's Nala?"

Slaven looked at the Lieutenants. "Who's Nala?" he growled at them. "What have you all been doing in my absence?" he snapped at the closest leopard, taking a chunk out of his neck, and causing him to whimper and jump back. The others moved away quickly. "Cowards," he snarled, before turning back to a grinning Zagane. "Nala is the huge wolf that has caused you so many problems."

The grin left Zagane's face. "The wolf is dead? I had hoped to kill him myself," Zagane said.

"Unfortunately, yes. I would have loved to have Nala watch me take Leandra in front of him," Slaven replied.

Zagane walked casually past him. "So, this is all that's left of the Runners?" he asked again.

Slaven nodded.

"Call the Captains in," Zagane ordered.

Animals darted off, and within minutes, they were back.

"Let everyone know that we are to hit them hard and fast, heavies on the first wave, but everyone else on their heels. I want this over quickly," Zagane ordered.

They all nodded and turned.

"And no one is to kill Gervais. He's mine!" Zagane called as they left.

Zagane moved forward and took his place in the middle of the line, behind the heavies, opposite Gervais, with Slaven on his right side.

When all the Death Dealers were in place, Zagane looked at Slaven. "Would you like to do the honours, Brother?"

Slaven nodded and took a step forward. "Death Dealers," he called to get their attention. "KILL THEM ALL!" he screamed, with years of pent up aggression in that one order … and they surged forward as one.

* * *

Gervais stood calmly, watching the Death Dealers take their place in front of them. He looked, for what must have been the hundredth time, for the markers. He and Nala had planned this for the last few months. Gervais had suspected there were Death Dealers in the camp, recognising a few of them in the horde in front of him, but the one that hurt the most was Slaven. He had been with them a long time, Mavis even nursing him back to health after what they'd suspected was a Death Dealer attack, yet now he knew it to be a ruse.

"Barrier Squad," he said calmly.

A group of monkeys stepped out of the Runners lines and stood around him. "Can you see some pretty blue shells out

420

in front of us?"

He had to suppress a smile as he saw Leandra's eyes narrow, seeking out the shells and then looking around and noticing other markers set in unnatural lines. The monkeys all nodded.

"You see their heavies aligned at the front?"

There were approximately twenty large animals: the gorilla from the alpha site, a stag, and a couple of scruffy wolfhounds amongst them. Again, they nodded solemnly.

"Your job is to stop them."

A wicked grin crossed their faces, none of the Runners that were left wanted to go down without a fight. They started to move out to the shells, pulling various weapons out of their belts, and he laughed.

"Wait, My Friends, I haven't told you the best bit."

The monkeys looked at him, quizzically.

"In the ground, in front of those shells, are ten wicked sharp pikes, as tall as three of you." He watched them look at each other, gauging the size. "Out in front is a stone which you can see just below the surface. Once the heavies reach that, you need to drop your weapons, and plunge your hand into the sand and pull up the pikes. They're already wedged, so you just need to raise them. Once the heavies hit the pikes, let them go and return to the front line."

He watched the fire dancing in their eyes.

"Do you understand me? I need you back in the front line once they hit."

It took a few moments, but each of the monkeys controlled the bloodlust, nodded, and took their places. He smiled and turned back to the Runners. He looked across them and addressed them in a calm, unconcerned voice.

"Runners, today, this battle ends the war for The Forbidden. Fight like your very existence depends on it because ..." his speech was cut short by Slaven's scream.

"KILL THEM ALL!"

He turned back raising his blade high, and above the cries of the Death Dealers, yelled his own battle cry.

"SEND THEM ALL BACK TO THE RIVER!"

* * *

Slaven smirked as he watched Gervais raise his weapon in defiance, the Runners didn't stand a chance. The sand shuddered under his feet as Gondo and the heavies pounded across the ground, closely followed by Vepar and Gremor's hordes. He wouldn't even have to get his nose bloody. He felt a bit disappointed at the thought, but consoled himself ... he would have some fun after. At which, his eyes cast to Leandra. She had calmly walked up to Gervais with that lumbering brute, Reg, beside her.

"They look too calm," he whispered to himself. His mind started whirring, thinking over, and questioning the lack of fighters left ... why were these specific Runners split-up from the group and hunted down? The Death Dealers weren't that disciplined, and the Runners' hunters were pretty good. His thoughts turned to Nala, taken down defending the young? They had left the alpha camp days before, they wouldn't be close enough for Nala to need to defend, he was the rear guard.

Before his train of thought coalesced into something meaningful ... the world went crazy. Everything seemed to happen all at once, almost like time accelerated.

Gondo reared back with a scream of agony, blood spurting from a wound in his neck. He fell back, crushing a wolfhound while taking out a stag's front legs ... all going down in a heap, and providing him with a view of a wall of wooden stakes that had greeted the heavies.

Over half of their numbers were lost in moments, leaving the remainder confused and disorganised now that Gondo was down. The rest of the Death Dealers had stopped at Gondo's deathly scream, looking around for instructions.

Vepar and Gremor were looking to Zagane for advice. The realisation hit him like a rhino, the Runners were ready, they had planned this. They weren't the prey, these were bait.

He had to stop Zagane. Before he could open his mouth to speak ... a cry of fury erupted from Zagane, and he knew there was no bringing him back to reason. He had to hope that Zagane's wrath, which he aimed at the heart of the Runners leading the charge, would burst this ambush wide open.

He took off as quickly as he could to join his brother in battle, allowing himself to become caught up in the charge, the blood and roars pounding in his ears.

He didn't hear the howl that signalled the trap closing.

* * *

"Stay where you are!" Nala growled, the noise shaking the ground around him.

Tergar stopped in his tracks before turning to face him and hissed, "Why?" It was evidence of Tergar's state-of-mind that he was challenging him, when all the other Runners had taken a step back.

He felt his rage growing. His alpha pack instinct was driving him, wanting to subdue the challenge to his authority, but a faint echo of Swiftwind's voice, which had grown weaker over the previous weeks, reminded him of Tergar's loss.

He sighed, and everything came back into focus. He felt more than saw the rest of the Runners take a collective breath. He wasn't sure whether it was Swift, or just the influence she had left, making him calm the situation.

He took a gentle step forward. "It's not what Midnight would want to happen."

The hurt look in Tergar's eyes made him wince inwardly. It was a low blow invoking the name of his lost mate, but he needed to stop Tergar from advancing, and jeopardising the whole plan.

"Midnight would also not want her friends slaughtered while we cower in the forest. The monkey has said they are surrounded, and Slaven is one of them," Tergar spat.

He decided to take a different approach. "I know, and everything hinges on us exacting this plan precisely as Gervais has advised," he said simply. Then added in a more menacing tone, "And Leandra is down there. So, don't think for one second that I'm not fighting the urge to get down there. To fight for her, and the rest of the Runners."

He saw that he was getting through, so decided to finish this.

"So, if you don't trust me, we can deal with this now and risk everything. Or, you can get back in formation, trust me, and wait?"

He held his breath as he watched Tergar fight his instinct, then his shoulders sagged in an all too human gesture on a panther.

As Tergar walked past, he spoke quietly for his ears only. "This ends today. We will avenge Midnight, and every Runner we have ever lost."

He smiled to himself as he saw Tergar stand a bit straighter, a vicious grin spreading across his lips as he joined the rest. He turned to the group. Over the preceding weeks he had arranged a pre-meet point with those he trusted outside his own Squad, which had left these thirty hunters. He was glad that he had not approached Slaven. His pretence for leaving his Squad with Leandra was to round everyone up, the fact that it probably saved them was a bonus. He would have loved to have them all at his side now. However, Gervais needed the best fighters to hold long enough for them to spring the trap.

The hunters all looked lean, eager, and not a little bit angry.

"It's nearly time, ensure everyone is ready. As soon as I say go, we go." he ordered, looking directly at Tergar. "And we go as if the hellions of the Riverbank themselves were on our tail. We hit hard and fast. Our brother and sister Runners are down there, giving their lives for us, to end this conflict with the Death Dealers." He then looked across them all, making eye contact with each one. "What we do today will decide the fate of the Runners and The Forbidden. I, for one, want it to be our future! Who's with me?" he growled.

Every hunter growled in response, their view echoing his own. He smiled as the fire blazed in each of their eyes.

Ben dropped down next to him. "Zagane has lost it, he will pass the marker in seconds."

He turned quickly. "Let's go save our brothers and sisters!" he roared as he took off, with Ben vaulting from the tree and landing cleanly on his back. As they dashed through the last trees towards the beach, he saw the scattered bodies of owls, rats, and foxes.

"Called themselves scouts," Ben huffed angrily.

Just then, he caught a brief glimpse of Fred dropping out of a tree and onto Tergar's back, before he was out into the open, and onto the beach.

"Always wants to be in the thick of it, that one," Ben observed proudly.

"Says you. I'm going to be target number one out there," he said, feeling the roll of the eyes from Ben.

"Don't worry, Nala. I'll keep you alive," he laughed.

The laugh was cut short as they received a final picture of the carnage that was the beach. The Death Dealers were swarming the meagre Runners, who were holding their own for the moment, although he saw numerous gaps in the line that the Runners were trying to fill from behind. Zagane was almost to Gervais, slowed down by the sheer numbers, his tusks tearing his own fighters if they were in his way.

He looked at the centre where the fighting was fiercest. He couldn't see Leandra. His heart skipped a beat as she suddenly rose out from a pile of rats and ferrets, two in her mouth. Joe was on her back, covered in blood, and plunging his tiny blade into anything that tried to attach itself to her from the side.

"You and your brothers have my loyalty ... and a place at my side for as long as we live," he whispered.

"Yes. Yes, we keep you alive," Ben mocked, but he could hear the pride in his voice as he watched his brother. "Don't you think it's about time we play the final card?" Ben asked.

He shook himself from his stupor. He had been so focused

on getting to the Runners he had almost forgotten. He raised his head and howled, louder than he had ever done before, feeling it reverberate through his bones, and the ground at his paws. Nothing happened straight away, and panic rose ready to take hold, thinking that his signal went unheard. He took a breath, ready to signal again, when he saw bubbles rise in the sea on either side of the Death Dealers.

Out of the water rose two massive creatures, both breaking the surface at speed and landing half on the beach, crushing the Death Dealers close to them. Their mouths opened wide, releasing a tide of adult River Runners, who poured out armed with picks, shovels, and pikes ... the tools of the Runner's farmer.

He only had a few seconds to register that Gervais had been right ... those at the sides were the weakest of the Death Dealers. The surprise of the creatures rising from the water ... and the speed of the attack ... meant the Runners were exacting a heavy toll.

Suddenly, he was into the battle himself, his jaws snapping left and right, taking legs from deer, and cutting the throats of monkeys. Ben was on his shoulders, slashing his blades from side to side. They quickly cut their way through the rear guard who were less keen for a fight. Numerous creatures ran at the sight of him, only for them to be taken down by the rest of the Runners ... there was no mercy given.

He began to think he would get to Zagane before he reached Gervais, when a line of animals appeared in front of him. They were led by a wolverine, who looked controlled and capable. Five little monkeys, similar to Ben, jumped up onto the back of a hyena that stood behind the wolverine, and loosened a volley of arrows. One hissed past Nala's ear, and he heard a yelp from behind as an arrow hit home. The monkey loaded the arrows quickly to loose again, when suddenly, one of them flew from the back of the hyena with a dart in his forehead.

"Shoot at my wolf, will you!" Ben screeched from his back.

"Runners!" he roared, as he bore down on the wolverine.

His roar was echoed by what felt like a thousand voices as he hit the wolverine head-on. Ben was thrown off his back and hit one of the Death Dealer monkeys square in the chest.

That was the last thing he saw before he was in a life or death struggle with the wolverine. He realised quickly that getting close to this animal was a bad idea. The wolverine was a short and stout creature, with a mouth full of sharp teeth, which were snapping at his neck, and two-inch claws that were like razors, trying to slash his underbelly as they rolled in the sand.

It was all he could do to keep the claws off him with his longer reach. He lashed out a paw, which caught the wolverine on the side of its snout, eliciting a cry of fury and causing it to double its attack. He felt a sharp pain across his chest before he was pushed over onto his back. The wolverine was up in a flash, stalking him, he had landed awkwardly, and was struggling to get up. A wicked grin crossed the wolverine's face as it raised its paw to strike, blood dripping from three of its claws.

"Time to die, Wolf."

He closed his eyes, hoping Leandra would survive and forgive him. The blow never came.

"You can open your eyes now," Ben's voice mocked.

Snapping his eyes open, he saw Ben leaning nonchalantly against the snout of the wolverine … which wasn't moving.

"I think I'll take up your offer, Nala. You would be dead in no time without me to look after you."

He laughed and pulled himself to his feet, realising his left paw had become trapped under a gazelle's leg. He marvelled at how something so simple had rendered him helpless and nearly cost him his life. Taking stock, he stood on top of the body of a huge stag and surveyed the battlefield. Fighting was sporadic across most of the field, with the Runners having decimated the smaller and weaker Death Dealers. They were retreating quickly back to the trees, likely hoping that Zagane would die, rather than catch up with them.

At the centre of the sandy outlet the battle was still raging. Zagane had broken through his front line and taken out two chimps, his tusk tearing into the belly of one, and his back legs crushing the face of another. As Nala watched, Zagane came face-to-face with Gervais.

Gervais growled and moved quickly towards Zagane, who at the same time dived forward, his tusks whipping wickedly at Gervais's midriff. A quick flick of the blade in Gervais's right hand moved him past Zagane with a slight graze on his belly, but he had opened up Zagane and raised his staff, ready to bring it down on his head. Before Gervais could deliver the blow, one of the wolfhounds clamped its jaw around his wrist. A roar of pain and anger came from Gervais as he turned on the wolfhound. Zagane was momentarily forgotten as Gervais brought down his blade, punching it deep into the wolfhound's skull while it was still latched to his arm.

His view became blocked then, as Slaven and another wolfhound tore in. He jumped down quickly, and Ben vaulted onto his back.

"Gervais is outnumbered, we need to get there, NOW!"

He took off at a sprint, with Ben squealing a war cry as they carved a path towards Gervais. He was almost to the spot where Gervais had been, when he was struck in the side. All he saw was a flash of gold on the chest, and for the second time in as many minutes, he found himself on the floor and at the mercy of his attacker ... whose blade was flashing down at him.

This time he kept his eyes open, and so saw the flash of black above him that intercepted the blade. Tergar's teeth tore into the bear's throat, driving him to the ground.

He jumped up to help, but stopped short. The bear's blade was sticking out of Tergar's chest and the bear's throat was torn and oozing blood ... both sets of eyes were vacant in death.

He looked away, there was nothing he could do for Tergar now, he was with Midnight. Instead, he turned to get to his friends ... before stopping cold.

Everything seemed to drop into slow motion, his hunter sense on overdrive.

Leandra, drenched in blood, was standing over the body of Slaven with Joe on her back, who was wiping his blade on his fur as Leandra's head looked up to watch something. Slowly, his eyes panned across the sand, barely registering Reg standing on the skull of the other wolfhound. His eyes had found Gervais and Zagane.

They were in a deadly dance, moving faster than anyone else, with Zagane lunging in, trying to tear Gervais to pieces. Gervais was trying to counter-attack with his blade, and divert the razor-sharp tusks. After one such attack, Gervais glanced up ... locking eyes with him, and breaking the spell as he winked and smiled before turning back to Zagane, who had begun another attack. This time, Gervais didn't try to avoid Zagane. Instead, he moved into the attack, impaling himself onto Zagane's tusks, which wedged deep into his stomach.

The pain didn't appear to register with Gervais as he leaned forward, whispering quietly into Zagane's ear.

But he heard it loud and clear.

"Our time is done … my Old Friend. A new dawn is rising, so we must enter the River." As Gervais spoke, he brought his blade up into the chest of Zagane. There was a roar of rage and pain issued from them both, and it felt like it shook the very fabric of The Forbidden.

Once the world stopped shaking, he saw Gervais and Zagane lay side-by-side on the beach. He rushed over, arriving at the same time as Leandra. Gervais's breathing was shallow as he looked him and Leandra in the eyes.

"Do a better job than we did," Gervais whispered.

A wracking cough came from Zagane. "They don't stand a chance. Even you don't understand the mantle they have to take on. They're doomed," he hissed with venom as he died.

He looked to Gervais, who smiled and told him, "I believe in you both."

He was confused, having no idea what was going on. He was only aware that his friend was dying before him. He whimpered as Gervais closed his eyes, smiling as his breathing stopped.

He listened to his own heart, beating fast, as he heard the last beat of Gervais's.

He started to raise his head … to howl a message to the River to expect a hero to arrive … when suddenly his mind was on fire. His eyes began to black-over as pain permeated every part of his body.

As the pain overwhelmed his senses, he was vaguely aware of a cry of pain from Leandra. It was her cries that helped him, more than anything, to fight against it. Opening his eyes, he saw her drop to the floor beside him, her eyes closed. He took a step towards her as the wave of pain in his mind amplified ... and he knew no more.

The End ... for now.

About the Author

Author Michael McGrail is more commonly known to his friends as Mike (he prefers this to his Sunday name, Michael.) He is a self-professed geek who loves nothing more than curling up with a cup of tea to read the latest fantasy book by his favourite authors, watching sci-fi on the TV, or playing with his friends on the Xbox.

Mike is a family man at heart, living with his wife and daughter in a small village in Derbyshire, England. When he isn't spending time keeping up with his daughter, reading, writing (assisted by his ever-faithful Cavapoo companion), he enjoys playing football and walking the said crazy Cavapoo through the beautiful countryside where he lives.

Unfortunately, his social media skills are laughable! So much so, that his daughter thinks he has been living in the Stone Age ... but he is trying.

You can keep up to date and marvel at his expertise on social media @

You can connect with me on:
🅕 https://www.facebook.com/Michael-McGrail-Author-104779601390420

Printed in Great Britain
by Amazon

18268396R00257